TWO WEDDING CRASHERS

A DATING BY NUMBERS NOVEL

USA TODAY BESTSELLING AUTHOR

MEGHAN QUINN

Published by Hot-Lanta Publishing, LLC

Copyright 2018

Cover design by RBA Designs

PROLOGUE

BECK

"Dude, you have to come. It's going to be the party of the century." Chris takes a sip from his beer and watches the dance floor, his elbows leaning on the bar behind him.

I bring my water to my lips before I say, "That's great and all, but I wasn't invited."

"You don't need an invitation."

"Chris." I give him a pointed look. "It's a wedding. It's not like a birthday or company party that I can get away with going to, but a wedding has seating arrangements and actual invitations."

"Semantics. Just hang out at the bar the whole time and pick off people's plates when they're not looking. Hell, I think it's a buffet, so you can grab a plate and eat in the bathroom."

"As much as scarfing down a wedding meal next to a urinal is appealing, I think I'll pass."

The music switches from a fast-paced salsa, to a slow, seductive melody. Couples on the dance floor immediately fall in step with the song, their moves unhurried and fluid. Hell, what I wouldn't give to be on that dance floor. As a guy, dancing alone to a sexy song reads a little strange, so I keep myself firmly planted next to

1

my good friend, Chris, who works behind the scenes at *Going in Blind*. He was the one who set up my profile six months ago, the one who keeps egging me on to try it again. But after the night I ran into Noely at the restaurant, right before she chased after someone else, it's been downhill from there. The girl I went on a date with that night was . . . blah. Zero personality. She tried to impress me with her cleavage-showing ways, which granted, I enjoyed because I am a man.

But there was nothing there—no spark, no urge to take her on my bike—so I said good night and went on my way. I wasn't ready. Noely had been right. I still had things to sort through. Noely was so goddamn gorgeous, so my physical attraction to her made complete sense. She'd been warm and funny, and I wish I'd been ready in some respects. But I get it now. I understand what she meant about emotional connection. She certainly set the benchmark though. Physically, of course. But she'd become my friend, and I knew that ultimately I really wanted that.

Since then, I've spent time learning about being single, and even though it's been good for me, to focus on the things that matter the most, supporting and building my charities, I've felt like I've been missing something.

And I think I know what it is.

Can you guess?

Sex.

Fuck, I miss sex. The last time I had anything remotely close to sex was with Noely. I'm pretty sure my balls have turned to dust by now; one wrong move and they're going to evaporate into the air for good.

Why haven't I been fucking my way through Malibu you ask? Because no one has snagged my attention. There has been no interest on my end, which is insane since I'm so fucking horny. I feel like my penis is going to fall off.

"Just think about it, man. You need a vacation. The wedding is in the Florida Keys at this fancy-ass resort that overlooks the ocean. You can crash the wedding, eat with your urinal, get your dance on, and have some crazy, no-strings-attached sex with one of the bridesmaids. There are at least three that are single."

No strings-attached sex, huh . . .

"Crash someone's wedding? You're serious."

"Dead serious." He takes another sip of his drink. "Justine and I booked two rooms in case we decided to take the kids, but if you go, we'll make it a parents-only weekend and leave the kids at my mom's." Turning toward me, looking sadly desperate, he says, "Please, dude. Please crash this wedding. Please take that extra room so I can have wild island sex with my wife. Do me this favor and grant me this one wish."

"Can't you find someone else to take the room?"

"Nope, I tried. And you know Justine. She's not going to eat the money on the room. So right now, we're taking the kids."

I run my hand over my hair, unsure. This is crazy. I'm not Vince Vaughn or Owen Wilson, primed and ready with a fucking bro code on how to crash a wedding. But, a mini vacation does sound good. And honestly, Chris has been there for me through the hard times. He and Justine do actually deserve this time away too.

"When?"

"Dude!" Chris pulls me into a hug and then holds my shoulders as he stares at me. "I can't even tell you how excited I am."

"I need the details first."

With a knowing smile, says, "Oh, you're fucking coming. It's a done deal."

Unfortunately, I think it is. *I think the final lure was hearing two words—fucking and coming.* Yeah, I got it bad.

Look out, unsuspecting couple. I'm about to crash your wedding.

Part One

THE MEET "NOT SO" CUTE

CHAPTER ONE

RYLEE

"I don't know what love is anymore." I flop across Victoria's stiff-as-a-board couch and drape my arm over my eyes.

"No shoes on my settee, please. How many times do I have to remind you?" Victoria, one of my best friends, huffs, while setting a tray of tea on the coffee table in front of me.

"This isn't the time for your fine china and delicate finger sandwiches." I turn on the couch and prop my head up. Jamming my finger into the settee with force, I say, "This is the time for vodka! This is the time we crack open that expensive bottle you have and do all the shots. No, not shots. Just hook me up with a funnel and start pouring straight down my gullet." I open my mouth, tip my head back, and point down my throat.

Victoria sits across from me and starts making a cup of tea, using teeny tiny tongs to pick up the sugar cubes. "One lump or two?"

"Did you not hear me? Vodka, Victoria. I need all the vodka."

"Inebriation is not a solution to your problem, Rylee." She plops two cubes into the cup and then pours tea on top. She's always served tea this way. She says the less splash the better. She holds the cup out to me and waits for me to pick it up.

"Alcohol won't solve my problem but at least I'll be less stressed."

"Until you start violating my toilet with last night's dinner." Victoria shakes her head, her nose turned up in the air. "I refuse to be a part of your drunken debauchery once again."

I reluctantly take the tea and sit up, keeping my shoes away from the fifty-year-old velvety fabric. "I puke once in your house and you're going to hold that against me?"

"Puke is such a vile word." She shakes her head, an absolute distaste in her mouth from repeating me. "And not only did you get sick in my house, but it was before that, when you were dancing around in my petticoat without permission."

Can you tell Victoria is stuck in the 1800s? My dearest friend is an author, just like me, but instead of writing raunchy, give-it-to-me-big-dick-daddy sex, she delights readers with non-fiction historical memoirs. I've read a few, talk about detail and research, this girl has it down pat. But after every book I read, I always ask, where's the sex, where's the romance? I know, I know, not every book is about love, but Benjamin Franklin most definitely poked his dick around—that's no secret—so it wouldn't hurt to write in some good old-fashioned bifocal banging. Am I right?

That's just my opinion.

Victoria thinks otherwise.

"Well, if you weren't so stingy with your petticoats then maybe I wouldn't have to dance in them without your permission." Taking a sip of my tea, I continue, "That's beside the point. We need to focus on the real problem, here."

Victoria's front door swings open and Zoey, the third leg to our tripod, waltzes in wearing her designer sunglasses, hair a complete disaster, and carrying two bags on each arm. "I'm here. I'm here and I brought all the things." She slams the door shut with her foot and flops on the settee next to me, her bags spilling across the floor. "I have booze, onion dip, Lay's chips, Hot Pockets, and Post-it Notes in a variety of colors." She rubs her hands together and looks between Victoria and myself. "Let's plot, ladies."

"I made finger sandwiches," Victoria points out. "Cucumber and tuna, so we don't need those microwaveable meat pockets."

"There is always a need for a Hot Pocket, especially when our friend is out of ideas." Zoey rips her sunglasses off her face and turns toward me, her face stern and serious. "How bad is it? Are we talking a little blip in the road or are we talking"—she swallows hard—"the big WB?"

Lips pressed together, eyes shut, I let out a long breath. "Total and complete WB."

The room stills, the air around us heavy as Zoey barely whispers, "Writer's block."

The word hangs there between us, the heaviness so incredibly foreboding none of us really know how to respond.

Zoey, or Z. Platt, is a children's author. She has a very popular series about Dilly the Dinosaur and the trouble he gets into. She's published with Penguin and cranks out five books a year while being mom of the year to her six children—yes, six—and before you ask, she does the illustrations as well. They are so beyond cute. *So in a nutshell, she is freaking talented.*

So being that Victoria and Zoey are both authors, they get it. They understand the weight of my words. They've been there before and when it happens, we rally behind each other. Despite our different writing genres, we always rally.

Victoria eyes her sandwiches, her face twisting with concern. "I'm not sure cucumber sandwiches on pumpernickel bread is going to help in this situation."

"I told you!" I flop my body back on the couch, careful not to spill my delicious tea. "You guys, I have no idea what I'm going to do. My publisher needs eighty thousand words from me in four weeks and I have nothing, literally nothing. No ideas, no characters, no plot, not even one idea of a hot sex scene."

Victoria and Zoey both gasp.

"I know, like I said, I don't know what love is anymore." I flop my non-tea holding hand across the settee.

"We can fix this; we got this." Waving at the tea and sandwiches, Zoey says, "Vic, clear this shit off the table, warm up those pockets, and bring some shot glasses. We have some plotting to do."

&

"I need a trope. I can't just write about the Wright Brothers."

"Why not? They're attractive in their own way." Victoria tips a bottle of vodka, pouring out more shots. This would be round five.

"Attractive in their own way, what does that even mean?"

Victoria shrugs. "Mustaches."

"Mustaches are NOT book-boyfriend material. Mustaches belong to the creepy boss the heroine has to deal with, or the wise old grandpa who tells the hero to follow his heart and get the girl, not the guy who's supposed to plow his rock-hard cock into the tightest canal he's ever experienced. Can you even imagine what a mustache would be like on a thirty-year-old?" I shake my head, envisioning it in my head. "There she is, the heroine, lying on the bed, completely naked, legs spread, breasts heaving, nipples hard, waiting for the man she's been dreaming of to finally take her up against the headboard, and in walks Zane, or Blaine, or Blake, whatever you want to call him, sporting a chunk of hair above his upper lip and nothing else, looking like the epitome of an eighties porn star. A thirty-year-old in today's society with a mustache saying: 'I'm going to eat your pussy so hard you're going to come all over my tongue,' doesn't really scream sexy to me. It screams . . . sexual predator." Thirty-year-olds and mustaches, just no, even if your name is Zac Efron. NO. Shave it, man. Shave it off.

"Mustaches are dignified," Victoria says.

"For older men."

Victoria huffs her disapproval.

"How about we drop the facial hair talk for now, table that, and come back to it later and think about an actual plot." Zoey holds a pen in her hand and a pile of Post-it Notes, ready to write down our ideas. The only thing we've written down and stuck to the wall is one Post-it Note that says, "Sex." Yup, since it's a romance novel, that's a given, but it made us feel good putting one thing on the wall.

"What about a stepbrother romance? My friend was raving about one the other day," Zoey says, looking excited about her contribution.

"Already did one. Remember Tag and Brittany?"

"Oh yeah, Tag fucked Brittany so hard on that log in the campground. That was hot."

"What about a librarian?" Victoria asks, making a good suggestion.

"Yeah, a librarian," Zoey cheers and snags a shot glass. "To librarians, those smart bitches and their books. God bless them." Talking to her shot glass, she says, "And down the hatch you go."

Getting into it now, Victoria adds, "Yes, she can be a librarian who falls in love with a traveling salesman who comes into town on a whim selling musical instruments."

"Should I name him Professor Hill?" I deadpan.

Nodding her head vigorously, Zoey says, "Oh great name. Hot. Professor Hill, do me on those books. Come on my pages, Professor Hill. I want to be fucked on words, right on these inked-up pages. I can see it so vividly." Zoey's eyes look wild as she licks her lips.

"Zoey." I interrupt her fantasies to lay down the bad news. "Victoria just described the plot for *The Music Man*."

"Wha—" Zoey throws her arms in the air out of pure frustration. "Victoria, for Christ's sake, that's the third time tonight. For the love of God, use your imagination."

Victoria shrugs and takes a shot, only her second. "I write non-fiction, so sue me."

"First it's *Gone With the Wind*, then it was *Casablanca*, now *The Music Man*." Zoey points her finger at Victoria. "I'm disappointed in you."

"It's not her fault. Don't turn on each other," I wave my arms around, as if I'm breaking up a fight. Sighing, I lean back and bring my shot glass to my mouth where I lick the vodka, as if I'm a cat lapping up milk. "This is pointless," I say over my licks. "I'm all dried up, a shriveled vagina with zero ideas."

"No, no, no, don't say that. Let's go over the tropes again," Zoey says, slapping my leg. "Something might spark."

"We've been through them five times already. There is nothing."

"Small town, uh, brother's little sister, roommates, my boss is my baby daddy."

I shake my head, even though *my boss is my baby daddy* does do something for my imagination, but just as quickly as the idea ignites, it fizzles out.

Downing my shot, I place it on the coffee table and hang my head low. "This is pointless. I should just email my publisher now and tell them there is no way I can fulfill my contract."

"No." Zoey slaps the settee, which awakens Victoria, her eyes sharpening from the abuse to her precious furniture. "We are not giving up, and what you need is a refresher of what love is."

"If you tell me I should set up a Tinder account, I'm going to punch you."

"I would never suggest that."

"You did last week when you said I was becoming a hermit."

"Well, for fuck's sake, Rylee. It's summer and you're wearing scarves inside your house with socks on your hands. A little Tinder action wouldn't kill you."

In my defense, I like it cold in my house, plus wearing socks on my hands feels nice, especially when I'm exfoliating and doing a deep conditioning on my hands. My fingers are the money makers. I have to treat them with respect, make sure they're well oiled and ready to type all the words. Now if only my brain would kick it into high gear.

"I'm not doing Tinder." I put my foot down. Tinder is not the solution.

"Well good, because that wasn't my idea anyway." Zoey bites into a Hot Pocket and talks with her mouth full. "What you need is to be in an environment of love where you can feel romance. I know you, Rylee, and the minute you're put in a new situation, you start observing every little thing from the way a man casually presses his hand on the lower back of the girl he's with, to the look a woman gives her man when they're at dinner, a look that's full of promises."

She's right. I'm an observer, a borderline voyeur at times, but it's for the good of the books. That's what I tell myself when I have my binoculars propped against my face, watching my neighbors from my window.

"Okay, so what's your suggestion?"

Zoey sits up, mischief in her eyes. This is going to be good. "Next week, Art and I are going to Key West for a wedding. My cousin is getting married to her college sweetheart. They are the sweetest couple you will ever meet. Tiffany and Del, seriously, their love is so cute. And I think you should crash it."

"Oh that's very improper," Victoria says, her lip curling from the idea.

"Yeah, I'm really not into that. I don't know them, so that would be awkward."

"That's why it's called *crashing* a wedding. I didn't tell you to ask them for an invite."

"Ehh, still a no from me." I cross my arms and mull over the idea.

"Think about it." When Zoey gets in this mode, there is no stopping her. "You fly to Key West for a few days, write off the trip as a business expense, and enjoy the sun while soaking up the romance. And who knows, maybe a little change of scenery and being in the presence of true love will help you come up with the most epic story ever."

"It is an idea," Victoria says, "but crashing someone's wedding is rude."

"The wedding is at The Hemingway House," Zoey adds, a hand on her hip and a look of arrogance on her face.

Annnnnd she just dropped a bomb on Victoria. "Ernest . . . Hemingway?" There is a shake in her voice.

Zoey nods, smarmy written all over her. "The one and only."

"Like the place where he wrote his novels?" I ask, feeling a little more intrigued.

"Yup. So think about it. Wedding, romance, beaches, Key lime pie, and Ernest's ghost hovering over you, whispering into your ear every idea your little heart can desire. I can't think of a more perfect place to get your writing groove back. Can you?"

I hate that she's made it almost impossible for me to say no to this idea. I'm not one to crash someone's wedding, not one at all since it's a special day full of close family and friends, but . . . romance and Hemingway vibes. I mean . . . what romance author would say no to that?

"I'm only going if Victoria goes," I blurt.

"Why are you dragging me into this?"

"Two seconds ago you were just salivating over the idea of being at Ernest Hemingway's house."

"Yes, I was because that would be an amazing place to not only visit but to get married in." She brushes a piece of lint off her chinos. "But that doesn't mean I'm about to crash the most important day of someone's life. I'll pass."

"Ridiculous," Zoey mutters as she gets up and walks toward the bathroom.

Victoria continues to pick lint off her pants, her turtleneck looking a little too tight around her neck right about now.

"Victoria . . ."

"I'm not going."

"Come on. I need this."

"Then go by yourself. I don't need to go with you. You're a big girl."

Sighing, I say, "You and I both know if I go with Zoey and Art, they're going to end up doing some couples thing like they always do, leaving me behind. I need a partner in crime, someone to help me stare at people."

"As appealing as that sounds, I'll pass."

"Victoriaaaaaaa," I whine, trying to think—aha! I've got it. "If you go with me to this wedding, I'll go with you to that historical ball thing you wanted to go to at the end of the month."

Lifting an eyebrow in my direction, Victoria asks, "You'll go to the Historical League's Annual Summer Solstice Ball?"

"Yes."

"And you'll wear a traditional dress from the 1800s."

"A replica of sorts." I swallow hard, starting to realize what I'm signing up for.

"You'll wear a traditional dress from the 1800s with gigot sleeves and everything?"

Goddamn you, gigot sleeves.

Forcefully smiling, I nod. "Yup. Bring on the gigots."

"Fine." Victoria tilts her chin to the side. "I'll go to your wedding, but I will tour The Hemingway House on my own. I don't need you rushing me through it. And I require my own room, as I refuse to share with you."

"Because I make fun of your sound machine?"

"Yes, I would rather sleep in peace than listen to your moaning about my machine all night."

So many jokes, so many sexual things.

"I didn't want to share a room with you anyway," I answer just to save face. Can't let Victoria think she holds all the cards in this deal, even though she does.

"Sure you didn't." Victoria starts gathering the plates and shot glasses when Zoey walks in clapping her hands.

"Did you girls figure it out?"

"We're going," I answer, hope blossoming inside me, hope for a possible book idea to finally come to mind.

"You're going?" Zoey's voice gets louder.

I match her enthusiasm, really starting to feel excited about my decision. Standing and throwing my arms in the air, I cheer a little too loudly, "We're crashing a wedding!"

CHAPTER TWO

BECK

"Would you like anything to drink before we take off, sir?"
"Oh, I'm good, thank you."
I've never felt so out of place in my entire life. Chris and Justine upgraded our flight to first class, even though I told them multiple times not to, but they didn't want me sitting in the back when they were "boozing it up with the yuppies." Their words, not mine.

My phone vibrates in my pocket. I've been waiting for this phone call so I answer on the first ring.

"Hey Cal."

"Beck, how are you doing?"

"Good, really good," I answer, watching the passengers board the plane. A mom and her baby sit in front of me, next to a girl who's buried in her computer. I hope she has noise-cancelling headphones in that huge, quilted bag of hers.

"I'm glad to hear that. What are you up to?"

Cal Pipkin, yes, that is his name, has been calling me every Wednesday around ten his time for the last eight years. I've come to grow quite fond of his rough, no-nonsense tone. At first it had terrified me, but now it puts me at ease.

"I actually just boarded a plane headed to Key West."

"Key West, huh? Looking to get a little R and R?"

"Yeah, something like that." No need to go into details with Cal.

"Are you going by yourself?" I know what he's getting at. He usually asks point-blank, but now, he beats around the bush, testing me.

"Chris and his wife are going with me. We're attending a wedding, and then we're going to have some beach fun."

"Chris is a good man." A good man who keeps me straight. There's no doubt in my mind that Cal is happy about this information.

"He is."

"Will alcohol be served at the wedding?"

Biting on the inside of my cheek, I nod even though he can't see me. "Open bar, sir," I answer, becoming formal with my sponsor.

Cal is a veteran who's spent his retired days coaching and sponsoring not only retired military but civilians who are alcoholics. Eight years ago, my life changed. Luckily, I met Cal, the strong voice of reason driving me forward.

"How do you feel about that?"

"Good. Strong. It's rare when I want anything other than water."

"That's good to hear." He takes a moment and then says, "I'm proud of you, Beck. Your confidence knowing there is an open bar at the wedding is commendable. Stay strong. I don't have any doubt that you'll do fine."

"Thank you," I say uncomfortably.

"You're welcome. I'll let you go because I'm sure you have to get off your phone soon. Don't be afraid to call if you need me, especially if temptation finds you."

"I will. Have a good one, Cal."

Temptation. Funny thing, it hasn't found me in over eight years. The cravings diminished the minute I found out what I did, who I broke, and who I destroyed. Perspective hits you right in the gut when you flip another human's world upside down, and fuck did it hit me hard.

I hang up and stare at my phone for a few seconds, taking deep breaths and slowing down my racing heart. *Give yourself a moment, Beck. I understand the nature of my wrongdoings. I am in a process of recovery. I am willing to make amends to those I've harmed. I have accepted my past decisions and whom they affected.* And as I often do when I get off the phone with Cal, I take a second to remember the little boy who haunts my dreams.

"Was that Cal?" Chris asks, leaning over the aisle, talking between boarding passengers.

"Yeah, just doing his weekly check in."

"He must have an alarm on his phone to remind him about calling you because honestly, I don't know how he remembers. I can barely remember to get the kids dressed in the morning. If it was up to me, they'd go to school in their pajamas."

"That's why you're not in charge," Justine says over Chris's shoulders. Growing serious, Justine asks, "How's Cal?"

"Good." I nod my head. "Just a quick check in. Never misses one."

"Did he ask about the wedding?"

A lady carrying a tiny dog in a bedazzled dog carrier stands between us so I wait to answer until she passes, her dog eyeing me through the mesh, his teeth snarling. Listen, dude, I'm not the one who put you in the damn thing.

"He did. He trusts me. A few years ago, he wouldn't have been as easy to get off the phone." Cal was relaxed as we spoke and knowing he also believes in me is all I need.

"He has no reason to worry." Justine leaves it at that, knowing my background and where I stand now, how I've drastically changed.

There is loud clanking on a keyboard in front of Justine and

Chris. I peek around the seat and eye a woman hunched over her computer, rapidly pressing the backspace on her Word document, muttering something to herself. One by one, her words vanish from the white screen on her laptop followed by a long sigh and a hand to her forehead.

She seems so annoyed, so I'm glad I'm not in her position. Whatever the hell she's doing, or trying to do for that matter.

Sitting back in my cushioned seat, I attempt to relax as the girl now brings her phone to her ear and starts speaking rapidly, just loud enough that I can hear her.

"You should have paid extra to sit next to me. I would have paid extra. I need you. I have no ideas." She pauses. "You're so cheap, Victoria." Pause. "No, I just deleted everything. It was pure shit. It wasn't even the least bit riveting. What?" She sighs. "My first sentence? Why does that matter?" More sighing. "It was . . . Look at the bottom of my shoe." Pause. "Yes, I know that's a terrible first sentence. This is what I'm dealing with, Victoria. I wish you were here. I need your bosom."

Eh?

"You can be on the phone right now, Victoria. The cabin door hasn't closed. Just give me . . . don't be such a square. You can be on the phone. Christ! Just give me a sentence, any sentence. Hello? Hello?" Sighing out of more frustration, she puts her phone in her lap and starts typing again.

Okay, I know I shouldn't be looking, hell, I shouldn't have even listened to that conversation, but now I feel invested. What is she trying to write and why does she need Victoria's bosom? And if Victoria is such a square, it doesn't seem likely she'd lend out her bosom to begin with. Is Victoria her lover? And what kind of a first sentence is "Look at the bottom of my shoe"? That doesn't seem like a great first sentence for anything.

Needing to know more about this girl and her rather comical situation, I study her computer in front of her across the aisle. Yup, I'm that person right now, and I don't even care.

She types a sentence and quickly deletes it. Curious, I start reading along with her typing.

Did you just walk in here naked?

Delete

Snakes, there are snakes in my bed!

Delete.

Ahoy, sailors. Is that a buoy in your pants?

Delete.

I just made apricot pie. Come on in and take a bite . . .

Delete.

Cats. Cats. Cats. Dog. I hate my life, this baby smells like a turd, and if the lady next to me elbows me one more time, I might use my computer as a crocodile device and chomp the hell out of her breast.

Delete

I snort to myself, kind of enjoying this girl's sense of humor and also slightly confused by the cats, cats, cats, and dog part of that sentence, even though it was entertaining.

From the look of it, this girl is going to have one hell of a long flight.

~

"Please put your trays in the upright and locked position as well as your seats. Gladys will be around to collect your trash before our final descent into Key West. Thank you for flying with us, and we hope you have a wonderful time under the sun."

Chris shakes my shoulder with a little too much enthusiasm. "Almost there, buddy. I can smell the jet skis."

"I can taste the pineapple rings you'll be eating off my nipples." Justine wavers forward, drinking the rest of her wine straight from the bottle. "Vacation, here we come."

I guess this is what vacationing with parents gone wild is like: pineapples and nipples. And we're not even off the plane yet.

"I'm going to eat those pineapple rings so hard."

Lips pressed together, I mutter, "Excited to share a wall with you two."

"Dude, we're going to bang all night long. Get ready."

"All the banging," Justine follows up, giving me an over-exaggerated thumbs up.

Wonderful. Just what I need, to hear my best friend and his wife having sex, especially when I'm horny as fuck.

More clacking comes from in front of me. It's been like that the entire flight, typing and then aggressive backspacing. Combine that with the toots from the baby and the incessant crying, this has been one magical flight. But I can't complain. The lady in front of me, the one trying to calm her baby down, has had it worst. I can't imagine what she must be feeling right now. *Harried.*

The girl with the black hair tied into the messiest of buns on top of her head, wisps of hair fanning around her head, slams her computer shut and rips her earphones out of her ears. Huffing, she stuffs everything in her backpack and then sits back and crosses her arms over her chest only to look out the window.

I want to tap her on the shoulder and tell her things could be worse, but knowing an unwelcome pep talk from a stranger will do no good, I sit still, trying to read her a little better. I don't know why I'm so interested in her, in her every move, but I don't think I've ever seen anyone so outwardly expressive with their displeasure in life. It's as if she thinks she's in her own little bubble, and no one can see what she's doing.

"First things first when we land, get me a piece of Key lime pie. I don't want anything else, I just want a pie shoved in my face."

"I want to try all the Key lime pies from every pie place and decide which one is best," Justine says. "I say we get an Uber and drive around to all the pie places, one at a time, picking up slices."

"Or we can rent one of those golf carts and do the driving ourselves." Chris becomes far too excited about this idea. "Putt Puttin' in our fucking golf cart for pies."

"Putt Puttin' for pies." They both high-five. Did I mention Chris had some drinks as well?

"How about you two check in to our rooms first and then you can go putting for pies after a nap and lots of water consumption." I give them a knowing look that straightens them up.

Chris, looking a little shameful says, "Good idea, water, nap, then pies."

At this new idea, Justine high-fives him again. "Water, nap, and pies!"

The plane gradually descends, turbulence shifting the cabin back and forth, up and down, every which way you can possibly think. The baby in front of Justine is screaming, her mom shooshing constantly, making me feel like reaching over to give her a break. Thankfully no one is annoyed in first class. Including the girl with the weird first sentences, most are more understanding than anything.

"Can I get you anything?" she asks, shouting over the screaming. "Want me to grab you a bottle?"

The mom turns to her, tears in her eyes. "Would you mind holding her for a second while I dig through my bag?"

"Not at all," the girl says, seeming a little apprehensive at first.

The mom hands over the screaming baby and the girl, unsure on how to properly hold a baby, extends her arms straight out in front of her, the baby held under the armpits, screaming. It's awkward to watch. The girl tries shooshing as well, tucks her knee under the baby's bottom and lightly bounces her. Sure enough, the baby quiets, the crying ceases.

I look around, and relief is written all over the passengers in first class. I want to give the girl a high five. She might not be good at writing first sentences for Lord knows what, but she sure as hell can calm down—

Blehhhhh.

Oh hell.

Without a second thought I cover my nose with my shirt—I'm quickly followed by other passengers—as I watch orange-colored liquid slowly drip down the girl's face and neck. It's almost as if her skin started oozing chunky orange liquid.

23

"Oh fuck, oh fuck, oh fuck," the girl says, holding the baby out as far as possible now. And of course, there's a happy smile on the baby's face.

"Oh no, she must have had a little bubble in her tummy. You burped it out of her." The mom takes the baby and coos into her ear. "Poor baby."

The girl sits there, arms extended, frozen in place, orange still dripping down her face and neck. Oh fuck is right. I smile to myself, a laugh popping out of me that I keep to myself.

Carefully, the girl rises out of her seat only for a flight attendant to scold her. "Ma'am, you're going to have to take a seat, we're about to land."

"But I have puke on me."

"I'm sorry, but the fasten seat belt sign is on."

"But . . . puke."

"Ma'am, please take a seat. Use a wipe?"

Fingers twitching, veins popping out of her neck, she takes a seat and looks to the mom who's holding some wipes to her. "Sorry about that, but hey, at least she stopped crying."

Dryly, the girl replies, "Glad I could help."

I don't know how I do it, but I manage to hold in the snort so close to escaping. Her tone. Her frozen form. *Oh shit. Don't laugh.* But then I glance at her again, and all I can think is, *poor baby.*

CHAPTER THREE

RYLEE

"I could have walked to the hotel by now. Where the hell is Zoey?" I seethe, trying not to focus on the dry puke encrusted on my neck, or how the humidity and sun have created a vicious cycle of liquid and drying baby puke on my skin.

To say my "vacation" has started off on the wrong foot is a complete and total understatement.

"She said she was drying off when you texted her," Victoria says before biting into an apple. "Can you sit down please, your pacing is giving me anxiety."

"I'm giving you anxiety?" I step right into Victoria's space and point at my neck, showing off the highlighted veins in orange. "I got puked on by what I can only describe as Satan's baby herself and haven't been able to fully wash it off my body. For the last half hour, I've walked around smelling like a garbage can, I have yet to be able to write one damn sentence for this book, and I was frisked from my tits to my crack by a rather unpleasant TSA woman. I'm two seconds away from throwing myself in front of one of those propeller planes to end my goddamn misery. So I apologize if I don't want to hear about your anxiety from my pacing."

Honk, honk.

Turning around, Zoey pulls up in a souped-up golf cart decked out in fringe.

Oh for the love of God.

"Hop in, sexy ladies." She honks the horn again. "Borrowed this from the hotel. Tops out at twenty-five miles per hour, so you two better buckle up." Looking closer, Zoey gives me a disgusted look. "What the hell is on your neck?"

"She got puked on," Victoria says, tossing her apple core in the trash can. "Don't ask her about it or she'll go on another tirade."

"Annnnnd you're disgusting." Zoey points at me and thumbs to the back of the golf cart. "You have the bitch seat in the back. We're going to need you to sit downwind from us."

"There's no seat belt," I complain when I sit down.

"Then make sure you hold on tight, because it's a bumpy ride, and don't let go of your luggage. Hubby is in the hotel room, naked and waiting for me. Wifey wants the dick so she's going to be zipping around pretty fast."

"Why not let us take an Uber then?" I ask, praying I don't fall off the back end of this thing as Zoey puts it into high gear and pulls out onto a main road. Oh hell, I'm going to die . . . with orange puke on my neck.

"I'm not a bad host. I invited you guys here, so the least I can do is pick you up. Honestly, Rylee."

Duh, such common knowledge.

From the front seat, I can faintly hear Victoria recount the flight, reflecting on her recent read about Amelia Earhart and the suspicions that she possibly didn't die in a plane crash but was captured by island natives. Semi-fascinated in the conversation, but bitter from my flight, I tune them out and hold on to the cart and my luggage as we drive along the coast of Key West, passing by palm trees, diving pelicans, and random roosters standing by the side of the road.

Odd.

Taking a deep breath, I soak in the sea salt air and feel the sun blazing on my exposed skin. This is supposed to be an adventure, a time to relax, an opportunity to spark the writing bug, to light that little fucker's ass on fire.

Instead of focusing on the bad, like the inappropriate diddle in security, or the regurgitated mango and peach combination plastered on my neck, I need to look forward to the next week here. This is going to be fun . . . it has to be.

It doesn't take long for Zoey to drop us at the hotel lobby where she parks the golf cart, tips a bell hop, and walks us into check-in. "I made reservations for us at Martinis on Duvall Street. We have about twenty minutes before we need to leave." She eyes my neck. "Make sure to wash up and don't be late. Meet by the beach café in twenty."

It takes all my energy not to wallop her in the boob for that comment. No, I planned on going to dinner with puke on my neck.

Counting to ten, I remind myself of my initiative to be positive.

Just for the record, before you say, "I hate this girl" I want you to know I'm usually really outgoing and fun. I love making people laugh, especially with my writing, but I'm going through a difficult time. Not being able to write, having to stand up in front of my author friends and tell them I have writer's block, hell, it wasn't easy. And this trip hasn't been the easiest ever, so please forgive me and my ornery outbursts.

Victoria and I run through check-in. We're staying at Southernmost Resort, which is located right next to the southernmost point of the United States. It's right on a beautiful beach and has the most incredible ocean-view rooms with balconies, which is what I chose, naturally. For writing purposes. I can see it now: my legs kicked up, computer on my lap, waves crashing below me, pure heaven and the perfect place to write.

Victoria, on the other hand, chose a garden-view room and

asked for a place close to the roosters, which granted her a ground-level spot. She's an odd girl, that one.

"Here is your key, Miss Ryan. Would you like help with your luggage?"

"I'm good, but could you point me in the right direction?"

"Yes, ma'am." The girl at the front desk lays a map in front of me and starts directing me where to go with a Sharpie. "Unfortunately, it is a little bit of a hike from here, but the view will be worth it."

She wasn't kidding. It takes a nice little dent out of my allotted twenty minutes to get to my room, which is on the far side of the resort but alongside the ocean. Crystal-blue ocean shines below me, and if I wasn't so scared of Zoey and her repercussions for being late, I would take the time to appreciate Mother Nature. Instead I hurry into my room, flop my suitcase on my bed, unzip it, and grab my toiletries.

Not taking a second longer, I strip down, leaving my gross airplane clothes on the floor, and practically skip to the shower where I stop mid stride.

In the shower stall is a black razor, with accompanying shaving cream. That's odd. Is that courtesy of the hotel? This place is fancy, but not that fancy. Spinning on my heel, I turn toward the sink behind me and spot a white and green toothbrush, tube of toothpaste, and men's cologne. Shit, turning toward the room, my eyes frantically roam the space, spotting a black suitcase in the corner.

Shit, shit, shit.

Naked, I cover my breasts with my arm and open the closet door only to come face to face with a few hung-up shirts.

Yup . . . I'm in someone else's fucking room.

And whoever this room belongs to is the neatest person ever because who honestly lines up their toothbrush and toothpaste tube perfectly on the counter?

Reaching for the phone, I call down to the front desk.

"Mr. Wilder, how can we assist you?" Oh yeah, totally not in the correct room.

"Uh, yeah, hi, this is Rylee Ryan. I just checked in. I was given the key to room 625 and it seems to be occupied."

"Oh dear, let me check." There is a pause on the phone and then the lady comes on the line again. "I'm terribly sorry, Miss. Ryan. We have you in room 626. Would you like to come down here and grab a new key?"

Is she kidding? The trek it took to get over here ate up enough of my time. I can't possibly take a shower if I have to run back to the lobby, grab a key, and run all the way back here.

"Would you mind bringing it to room 625? I have dinner plans and have to get changed."

"Oh, of course. I'll send someone up with a key right away."

"Thank you."

I hop around naked, eyeing my pukey clothes on the floor and the shower in the other room. Twisting my lip to the side, I try to decide what to do. I can be super quick, like really fucking quick. I just need to scrub the puke and throw on a dress, simple. Two minutes tops. The water doesn't even have to be warm. I'll write a polite note to Mr. Wilder—whoever that is—leave him five dollars as a kind gesture and quietly leave. No problem with that. Right?

Right.

Turning on the shower, I hop in before the water can warm up and hiss from the frosty temperature. I douse soap all over my hands and scrub my neck and body vigorously first, which normally I would wash my hair first but . . . puke. Once I'm satisfied with the amount of scrubbing, I wash my hair, condition it in a minute, do one more soap scrubbing all over my body before rinsing and turning the shower off. Two minutes.

Just in case Mr. Wilder is sitting outside the bathroom, I peek my head out the door, towel wrapped around my body, and call out, "Hello?"

When there is no response, I check that the coast is clear then strut to my suitcase and find a simple black sundress. Not bothering to look for underwear or a bra—I really don't need one with my perky B-cups—I lay out my dress and dry off.

29

Hopefully Mr. Wilder doesn't mind me using one of his towels or his room for that matter. *He's probably some old dude away on his golfing vacation.* I hope I don't give him a heart attack.

I drape my towel over the bed and run my hands through my naturally wavy, black hair. This will have to do. Picking up my towel one more time, I scrunch my hair, trying to soak up all the water just as the hotel door swings open, light blaring through, a tall, dark silhouette shadowed in the doorframe.

I still, frozen from the tips of my toes to the hand scrunching a towel in my hair.

Toned calves and legs are covered by black board shorts, slick to his thighs, a bulge prominent. Narrow waist where his board shorts ride low on his hips, a black shirt dancing across his broad chest, cinching sleeves cuffed over his biceps, and a V-neck providing a glimpse of how far his tan extends. Head cast down, eyes transfixed on his phone in front of him, he doesn't notice the naked girl standing in the middle of his hotel room. He stuffs his keycard in his back pocket and looks up, startled.

I scream.

He grumbles something unintelligible as I point out the obvious. "Ahhh, my boobs are naked!" It might be a little concerning that I consider my boobs to be the only things naked at this point.

As quickly as I can, I cover my body, towel making a poor attempt to hide my girly bits.

The man turns away, covering his eyes with his arm while muttering, "Oh shit."

"What the hell do you think you're doing?" I ask, struggling with my towel. I know damn well the man in front of me must be Mr. Wilder, and this is in fact his room, and I'm the one intruding, but I still feel the need to place the blame on him for walking in on me naked.

"Grabbing my sunglasses," he says, his voice terrified but also deep and rumbly. "What the hell are you doing here?"

Still trying to cover myself, I scramble to grab my dress and back up to the bathroom. "Washing my neck," I answer, nervously, boobs swaying with my erratic movements.

Eyes still covered, he keeps his back toward me but straightens up. "Washing your neck? Is that code for some kind of weird Key West thing?"

I back into the bathroom and make quick attempt of putting my dress over my head and righting it so everything is covered up. Hair still damp as well as my body, I step out into the room and clear my throat, dress sticking to my damp skin. "No, it's not code for anything. I really had to wash my neck."

"And you chose my room to do that in, because . . ."

Bending down, I shove my dirty clothes in my bag and zip up, giving Mr. Wilder the heads-up that I'm dressed. *At least he's a gentleman . . .*

When he turns around, he eyes me up and down, his gaze curious and heated when he sees just how hard my nipples are from the cold shower . . . and the unexpected peep show.

"I didn't choose your room to take a shower in." I move my suitcase to the floor and pull up the handle. "The hotel gave me the key to this room by mistake, and since I had puke on my neck from the airplane—long story—I decided to take a quick shower while I waited for my room. I apologize for taking up your space, but I think we're skipping an important detail here." I cock my hand on my hip. "You saw me naked."

"No, I didn't," he retorts rather quickly, despite the slow grin that spreads across his face.

I'm calling bullshit. "You totally saw my boobs."

"I really didn't. Your scream scared the shit out of me. I didn't have enough time to see anything before you covered up."

Eyeing him suspiciously, I ask, "You promise you didn't see anything?"

"Promise."

Hmm. "Okay, because being hotel neighbors and all, that would be extremely awkward if you saw me naked."

"Good thing I didn't then." He rocks back on his heels, hands in his pockets, unsure of what to do. Finally he reaches out to the desk next to him and holds up his black Ray Bans. "Just needed my sunglasses."

"Just needed to wash the puke," I add, not knowing what else to say.

He nods. "Okay then." He points to the door behind him. "I'm going to go then."

"Me too." We walk out together just as a hotel attendant makes his way down the outdoor hallway of the hotel. "Thanks for the shower."

"Yup, anytime." He smiles at me, giving me one more once-over.

I point my finger at him. "Promise you didn't see anything."

He holds his hands up in defense. "Promise. I have no idea what your naked tits look like."

"Well, thank God." Although, looking at this guy, maybe I wouldn't mind if *he* saw my naked bits . . .

CHAPTER FOUR

BECK

F or the record, I totally saw her tits.
    Fuck, did I see them.
    An entire eyeful of gorgeous breasts. They were small, round, perky, with tight rose-colored nipples. Hell. Two hours later and I'm still thinking about them.

Not to mention the girl they're attached to is the same girl who sat diagonally in front of me on the plane. What are the odds? When I went to get my sunglasses in my freshly unpacked room— just the way I like it—I never expected to run into a naked woman, but I'd be lying if I said I didn't like it. I only wish it wasn't under the most awkward of circumstances. I would have loved to ask what her name was, to ask her what was the deal about her first-sentence issues, or to even ask her how her day was going since the puke show.

From the look of it, not good.

"You sure you don't want to go with us?" Chris asks, his arm draped over Justine.

I shake my head. "I'm good, man. You guys go have fun getting pies. Just be careful, okay?"

"We will. Do you know your way back to the hotel?"

"It's a straight shot down Duvall and make a left. I'm good. Seriously, you two go have fun." I give Chris a fist bump. "Parents night out."

"Wooo," Justine cheers, her arm flying to the sky.

I high-five her then wish them a good night. It's almost eight o'clock and way too early for me to go to bed, but I have a good mystery book calling my name and a balcony waiting to be sat in. Sounds like a perfect night to me.

I make my way to the resort and cut through one of the pool areas. The resort has three pools, but this is the biggest one with its cascading sides, cement fish spouting water in the air, and poolside bar. The lights are dim, the water of the pool reflecting a bright teal glow, and faint music plays in the background. Everyone must be out to dinner, or down at the bars, which is so not my scene.

Closing the gate behind me, I nod at the bartender as I make my way through the pool area only to see a woman sitting at the end of the bar by herself, casually stirring a drink, legs crossed, long ebony, wavy hair lusciously falling over her shoulder.

I know that hair.

I know those slight shoulders, the smooth, freshly showered skin.

Pausing in my path to my room, I also recognize those perfects tits, small but also full. Before I can stop myself, I'm walking toward her, a bit of pep in my step and a need to know more about her.

"Can I get you anything?" the bartender asks as I walk up.

"Water is great." My answer pulls the woman's attention as I take the seat next to her. Turning in her direction, I hold out my hand. "I don't think we formally met. I'm Beck."

She eyes my hand and then looks me up and down, a knowing glint in her eyes. Sighing, she mutters, "Didn't see my boobs, my ass." She shakes her head and then takes my hand. "Rylee, nice to meet you." She takes a sip of her drink and stares at the water the bartender sets in front of me. "Not much of a drinker?"

"Not really."

"Me neither." She downs the rest of her drink and cringes. "But after today, I'm pretty sure I should be allotted an entire pint of vodka."

"Rough day, huh?"

"You could say that." She spins the ice cubes in her drink with her straw.

"I was there, you know? I saw the hell you lived through," I say, as if it was Doom's Day. "I could almost have predicted what happened to you, and if I could have stopped it, I would have. But that baby was too fast on the trigger, and I couldn't block the spewing of orange."

Perking up, she looks me square in the eyes. "You were there?"

I nod. "I saw it all happen. Witness number one, right here." I point to myself. "There was nothing you could have done. That baby hosed you. You took one for the first-class team, burped the hell out of that baby."

"You *were* there." She presses her hand against my forearm. "You were witness to the bullets of mango and peaches pelted at me."

"I can still see it in my mind in slow motion." I shake my head. "Damn shame. That sweatshirt will be stained for years to come."

She agrees, playing with my humor. "It was a good sweatshirt, so warm, so thready."

I pound the bar and then throw a fist up to the sky. "Damn you, puke, damn you." With disappointment heavy in my voice, I add, "Another innocent article of clothing bites the dust. When will it end?"

"It's a never-ending crime wave." Her hand squeezes my arm.

"Such a fucking shame." I sigh and lift my water to Rylee. "To your sweatshirt, may it be known as endlessly comfortable and practical."

"To my sweatshirt." We clink glasses and I take a sip of my

water while she plops an ice cube in her mouth. Sighing, she says, "I think I should have a burial for it."

I ponder that idea for a second and then suggest, "An at-sea burial."

As if she was thinking the same thing, she replies, "I can't imagine saying goodbye any other way."

I drink the rest of my water, guzzling it down with one tip. I set the glass on the bar in front of me and say, "Okay, let's do this."

Caught off guard, Rylee sits up. "You're serious? You want to bury my sweatshirt?"

"You tell me. Do you really think you can OxiClean that stain? That puke was neon. But if you have confidence in your stain-removing skills, by all means, soak the shit out of that thing and pray to the heavens you can make it less neon orange and breathe life back into those well-deserving threads."

She nibbles on her bottom lip and says, "Would you judge me if I admitted that my domestic skills are less than stellar?"

I lean forward myself. "Would you judge me if I said I still turn my clothes pink on occasion?"

Giggling, she shakes her head. "No, I wouldn't judge you in the slightest."

"Good." I clap my hands together. "So are we doing this? An at-sea burial?"

"I think we are." She tosses a few bills on the bar and hops down from her stool. I do the same and realize for the first time how much taller I am. Taking me in, she says suspiciously, "You're not some psycho killer who's going to toss me in the ocean with my sweatshirt, are you?"

Playing around, I add my own question. "Are you some murdering mistress trying to lure me in with your sweatshirt mishap only to shank me in the back with a bottle opener you jimmied into a knife?"

She narrows her eyes. "That too specific. It's like you've banked that way to off someone in your mind for far too long."

"You didn't answer my question."

"You didn't answer mine," she counters, head tilted up.

I very well think I might have met my match. Saucy, I like it.

"If I was a psycho killer, don't you think I would have attacked you while you were naked, or at least waited outside your door once you left to capture you and bring you to my creepy-as-fuck lady lair?"

"That's not reassuring at all." Her hands are on her hips now.

Rolling my eyes, I say, "I'm not a psycho killer."

"Prove it."

Okay, like that's easy. How does one prove they're not a psycho killer?

Searching through ideas, I finally pull my phone out and dial Chris, who answers after the first ring. I put the phone on speaker so Rylee can hear the entire conversation.

"Woooooo, dude you're missing out. We're getting all the pies. Fucking pies for days."

Rylee raises an eyebrow at me. "Chris—"

"Coconut Key lime pie in my mouth, right in my mother fucking mouth. I'm owning this bitch."

"Chris—"

"Beckkkkkk, you're missing out," Justine wails into the phone. "Don't worry. Even though it's parents' night out, we'll still bring you a piece, because we're parents after all and if anything, parents are considerate fucks."

"The most considerate fucks ever," Chris adds.

Rylee covers her mouth. She's barely containing her laughter, and I'm digging her sense of humor.

They're high, on sugar. Wouldn't be the first time. This is what they do when they're free of their kids. They eat as much sugar as they can. They won't let their kids have any, which only deprives them. So whenever they're childless, they binge and they binge hard.

They'll regret it in the morning. As always.

"I'm happy for you guys, sugar it up. Just real quick, can you tell this girl I met that I'm not a psycho killer?"

"You met a girl?" Justine excitingly squeals.

"Dude, is she hot?" Chris asks, causing Rylee to blush.

Keeping my eyes trained on her, I say, "Super fucking hot, and she's on speaker phone so if you can just give her the thumbs up that I'm a good guy, that would be awesome."

"Look him up," Justine calls out. "Beck Wilder, that's all you have to type." I roll my eyes. *Oh great.*

"Yeah, and ignore his haircut. It's recent, so don't let the buzz cut steer you wrong. He has luscious locks when he grows them out."

"So luscious," Justine chimes in. "I don't know you, lady, but I'm going to tell you right now, you'd be stupid not to get to know this man. Trust me." And with that, they hang up, making my phone turn black.

In their world, that's like dropping the mic. Ridiculous.

"Well, I guess I need to look you up." From the way she's nibbling on the side of her lip, she's curious.

I lean against a pillar next to the bar and cross my arms over my chest. "I'll wait."

Giving me a suspicious look, she pulls her phone from a pocket in her dress and types across the screen. I give her a few minutes, let her read until she pockets her phone and mimics my stance. "You're into philanthropy, huh?"

"Can't get enough of helping others, especially families in need."

"I can see that. You raised over fifteen thousand dollars for families who needed help during Christmas."

"It's a passion of mine." I shrug my success off, even though I'm damn proud of it. Anything to help, anything to ease the ache in my chest that I carry daily.

"That's a sexy passion," she admits without stumbling over her words. She's confident, I like that.

"What about you? You clearly can tell I'm not a psycho killer, despite the recent haircut."

"Yeah, about that. What made you buzz it all off?"

I rub my head, feeling the short strands stumble over my fingers. "Wanted a change, was going to warm weather, so I buzzed it."

Her eyes fall over my haircut, observing, taking it in. "I like it. You have a nice-shaped head."

Chuckling, I say, "Can't hear that compliment enough. Now stop avoiding the question; are you going to shank me or what?"

"I'm not going to shank you."

"Yeah"—I nod at her—"prove it."

Rolling her eyes, a smile twitching at her lips, she pulls out her phone and puts it on speakerphone, letting it ring out loud. Mimicking the phone-a-friend, I like it.

"What?" A groggy female voice answers.

Slightly cringing, Rylee says, "Victoria, uh hey, sorry to bother you, but can you please tell a guy I met that I'm not going to shank him."

Grumbling, the girl who Rylee spoke to on the airplane fumbles with the phone and then says, "Dear sir, stay as far away from the wild beast that stands before you. She will shank you if you look at her wrong, and she's been known to annoy friends when they're trying to sleep. She might be pretty, but she's a gold digger, a certified clinger, and shows no concern in stealing your wallet and leaving you high and dry. My advice to you is run and run fast." And then she hangs up the phone.

Before a furious Rylee can respond, I throw my head back and laugh, a good hearty laugh, the kind of laugh I haven't laughed in a while.

"Well, that didn't go as planned."

"Yeah, your friend didn't paint you in the prettiest of lights. I'm actually a little more nervous being around you. A certified clinger? I'm not sure I'm ready to have a live-in girlfriend, someone who apparently likes to steal wallets and annoy friends while they're sleeping. That's some inconsiderate shit right there." Thankfully the humor in my voice makes Rylee smile.

So goddamn pretty.

"Victoria is super cranky. Let me try a different friend. Hold please." She holds up her finger and types away on her phone. It rings twice.

"Thank God, I was just about to call you. What is that sex position you wrote about in your last book, the one where the guy is scissoring his legs—"

Rylee hangs up, her face bright red as she sticks her phone back in the pocket of her dress. "Uh . . . wrong number."

"No way." I reach into her pocket and pull out her phone. Thankfully the lock screen isn't up yet as I pull up her call history. The last number reads *Zoey Best Friend Forever*. Turning the phone toward her, I say, "Doubtful that was a wrong number." I hand her back her phone. "Are you an author?"

Relenting with a sigh, she says, "I am, and if you ask if I write porn I'm going to kick you square in the balls. Like toenail to taint."

Fuck, she's funny.

"Turn down the sauce there, lady. I wasn't about to ask you about porn. Jeeze." I look around and then lean in. "So . . . do you write porn?"

Her head falls back and she rolls her eyes, hard. "No! I write romance. There is a huge difference. Yes, I write sex scenes as my friend Zoey so beautifully revealed, but if you take the sex out of my books, there is still a funny, romantic, and witty story to be read."

"There are storylines in porn."

She points her finger at me. "No, there is not. Boss banging his secretary until she puts more toner in the copier is not a storyline."

I laugh. "Could be."

"It's not." She folds her arms and looks away.

"Okay, so tell me your author name. You got to look me up, so I want to look you up now."

She eyes me suspiciously. I'm guessing she's really giving thought to whether or not she should show all her cards with me.

Luckily, I win out because she says, "My author name is my real name, Rylee Ryan."

I type her name into the search engine on my phone. The first thing to come up on my results is her website. I click on the link and instantly see a picture of her, sitting cross-legged on a bright purple couch, books on either side of her, and a giant smile on her face. I turn the phone toward her. "Are all of those books yours?"

She nods, a blush staining her cheeks. "I'm a fast writer."

"I can see that. Damn." I click on the link about her books and take in all the shirtless men on the covers. "I'm going to take a wild guess and assume you like abs."

"Love them and pecs. Seriously, there is nothing more sexy than a man with strong, thick pecs." She cups her hands as if she has a pair of those "strong, thick pecs" in her palms.

I raise an eyebrow at her. "Is that right?" She licks her lips and nods, making me chuckle. I check the rest of her website out and then pocket my phone. "Everything checks out to be normal, so if you try to shank me, I might go *Misery* on you and Kathy Bates your little ass."

"I think I can take you."

"You can try, Saucy, you can very well try."

CHAPTER FIVE

RYLEE

I'm on a pier, at night, the ocean rippling beneath me, standing next to a sexy man. Strike that. An extremely sexy man I know practically nothing about, and we're saying goodbye to a sweatshirt encrusted in regurgitated mangoes and peaches. When I signed up for this little getaway, I never envisioned my first day going this way.

"She was good while she lasted, wasn't she?" Beck asks, looking out into the ocean where my sweatshirt ashes now rest.

"She provided so much warmth."

Scooting closer to me, Beck's woodsy cologne mixes with the ocean breeze and sends a thrill of chills up my spine. He wraps his arm around my shoulder, pulling me in close. "Such a beautiful ceremony. You did her well."

"I couldn't have done it without you," I joke, feeling a little awkward now that we've bid my sweatshirt adieu.

He sighs and turns toward a small part of the resort next to the water where they brought in sand, lawn chairs, and hammocks for a very resort-like ambiance. "Care to join me in the hammock?"

"Sounds a little naughty."

He squeezes me for a second before releasing his grip on my shoulder. "I promise to keep my hands to myself." *Why do I think I might regret that?*

He guides me down the tanning pier to the sandpit, his hand on my lower back, his strong presence making me feel comforted, like I'm in good hands.

Who is this guy and where did he come from? And why is he single?

It's like I plucked a hero from one of my books and set him in this picturesque setting.

He's everything I would write about when it comes to one of my male characters . . . besides the buzzed hair. I've always been partial to a styled haircut on a man, so the buzz is different. Hot in a way. Pushing past his hair, he has it all: the penetrating eyes, the witty banter, the easygoing, addictive personality, and he's all muscles, at least from what I can tell. Plus he has this rebel quality to him, dark and sultry in a way that has me curious to find out his story.

"I can't remember the last time I was in a hammock," Beck says, holding it still so I can climb in.

I hop in, not being the slightest bit modest because frankly, what's the point? Beck has already seen it all at this point, no matter how much he wants to deny it. Although, at least I put panties on before I went to dinner.

"I had one in my backyard growing up. I spent hours reading in it."

Beck joins me, a little clumsily which makes me giggle. Once he rights himself, he lets out a pent-up breath and his shoulders visibly relax next to me. "That hammock mounting could have gone wrong so fast. I mean, I could have flipped you right out of this damn thing and sent you straight into the sand beneath us."

"I'm glad you were able to mount somewhat gracefully"—I pause and suggestively wiggle my eyebrows—"because eating sand doesn't sound quite appetizing right now."

He grins. "Does it ever?"

"Maybe." I smirk and then look at the bright stars above us. "What brings you to Key West, Beck?"

I feel like that's a question I should have asked a while ago but with the whole naked hotel room exposure—which I have yet to tell my friends about—and the sweatshirt burial, we haven't had a real chance to get to know each other. Not that I'm complaining all too much. What I know about Beck so far is that he's a gentleman and likes to have a good time, even if that means torching a sweatshirt and sending it on it's way.

There aren't many people I know who would stand there, hand over heart, talking about the thread count of a sweatshirt while fake crying.

The corner of my lips pull up just from the image of Beck wiping "tears" from his eyes with the back of his index finger.

"Do you want the truth, or do you want a fabricated lie that will cause you to fall madly in love with me?"

Chuckling, I answer, "Both."

"Fair enough." Beck pushes his foot against the sand below us, sending the hammock into a relaxing swing. "Want the truth or the lie first?"

"Hmm, how about I guess which is which."

"Ah, things are about to get exciting." He chuckles and rubs his hands together. "Okay, reason number one." He clears his throat. "I'm attending a wedding this coming weekend, a wedding I wasn't invited to, but my friend begged me to attend because he wanted to bone his wife without children around. It doesn't make sense, but hey, I'm a good friend so here I am."

Errr, that's eerily familiar. I swallow a little harder than expected. There is no way he's crashing a wedding like me. That's only something a desperate author does in order to find signs of love again. "Okay, reason number two."

"My sister is getting married this weekend and I'm giving her away. Our dad passed away a few years ago from a heart attack, and even though we'd been estranged for two years, she asked if I would be a part of her wedding. So here I am."

Silently he swings us, my mind whirling with what the truth could be. Both stories were told so effortlessly, so he's either a really good liar, or some kind of con artist. I should be scared. I should go to my hotel room right now, wishing Beck a good night, but I don't, because I'm intrigued by this man. Behind the good looks and intelligence, there's something beneath the surface, something dark that makes understandable the age in his weathered eyes.

Because of that, I go with option number two. It seems the most plausible, because who really crashes weddings? Only crazed women with the tendency to sit in a bush with a notepad and pen and take notes while staring at couples and listening in on their conversations.

Research and all, it comes at a high price, like spikey branches to the tush.

"Hmm, I'm going to go with reason number two."

He nods and says, "I knew you were going to say that, but you're pretty little self is wrong. I don't even have a sister."

Stunned, I prop myself up as best as I can on the loose woven thread of the hammock and stare him down. "You're here to crash someone's wedding?"

He winces. "Uh, yeah, kind of."

"Unbelievable." I shake my head in disbelief and lie back down.

"Now before you judge me and give me a lecture about RSVPing—"

"I'm not judging you." I turn toward Beck, the hammock making the shift slightly difficult. "I'm just a little . . . surprised."

"I don't plan on eating any food." He bites his bottom lip. "That's a lie. I plan on eating a lot, but hey, I'll bring the party to the dance floor. If anything, I'm bringing them the gift of dance, so you can't be mad at me for that."

"I'm not mad." I laugh, still surprised. "I'm just trying to comprehend this." Looking him square in the eyes, I say, "I'm here crashing a wedding as well."

This causes Beck to sit up, his brawny chest straining the fabric of his shirt. He intently studies me, his eyes flitting back and forth until he finally asks, "You're serious? You're really crashing a wedding?"

I press my lips together and nod.

A sharp laugh escapes Beck as he lies down on the hammock and sends our swing into more of a frenzied movement. "I'm just going to assume, given our luck of baby puke, naked encounters—"

"I knew you saw boobs."

"I didn't see . . . ah hell, what's the point? I totally saw your tits and fuck, woman, they're hot." I blush . . . horrendously, my face heating up along with every vein in my body. "But like I was saying, with our luck, we're going to the same wedding."

Clearing my throat, trying to move past the part where Beck just made my nipples harden and pop out like turkey thermometers, I lamely say, "Yeah, that would be our luck."

"Let me guess, wedding is on Saturday at The Hemingway House."

Cue another rush of heat to eclipse my body. "The one and only."

He nods and lies there silently for a second before saying, "So what you're telling me is that I have a date for the wedding Saturday night."

Not expecting him to say that, I laugh out loud and for some reason say, "I'm wearing teal, in case you want to match and take couple pictures. You know, might as well do the whole couple thing up, right?"

This garners, a deep, low, rumble of a laugh from Beck. "Thank God I packed grey pants with a white button-down. There won't be any kind of clashing in those couple photos."

"Nope, not even in the slightest."

Still swinging, I say, "This is weird."

"Nah, it's fitting. Got to live life to the fullest, Rylee, because you never know when it will be taken from you." Sitting up, his statement confusing me, he holds out his hand, and nods toward the building. "Come on, I'll walk you back to your room."

I allow him to help me to my feet. I stand there, being towered over by this stranger, this mystery of a man, my apparent wedding date for Saturday, and even though he wants to walk me to my room, I'm not entirely ready for this night to be over.

With a slow, leisurely pace, we walk side by side, the ocean rolling into the shore to our right, filling in the silence. "Have any touristy things planned while you're here?" I ask, feeling kind of dumb from my question, unsure of what to fill the silence with.

"Nothing planned. Just kind of winging it." Why does that not surprise me? Beck seems like the guy who on a Wednesday, drops everything and flies to Tahiti because he wants to, hence, crashing a wedding. At least I have a somewhat sound reason for crashing. You know, rekindling my romantic brain and all.

"Me too. If Victoria doesn't want to tear me open with her pre-historic mammoth claws tomorrow, I might try to convince her to go sightseeing with me."

"Yeah? Going to tour the island? You know it's only a two-by-four, right?"

My brows pull together. "What do you mean a two-by-four?"

We stop in front of our rooms, the doors only a few feet apart. Hands in his pockets, looking sexy with his mouth quirked to the side, and his short haircut emphasizing his lovely hazel eyes, he says, "The island, it's only two miles wide by four miles long. It's incredibly small, so I think your sightseeing will only last a few hours at the most."

"Huh." I ponder this. "Shows how much research I did before I came here."

Chuckling, he answers, "A little ill-prepared, but there is nothing like a good adventure that gets my blood roaring. I'm right there with you, Rylee. I did zero research before hopping on a plane down here." I laugh. I'm learning that Beck is Mr. Impromptu. Why bother spending hours in front of a computer planning his trip? Shrugging, he continues, "Who knows, maybe we'll run into each other tomorrow." With that he tips my chin with his finger and says, "Have a good night." Pulling a key card from his back pocket, he enters his room, fist raised to the sky and shouting, "Long live your sweatshirt."

The declaration to my burned-up threads makes me snort inelegantly, but before he can see the snot spray unattractively from my nose, his door closes.

Thank God for quick-closing hinges.

I wipe my nose, pull my key card from the bra of my dress, and enter my room.

How strange. This random man, who not only witnessed puke apocalypse on the airplane, but also walked in on me while I was naked in his room, who then shared a weird sweatshirt burial, is now resting his head only a few feet away from mine. It's weird, almost like Cupid is waving his bare ass in the air, laughing and shooting darts in my direction.

That fucking chuckling cherub.

I wave my finger to the sky. "Nice try, dude. Guess who's not interested? I came here to witness love, not dive deep into the emotion myself."

CHAPTER SIX

RYLEE

"Think you have on enough sunblock?"

The paste-covered human next to me glares from beneath her sunglasses and sun hat, as well as an inch of sun block that has yet to be rubbed into her body. It's like she's making a seven-layer dip of only her skin and sunscreen.

"I'll have you know, skin cancer is not to be toyed with. It's a serious thing."

"Well aware, that's why I'm wearing sunscreen, but it's okay to show a little skin."

"Better to be safe than sorry." She caps off her bottle and sets it inside the pink and green Vera Bradley bag next to her. "Butterscotch candy?" she offers, the crinkling of the wrappers mixing with the ocean waves crashing a few feet away, as well as the playful sounds of kids around us.

"I'm good. Thanks." I down half of my water bottle and let the sun warm me up to my very core. "My body is not used to this kind of heat." I can feel myself sweating in areas I was unaware had sweat glands.

"Yes, a far cry from Maine for sure. But the sun is lovely, isn't

49

it?" Victoria stretches her lily-white arms and tries to soak in the rays . . . which is impossible with the amount of cream covering her skin. "So what was last night's phone call all about? You interrupted a very intriguing dream of mine."

"Sorry." I cringe, knowing how much Victoria relies on her dreams for her writing. She always tells me her best ideas come while she's sleeping. "I met this guy yesterday—"

"Already scouring the streets, are we?" There is a light, playful hint in Vitoria's voice.

"Ha, no, believe me, meeting this guy was all by chance."

"Ah, there you two are." Zoey's voice startles us from behind. "I've been texting you. The hubs went on some early morning fishing trip and has been gone all morning, and I just rolled out of bed looking for coffee." She takes a giant sip from a Frappuccino in her hand. "Ah, that feels good. What are we talking about?" She flops a giant beach bag next to me and pulls a lounge chair through the sand to saddle up close to mine.

Keeping her eyes closed, the brim of her hat covering her face, Victoria says, "Rylee was just telling me about a man she's seeing."

"Say what?" Zoey cranes her neck to the side like it's made of elastic.

"I'm not seeing him. Jesus, Victoria. We just, hung out . . ."

"Why did you trail off like that? Did you guys have sex last night?"

"I think they did. She called me for a recommendation. I told the guy to run for his life."

Zoey clutches her chest and laughs entirely too loud. "You did not."

"Unfortunately she did," I mumble, pulling my legs into my chest.

More laughter, from both of them now. Can you hear my heavy sigh?

"Oh that's so great. So what happened after you failed to get a recommendation?" Zoey pauses and then whacks my arm. "Hey, why didn't you call me? Am I not good enough to give you a sex-a-mendation?"

"I tried! You answered the phone asking about scissoring with Art."

Zoey nods, the corner of her lips turns down in agreement. "It's frightening how accurate that is. Okay, so I was hyper-focused on my own pleasure. What happened after Victoria cock-blocked you?"

Sitting up some more and crossing my legs, I say, "For the record, I wasn't looking for a sex-a-mendation. I was just trying to prove I'm not a psycho killer."

"Smart man." Zoey nods and sips on her drink.

"Well, you know after he saw me get barfed on, and then after the whole naked thing, he came up to me—"

"Wait." Zoey and Victoria both sit up and lean over to look at me. "What naked thing?"

"I don't really want to get into it. Let's just say there was a mix-up with hotel rooms, and I wanted to get the puke smell off me."

"I'm so confused right now," Victoria says. "I thought there was no sex."

"There wasn't. We didn't have sex or even kiss. He just saw me naked."

"Talking about me?" A deep voice pulls our eyes off each other and toward the man standing in front of us wearing a pair of low-slung black board shorts and nothing else besides a long necklace around his neck that's made of leather and a small gold key. His tan skin glistens under the sun, the contours of each and every one of his muscles flexing tightly with every move. His smile stretches across his face, his eyes are full of intrigue, and his hair begs for me to run my hand over the short strands.

Turning toward me, thumb pointed at Beck, Zoey asks, "Is this the guy you wanted the sex-a-mendation for?"

Want a sure-fire way to make me blush? This, this right here will do it.

My cheeks heat up, my ears burning with embarrassment.

"Sex-a-mendation, huh?" Beck scratches the side of his jaw, his eyes trained on mine. "I wasn't aware that's what we were calling friends for."

"It wasn't. There was no sex involved. None." I can feel my forehead start to sweat. Damn sun. "Just making sure we weren't going to murder each other, that's all. Sex is off the table. There will be no sex."

"No? That's a damn shame." Beck smiles and then leans over to shake Zoey and Victoria's hands. "Ladies, nice to meet you, I'm Beck." Zoey and Victoria introduce themselves, their mouths agape like fishes out of water as they stare at the mound of muscles in front of them. Hell, I don't blame them.

"Beck, wow even your name is hot." Zoey pokes me in the side with her elbow. "You should use that name in one of your novels."

"I agree." Beck wiggles his eyebrows. "Maybe he could convince the heroine to go sightseeing with him in the book."

"Ooo, that's a good idea." Zoey picks up my bag and puts it on my lap. "Rylee was just leaving to go tour the island."

"No, I wasn't."

"Yes, she was," Victoria chimes in. Traitor. "She wants to rent a Vespa. She tried to get me to get on one but I refused. You seem like a gentleman who knows how to handle that kind of machinery. Why don't you go with her?"

"Beautiful idea. Grand actually," Zoey adds, and after digging through her purse, lifts a five-dollar bill to the sky and waves it. "Ice cream is on me."

I eye the bill, hating both my friends right now. "We're going to need more than five dollars."

"Here." Victoria tosses a twenty at me. "Have fun."

"See, all set. Just tuck those bills in your bra with your license and go have fun." Zoey starts pushing me off the edge off my lounge. "Go on. Sightsee with the hunk. Thank us later."

"You know he's standing right here," I grit out in utter embarrassment.

"Oh, don't mind me." Beck rocks on his heels and crosses his arms over his chest. "I'm just here for the free ice cream and great company."

"How can you turn down free ice cream?" Zoey now waves both bills in front of me, a knowing look on her face.

Sighing, I snag the money from her, stuff it in my bra top along with my phone, room key, and ID and stand from my lounge chair. I point at Victoria and say, "You're in charge of my bag." Turning toward Beck, I say, "You're in charge of renting the Vespa, come on." I grab him by the hand and pull him toward Duval Street.

Thankfully I'm wearing a little black cover up over my white bikini because driving around in nothing but a bathing suit isn't on my to-do list today. Although, it seems like it's on Beck's.

"You know, you don't have to sprint. We can walk leisurely."

Noticing my giant and very awkward steps propelling us forward at an alarming pace, I slow down and straighten myself. "Eh, sorry. Just wanted to get out of there before those two said anything else embarrassing."

Beck nudges me with his shoulder. "Oh come on, they weren't that bad. I liked them."

"Yeah, because they practically pushed me into your arms."

"Into my arms? I would have remembered that." His smile is devilish and I'm very much aware of how that little tilt of his lips affects me.

"Don't be cheesy."

"Not cheesy when it's the truth." Nudging me again, he says, "And what's with this tough front you're putting on? I catch you talking about our night and now you're acting like you want nothing to do with me? That's not the truth, right?"

Man, is he upfront. I don't think I've ever had a man call me out like that before. I should have known after one look at Beck that he was going to be different than I'm used to.

Letting out a long breath, I turn toward him, stopping him on the sidewalk and say, "That's not the truth. I'm just . . . aware of our situation, and it makes me nervous."

"Aware of our situation. What does that mean?" He takes a step forward, closing an immense amount of distance between us.

"You know." I gesture between us, my nerves jumping. "This, uh, attraction."

"What about it?" He places his hand on my hip, and legit, my mouth goes dry.

It's just a hand on my hip. It's not like he stuck his hand down the back of my swimsuit and started massaging my ass. No, it's a hand to the hip, but with the way he so powerfully grips me, and his unwavering stare, he has my body tingling, anticipating so much more.

Wanting to be honest, since he gets to the point, I say, "I'm not looking for anything serious, or to start anything with anyone. I'm here to write, to be immersed in love, and then be on my merry way. That's all."

A larger smile splits his lips. "Sounds like a plan, but I see some holes in it I would like to fill."

"Beck——"

He places his finger over my lips, shushing me before I can protest. "Listen, Rylee. I didn't come here to fall in love. I came to have a good time and live in the moment. I find you sexy as hell, interesting, and someone I want to spend some island time with. I'm not looking for anything serious either, but to hell if I'm going to take you as my wedding date and not spend some time with you beforehand."

I snort, just like last night and quickly cover my nose. How grossly unattractive. When I glance at Beck, he doesn't seem to think so from the heated look in his eyes.

"You want to spend some time with your wedding date, huh?"

He nods. "You got it, Saucy."

I press my lips together, trying to mull this over. "Nothing serious. Just fun?"

"Living in the moment is what I like to call it. Saying yes, rather than no."

I can jump on board with that. It might be good for me actually, to step outside of my little box I like to bury myself in, and actually experience life with nothing holding me back.

It almost seems . . . freeing.

Before the worrisome side of my brain kicks in, I say, "I would love to live in the moment with you. But no strings attached, right?"

"None. Just the memories of two wedding crashers and the remnants of an island tan."

It's my turn to smile. "Then what are we waiting for? It's time to see what this two-by-four island is all about."

Beck links my hand with his. "That's the girl I was looking for."

"**Y**ou're kidding, right?" Beck stares me down, disbelief in his eyes.

"Dead serious."

Pulling me away from the counter, from the prying eyes of the rental worker, he says, "We're not sharing a Vespa, and if we did, you sure as hell wouldn't be the one driving."

Hand on my hip, I reply, "And why the hell not?"

"Uh, so many reasons."

"Name them." I challenge him.

"Well, for one I have more experience. I own and drive a motorcycle." Of course. I could have easily guessed that from the way Beck carries himself. "Also, I'm much bigger than you. Bigger in the front to cushion any blow we might have."

"That's a lie. No way that's a thing."

"Well, it is in my head."

I can tell he's not going to back down on this, but too bad, I'm just as stubborn.

"I'm driving."

"Fine, then we'll get two Vespas."

"No." I shake my head. "Then we won't be able to talk to each other. Plus it's a waste. We could easily get the two-seater and pay less as well."

"You're not driving us."

"I'm driving."

"No, you're not." He matches his hands on his hips to mine.

"Yes, I am."

Stewart, the man in charge of the rentals clears his throat, drawing our attention. "Can I make a suggestion since it seems like you two are having a hard time deciding who's going to drive?"

An outsider. Hmm, he might be partial. "Yes, Stewart, we would be delighted to hear your suggestion." I turn toward him, interested in solving this little dispute.

Reaching into his pocket, he pulls out a quarter and says, "Flip a coin to decide." Duh, that was easy.

"Brilliant idea." I snag the coin from Stewart and hold it up. "Would you like to call it, Beck, or shall I?"

"We are not flipping a coin to decide." Beck tosses his ID on the counter and says, "I'm driving."

Stewart, the beautifully hairy man takes one look at the ID in front of him and then folds his arms over his chest. "I believe the lady wants to flip a coin."

"Yeah, Beck, the lady wants to flip a coin." I stand there in my black cover-up, at least eight inches shorter than Beck, chest puffed, and putting up one hell of a fight.

Eyeing me, Beck asks, "You're not going to back down, are you?"

"Nope."

"But you could kill us."

I shrug. "What happened to living in the moment? Here's your moment, Beck, flip a coin and decide your fate."

Sighing heavily and running a hand through his short strands, Beck says, "I'll call it in the air."

Giddy, I flip the coin and Beck calls out, "Heads." I catch the coin and flip it over to the back of my other hand. Beck, Stewart, and I all lean forward, eyes trained on the fate of the toss.

With a touch of flair, I lift my hand and reveal the coin.

"It's tails," Stewart declares with far too much excitement for being a third party in this little disagreement. "She's driving, dude. I'll take your ID, Rylee."

Feeling like I won the lottery, I hand over my ID and lean on the counter while I smile all too brightly at Beck, who seems to be . . . yup, grinding his teeth. He's not happy, and for some reason, I really like seeing that.

Tapping his cheek, I say, "Just think of it this way. You get to hold on to me. Now that's something to look forward to."

Bending toward me, Beck whispers in my ear. "Damn right I do, and if my hands accidentally rub against those sweet tits of yours, then so be it."

Cue gasp and beet-red face.

Damn him!

~

"You have to ease into the brakes, or else we're going to fly over the handle bars."

"It's more fun this way." I hit the brakes at a stop light, jerking the Vespa forward and causing Beck to grunt behind me.

"Woman, as much fun as you think it is to crash my cock into your backside, we're going to have a serious problem if you continue to do that."

From over my shoulder, I ask, "Getting excited, Beck?"

His jaw ticks, his hands on his thighs, the strain in his neck evident. "Don't play with me, Saucy."

"Isn't that what this is all about? Playing?" The light turns green and I slam on the gas pedal, sending us into a speedy fifteen miles per hour down the colorful road of Duval Street where flags hang from buildings and palm trees offer a brief shade to passersby.

Wrapping his arms around my waist, his entire chest eclipses my back as he brings his head forward and speaks into my ear. "Are you going to be a tease this entire time?"

My inner goddess smiles. "Count on it."

His chuckle rumbles against my back. "Fair enough, but be warned, two can play at that game."

"I'm looking forward to it."

I direct the Vespa down the road, the wind breezing through my hair, Beck's hands roaming from my stomach to my thighs, depending on how close he's leaning against me. I can only imagine how he must look behind me, a massively attractive and larger-than-life man gripping me, his arms flexing under the beaming sun. From the stares we're getting from tourists on the streets, I'm going to guess he either looks ridiculous, or the women who have their mouths open as we pass by are a tiny bit jealous.

Hell, I don't blame them.

Believe me when I say this, I don't do "non-committal flings" often, or ever for that matter, but there's something about Beck and his *live life* motto that has me throwing caution to the wind and experiencing something new, something crazy out of the box for me, something I know will stick with me for years to come.

So why the hell not just experience rather than worry?

Maybe it will spark my imagination.

Maybe this little break from reality is just what I need.

"Where we going, speedy?" Beck grips my hips, pulling my attention from another red light.

"Uh, straight?"

"Straight?" He laughs. "Well, if you keep going straight you're going to end up in the ocean. I don't know about you, but drowning this rental wasn't on my list of things to do today."

Such a smart-ass. "Okay, then what was on your list?"

"Let's go to Mallory Square. It's up there on the left." He directs me with a point of his finger toward a parking lot.

Making the turn, I rumble our bike over the uneven concrete of the road and park between a red Ford Mustang convertible and a black Hummer. I give our "whip" a once-over and talk over my shoulder to Beck. "We look a little ridiculous right now."

"Slightly. But what's really going to get us into some trouble is people thinking this spot is empty only to realize you parked this hot two-wheeler here instead."

"Ugh, I hate people like us."

"I'm partial to park whatever you want, wherever you want." Beck hops off the back of the Vespa and holds his hand out to me.

"That's because you drive a motorcycle. You're the person everyone hates."

He shrugs. "Couldn't care less what everyone thinks. Plus, I park in the back to avoid a kick to my bike from angry car drivers."

"Ah, smart." After Beck helps me off, he pays for parking and tucks the slip in a crack near the speedometer.

"Come on, Saucy." *Saucy.* No idea why he's sticking with that, but it's kinda cute. He takes my hand in his and guides me past a brick house labeled restroom that smells like a place to dispose of excrements, and down a little narrow path where we come across a bunch of little kiosks selling your typical touristy island souvenirs. "Are you a souvenir kind of girl?"

"Sometimes, depends on the souvenir. It has to be good, something I wouldn't be able to get anywhere else, and I'm not talking about your typical location-branded shirt or mug. It has to be super unique."

"Something off the wall?"

"Exactly."

Beck stops in front of a kiosk full of musical instruments particular to the island like bongos, maracas, and didgeridoos. Not that a didgeridoo is necessarily an island instrument but contrary to popular belief, I don't see didgeridoos sold everywhere. Beck picks up a rainmaker and turns it upside down so the beans start bouncing off the pins inside the tube. "Tell me, what unique souvenirs have you bought before?"

Okay, let's pause for a second. You know how I said I only buy a souvenir if it's super unique? That's true, but what I left out is the massive collection of a certain souvenir that I have at home. And when I say massive collection, I mean a good shelf full of a particular item I seem to find everywhere I go, or that my readers have purchased for me.

Interested? Want to know what it is?

You're thinking silver spoons, aren't you? Tiny silver spoons labeled with each location, right? Even though they're cute, that's not it.

Not spoons, not mugs, not keychains, or magnets. No, this is unique, a special find you can only locate in a quirky store.

And there is always one quirky store in a touristy town, and you just have to find it. It's the store that carries those dolls that come alive at night, but also Christmas ornaments, local hot sauce, kitchy oven mitts, and . . . hunks.

Yes, hunks.

How do I explain this? They are little glass or plastic man figurines turned into something special like an ornament, or a bottle opener, of a wine glass ornament. They are always shirtless, hunky, and so goddamn amazing that whenever I see one, I add them to my collection. It's an immediate purchase for me.

My favorite of these glorious gems is my collection of hunky mermen ornaments. You would think, wow, there mustn't be much variety of those. Oh by golly, are you wrong. I don't think I will ever own all of them and it makes me sad. I want all the hunky mermen. Is that too much to ask?

Sigh.

"Why are you smirking over there?" Beck pokes me with his rainmaker.

"Oh, uh, just having a good time, you know, making rain." I shake a rainmaker and put it back in the bin.

"Yeah, that's not the truth. There's a souvenir you collect that you're not telling me about."

Is this man a mind reader? God, he's too damn perceptive. I have a feeling there won't be much I'll be able to get past him over the next few days. None of my ex-boyfriends have been particularly perceptive, so to them, I appear to be an open book. They don't know there has been so much I've never bothered to share.

"Maybe," I say coyly while walking over to the next kiosk that has woodcarvings. I pick one up and admire the craftsmanship.

"And are you going to tell me what this souvenir is?"

"Nope."

"Then how the hell am I supposed to help you find it?"

I turn toward him, putting the woodcarving back in place. "Oh Beck. I don't search out the souvenir, the souvenir finds me."

"Bullshit, you're looking for it right now, aren't you?"

Yes.

"No. If my special souvenir is here, it will be kismet if we meet up."

Beck shakes his head and walks me toward a shell shop. "I don't believe that one bit. You're on the prowl. I can feel it. You're searching, but what could it be?"

"You're never going to guess. Believe me. This isn't your typical souvenir."

"You've made that point. Don't worry, my mind is set on unique, out-of-the-box objects like this." He picks up a ball cap that has a helicopter on the top. Placing the hat on his head— entirely too large for the child's headwear—he spins the helicopter and exudes that devastating charm of his. "You collect these hats, don't you? You have at least fifty of these that you line up along a stretch of your hallway and try to spin them all at the same time."

Hands on hips, I cock my head to the side. "Do you really think I have time to do such a thing?"

Unapologetically he shrugs. "Hey, I don't know what you do with your personal time."

I snag the hat from his head and flip it back into its box. "Not that."

"All right." Picking up a conch shell, he brings it to his ear and says, "Shells seem too basic to collect. Unless"—his eyes light up with humor—"you collect dick-shaped shells. That's unique and a very hard find. That takes some examining."

Chuckling, I shake my head. "No dick-shaped shell collection, although, now you have me thinking I probably should start collecting them." I peer my head around. "See any?"

"Not yet, but if I do, you can bet that pretty ass of yours I'll be the first to start that collection for you."

"Ooo, don't get me excited, the disappointment would be heartbreaking."

Beck studies me for a second, his hand rubbing against the light scruff on his chin. "You know, from your excitement over a dick-shaped seashell I'm going to guess your little souvenir has something to do with an adult souvenir, something . . . sexy perhaps?" There's no way he'll figure it out, at least I hope he doesn't.

I give him no inclination to whether or not he's right, instead, I turn my back and pick up a black pokey shell and examine it.

"Aha, I'm right, aren't I?"

"No." I try to hide my smile, but it's impossible when Beck is standing next to me, playfully poking me in the side.

"Oh, I'm so right. Okay, sex souvenirs. Hmm, where do we find sex souvenirs?"

"Can you not say that so loud?" I pull on his hands that are rubbing together as he looks around.

"What? You don't want people know you're looking for sex souvenirs?"

Feeling my face getting red, once again I say, "I'm not. That's something you made up."

"No way. You are so looking for sex souvenirs." A worker walks by us just in time for Beck to gather his attention. "Dear sir, would you mind helping us?"

"Of course, sweetheart," the man replies in the deepest New York accent I've ever heard with a hint of drag queen. And from the Hawaiian shirt and heels he's wearing I'm going to guess I'm right. I heard Key West is very gay friendly and has some of the best drag shows ever, and boy, does it seem like they were right. I'm intrigued.

"My friend over here, the cute one"—the worker eyes me up and down and smiles, hands clasped together at his chest—"is looking for a sex souvenir, do you have any?"

The man laughs as I feel a strong urge to climb into the shell I hold in the palm of my hand. I'm going to kill him.

"Oh honey, we don't sell condoms here. Go to CVS around the corner."

At my very blank and confused look, he adds, "Don't you realize you're supposed to be her sex souvenir?"

The man pats Beck on the back and walks away, or more like sashays. Spinning on his heel, Beck faces me and asks, "Am I your sex souvenir, and I don't even know it? Oh my God, do you have a punch card or something, a form I have to fill out? Are you going to take a picture of me with a Polaroid camera, have me sign it, and then hang it with your other sex souvenirs?" He clasps his hand to his chest in disgust. "Am I merely here to be your . . . fuck toy?"

Oh for heaven's sake!

CHAPTER SEVEN

BECK

"You can't possibly be getting that?"
"Why the hell not? She's fucking beautiful. The minute I saw her, I knew I had to have her." I dangle my newfound item from my finger, loving every last inch of her.

"It's a drag-queen sea turtle with glitter everywhere," Rylee deadpans.

"Yeah, and she's fucking gorgeous. Look at her turtley tits and pearls. That's classy."

Rylee's eyebrows rise. "You think that's classy? I might be a little terrified. What sea turtle has breasts, let alone lips like that?"

"The best kind of sea turtles." I take the ornament to the counter and pull out my wallet. Thankfully the island is full of partially dressed tourists or else I'd feel really out of place with no shirt. The vibe is pretty relaxed here, and I'm not going to lie, I fucking love the way Rylee keeps sneaking glances at my bare chest. She's totally contemplating making me her sex souvenir.

"Oh you found our most popular ornament, isn't she beautiful?"

"Did you hear that, Saucy?" I nudge Rylee, who's leaning

against the register counter with her arms crossed. "Most popular ornament."

"I heard her. Seems like you're not the only deranged person here." She mumbles the words just loudly enough so only I hear them.

Dragging her into my body, I wrap my arm around her waist and haul her close to my chest. Her lavender scent—shampoo maybe—makes its way around me, wrapping, squeezing, engulfing. "We're on our honeymoon," I say, rubbing my fingers over her soft skin. "I'm getting this ornament so my new bride can remember this special occasion. When every Christmas rolls around, she'll remember the day we said I do whenever she looks at this sea turtle."

"Oh what a beautiful memory. You found yourself a good one," the clerk says as she rings up Pearl, my sea turtle. Yes, I'm calling her Pearl. My initial instinct was to call her Turtle Titty Tata, but Pearl has the elegance and class she deserves.

"I tell her that every day." I hug Rylee and kiss the top of her head. She's stiff but with a light peck to her head, her body molds to mine.

"No souvenirs for the lady?"

"Nah, nothing for my girl." Rylee gently wraps her arm around my waist for a brief moment, almost like she's unsure about her touch. "She told me earlier that the wild honeymoon sex we're going to have will be souvenir enough."

"Oh dear." The clerk fans herself. "Well, I don't blame her." She takes my card and swipes it. "I don't know why you two are even out in public right now." She hands me my card back and nods at Rylee. "With a man like that, I would be hanging out in bed every chance I get."

If only I could see Rylee's burnt-red face right now, it would make this moment so much better.

"We have to come out for air at some point, you know?" I wink at the clerk, who blushes herself as she hands me my wrapped up Pearl in a bag.

"Enjoy, you two. And congratulations."

"Thank you." I wave to the clerk and leave the shop, Rylee in tow.

When we reach the street, Rylee continues to walk when I half expected her to confront me. Her little legs propel her forward, leaving me in her wake. Running up to her side, I catch her hand in mine and say, "What's the rush?"

"I want pie." She forgoes eye contact and crosses the street, barely checking for traffic, and heads straight toward a small yellow building with a sign that says "The Original Key Lime Pie Bakery."

Hell, if she wants pie, so do I. After listening to Chris and Justine talk this morning at breakfast all about their pie binge, I'm craving some. And from what they told me, this bakery has the best Key lime pie, especially the one with coconut.

My taste buds are already watering.

When we walk in, it's not the kind of bakery I'm used to. I expected a wall-to-wall bakery cooler of goodies, but instead, it's packed full of Key lime-flavored everything, packaged and branded for all the tourists. I give the treats a glance, but when my eyes become glued on the pies in the back under a glass case, I'm like a tractor beam to the goods, right next to Rylee, who's already ordering.

"Yes, one slice of each, please."

"Oh, you're a hungry one, aren't you?" the lady asks.

Rylee grabs my arm and drapes it over her shoulder, snuggling in close. Her cheek rubs against my chest, practically purring. What is she up to?

"Something like that." Smiling at me, she turns back to the lady and says, "We're on our honeymoon."

"Oh really? Congratulations, that's wonderful. Are you having a nice time in Key West?"

"It's beautiful here," Rylee gushes. "Just wish we spent more time in the bedroom, if you know what I mean."

"Oh dear." The poor older lady looks shocked.

Rylee sighs heavily and then pats my abs. "He might be a pretty thing to look at, but he's having a hard time getting an erection. Hence all the pies. Kind of eating my sorrows. Married a bit of a dud, rather than a stud. But hey, that's okay. That's why they make dildos." Rylee takes the bag from the incredibly stunned woman and links her hand with mine. "Come on, sweetie, maybe the sugar rush will help your peenie get happy."

Peenie?

Dildos?

Dud rather than a stud?

What the hell did I get myself into with this woman?

I've met my match.

Stunned, I follow a very happy Rylee out the door, avoiding the raised eyebrows of disappointment from every woman I pass.

Touché.

Tou-fucking-ché.

~

"Where do you live?" I raise a glass of water to my lips and await her response, genuinely interested in her answer.

She bites down on a ketchup-covered fry and says, "A small town in Maine called Port Snow. It's kind of like Key West, in the way it thrives off its tourists."

"Port Snow, sounds like a magical place."

She nods. "It's beautiful, but the winters can be bitter. We're right on the coast so we get the whip of the cold ocean breeze, and if you're not wearing the proper gear, you can freeze your nipples right off."

"Shit, not the nipples." I mock horror, bringing my hand to my chest.

She leans forward, fry in hand. "Yes, the nipples."

"That's fucked up." She chuckles and it's so intoxicating that I can easily see myself getting drunk on that sound. It's been an amazing day, hanging out with Rylee, ribbing with her. The heated glances, the small touches, the one-upping each other. Fuck, she's fun. "Other than nipples freezing off, you like it there?"

"Yeah. It's where I grew up. Everyone is in each other's business, but we also look out for each other. My best friends live there and so does my family. They own an art gallery that surprisingly does really well. The tourists flock in during the summer, scoop up all the lighthouse pictures, and then take off, taking a little piece of Maine home with them."

"That's pretty cool. Where do you get the pictures from? Anyone in the family an artist?"

She shakes her head. "My mom dabbles in different aesthetics, but she's never wanted to sell any of her pieces, because she doesn't think they're sell worthy even though we beg to differ. We commission all the pieces from local artists and artists from around the state."

"So where did the writing come in?"

Smiling, she dips another fry in the shared ketchup bowl we have between us and pops it in her mouth. "I was always into telling stories, but it wasn't until I went to a creative writing class in college that the urge to tell stories really bit me, and I think it's mainly because my creative writing teacher said I wasn't very good at storytelling."

"She said that? Man . . ." I lean back in my chair. "What a bitch."

"Tell me about it. She gave me a C in the class." She scrunches her nose, crinkling the skin and it's cute. Adorable. Sincere.

"And now you're a successful author. Good job for sticking it to her."

Rylee leans back in her chair as well and folds her arms over her chest, amplifying her breasts but instead of staring, I keep my eyes fixed on hers—despite the *strong* temptation to check her out. I have yet to be up close and personal with her sexy tits, but if the opportunity presented itself, I'm there. "I wish. I have no idea where she is, or else I would send her a few signed paperbacks with a copy of every single paper she gave me a bad grade on."

"You kept them?"

She nods with a smirk. "Have them laminated in a folder."

"You did not laminate them."

"I did," she answers, almost seeming bashful now. "Sometimes, you have to hold on to the things that tried to tear you down, because it's good to be reminded why you're going to succeed."

Studying her, I tilt my head slightly to the side, trying to get a good read on this woman who almost seems like a dream. Sexy, smart, sassy as hell, with enough wit to keep me on my toes. She quite possibly could be too good to be true. Wait, she is, because she lives in Maine. I live in California, and this is a no-strings-attached fling.

But still, I can tell already she's going to be a hard one to let go at the end of this.

"What's that look on your face for?" she asks, motioning in my direction.

I rub my hand along my jaw, feeling the rough bristles against my fingertips. "You're sexy."

"Oh . . . that's not what I thought you were thinking." Her cheeks turn a pretty crimson color. I really like that even though she can hold her own in a battle of wit, she still shows moments of innocence.

"And what did you think I was going to say?"

"I don't know, not that."

"Well, it's true." I lean forward, eyes focused on hers, loving the way her eyelashes flutter with every glance she gives me. "One thing you'll find out about me, Rylee, is I don't lie. I say what's on my mind."

"Is that so?" Her fingers twist and pull on the napkin in her lap.

I nod, watching how her eyes light up, ready to strike with that saucy mouth of hers.

"Then how come you told me you didn't see me naked initially but then told me differently later? Hmm?"

Goddamn that smile. Makes me want to take her back to my

room and kiss it right off her face until she's moaning my name, writhing, begging for more.

"I was sparing you from embarrassment. You clearly were not super excited that I saw you naked."

"Uh, who in their right mind would be excited about a stranger seeing them naked?"

"I couldn't care less about someone seeing me naked. You know, wearing nothing is how God intended it." I take a sip of my water. "Clothes are just accessories. It's what's beneath us—our true selves—that matters."

Rylee rolls her eyes at my corny philosophy. "Please, you're just saying that because you're an Adonis under your clothes. Let me guess, you have hairless balls, a big penis, and thighs that can crush a walnut."

Laughing, I say, "I don't know about the walnut thing, but the other two assumptions are spot on. Care to take a gander to see if I'm lying?"

"God, no. That is such a guy thing to say." In a deep voice, she mocks me, "*Hey, girl I find attractive. Why don't you come pull my pants down and stare at my penis and balls? I think they're amazing.* Balls and penises are not all that great to look at. I would rather play with an eighty-year-old-man's ear hair than examine balls and penis."

"You don't find the male genitals attractive?"

"Not even in the slightest. You have a flesh tube right above a dangling sac of skin full of milky white crap that is less than pleasing to have in your mouth, dripping down your legs, and in your vagina."

Caught off guard from her candidness, I take a sip of my water, eyeing her from over my glass. "I don't think it's the male genitalia that you find repulsive—"

"I never said repulsive. It's just not something I want to have a staring contest with, that's all."

"Either way," I cut in, "I don't think it's the dick's fault. I think it's the men you've been with, because I'm going to tell you right now, when my come is dripping down your thigh, or across your stomach, or in your mouth, you're going to crave it." Leaning forward, my voice dropping lower, I say, "And remember, I don't fucking lie."

Tossing some cash on the table, I stand from my seat, pick up our shopping bags, and hold my hand out to Rylee. Shakily, she takes it and once again, we hop on our ride for the day. This time, though, she's sitting in the back. I refuse to ride on the bitch seat anymore.

"What do you think you're doing?"

"Pulling an alpha move on you, and you're going to let me. Hop on, Saucy. It's time I showed you the island."

With little hesitation, she straddles the bike and wraps her arms around my waist, her fingers barely caressing my abs. Fuck, just the way I like it.

～

"You're cheating!"

"I am not."

"Yes, you are," she accuses me, swiping the dice before I finish entering my score.

"How the hell am I cheating?"

Shaking the dice in her hands, she watches me suspiciously. "At the moment, I'm unclear how you're cheating, but I will find out. And when I do, ohhhh boyyy, are you in trouble. I'm coming for you, Wilder."

"There is no way someone can cheat in Yahtzee. It's all luck."

"Oh yeah? Then why do you yell Yahtzee every time you throw the dice? Are the dice voice controlled?" She tosses the dice on the table and yells Yahtzee at the top of her lungs, shaking the water glasses perched on the table. When the dice stop, they reveal a load of crap.

"Damn it all to hell." She tosses her arms in the air.

"You can't cheat in Yahtzee."

"Clearly I can't, but you can." She looks under the table. "What do you have under there? What are you playing with? Do you have some kind of dice flipper like in the movie *Ocean's Thirteen?*"

"You're losing it, Saucy."

"How can someone have five Yahtzees in one game? What are you playing with?" Standing from her chair, she pushes me so I'm sitting back in my seat and lifts my hands from my lap. "What's this piece of paper? Does it have Yahtzee secrets on it?"

I toss the rolled-up piece of paper and hit her between the eyes. She huffs as I say, "It's my straw wrapper. Can you please undo the calamity that is your mammary, take a seat, and finish your turn?"

Eyes on fire, a fierce pinch to her brow, she puts a hand on the table and leans into me. "What did you just say to me?"

Nervously laughing, I play with my water glass and say, "I, uh, asked you to calm your tits, you know, adjust your bust before it combusts."

Her tongue runs along her teeth as she straightens. I don't think I like the wild look in her eyes, like she could easily pull a shiv from her back pocket and stab me in the thigh with it.

"Let me get this straight. You're the one cheating and you tell ME to calm my TITS? Is that right, Beck? Is that what I'm hearing?"

Wow, talk about sore loser. Note to self: don't play games with Rylee unless I can purposely lose.

"Well, for one, yes, that's what I'm saying, and two, I'm not cheating." Call me stupid, but I'm not one to back down from an angry female. If anything, I like to push them even harder, because fuck if it isn't fun. *Especially when they're hot like Rylee and easily riled.*

"Beckford Wilder, don't you dare lie to me."

Holding back the laugh that wants to spring out of me, I answer, "My name is Beck, but I like how you tried to add a little finesse to it. And what did we just talk about? I don't lie. I'm not cheating."

"Yes, you are."

"No, I'm not."

"Yes!"

I calmly fold my arms over my lap. "No."

"Ugh, you're infuriating."

"And you suck at Yahtzee."

Ooo, did you just see that fireball? Holy hell, I swear one just popped out of her eyeballs.

Steam is billowing from every orifice of her body. At least it seems like it as her hands flex at her sides. Is she going to . . . punch me?

"Is everything okay here, miss?" the waitress asks, looking a little frightened herself.

Hell, I don't blame her. I'm two seconds from hopping behind the bar and ducking for cover, because I'm nervous her bust is truly about to combust.

Exploding nipples, take cover!

Whipping her head to the side, Rylee points at me and says, "Do you smell that? He won't stop farting, and I can't take one more second of it."

Say what?

The waitress lifts her nose, her nostrils sucking in the air around us. Oh for fuck's sake. "Oh, I do smell something."

Okay, for the record, I haven't been farting. I wouldn't do that. I'm all male, but I'm not a moron. Rule number one: don't fart when with a woman you want to fuck on the beach. It's common sense.

"You smell nothing," I scoff. "Rylee here doesn't like how I'm beating her at Yahtzee. If anyone should be offended it should be me for the cheating accusations she's throwing my way. I'm an honest man, a man of integrity, and I would never cheat when it comes to anything, especially such a vivacious and exhilarating dice game. No, I like a true, honest, and hard-earned win, something I can be proud of for many years to come." Tapping the table with my index finger, I continue, "This day will be marked in memory as the day I scored over six hundred points in Yahtzee, a day of infamy."

The waitress and Rylee exchange glances after my little speech only to be followed by Rylee rolling her eyes and saying, "No one asked you."

The waitress walks away and Rylee retreats to her side of the table, but not before I snag her arm and pull her onto my lap. A sound of surprise escapes past those luscious lips as she pushes stray strands of her silky hair out of her face.

Not able to control myself, I graze my hand up the length of her arm, over her shoulder, to the dip in her neck, our eyes connected the entire time. "Do you really think I'm a cheater?"

Her eyes search mine, her body leaning into my touch. "A cheater?" She gently shakes her head, becoming serious. "I don't think you actually have that bone in your body."

Cupping her face, I stoke her cheek with my thumb, once, twice, three times. Her eyes flutter shut, her lashes long and black, curled at the ends. When they open, I'm met with beautiful blue eyes, sincerity ringing through them. There's a depth to them, slightly weary, hopeful . . .

A shaky breath escapes her when I grip her hip, my fingers, just the tips, skimming her backside. She's sitting sideways on my lap, one of her palms pressing against my chest with the other snaked to the back of my neck. Our light and jovial energy slowly morphs into something more sensual, more seductive.

Her pink tongue peeks out and wets her lips. One swipe, then two. Glistening under the sun, plump and ready for me. So tempting.

She leans forward, her nose mere millimeters from mine, her breath mixing with mine, her body humming with anticipation. Lightly her fingers play with the short strands on the back of my head, her nails scraping against my skin. Feels so fucking good.

Clearing my throat, I lick my lips as well, prepared to take what I want, her mouth pressed against mine, my tongue sliding across hers.

I inch forward, our foreheads pressed together, her fingers digging into my skin, my hand a death-grip on her hips, not wanting her to move an inch away. Just one quick taste to hold me over, something to solidify this day, to calm the restlessness churning inside me.

Just a few more inches.

Three.

Two.

My skin ignites, my stomach dropping with anticipation, my heart hammering, causing my pulse to skyrocket. Her scent, her soft skin, her goddamn heaving chest . . .

"Would you like a refill of water?" the waitress asks, killing the mood immediately when Rylee is snapped out of the moment. She jumps off my lap and stands, fumbling with her shorts and straightening her outfit.

"Bathroom. I need to use the bathroom." She points in a direction and the waitress points her in another.

"Around the corner."

"Yup. Okay, going to pee. Bye."

She bolts off, walking as fast as her little legs will allow her. Exhaling heavily, I glance at the waitress, shoulders slumped. "Great timing."

She winces and holds up my cup. "Refill?"

I wave my hand at her. "Sure. Fill me up."

~

"**W**here do you think you're going, Saucy?"

She pauses at her door and innocently puts her keycard down. "Uh, I was going to go to bed."

"It's ten. Spend a little more time with me."

She chuckles. "I spent almost the entire day with you." And yet, it doesn't feel like that at all. I want more time. I want to recreate the moment we had with her on my lap, but this time without a pesky waitress asking about refills.

"Yeah, and I still feel like I don't know you." I nod toward the hammock below us and say, "Come on, join me." She's hesitant so I add, "There will be no games played, no farting—even though there was none to begin with—and I promise to only hold your hand. Come on, I won't bite. Have a swing with me."

She sighs. *Yes, she's giving in to my charm.* "You know, it's hard to say no to you."

"Good. That's the way I like it. And remember, we're all about saying yes on this trip. Right?"

"Right."

She takes my hand and we head toward the stairs that lead to the hammock we spent some time in last night. Mentally, I mark the space as "our spot." Lame maybe, but hey, live in the moment . . .

"There you are, we've been looking for you all day."

Chris and Justine round the top of the stairs, hand in hand, and as they take in Rylee standing next to me, giant smiles light up their faces.

"Oh, and who might this be?" Justine asks, looking all too giddy. "Is this the girl we vouched for last night?"

Knowing this is going to lead to an embarrassing interrogation, I throw in the towel. At this point, there will be no stopping them.

"Chris, Justine, this is Rylee, the girl you spoke to last night."

"Ooo," Justine cheers and hops in place. "We did a good job then, didn't we? He's a good guy. We were right, weren't we?"

Rylee gives me a side glance, a smirk pulling at her lips. "Yeah, he's all right. Likes to cheat at Yahtzee, but he has to have some sort of fault, right?"

"I didn't cheat," I reply, exasperated.

"Oh sweetheart, the man has many more faults, just wait." Chris grips her on the shoulder. "I could keep you up all night, running down the list of his faults."

"Not necessary, dude. I'm sure she'll figure them out."

"So is this love?" Justine peers at us, her eyes watery, hands clasped together now, almost as if she's praying for us to make babies right in front of her. She's obviously had a little too much to drink again tonight. *Parent-free vacays.*

"Babe, don't you think that's a little soon?"

"No way, he fell in love with Christine in a day." The moment the words leave Justine's lips, she cringes. I don't ever talk about Christine, my first marriage, and divorce, because it's better for me to stay away from volatile memories that lead to dark places.

Playfully, Rylee squeezes my hand and says, "Oh my, who's Christine? Is this my competition?"

Sobering up from the kick back to reality, I clear my throat. *Fuck. No.* "Not even close." Looking at my watch, I say, "You know what, it's getting kind of late. I'm going to take a raincheck on the hammock." I release Rylee's hand, not missing the confusion in her eyes.

I know what I'm doing. I can see from afar how I'm turtling in on myself and hiding from the world, from the truth of my life. But I know myself well enough that if I go to that hammock with Rylee, she'll ask about Christine, and I'm not ready to go there. I'm not sure I'll ever have that conversation with Rylee. This is a fling, a short stint of fun in our lives, no use dragging it down with my past.

My sordid past that will keep me up all night.

"Are you sure?" Rylee asks, concerned.

"Yeah. Kind of just hit a wall." I glance at Chris and Justine particularly. She looks like she's about to cry. When we make eye contact, she mouths, "I'm sorry." I give her an understanding nod and a curt wave. "I'll see you guys in the morning." Turning toward Rylee, I say, "Have a good night. Thanks for today."

Without another word, I make it inside my hotel room and flop on my bed, my gaze cast toward the ceiling, forcing my eyes to stay open, to focus on the texture of the paint, of the color of the blades attached to the ceiling fan.

If I close my eyes, I'll see it all. I'll see the shattered cars, the crimson-tinted asphalt, the deployed and battered airbags, and the lifeless form in the driver's seat of the car.

The car I hit.

I can't.

I can't close my eyes.

Sirens sound off in the distance.

I hear the crunching of the jaws of life.

Yelling from first responders to clear onlookers.

My breathing picks up, becoming labored as my body starts to involuntarily shake.

Fuck.

My mouth goes dry. The smell of alcohol hits me, even though I know there is none in my room. My palms become clammy, and a cool sweat breaks out along my skin. I'm drifting, and fast. Not wanting to head into the space I know will eat me alive for the rest of my trip, I do the one thing I know will calm my racing heart.

Reaching into my pocket, I pull out my phone and press down on speed dial one.

Two rings, that's all it takes.

"Beck?"

I swallow hard, my hand rubbing my brow, trying to rid it of the thoughts crashing uncontrollably through my mind. There is some muffling over the phone and then the distinct sound of a door being shut. Cal comes back on the line. "Talk to me."

Breathe. Fucking breathe. "I don't know what's happening. Justine mentioned Christine, and all of a sudden, my mind started tumbling in on itself." I take a deep breath. "Christine has never been a huge trigger point for me, but for some reason, the mere mention of her name has my stomach flipping and my heart racing."

"Where are you?"

"In my room."

"Anything in there that can get you in trouble?" Cal always gets straight to the point. *Thank fuck.*

"No, sir."

"Good. Go grab a cup of water, and then let's recite the serenity prayer."

Doing as told, I fill a coffee mug full of tap water, take a few big gulps, and then set the cup on the table.

As if second nature, Cal and I both start reciting the AA serenity prayer.

"God, give me the grace to accept with serenity the things that cannot be changed. Courage to change the things which should be changed and the wisdom to distinguish one from the other . . ."

CHAPTER EIGHT

RYLEE

K *nock. Knock.*
. . .
Pound. Pound.
. . .
Pound. Pound. Pound. "Rylee, I know you're in there. Open up."

"Mmm," I grumble, shielding my eyes from the light peeking through the blinds.

"Rylee, open the door." *Pound. Pound. Pound.*

I turn away from the door and cuddle closer into my pillow.

"Ouch, I, uh, I was stung by a jellyfish, quick come here and pee on my leg." More pounding.

"That's a lie," I shout.

"Ehh, you're right. But now that I know you're in there, open the door. I have coffee . . ."

Damn him. Damn him and his coffee-fetching ways. Peering an eye open, I take a look at the clock. It's half past ten? Wow, that's later than I usually sleep in.

Maybe because I was up all night wondering who this Christine girl was and why the mention of her name made such an impact on

Beck. And then I chastised myself for half the night, reminding my little wandering brain that this is a fling, and I don't care about Christine or why Beck shut down. Because in a few days, I won't see this man again.

Needless to say, my brain is tired, my body is exhausted, and the only reason I'm flipping my bedding off my body is because I want coffee. Because I NEED coffee.

I open the door to my room, run my hand over my face, and hold out the other. As if I was locked and loaded with the Jedi force, the cup of coffee magically appears in my hand and I take a long sip without ever truly opening my eyes.

The hot liquid scalds my mouth, making a wave of warmth down my throat.

Clearing his throat, Beck says, "Uh, mind if I come in so we can shut the door?"

"Whatever," I mumble, drinking more coffee.

The door shuts with a slam, and I can feel Beck's presence inch closer and closer, his breathing almost erratic, heavy.

I peep an eye open, just one, and look him up and down. Long legs clad in a pair of khaki shorts with a black shirt spanning across his developed chest, thick and strong. Simple, but sexy. He's all male, every inch of him, especially when he looks at me like that, as if he's about to devour me in seconds. My nipples harden, the breeze of the fan igniting goosebumps over my skin, and I'm more than aware of the carnal way he's casually licking his lips and the hungry spark in his eyes.

Hands clenching his sides, his voice strained, he asks, "Do you always sleep topless, Rylee?"

Huh?

Topless?

Coffee halfway to my mouth, I look down. Well by golly, take a look at those tits, out in the open for everyone to see. Laughing nervously, I slowly cover them with the hand that's not holding my coffee and say, "In Key West I apparently do. But hey, at least I'm wearing a thong. I have that going for me."

Looking very uncomfortable, Beck pulls on the back of his neck. "It's not easy for a guy to have a door opened and a hot girl appear, topless. Do you know what kind of self-control it takes to not press you against the wall and suck your nipples into my mouth?"

Cue the wave of heat scorching up my spine. A slow, beating pleasure thrums between my legs from the thought of Beck's mouth on my breasts. Hot and tingly, I ache for his touch.

Yeah, I wouldn't mind that at all.

Not one bit.

"Have at it," I say right before I take another sip of my coffee, feeling less modest than before. He's seen them already, so it's nothing new to him. "Just don't knock this coffee out of my hand when you're doing all the sucking. And hey, do you mind if I lie down while you do it. I still feel sleepy."

I go to lie on the bed to cuddle with my cup when a strong arm wraps around my waist and pulls me against Beck's very strong and tightly corded body.

Well, good morning to me.

"Listen here, Saucy." His breath tickles my exposed skin. "I'm not about to devour those delicious tits of yours while you're half awake. So what's going to happen instead is you're going to hop in the shower, wake yourself up, and then we're going on a helicopter ride."

Errr, did I just hear him correctly? A helicopter ride?

"Repeat that?" He's so close, I have to bend back to look at him, and when I do, I'm met with a pair of hazel eyes that for some reason, I never noticed the depths of before. They're beautiful with a gold center and green wrapped around the outer edge. The corner of his eyes look weathered, but his actual pupils are bright and full of hope. I don't think he's kidding about this helicopter thing.

"I'm taking you on a helicopter ride around the island and out to sea to explore some marine life."

"You're serious?"

He nods. "I am, and the helicopter takes off in thirty minutes, so you have about ten minutes to get ready."

Hell. Taking my thong off is going to require at least five minutes from the pace I'm moving this morning.

"Come on." He ushers me to the bathroom, turns on the shower and smacks my ass before taking my coffee and exiting the shower area.

"Excuse me, I need my coffee back."

He steps away when I try to grab for it. "You'll get it once you're ready to go."

"That's devil-level torture right there. You realize that, right?"

"I'm aware of the dangerous position I've put myself in by taking your coffee, but I'm also aware of how much fun you're going to have, so I will do almost anything to get you moving. Now hurry up, Rylee, we have some flying in the sky to do today."

And just like that, he shuts the door, leaving a small smile on my face.

And there he is.

The Beck I've come to know over the past two days.

Free-spirited.

Happy.

In his element.

The man who's propelling me into the shower so I can spend a few more hours during this vacation with him, soaking up his ability to live life to its fullest.

∾

The Uber ride to the airport is quiet. Beck spends most of the time staring out the window at the ocean, his hand pressed into his lap instead of linked with mine.

I'm tempted to ask him about last night, to question him about Christine, but I refrain, not wanting to set him off again. *This is temporary, so don't get too emotionally involved.* Although, my creative mind is running a mile a minute, trying to figure out why Christine is such a hot-button topic for Beck.

Is she an ex-girlfriend? Someone he never got closure with?

Is she a current girlfriend he never told me about? I sure as hell hope not. *Surely his friends wouldn't encourage me about him if he had a girlfriend.*

Is Beck a widower? I think it would break my heart if he was, which is another reason why I'm keeping my mouth shut and turning off that rabbit trail of questioning sounding off in my head.

When we arrive at the airport, we're directed to the private section where a cute Australian blonde with a killer accent greets us. Our pilot.

"You must be Beck, and this is your new bride." *Oh here we go again, Beck and Rylee, the newlyweds.*

Beck reaches out a hand and shakes it while squeezing me close to his side. "And you must be Callie. Pleasure meeting you."

"Pleasure is mine. I'm excited to be your pilot and tour guide today. Newlyweds are my favorite; they're probably the most fun since they're in a constant state of bliss."

"Totally in a fog of bliss, aren't we, baby?" Beck gently runs his nose along my cheek and up to my temple where he places a kiss, causing my stomach to drop and my toes to tingle. It's only one kiss, but when it's combined with his velvety voice, his grip on my arm, his all-encompassing scent, and the press of his soft lips, I have pins and needles and am begging for more of his lips on mine.

Controlling my rapidly beating heart, I nod. "Totally." Reaching out my hand, I shake Callie's and introduce myself.

After we exchange a few pleasantries, we load into a golf cart and Callie drives us to her bright yellow helicopter that is much smaller than I would have expected. When she starts to run through her safety checks, I lean into Beck and say, "I thought you didn't lie."

"When did I lie?" he asks, genuinely confused.

"Uh, pretty sure we're not married, and we're not on our honeymoon."

He chuckles. "Eh, that's more of a joke than anything. I mean, it's a given at this point that we're married. We've been through so much together already. Puke apocalypse, a funeral, nakedness, the Yahtzee chronicles, and of course the adoption of Pearl Turtle Titty Tata."

"Hey." I point my finger at him. "That turtle is entirely yours. I took no part in giving that thing a home. Pearl is all on you."

He presses his hand against his heart. "You know, it really hurts when you don't love our child. We birthed her together, and for you to just pass her off, as if . . . as if she's some monstrosity, that doesn't sit well with me."

I pat his cheek and playfully say, "You'll survive."

"Okay, all set," Callie calls out, pulling our attention away from each other. "Hop up on the platform, and I'll take a picture of you two."

Before I can tell her we don't need a picture, Beck hands her his phone and picks me up into a cradle position. He effortlessly hops up on the platform, holding me close to his chest and nods at the camera. "Smile, Saucy."

Without giving it a second thought, while my hands are wrapped around his neck, I smile.

"Ugh, you two are just too adorable." She hands Beck back the phone and then gets us situated in the helicopter.

Let me just tell you this. Beck is a tall, broad man. Easily he's six two, six three, which is even more pronounced given the way his body is crouched and stuffed into the small space of the helicopter's backseat. It's almost comical.

Callie takes some oil from under one of the seats and pours it into the engine as Beck hands me his phone. "Plug your number in there so I can send you that picture."

I raise an eyebrow at him. "You want my number?"

"Yeah, I do. Don't give me a hard time and plug it in."

"How can I trust you? How do I know you're not going to sign me up on a dozen telemarketer's lists?"

"I make no promises." He winks and then nudges me. "Come

on, just give me your number so I can send you the picture . . . and bug you in the middle of the night with meaningless text messages."

"Ooo, meaningless text messages, now that's what I'm talking about." I enter my phone number along with my name.

In seconds, after I hand Beck his phone back, I receive a text message from a strange number. When I open it, I read the text out loud. "Your husband thinks you look sexy in that dress."

This man.

Wanting to accept his compliment, I say, "Thank you."

Pinching my chin with his forefinger and thumb he replies, "I mean it, Saucy."

Those hazel eyes, that voice, the sincerity in his every movement . . . Yup, Sunday is going to suck . . . when I have to say goodbye.

"Honestly, I think it was really rude of the marine life to hang out on your side of the helicopter and not mine." This was my first time ever riding in a helicopter, or taking an aerial tour of an island and ocean, and of course, I had to lean over Beck's lap the entire time to get any good glimpses at sharks and turtles. And I think you and I both know Beck had no problem with having me in his lap. Then again, when he was lightly stroking my hair, leaning over with me, talking about all the different animals we were seeing, it was sweet; an intimate moment I can still feel.

Beck and I walk hand in hand down Duvall Street, one of the main touristy strips in Key West, looking for a place to eat. We had the Uber driver drop us off at the opposite end of our hotel so we could scour our options.

And just like a married couple, we're having a hard time agreeing on a place to eat. It's funny how alike we are sometimes— both hardheaded and willing to do whatever we can to get our way. Apparently pressing my breasts against Beck's arm has no effect on him. That's why we're not eating at the cute little French bakery place I wanted to try. He was against it because it was more of a breakfast restaurant than anything, and he wanted meat.

Ugh . . . men.

"It's because I paid off all the sharks to show up on my side before we took off."

"I knew it. I knew you bribed those swimming elasmobranch fish."

"Hey." He tugs on my arm. "Way to pay attention."

I chuckle. "Honestly, normally I have a hard time paying attention to tour guide things because my mind wanders at an extreme rate, but Callie's accent entranced me, and all I could do was listen."

"Yeah, she was pretty to look at, wasn't she?"

Mouth agape, I look up to Beck who's smiling devilishly. I elbow him in the ribs. "Your wife doesn't approve of such meandering eyes."

"Ah, so you admit it, we're married."

I huff in annoyance. "In your dreams, Wilder."

"You're right. You're in my dreams, Saucy."

Eyeing him, knowing about his kind, I say, "Oh no, you don't. I write about men like you, with your quick, sexy comebacks, your ability to whisper naughty things into a girl's ear to make her drop to her knees. Yeah, nice try, Beck, but I can see past your ways. I know your type, and it's not going to work."

"What's not going to work?" He pulls my hip against his and brings his mouth to my ear, immediately erupting chills all over my skin. "Do you mean this? *This* is not going to work, this pull we have? What about my ability to make your nipples hard with only the rub of my nose against your cheek?" God, he's so right. "Don't fool yourself, Rylee. You might want to believe you can resist me, but it's not going to work for long, because don't forget . . . I am your husband, after all."

Oh Jesus.

Laughing, I push him away and start to walk.

And then it happens.

Oh my souvenir dreams! They have been answered.

Is that . . . is that a hunk?

Unaware of my halt, Beck runs into my back and sends me flying forward, but before I can fall face first into the pavement beneath me, he lifts me upright. "Damn, Rylee. I almost flattened you. What has you . . .?" He pauses and I can tell the minute he sees what I see. "You've got to be kidding me. That's it, isn't it? That's your souvenir."

I walk toward the hunk, arms extended, stars in my eyes.

This isn't any ordinary hunk, either. No, this guy is special. He's a bottle opener, but he isn't just a beautiful shirtless, glass of a man.

No, he . . . oh God, I might cry I'm so excited. He is holding a present over his crotch. He's a freaking dick-in-a-box, shirtless hunk bottle opener, and he's about to be all mine.

"Oh he's magnificent. Just perfect," I mutter to myself, turning him over and checking out every last inch of him. I hold him to my chest and squeeze tightly. "You shall be named Justin."

"Ahem." Beck clears his throat next to me, interrupting my little love fest. "Am I going to have to have divorce papers cued up here?"

"Maybe, I mean, look at him." I hold him up carefully. "He's perfect. God, everything I want in a hunk. The muscles, the suggestive naughtiness, and he moonlights as a bottle opener. Pretty and useful, doesn't get better than that."

"And you named him Justin, because . . ."

"After Justin Timberlake, of course. You know, the whole dick-in-a-box thing."

"Ah, yes. So I'm going to take a wild guess and say you have a bunch of these lying around your house."

"I wish." I shake my head. "No, I only have a little shelf. They are hard to find, so I haven't been able to purchase many, but the ones I have, oh God, I love them so much."

"Yeah . . . okay." He scratches his jaw. "Do they all have names?"

I cringe, starting to realize how insane I sound. "If I say yes, will you judge me?"

"I think it's fair to say that I'm allowed to judge you at this point. You hugged a shirtless male figurine in the middle of the sidewalk, and there is no getting around that without someone passing judgment."

Laughing, I nod. "I'll give you that."

"Okay, let's get Justin so we can continue to bicker about where to eat, because I'm starving."

Beck pulls his wallet from his back pocket, but I stop him. "You don't have to buy this, I got it."

"No, allow me." He squeezes his arm. "The least I can do is purchase Justin for you so whenever you look at him, you're reminded of me, and hopefully . . . hopefully, I'll rival him a little in your head."

Hell, Justin might be my new hunk, but Beck has zero competition as my new man. *It's a shame I only get to keep one of them.*

～

eck: Are you awake? You better say yes because I don't hear you snoring unlike the last two nights.

I read his text message and scoff. I don't snore . . . at least I hope I don't. God, I'd be mortified if I did, let alone so loudly that Beck can hear me through the wall.

Rylee: I don't snore.

Beck: Ah, I knew that would get you to respond. No, you don't snore, but I bet you're a moaner.

I smile at my phone and turn to my side, getting in a comfortable texting position. Funny thing is, at this point, I can't remember if I'm a moaner or not. It's been a while since I've been given the chance to moan.

Rylee: Too bad you'll never find out.

Beck: Keep telling yourself that, Saucy. Are you topless again tonight?

Rylee: Nope, bottomless.

Beck: *Are you ever fully clothed?*

Rylee: *I like to keep things interesting, switch it up. I like feeling the sheets on different parts of my body.*

And just like that, my body heats up as my legs begin to rub together. I barely said anything, but the thought of the cool sheets rubbing against my exposed skin has my body prickling with awareness.

Beck: *That's fucking sexy. Want to know a fun fact about me?*

Rylee: *Sure. Lay it on me.*

Beck: *I don't wear underwear.*

Rylee: *Like, none?*

Beck: *None. Haven't owned a pair in a really long time.*

Rylee: *Really? That's . . . hot. So does that mean you sleep naked?*

Beck: *Why don't you come over and find out for yourself.*

Oh hell, I should have known that response was coming, and still, my face flushes. Beck seems like a guy who sleeps naked. He also seems like someone who knows their way around a women's body, which can be lethal.

Rylee: *I think I'll leave the answer up to my imagination.*

Beck: *Scared of what this possibly could feel like between us?*

Rylee: *Terrified.*

And that's the truth. It's one thing hanging out, flirting, acting like we're on our honeymoon, but it's a whole new level taking this faux relationship, this faux-ship to the physical side. Yeah, there have been little touches here and there, and maybe he's seen my breasts far too many times for my liking, but we haven't crossed *the* line I'm afraid to cross, because I know the minute I do, there will be no ridding this man from my memory.

Right now, he's fun, a mere encounter that maybe I won't remember when I'm older. But I know the moment Beck gets his hands on me, the moment he's naked, thrusting inside me, I'll be a goner. It will be forever branded in my memory, and I'm not sure I'm ready for that . . . or want it.

So I'll continue to share a wall with this man, rather than a bed. It's the smart thing to do.

The responsible thing to do.

The surest way to cock-block myself.

And Lord knows I need all the cock-blocking in the world.

My phone beeps, and from the preview I can tell Beck sent a picture.

Oh God, please don't let it be a naked shot; please don't be a naked shot.

I know what you're thinking. You're crazy, woman! Beck Wilder, naked, show me the dick pic, right? Well, internally my horny self is screaming to have the chance to run my cheek along a dick pic of Beck Wilder, but the responsible part—the part we just discussed—knows a dick pic will lead to all the above we're trying to avoid. You know, the unremovable imprint of this man in my mind. Let's not forget that.

With one eye open, I cautiously open the message to find a picture of Beck lying on his bed, one hand behind his head, showing off his gloriously naked and toned chest. But it's not the sinew of his pecs that's making me melt, or the flex of his bicep that doesn't go unnoticed. No, it's the devastatingly handsome smile he's sporting. Straight white teeth, tiny, almost unnoticeable dimples, and a small crinkle in the corner of his eyes.

Damn him.

I read his text that came along with the picture.

Beck: *Your turn.*

My turn? What exactly is he looking for here? Does he want a topless picture too? Because there is a huge difference between a topless picture of a man versus a woman. And, I'm not the kind that texts naked pictures to strangers, well stranger-husbands.

Nixing the naked idea, I go for goofy, because there is no need to drive up the sexual tension between us any further, especially since my pelvis has a mind of its own and is casually gyrating beneath the sheets.

I'm about to take a picture when another text arrives from Beck.

Beck: *I'm waiting . . .*

Insufferable man!

Now he really isn't going to get the photo he was hoping for. Instead, I take a chunk of my dark black hair, place it under my nose like a mustache, and snap a picture. Nothing like a little hairy Mary to get those engines revving.

I press send and wait.

I'm not going to acknowledge how giddy I am to hear his response, or how I'm kind of hoping I can hear him laugh through the walls, or how my hips are still gyrating as I stare at the picture he sent me. After what seems like forever, he texts me back.

Beck: *I see what you're trying to do here, but just a warning to you, Saucy, no matter what you do, I will always find you sexy, even with a semi-believable mustache.*

My heart starts thumping, my skin tingles, and for once in my life, I actually feel like a character in one of my books.

I don't know if I should be excited, or completely terrified.

And like a reader, I'm keen to see what happens next.

~

B**eck:** *Are you awake?*
    Rylee: *Can you hear my TV?*
Beck: *Just some muffling. What are you watching?*
Rylee: *Key West morning news.*
Beck: *Anything interesting happen?*
Rylee: *Not really. Only talks of the rooster population. What are you doing?*
Beck: *Wishing you were over here, snuggling with me. How can I convince you to get over here?*
Rylee: *I'm too warm in a blanket cocoon.*
Beck: *What if . . . I pick you up in your blanket cocoon and bring you over here?*
Rylee: *At that point, you should come snuggle over here.*

Within a few seconds, I hear Beck's door open and close and

then there's a light knock on my door followed by Beck saying, "It's me, Rylee."

Smiling, I shake my head and quickly hop out of bed to open my door. I don't wait for Beck to enter, but simply hop back in bed and pull the blankets over me. I blast my air conditioner at night because I hate a warm room and waking up to the artic chill reminds me of home.

I peek over my blankets to see Beck enter the room, shirtless and wearing a pair of gym shorts.

I don't wear underwear. His text plays on replay in my head as my eyes focus on his crotch, the bulge so evident against the thin fabric, a very revealing outline, so revealing I can feel my entire body start to blush.

Thick and heavy.

Oh. God.

Nodding his head at my little cocooned body, he says, "Scoot over, Saucy."

Mouth dry, body humming, I watch Beck slowly strut toward me, his torso moving with each step, abs flexing, hard arms swaying by his side, that bulge . . . shifting.

I must still be in a dreamlike state because one of the most handsome men I've ever met is crawling into my bed.

Wrapping his arm around me, he scoops me into his side and lays my head against his chest, his fingers stroking through my hair, massaging my scalp.

"You're so fucking warm, like a little heat box in this freezing room."

"I like it chilly when I sleep. I feel comforted when the tip of my nose is cold. Is that weird?"

He presses his fingertips into my scalp, slowly working them into my skin. "I think it's cute actually."

A little nervous but feeling courageous from the way Beck is touching me so intimately, I press the palm of my hand against his chest and hold it there for a second, feeling the beat of his heart. He doesn't move—he doesn't even flinch when I touch him—

almost like he expected it, and it's a weird feeling, a weird quiet moment.

So far almost all of our interactions have been lighthearted, joking, but this morning, there is nothing funny about this moment. It's comforting, easy, natural.

Is that weird? To feel so comfortable with him so soon?

"Do you watch the news every morning?" Beck's morning voice rumbles over my body, sultry and sexy.

Clearing my thoughts, I take the moment to snuggle in a little closer. Just this time, I'm giving myself a chance to soak this in, the comfort of another human. "No, I usually play music while I make breakfast and get ready for the day."

"Make breakfast, huh? What is breakfast normally for you?"

I smile to myself. "Cereal. I'm really good at making it."

He chuckles, the lift of his chest shaking beneath me. "Culinary expert in cereal. That's my kind of girl."

"It takes a lot of knowledge to know how much milk to put in a bowl without turning the entire meal soggy. So much practice and trial and error has gone into this formula."

"I can believe it. What's your favorite?"

"Depends on the day, but my go-to is Peanut Butter Captain Crunch, followed closely by Fruity Pebbles and Cocoa Krispies. It's so hard to decide. Although, I do have at least four boxes in my cupboard currently."

He's silent for a second and then says, "I never would have pegged you for a sugary cereal girl."

"Oh, I'm a whore for sugary cereal. I want them all. I have Lucky Charms, Fruit Loops, Peanut Butter Captain Crunch, and Apple Jacks at home right now. It's been hard eating things like eggs and bacon while I've been here. I only want cereal."

His fingers twist in my hair now, lightly pulling on the strands. That feels so damn good.

"Have you always been addicted to cereal?"

I shake my head. "No. My mom was amazing and made me a nutritious breakfast every morning, which meant I never got to have any kind of trash cereal. Once I went to college, I became an addict and haven't been able to quit my addiction yet."

"And is it always sugary cereals? What about shredded wheat? Surely you add a little health in there."

"If it's frosted shredded wheat, I'll eat it, but I won't be happy about it."

Beck's laugh fills the room followed by his lips pressing against the top of my head. "Fuck, I like you, Saucy."

I bite my bottom lip, a smile pulling at the ends of my mouth. *I like you too, Beck.*

CHAPTER NINE

BECK

"Ladies, care if I join you?"

Victoria and Rylee look up from their reading devices and take me in. Rylee's perusal is much longer than Victoria's, who buries her head back into the words in front of her and mumbles, "Do what you want. I'm reading."

Rylee, on the other hand, folds the cover to her e-reader over and blocks the sun from her eyes when she speaks. "I don't know, do you have snacks with you?" Ever since this morning, after crawling into her bed and talking and enjoying each other's company, I can't seem to get her out of my damn mind. And from the little sparkle in her eyes when she looks me up and down, I'm going to guess she's having the same problem.

I hold up my empty hands and she tsks at me. "No, but don't let that deter you. I can order some beachside food from one of the servers. Care for some crab cakes?"

"I love crab cakes," Victoria says in a monotone voice. "Make sure they give us extra tartar sauce and a lemon water. I'm parched."

"Diet Coke for me and some loaded waffle fries," Rylee answers with a wink. Fuck, I want to take her back to her hotel room and cuddle her some more. Scratch that, I want to do more than cuddle her.

Resigned with only getting food, I snag a lounge chair, put in an order for some snacks, and sidle up next to Rylee, who's wearing a killer white bikini with the smallest triangles covering her mouth-watering breasts. She's slowly killing me with every outfit I see her in.

I'm a patient man, and last night when I was texting her, I wasn't actually looking for her to come over. I knew she wouldn't. She's still reserved despite how I'm pushing her to live in the moment. And that's okay. I wanted her to know that I'm still very interested in her. I would have been shocked as hell had she knocked on my door, and a part of me, a rather desperate part of me, wished she had.

But instead of a late-night visitor, I went to bed with a massive hard-on, very aware that only a thin wall existed between Rylee and me, which made things even more tortuous. And what made things worse was that Rylee understood not to ask me about Christine. *She gets me.* Gets that talking about the previous night with Justine spilling the beans would have made me uncomfortable.

It's why I ended up thinking about her in the shower and relieving some of the built-up tension inside my body. And hell, it had helped. It *had* helped until I spotted her lying out next to a sunscreened Victoria, looking dangerous with her jet-black hair, white bikini, and toned legs.

When I take a seat on my lounge chair, Victoria asks without even looking up, "Did you get extra tartar sauce?"

"I ordered all the tartar sauce they have."

"Thank you. I really like it."

I can tell.

"Not a problem. I also ordered some tacos, in case you ladies wanted something extra to nibble on." Lowering my voice so only Rylee can hear me, I say, "Lord knows you didn't nibble on anything last night."

Looking sly, Rylee adjusts her body, her breasts pushing up toward the sun—fuck—and she says, "How do you know that?"

"I know that because my bed missed you."

"Just because I didn't go to your room doesn't mean I didn't go to someone else's place."

Okay, you and I both know she didn't go anywhere else. Hell, I was so quiet in my room last night, trying to hear her, that I would have immediately noticed her moving around, let alone leaving her room. The doors here are heavy and loud. I see what she's doing so I'll play with her.

"Yeah, have a midnight booty call? Tell me about it."

I move to the side of my lounge chair, prop my elbow on the armrest, and place my chin in my palm, eager and waiting for a little story time.

Shaking her head in mirth, she says, "Oh yeah, had a sex-feast last night. An all-nighter. I can barely walk this morning, let alone stay awake." She fake yawns and then turns toward me, her breasts smashing together, forming an endless amount of cleavage.

Fuck me big time.

"It was wild."

"Sounds like it. I'm surprised you're able to make an appearance after the pounding you must have taken."

"Hey, I live to please the people," she says, lifting her shoulders. "Couldn't leave Victoria out here all by herself, now could I? Who would be here to help slather the sunscreen on her back?"

"She could have asked me," I offer and pop up my head to take a gander at Victoria, who tilts her head to the side, eyebrow raised. "I'm a really good slatherer. These big hands don't miss an inch." I hold up my hands for both the girls to see.

"Those are big hands," Victoria offers. "Next time I'll be sure to ask you."

"No, you won't," Rylee says rather too quickly for her liking, or at least that's what it seems from the scowl on her face. "I mean, I'm your slathering girl, you can't give that title to someone you don't know."

"I do what I want, and if I want Beck's man hands on me, that's what I'm going to do." Looking down at her legs, Victoria continues, "You know, I could really use another layer on my knees." She pops open the sunscreen from her bag and holds it in my direction. "Beck, would you mind?"

Seeing the smirk on her lips, I hop out of my lounge chair. "I'd be happy to."

Just as I'm about to reach for the sunscreen, Rylee leaps out her chair, swats the sunscreen from my hands, and points back to my lounge chair. "Don't even think about it. Those man hands are to go nowhere near Victoria. If they're touching anyone's knees, they're touching mine."

Victoria snorts and goes back to her reading, while I have a hard time containing my smile. Irritated with herself, Rylee whacks me in the abs and says, "Don't you dare think about laughing."

I hold my hands up in defense. "Wouldn't dream of it. But can I point something out?"

"Not if you want to hang out with us for the rest of the afternoon."

"Fair enough." I chuckle, which garners a death glare from Rylee.

"You are so going to bang that man by the end of this trip if you haven't already," Victoria mutters.

And yup, I laugh. I laugh so fucking hard.

~

"So you're all authors?" I motion with my finger to Rylee, Victoria, and Zoey who joined us an hour ago.

"Yup. We met at a local writer's meeting in our area. It was the three of us and two older women," Zoey answers. "Since we live in such a small town, there aren't many authors, so we mixed our genres."

"Makes sense. What do you write, Zoey?"

"Children's books."

Kind of shocking given the mouth on this woman. I never in a million years would have guessed she writes children's books. I think it's her goal in life to fit in as much inappropriate talk in a conversation as she can.

"From the way your jaw is practically tickling the sand, I'm going to guess you weren't expecting that."

"Uh, not really." I pull on the back of my head. "No offense, but I think you're more crude than most guys I know."

"No offense taken, I'm honored actually."

"Honored about what?" Art, Zoey's husband, asks as he drops next to her and starts handing out drinks. I take my water and sip on it with a nod of gratitude.

"Beck here thinks I have a potty mouth."

"She does, and I kiss her potty mouth every day." To prove us right, he leans over and gives her a peck.

"I'm not knocking the potty mouth; it's entertaining. It's just contrasts what I had in mind for an author of children's books."

Zoey tips her drink in my direction. "It's all about the filter. And if you think I'm bad you should read some of Rylee's stuff. Talk about making you blush."

I raise an eyebrow at Rylee. "Is that right? You write some some provocative and racy shit, Rylee?"

Unabashedly, Rylee pinches my cheek. "Yep. Hot-as-fuck sex scenes in every book."

Well damn. "It's true. I can't read them. She writes cock way too many times. I blush." Victoria pulls on the brim of her sun hat.

"Looks like I might need to download some books onto my Kindle."

Surprised now, Rylee asks, "You have a Kindle?"

"Don't let the looks deter you. I'm a reader. Preferably I like mysteries, autobiographies, and I've dabbled in history as well."

"I write history." Victoria pops straight in her chair, and her eyes light up like I've never seen before. "What kind of history do you like to read? I'm working on a piece about Amelia Earhart right now."

"Really?"

"Yeah. I'm working with another historian and some researchers who are tracking where her plane crashed, and if she truly died on impact, or if she was captured."

I point at Victoria. "Oh, I saw a piece about that on the History Channel. They were talking about a picture that was found and if it was her in the picture."

"Yes!" Victoria sits on the edge of her chair and fans herself. "Oh gosh, I'm all worked up. Wasn't that History Channel special fascinating? I've watched it at least ten times."

"Fucking captivating."

Victoria starts to fill Zoey and Rylee in about the special, and I can't help but smile, because even though they all give each other a hard time, they still show interest in each other's very diverse work. They listen intently and pose questions, which only spurs Victoria on. The passionate way she speaks is inspiring.

A historian, a children's book author, and a romance novelist . . . there is a joke in there somewhere.

On a high, Victoria takes off toward the bathroom, leaving the four of us. When I decided to come on this trip, I never thought I'd find a group of people I enjoyed hanging out with so much, but damn, these are my kind of people.

"So what book of yours should I read?"

Rylee shifts so her head is facing me, her back to the sky, her ass looking so fucking good. "Are you really going to read one of my books?"

"Hell yeah. I want to see what these girls are talking about."

"I don't know if you can handle it."

I wiggle my eyebrows. "I bet I can. Lay it on me. Give me your dirtiest book."

"You're going to chub out easily."

A rumble of a laugh escapes me. "Chub out, huh?"

"Big time. I get super turned on when I'm writing, which only makes the book that much better. Believe me, you're going to get all hot and bothered."

"Can't fucking wait." I stand and pull my keycard from my back pocket.

"Where are you going?" she asks, giving me a once-over. Yeah, I fucking love it when she does that.

"Getting my Kindle. I have to start this book right away."

I shift in my seat and clear my throat for what seems like the twentieth time in the last five minutes.

Fuck, I'm getting hard and board shorts don't hide shit.

Running her finger along my forearm, Rylee asks, "So, do you like it?"

Swatting her away, I close the e-reader and shrug. "It's okay. Not as hot as you led me to believe."

"This coming from the man who never lies."

Damn it.

Sighing, I roll my eyes and lean closer so only Rylee can hear me. "Every time Jane moans, I swear to Christ it sounds like you in my head, and it's turning me on so much I'm in legit pain over here."

Thankfully, I'm lying on my stomach, so any evidence of my hard-on is shielded right now, but hell if having my dick pressed against the lounge chair isn't causing me to have some serious pain.

"Yeah?"

I nod and bite my bottom lip. "It's so bad that I'm seconds away from humping this goddamn chair for some relief."

Rylee covers her mouth and giggles. "I warned you."

"You could have warned me to not read it in public."

"Hey, that's your doing." She takes a sip of her pina colada. "But since I feel bad, I'll help you out."

"Yeah?" I raise my brow in excitement. "Want to go to my room?"

She chuckles and shakes her head. "Not like that. I'll help you take your mind off the . . . moaning."

"I would rather go to my room with you. It's not that far. We can tell everyone I'm going to show you the seashell collection I've started since I've been here."

"Or, I can ask you some questions to get to know you better."

Sighing, I drop my head to the lounge chair and say, "Fine. Ask away."

"Yay." From the corner of my eye, I can see her adjust herself so she's now facing me, sitting cross-legged. Yeah, no way in hell am I going to be lifting my head anytime soon, not with the way I can see how small her bikini is. Nope. "So you know I live in Maine, but you never told me where you live."

"Near Los Angeles."

"Huh, really? Well, I guess that explains the amazing tan you have." She pauses for a second and then says, "We couldn't live further away from each other."

Isn't that the truth.

"Kind of interesting that we met on a little two-by-four island."

"Magical for sure." Smiling playfully she says, "Now I want to know what you do, but I want to guess, so give me some clues, and I'll try to figure it out."

"Do you really think you can guess?" *Do I really want her to guess? How do I explain that at my age, I barely have a college degree?* I hate these types of questions.

"Possibly. I kind of have you pegged as a rebel, so I feel like I can gather a general read on you, and with a few hints, I feel confident I can guess."

Feeling my body start to relax, I say, "Okay, how about if you guess correctly, you get to decide what we do next, and if you can't guess it, I get to decide what we do next?"

"Yeah right, like I'm going to let that happen," she scoffs. "First of all, who's to say you'll give me honest clues, and second, if I lose I know exactly what you're going to say we do. And we are not doing that."

"And what is *that* exactly?"

She gives me a get real look. "Please, it's what men think about every five seconds."

"How little you know me." I shake my head in mock disappointment. "I actually had an idea, and it has nothing to do with removing our clothes."

"Doubtful."

"Try me," I counter, flipping to my side, my hard-on under control now. *Don't look below her neck, Wilder. Eyes up.*

She studies me, her eyes bouncing back and forth between mine, looking for any indication that I could be lying, but she should know that I don't lie. "Okay, fine. Let's play your little challenge. But I'm going to warn you right now, when I win, you're going to have one hell of a time being my little cabana boy and feeding me grapes while you wave a palm leaf above me."

"That's your idea of fun?" I ask, not too opposed to the idea.

"Oh yeah, hot guy fanning and feeding me, I call that a good time in my book." *That wasn't the good time in her book I was just reading about . . .*

I chuckle and then nod at her. "All right, are you ready?"

Cutely, she rubs her hands together. "I'm ready."

Thinking about my job, I try to be as vague but specific as possible, if that makes sense. I'm not going to lie. I want to win this. I have an idea that will not only be fun, but give me a chance to have my hands all over Rylee, something I truly need right now.

"I work with my hands."

She looks up to the sky, a calculating expression on her face. "Okay."

"I work by myself."

"Okay."

"Instead of a computer, I have shelves upon shelves of books on horticulture and habitats."

That last clue throws her for a loop. She twists her lips in confusion, her brain working hard. And just for the hell of it, I'm going to throw one more her way to really confuse the fuck out of her.

"Most days I'm caged up with people staring at me from behind a glass wall."

"What?" Her brow knits together. "What kind of profession cages you . . .?" She pauses as if she's figured it out. A giggle passes over her and she leans forward, looking around for any eavesdroppers. "Are you . . . are you a jungle stripper?"

"A what?" I laugh. "Where the hell did you come up with that?"

"So you're not a jungle stripper?"

"I don't even know what a jungle stripper is. Is that a real thing?"

"Well, I don't know, you tell me. You're the one behind a glass with habitat books. It almost seems like you strip and educate about the jungle at the same time, you know, using your hands and whatnot."

I can't help it, I full-on belly laugh, clutching my stomach. "Oh fuck, that's amazing."

"So, that's a no?" She's so fucking adorable.

"That's a hard no. Sorry, detective, but you lost."

She huffs and crosses her arms over her chest. "It's not my fault that you do something super weird. I was going to say you were a mechanic that refurbishes motorcycles, because that rings more true than whatever freak shit you're doing behind glass walls with onlookers. Are you a sex-a-bitioner? Are you fingering women behind glass windows?"

Cue more laughing.

I shake my head. "Is that what it's like to talk to an author? You immediately think of the weirdest things because your imagination runs wild, therefore skipping over the easiest answer?"

"Easy answer?" She nearly hops off her chair from her question. "There is no way there is an easy answer to the hints you—"

"I'm a muralist for local zoos and museums." Once my words register in that beautifully creative mind of hers, her plump lips form an O.

"Huh, well . . . that does seem like a simple and very innocent answer." She gently rubs her hands over her thighs.

"Yeah, it is . . . you fucking perv."

She laughs and shrugs her shoulders. "Hey, it's my line of work to be a perv, so I'm okay with this. So a muralist, damn, that kind of turns me on. I'm assuming you must be really good with your paint strokes."

"I excel at stroking, yes."

Rolling her eyes to sky, she says, "Now who's the perv?"

"I have no shame." Sitting taller, I say, "Now it's time for my reward. Are you ready?"

"Should I be scared?"

I stand, take her hand in mine, and help her to her feet. "Nothing to be scared about." Turning to Zoey and Art, I ask, "Are you guys available for a little game."

"Yes," Art answers with a little too much excitement. "I know we're supposed to be relaxing but there is only so much lying around I can do. What do you have in mind?"

From over my shoulder, I thumb toward the sand and say, "How about a friendly game of cornhole? Me and Rylee against you and Zoey."

"Oh, I'm so in." Zoey pops out of her chair. "You guys are going down."

CHAPTER TEN

RYLEE

W hen you think of a friendly game of cornhole, what do you think of? Friends having fun, tossing a bean bag back and forth, trying to make it into a hole, right?

Wrong.

Not the way Zoey plays.

The sheer determination flowing through her right now as she stretches her quads is rather frightening.

And Art, he's even worse, he's on their side doing knee-highs and windmills with his arms. This isn't the Olympics for fuck's sake, and we're not preparing for an epic chase to the gold. We're one beer bong short of a frat party.

"Uh, they seem pretty serious over there."

Beck places his hand on my lower back and nods. "Yeah, I'm afraid they might be far too into this. Have you played before?"

"Of course."

"Are you any good?"

"Ha! Of course I'm not. Sorry, dude, if you were looking for a ringer, I'm not your girl." And that's the truth. I might be able to write one epic sports scene with all the balls being thrown and caught, but to hell if I can do it myself.

"That's okay. I'll just have to help you out." His hand that's on my lower back slides around my waist, his fingers grazing the waistline of my bikini bottoms, the touch light, fuel to the flame burning inside me.

Why am I holding out on this man again?

Because to hell if I can remember my reasoning right about now with his touch relentless and unforgiving.

"You guys can start," Beck calls out. Bending down, his hand disconnecting from my skin, Beck picks up some beanbags. "We're going to play teams on the same side. Rylee needs a little guidance."

"That's fine," Zoey calls out, getting in a tossing position. "Al-eee-oop!" she shouts as she starts tossing her four beanbags, none of them coming even close to the hole. Ha, that girl is all talk. "Just a warm-up, don't worry. I'll be sinking those bags like LeBron James in no time. Watch out, bitches."

"Yikes." Beck laughs next to me, the sound so intoxicating, deep and satisfying in all the right places. "All right, we're up, Saucy. Do you want to go first?" He's so close, he's almost whispering, his breath sweetly caressing over my already-tingly skin.

"Sure." I go to toss one when Beck stops me.

"Hold up there, killer. Let's get you into position so you can actually sink some."

"It doesn't matter."

"Oh, it matters, because we need to beat those turkeys over there. Now let me show you how to do this." Can we agree that Beck calling Art and Zoey turkeys is kind of adorable? Love it.

Beck presses his body flush against mine and slowly runs his hands down my arms, immediately turning my nipples hard. His chest rounds my back, the tightly wrapped sinew flexing across my body. Rock hard and solid, he's like a brick wall protecting me from the outside world. But it isn't just the way his body is pressed against mine or the way his hands feel so right grazing along my skin. It's the way he's teaching me by speaking directly into my ear, soft and patient, and the way he smells, all male and delicious. Lord, help me, don't get me started on the lethal pheromones excreting from this man.

"Feel this, Rylee? This swing? This is the exact kind of swing you want. Smooth. That's right, Saucy, just like that." He's whispering, his hand is swishing my arm back and forth, his body so tight against mine that I'm seconds from combusting, from exploding from the heat coursing up my spine.

"Think you can do this?"

I swallow hard his breath tickling my cheek. "Yes. I think I got it."

"Good, give the first one a toss." He doesn't give me much room at all. In fact, he's still glued to me when I toss the bag, sending it skyrocketing across the small part of the beach. Oh hell.

"Uh, not quite where we wanted it to land."

"Looks like you need to do some more warm-ups," Zoey taunts. "Maybe a little less sexual tension over there and you won't be sending beanbags to the moon." She's going to get a throat punch after this. It's bad enough I'm trembling from having Beck's hands all over me. I don't need her pointing it out as well.

"Don't mind her." Beck attempts to soothe me, getting back into position. "Just keep it smooth and your arm straight. Float her right in the hole."

The next three bags come close to the wooden block but they're still losers, but it's okay because Zoey didn't sink any, so we continue to be tied. That's until Art steps up and sinks two bags right in the hole. Well, damn.

"We're losing," I state, feeling like we really need to win for bragging rights. I know if we lose, Zoey will never let me hear the end of it. If anything, we need to win to shut her up.

"Don't sweat it, Saucy. You have me on your team." Beck gives me a confident smile as he positions himself to throw, but instead of tossing the bags underhand like me, he flicks them from the side, spinning them in the air, and sinking all four bags.

I know it's just cornhole, that we are tossing fabric corn-filled squares around, but there is something to be said about how hot Beck looked just now. Shirtless, tanned, hazel eyes laser focused on the board in front of him. His posture is casual, like he owns the game, and he doesn't flinch after we score four points.

"Oh hell," Zoey says. "This guy's going to slaughter us."

Wiggling his eyebrows at me, Beck takes a sip of his water and says, "Told you not to worry. I got this."

And he did. He carried our team through the game scoring point after point, not even giving Zoey and Art a fair chance.

We are one point away from winning, and I have one bag left. We could not make any and still be far enough ahead that our opponents have no chance at winning, but still, I feel like this is it. I have yet to score a point for us and for some reason, I really want to contribute.

Taking a deep breath, I keep my eyes focused on the hole, envisioning sinking my bag.

"You can do this, Rylee. I believe in you," Beck says, cheering me on, leaning forward and whispering in my ear. "Did I mention you look fucking good in that bathing suit?"

Losing my concentration, I turn to look at him over my shoulder. He's close, once again, hovering over me, his hands low on my hips.

My breath catches in my chest when his fingers slip under the fabric of my bikini. Instead of tensing, my shoulders relax from the slow circles he's drawing along my skin, the pads of his fingers running along the front of my hipbones.

Oh fuck. A low throb starts to beat between my legs, my knees becoming wobbly and my need for this man growing stronger and stronger with every wicked look he gives me. Every touch. I can't imagine how he'll make my body hum if he has full access to it, if he has it stretched across his bed with my legs spread, ready for his next move.

"Wh-what are you doing?" I ask, having a hard time steadying my voice.

"Trying to help you loosen up."

"Well, you're not doing a good job. You're turning me on."

"Even better," he says in an extremely deep and seductive voice.

"Beck . . ."

"Hmm." His breath caresses my heated, sun-soaked skin, his fingers toying with all my nerve endings, shooting sparks of awareness all the way from my stomach to my toes.

"I . . ." I swallow hard, my body melting into his touch, wanting to fall into his strong hold, beg him to take me upstairs to his room. "I want to m-make this shot."

"Then do it, Saucy." He presses a light kiss along my neck, bolting me upright, my breath hitching in my chest. He runs his hand under the waistline of my bikini from the front of my hipbone, to my back end where his fingers caress the top part of my ass before he pulls out and says, "You got this."

I so desperately want to make this, not just to shove it up Zoey's ass, but to see the kind of congratulations I'll receive from this all-consuming man. Focusing, I swing my arm back and then bring it forward sending the corn filled bag toward the other board. As if in slow motion, I watch it fly over the sand, the air around us stilling as it effortlessly slides across the board and through the hole, scoring our final point.

In shock, I scream, throw my hands to the sky and start running in place. "Ahhh, I did it!"

Zoey kicks the sand in front of her, sending a chunk into Art's stomach, and then proceeds to stomp off, not wanting to stick around to watch me celebrate. That's the exact reaction I expected from Zoey. Although the height she got on that sand is impressive. Poor Art.

Wanting someone to cheer with, I turn to find Beck standing behind me, a look of pure pride on his face. Not even giving it a second thought, I leap up into his arms and straddle his waist with my legs. I grip the back of his neck and say, "We won. I did it. I scored a point."

"I saw, Saucy, and it was sexy as hell watching you score that final point too."

"I can't believe I did it. I did it!" I'm bouncing in his arms, feeling indescribably happy.

"You did." Beck's hands grip my ass, tightly, and I could care less at this point. I'm on cloud nine right now."

"Oh just kiss and get it over with," Victoria says, passing us with another plate of crab cakes and a jar of tartar sauce in hand.

Got to love my friends.

"I think she's right. We should just *get it over with* and kiss," Beck suggests, looking too adorable with his prideful smile and playful eyes.

What I wouldn't give to kiss him right now, but I won't. Not here, not with everyone surrounding us. Despite how much it pains me, I pat his cheek and say, "I don't get involved with teammates. Sorry, dude."

"What?"

I hop off his body despite his attempt to keep me there *and* despite my raging hormones. "Never fool around with teammates; it's the cardinal rule. You're completely off limits now. Sorry."

I start to walk away, giving Beck a good show, when he comes chasing after me and snags me around the waist.

"Fuck that. You're no longer on my team then." Leaning in close, he places a kiss on the side of my cheek. "Because there is nothing that's going to get in my way of taking what I want. And what I want is you, Rylee. I want all of you, all night. It's going to happen, the only question is . . . when."

From the heavy throb between my legs and the way my stomach is bottoming out from every word muttered from his mouth, I'm assuming it will be soon. It's going to happen so freaking soon.

"You're really going to sit over there?"

"Yup." I take a bite from the Key lime candy I bought earlier. The tart flavor hits my tongue followed by the richness of dark chocolate. The sun set a few hours ago, and the moon casts a glow against the rippling water in front of us, barely giving us a glimpse of the dark ocean waters. It's gorgeous here. Peaceful, the perfect place to come and relax.

"You're being ridiculous."

"Nope, being cautious. I'm not stupid. I've seen the way you've been looking at me all day, and after reading my book, there is no way I'll be able to keep my clothes on if I sit over there with your alpha self oozing out of your every pore. It's why you refuse to put a shirt on. I know it."

Seriously, the man has only worn a shirt once around me. *I get it, Beck, you're hot, all corded muscle and pretty pecs. Yup, you're a walking orgasm.*

Chuckling, he says, "Maybe I don't have a shirt on because it's humid as fuck here, and I'm not into the whole sweating through my clothes thing."

"Orrr, you're trying to drive me crazy."

Leaning over the railing that splits our two balconies, he asks in a low voice, "Is it working?"

"Not even in the slightest," I answer defiantly with my arms crossed over my chest.

The loudest laugh pops out of his deliciously seductive mouth. "You're not fooling anyone, Saucy."

Slightly irritated that his laugh turns me on so damn much, I say, "You know, we don't always have to talk about sex. We can talk about other things."

"Yeah, like what?"

"Uhhh." Think of something. Pecs, penis, abs, arms, all the muscles in your arms, shoes, your big hands—

Shoes?

Yes, shoes.

"Shoes," I shout, startling Beck in his chair from my sudden outburst.

"What?" he asks, laughter in his voice.

"Do you wear shoes?" Oh for fuck's sake. Trying to save my idiocy, I add, "You know, since you don't wear underwear, I was just wondering if you wore shoes."

From the way his lips are pulled up in the corners, he's confused and entertained, but he lifts his foot off the propped position of his balcony. "Yup, I wear shoes."

Duh. Everyone wears shoes.

"Those are sandals." Might as well keep digging the grave, go all the way, because if anything I'm thorough. "Sandals are a footwear, not a shoe."

"Thanks for the definition." Beck chuckles some more. Turning to face me, he places his arms on the rail that divides us and rests his chin on his arms, his eyes easing the tension building in my shoulders. They're so beautiful, hues of green and gold, so calming, so relaxing. "Do you wear shoes, Rylee?" The way he asks the question, so soft, so deep, I can feel myself getting sucked into his little world, his sexual web.

I nod, the air around us electric, the sexual tension almost making it hard to breathe.

"Good to know." He reaches over the side and grabs my hand, pulling me to my feet as he leans back.

With his head, he nods over to his side, indicating his intentions of bringing me over to his part of the balcony.

"Get on over here, Saucy."

"But we're having a conversation." I bite my bottom lip, knowing very well that our topic of conversation was the absolute pits. Shoe talk isn't all that riveting.

"We can converse over here. You can tell me all about the shoes you like to wear."

Weighing my options, knowing I won't be able to resist him much longer—even though I know I should—I take a deep breath and let him help me over the rail. When I go to sit on the chair next to him, he stops me and pulls me down on his lap so I'm straddling him.

I take in our little setup and raise an eyebrow at him. "I don't think this is a conducive position for a conversation."

"I think it's perfect." Scooting back in his chair, he props his legs up on the balcony rail behind me, and places his hands on my thighs. "See? Perfect. I'm comfortable, you're comfortable; we're good." Running this thumbs along my thighs, he says, "Now tell me about your shoes. I'm here to listen. Lay it on me. I want colors, heights, and detailed descriptions about any prints you might have."

"Stop." I playfully whack him on the stomach. "I'm nervous, okay?" The words leave my mouth before I can stop them. I twist my hands in my lap, embarrassed about my small confession.

I'm sure you can tell by now that I like to play it cool, that I put on a front. But in all honesty, the reason why I've been trying to keep my distance from Beck is because I don't want to give my heart hope. Because the disappointment that would follow is too crushing. And I know this man could easily give me hope, with one press of his lips against mine, I know he would give me hope for not necessarily love—because that's entirely too early to say anything like that—but hope for my future, for the future that with every call from my doctor seems to be slowly slipping from my grasp. *I'll never be enough.*

Calming my breath, keeping my heart from beating at an abnormal pace, I add, "I don't do things like this with people I don't know. I'm not a vacation-fling girl. Despite how much I try to show you how relaxed and chill I am, I'm a ball of nerves inside." My head falls in front of me, my eyes focused on my hands as they twine together.

Lifting my chin so I'm forced to meet Beck's soulful eyes, he cups my face and softly says, "Rylee, there is no need to be nervous. I might be flirting with you, but there is no way in hell I would ever do anything to make you feel uncomfortable. Never would I want you to feel like you're being forced into anything."

Hell, now I feel guilty. I don't want Beck thinking he's forcing me into anything. That's not the case at all.

"I'm sorry if you felt pressured. That wasn't my intention—"

I silence him with my finger to his lips. "You didn't pressure me in any way. If anything, you've made me feel sexy, irresistible, a feeling every woman wishes for. I only want you to know I'm nervous, that's all."

Beck—kind, funny, good-looking, attentive, thoughtful—he's the fantasy. No man has ever looked at me the way I've described *the look* in my books. Yet, somehow . . . Beck does, and it doesn't make sense. I'm never the heroine. There hasn't been a glimpse of a happily ever after for me. And there may never be . . . "You're the kind of man I write about, Beck, not the kind of man who finds me attractive."

"Fuck that shit." His features turn angry, his grip tightening. "Do you realize the minute I first saw you, it was hard for me to swallow, to even focus on what I was doing? Baby puke and all, I was immediately attracted to you. And then I somehow earned the privilege to get to know you, to hang out with you. Not only are you beautiful, Rylee, but your personality is a huge turn-on."

My face heats up, my palms start to sweat, and I realize for the first time I'm not good at this. I'm awkward as hell, I don't know how to take a compliment, I don't know how to act around an extremely attractive man who's interested in me, and I have no idea what to say other than to put myself down. I want to argue with him, tell him he has no idea who I really am, what I suffer from, and he should stay far away from me.

"This is crazy," I say softly. "What's going to happen here? We have sex and then go our separate ways?"

"No," he answers matter-of-factly. "We sit here and talk. We sit here and enjoy each other's company. We sit here and take in the moment, the waves whispering against the rocks beneath us, the moon casting its light on us, and the subtle smell of paradise drifting past us. Soak it in, Rylee. Stop thinking, and just experience it."

Before I can answer him, he turns me around on his lap so my back is against his chest. He relaxes my head against his shoulder and uses one of his legs to kick up mine so they are propped up like his. He wraps both of his arms around my waist and holds on tightly, his mouth a mere inch away from my ear.

"Relax, Rylee and just feel."

Closing my eyes, taking Beck's advice, I feel.

The beat of his heart against my back.

The pressure of his hands on my waist.

The light brush of his leg against mine.

The even rhythm of his breathing.

The way my body so easily melts into his.

My heart beats with his, the matching cadence soothing.

My cheek pressed against his cheek, the brisk scrape of his stubble across my soft skin.

His powerful thighs holding me up.

His soft, yet deep and velvety voice rolling from his lips to my ear.

"Tell me something only a few people know about you."

To relax me even more, his fingers find their way under my shirt and seductively stroke my hipbone. God, that feels good.

"Something they know?" I try to concentrate on his question, even though all my brain wants to focus on is the tortuous circles. "Okay." I clear my throat. "I like to write at this little coffee shop in our small town. There is a specific chair I write in that I swear to you is magical. I've written some of my best sex scenes in this chair. I mean, if this chair could talk, it would make you blush."

Beck chuckles into my ear.

"You have a lucky chair."

"I do," I answer, my body more relaxed than ever. "But that's not what I'm about to tell you."

"No? There's more?"

"Yes." I pause. "I want it to be known that I'm not proud of this, but I was desperate, okay?"

"Okaaay," Beck drags out in curiosity.

"Promise not to judge me?"

"If you tell me you started diddling yourself in the coffee shop to get yourself turned on to write a sex scene, I very well might judge you, and you can't take that away from me."

Laughing, I playfully pinch him from behind, causing him to shift in his seat.

"Hey, watch it."

"I didn't diddle myself in public. God, what is wrong with you?"

His chest rumbles against my back. "What the hell am I supposed to think? You're talking about this sex chair and how I'm not supposed to judge you for something you did in it. I think everyone would immediately think you diddled yourself in the chair."

My eyes roll to the sky. *Sex chair. Gah!* "Men, so disgusting."

"Okay, so if you didn't diddle yourself, what did you do?"

I shift so I'm back into my comfortable position. "I was desperate to get through a sex scene, so I walked to the coffee shop, Snow Roast, to sit in my inspiration chair—not sex chair—and when I arrived there was an old lady sitting in it, sipping her coffee."

"Oh Jesus, I think I know where this is going."

"I told you I wasn't proud of what I did."

"How did you get her out? Please don't tell me you got into a fistfight with an old lady over a sex chair."

"Inspiration chair," I say rather aggressively. "And no, I didn't fight her. God, I'm not an animal. You see, we live in such a small town that I know almost everyone, and it wasn't my first encounter with Mrs. Braverman. She's known to be a squatter. She will spend hours sipping a cold cup of tea, staring off into thin air, not having a worry or care."

"So you punted her out of the chair."

"No!" I hold back my smile. "I told her there was a flash sale at Wicks and Sticks."

"Wicks and Sticks?" Beck's thumbs continue their pursuit across my skin.

"It's a candle and incense store in town. Mrs. Braverman is well known for hoarding her scents . . ."

"Oh Rylee." I can feel Beck shake his head. "You fooled that old lady."

"I fooled her so hard." I giggle. "And she snapped out of my chair, grabbed her cane, and booked it down the street."

"You monster." Beck chuckles.

"To be fair, I felt really bad while I was writing one of the hottest sex scenes ever. To make it up to her, I gave her a gift basket of candles and incense afterwards."

Beck squeezes me. "I guess that's fair. Still, fooling an old lady. That's just low."

"I told you not to judge me."

His stubbled jaw runs along my cheek as he whispers, "Sorry."

Chills scream their way down my arms and legs, my nipples pucker, and just like that, with one word, all humor vanishes from our little conversation and awareness of this all-consuming man wrapped around me hits me hard.

Gathering myself, I say, "Tell me something Chris and Justine know about you."

"Hmm." His thumbs hook under the waistband of my shorts, playing with the lower part of my hipbones. His touch spurs on my pelvis, needing to rock, begging for him to go lower. My toes curl in my sandals and my back slightly arches, reaching for more. "Something they know about me."

His mouth doesn't stray from its position against my ear, and his hips start to slowly move underneath me, his legs tangling with mine. Involuntarily, one of my hands hooks the back of his neck as I hold on tightly to him, feeling like I need support from the onslaught of sensation I'm feeling.

I hear him say something, but it doesn't register in my brain, which has turned to mush as his thumbs stray from my hipbones to right above my pubic bone.

There is no denying how turned on I am, how wet I am from

his mere touch, how much—despite my reservations—I want this man.

With each stroke, my head turns farther and farther to the side until our noses are touching, Beck's head bends forward to meet me halfway. My eyes flutter shut for a brief moment before I open them and am captured by those flecks of green and gold.

The air stills around us, our breath mixing, swirling between us, our lips so close.

One swipe of this thumb.

Another one.

I can't breathe.

I can't focus.

Another swipe, my head leans even closer, my tongue wetting my lips.

One more swipe . . .

My heart hammers in my chest, my skin prickling with awareness.

Beck brings his mouth even closer, only a whisper away now, and he waits.

Holding still.

His breathing feeling erratic beneath me.

One.

More.

Swipe.

And I'm gone.

I bring my mouth to his, slowly parting my lips ever so slightly, just enough to maneuver my mouth across his.

A low, provocative moan escapes Beck as one of his hands snags the back of my head and holds me in place, almost as if he lets go, I'll disappear.

Needing more, I shift on his lap so I'm straddling him once again, my hands on his bare chest, feeling the powerful sinew that holds him together.

Our lips press and mold, mingling, taking, begging . . .

Desperate.

Beck's tongue runs against my bottom lip, eliciting a moan from deep within me, lighting a fire so hot, so wild, my hands start to travel up his neck to his cheeks where I grip him, positioning his head so when I open my mouth, I can expertly dive my tongue onto his.

He groans, his lap shifting against mine now, his hard-on pressing against my wet and throbbing center. I match his rocking, using my position on his lap to take advantage of his length I can feel through his board shorts.

This is exactly what I didn't want to happen, but God, am I happy it has. Maybe I really should live in the moment, maybe I should take advantage of the opportunity, maybe I should...

"Woo, yeah, get it on!" Zoey screams from below us, immediately shooting me off Beck's lap and into the rail behind me, causing me to lose my balance.

With cat-like reflexes, Beck catches my arm and steadies me, his eyes aware but heady with lust, his breathing as erratic as mine.

"Don't let us disturb you," Zoey calls out once again. "Just taking a midnight stroll."

"Yup, that's great." I give her a thumbs up with one hand as the other is holding on to Beck, our eyes never breaking contact.

"Have a good night, you two." She makes an obnoxious catcall and then disappears with Art, I'm assuming. Thanks, Zoey. Thanks a lot.

After what seems like forever staring at Beck, disbelief in my mind, he beckons me back to his lap with a little tug of his hand, but I resist, feeling like the moment has passed. *Hating that the moment has passed.*

"I should get to bed. Big day tomorrow and everything. Never crashed a wedding before. Should probably do some research on how to do it. Don't want to be that wedding crasher who doesn't follow protocol. Maybe I should watch the movie, really brush up on my rules. What does Vince Vaughn say?" I bite my lip and try to think back to the movie. "Rule number seventy-six: no excuses, play like a champion."

"Rylee . . ."

I point at Beck and say, "You should catch up on the rules too. I want to make sure my date doesn't screw this up. I refuse to be kicked out of a wedding because you didn't pay attention to details." I steal my hand back from Beck and before he can stop me, I hop over to my balcony. "Don't forget, rule number seven: blend in by standing out." I touch my nose and then point at Beck again. "Blend in by standing out, don't forget that." I trip over a chair on my blind pursuit to my door. "Ouch, rule number fifty-five: watch where you're going." I unattractively snort. "Rule number eighty-two: leave the snorting for the pigs."

Rule number five hundred: *shut the hell up, Rylee.*

"Okay, yup, good night." I give him a solid salute—because that's what awkward people do—and head into my room but not before I can hear Beck blow out a long breath and mutter, "Fuck."

Yeah, I'm right there with you, buddy.

Part Two

RULE NUMBER 7: BLEND IN BY STICKING OUT

CHAPTER ELEVEN

RYLEE

"There she is, master humper of Key West."

"Shut up," I say, flopping next to Zoey, my head pounding as if a hammer is trying to make its way through my skull. I steal Zoey's coffee and take a big gulp.

Victoria spreads jam across her wheat toast and asks, "Master humper? Did I miss something last night?"

"Yeah." Zoey grabs my shoulders and shakes me, making my stomach roll from my migraine. "Our girl here totally got some last night."

"With Beck? I like him, he's a swell guy."

"You should have seen them, Victoria, it was super hot. Art and I went back to our room and had some of the best sex we've had in a while. Isn't that right, honey?"

"Can you not talk about our sex life with your friends?" Art has a forkful of scrambled eggs partially lifted to his mouth, a look of utter embarrassment on his face.

"Oh sweetie, they know all about how you please me. This is not new information to them, but you're cute for turning red." She pats Art on the cheek and helps lift his fork to his face to encourage him to keep eating. I would do the same, and tell him to ignore the rest of this conversation; better yet, run for your life, Art. *Run.*

"First of all, don't tell me about getting off from watching me kiss some guy, that's extremely disturbing, and concerning."

"We didn't get off over you two. God, full of yourself much? It lit a spark in us, like it was a competition, like who could fuck harder." Zoey leans back in her chair and twirls a strand of her hair. "Let me tell you, Art fucked hard."

"For the love of God, woman," Art mumbles, face beet-red and buried in his plate, avoiding all eye contact.

"Well, good for you," I answer awkwardly. "And for the record, Beck and I didn't do anything last night."

"Bullshit, you two were clawing at each other."

"In public?" Victoria's nose scrunches up. "Rylee, a little modesty. I know he's attractive, but to hump people in public is just beneath you."

"We didn't hump in public, we . . . humped on his balcony."

"You should have seen it, Victoria, her hips were moving like a jackhammer."

Oh God, were they? I sure as hell hope not. How embarrassing. Did Beck think I was hammering my hips into him? Honest to God, I can't remember anything besides the way he tasted on my lips, like the best kind of addiction I could ever experience.

Not going to let Zoey get away with embellishing the story, I say, "There was no jackhammering. There was kissing and light hip action. We stopped once you started catcalling up to the balcony. Thanks for that by the way."

"What? You stopped? You weren't supposed to stop; you were to keep going. Why the hell did you stop?"

I take another sip of her coffee and slouch back in my chair, closing my eyes, willing my headache to dissipate. It's a tension headache no doubt. "You killed the mood."

"Oh no, don't you dare blame this on me. This is all on you." Zoey turns to Art and says in a sweet voice, "Darling, why don't you take your little fruit cup and go eat by the ocean. What a delightful experience that will be."

Art grumbles and stands from his chair, picking up his fruit cup and a spoon. He's a good man, putting up with Zoey. I barely put up with her, and she's my friend. I can't imagine being married to her, although, I think they do balance each other nicely. Art grounds her, and Zoey pushes him out of his shell. It's a good pairing.

Once Art is out of earshot, Zoey grips the table and turns to me. I can feel her eyes blazing, scorching laser beams in my direction. I block my sight from the world, but there is no denying the wildness exuding her. She's about to give me one of her "lessons."

"What the hell are you doing?" Yup, here it comes. "You are single and in paradise, living it up in the sun, getting all tanned, and there is a gorgeous man interested in you, practically panting every time you walk by. If I were you, I wouldn't be sipping my friend's coffee and whining about your humping parade coming to a quick end. I'd be hauled up, fucking said gorgeous man every chance I had. Hell, I would make a fuck-it list of everywhere I wanted this man to do me while on this island, including against a palm tree making it rain coconuts, in the ocean with fish as my witness, upside down in the shower, soap beating my eyes, and let's not forget on a piece of driftwood while sharing a piece of Key lime fucking pie! This is your last day here, what are you waiting for?"

I sigh and bite my bottom lip, trying to will back the tears threatening to fall. Zoey knows me better than anyone. She knows I'm not a girl who can simply *fling*. I'm just me. And Beck will probably avoid me like the plague after last night's excruciating exit. "Why start something when I know it's not going to go anywhere?"

"Uh, it's called endless orgasms and that man is handing them out like candy on Halloween. Who cares about starting something? Just have fun, Rylee. You deserve it after what you've been through this past year."

And the tears fall.

This past year. Hell, how I endured it, I have no idea.

"She's crying," Victoria says stiffly. Victoria doesn't do well with emotions, and I know I'm making her extremely uncomfortable.

Zoey sighs next to me and places her hand on my arm. "Sweetie, why are you thinking about this so much? Just have fun, have a vacation fling, throw caution to the wind."

I wipe my tears, seeing how soft Zoey's eyes are, understanding etching her features. Victoria, on the other hand, is trying to avoid me at all costs. I'm used to her dismissing anything that deals with feelings, so I'm not the least bit hurt.

"I'm nervous because I like him." *And* the truth comes out. "I don't want to have a taste of something I'll never have again. You know?"

Zoey squeezes my hand, pressing the palm of her hand to the back of mine. "I can understand that, but you and I both know, you only live once, why not live life to its fullest? No regrets, right?" She tips my chin up. "Will you regret throwing caution to the wind and having the night of your life? Or will you regret more never truly finding out what it's like to be with such an enigmatic man?"

I know what my body wants. It's practically thrumming for him right now, but can I truly put all thoughts to the side and have a passionate night?

Zoey is right. I think of all the regrets I could possibly face, and not being consumed by Beck for one night would be one of them. A huge one.

Massaging my temples, I take deep breaths as I calm the pounding in my head. "I need some medicine and my bed."

"Headache?"

"Yeah." I stand but Zoey grabs my hand. "Let us know if you need anything. Wedding is at five."

"I'm arriving an hour early," Victoria says, finally looking at me again. "I want to soak in Ernest Hemingway and his environment.

I doubt I'll stay for the reception. I'll pay my respects to the couple and take off."

"Okay. I'll see you girls later."

"Hey," Zoey calls out before I can walk too far away. "Are you going to be okay?"

I barely nod, not wanting to shake my head too hard. "I'll be good. Thank you."

When I reach my room, I take three Ibuprofen, down another cup of coffee from my hotel room coffee maker, and rest my head on my pillow, blocking out the sun and the rest of the world.

The bed dips and for a second, it almost feels like I'm on a boat, the waves peacefully floating me up and down. It isn't until I feel a warm hand press against my cheek that I realize I'm in a bed with someone hovering over me.

"Hey there." Beck's voice drapes over me like a warm blanket. "How are you doing?"

Peering my eyes open, I spot him immediately, his brow etched together, genuine concern on his face. "Wh-what are you doing here?"

"Victoria gave me her spare key to your room when she told me you weren't feeling well. I wanted to come check on you."

I would expect Zoey to do such a thing but not Victoria, unless Beck once again wooed her over, and I wouldn't put it past him.

"I brought some food and tons of water, also some more Ibuprofen and a Mountain Dew in case you needed some caffeine."

Right past Beck is a small cart with food, Ibuprofen, a bottle of Mountain Dew, and what looks like six bottles of water. God, he's sweet.

"You didn't have to do that," I say while rubbing my eye. "But thank you, that was really sweet."

"I had to make sure my date was feeling better for the wedding. I didn't want you miserable, and I know how important it is for you to go to this wedding. So, here I am. How are you feeling now?"

I pause, giving myself a second to adjust to the semi-intruder and waking up from a very long nap. There is no pounding in my head, only a faint "off" feeling, which could be from the nap or could be the recovery from a migraine.

"I seem to be feeling better." I sit up and Beck helps me by propping up my pillow behind me.

"Does that mean you're up for some food?"

"Depends on two things. What time is it and what did you bring?"

Beck pushes a long strand of hair behind my ear, the gesture so gentle, as if he's been doing that for years. "It's a little past two and I brought burgers and waffle fries, figured the grease might help you out a bit. But now I think about it, grease helps with a hangover headache, not a migraine."

I shrug my shoulders. "I bet grease helps with anything. I'm ready for it, bring it on."

"Mind if I eat with you? I'm starving."

"Of course not." I toss some pillows to the ground and pat the bed next to me. "I'm not about to make you eat lunch by yourself when you brought me food. That would be very rude."

"Very rude indeed." With ease, Beck brings the food and drinks over in one swift transfer, balancing all the liquid like a professional. Placing a tray on the bed, he hops up next to me, his long legs stretching out further than mine. Instead of the shirtless, board-short wearing man I've gotten to know, Beck is dressed in a pair of dark jeans and a plain white T-shirt. The sleeves cling to his arms, and the tan he's acquired makes the white of the shirt pop.

And then there is just something about a man not wearing socks and shoes with jeans. Something about him being barefoot in jeans is a bit of a turn-on for me. And even though I'm still feeling a little off, I'm not feeling off enough to not notice how extremely attracted I am to the man next to me.

My conversation with Zoey floats through my mind as Beck

opens up the plate covers, revealing two giant burgers and waffle fries. Live in the moment. It's what Beck has said to me over and over again in the last few days, every chance he's felt my resistance.

I think maybe it's time I truly listen.

"Thank you for bringing this over. You're the best fake wedding date ever."

"Not fake, Saucy, there is nothing fake between us." He winks and then takes a huge bite of his burger. Talking with his mouth full, he asks, "Do you want to watch some TV?"

I chuckle. "I mean we've done everything else together for the most part, might as well watch some TV like an old married couple."

Leaning over me, his broad body pressing against my petite frame, he snags the remote from the nightstand on my side of the bed and says, "Believe me, we haven't done everything together. If we had, you'd know it." Turning on the TV, he shoves a waffle fry in his mouth and adds, "What do you want to watch?"

"Not too particular, just no sports."

"Not that kind of guy, so no worries there."

A little surprised, I pop a fry in my mouth as well and ask, "No? Not a huge sports fan?"

"Nah, fell out of touch with life for a bit. During that time, I read more than anything so, I've become a reader."

"Fell out of touch with life. What does that mean?" I know I'm being nosey, but I don't care.

"A story for another time," he answers, shutting down the topic before I can ask him more. "How about Seinfeld? Does this work?"

"Uh, yeah, that's cool."

Still reeling from Beck's little hint into his life that I shouldn't care about, I take a bite from my burger while he opens a bottle of water for me. "You're going to want to drink up, hydrate as much as you can. I've had migraines before and they're killer. Do you get them often?"

"Not really. I think this was more of a tension headache than anything."

"Tense?" he asks the question so casually, as if he already knows the answer.

"Just a little." I shy away, not wanting to look him in the face. Is he going to bring up last night? I hope not. I'm not in the mood to hash things out.

"So what happened last night? You kind of ran away from me."

Well, there goes hoping. Should have known he'd bring it up. Beck doesn't bullshit around, and if there is anything I've come to understand over these past couple days it's that he gets straight to the point. He doesn't tiptoe, or neglect an issue for that matter. Yet, in some ways, I'm annoyed too. He ran off on me the other night with one mention of Christine, whoever she is, and hasn't offered any information about why *he* ran. Clearly, it was a hard topic, as he does seem to call a spade a spade. How do I play his question now? He'll been angry if I put myself down . . .

"Yeah, about that. Weird, huh?" I answer, trying to play coy.

"Really weird." He chuckles. "Especially since we were having a good time. One second, I had your sweet mouth all over mine, and the next, I was staring at your retreating back. I thought I'd get a solid kiss good night, but you stole that away from me before I could take it."

"Gosh," I shake my head, "What a bitch move."

This makes Beck laugh wholeheartedly, from the depths of his rock-hard abs. The sound eases the tension I've been feeling. I've been overthinking this. I feel like I was given this opportunity to experience this man, to allow him to help me step out of my comfort zone, and instead of holding back, I should take a chance on what I can only imagine will be a night I'll never forget.

Forget my reservations.

Forget what the future will hold for now.

Forget the last year and all the doctor visits.

And forget about the end of this trip.

Just focus on the here and now, because that's the only thing I can control.

And right now I want to feel. Not think.

CHAPTER TWELVE

BECK

I give myself one more once-over in the mirror and adjust the collar of my button-up shirt. The air has cooled down thankfully, so the grey pants and white dress shirt I'm wearing actually feel comfortable, not stifling. But just in case I get a little hot, I unbutton the top few buttons of my shirt, giving myself a little airflow.

I spray on some cologne, making sure not to apply too much, and check my dress shoes—all tied. Looks like I'm ready. Then why the fuck do I feel so ill-prepared?

Maybe because over the last few days I've become somewhat attached to this little raven-haired beauty. I know tonight is the last night I'll see her; she leaves early tomorrow morning, and my body is already aching over her departure.

Fuck, this wasn't supposed to happen. I wasn't supposed to grow attached to anyone on this trip, and yet, it's happened.

When I saw Victoria without Rylee by her side today at the pool, I immediately grew concerned. It didn't take very long to get information out of Victoria about Rylee's whereabouts or a key to her room. Victoria and I could be friends, which I appreciate.

I didn't think twice about getting things to help Rylee feel better. It felt like second nature, and if that isn't fucking scary, I don't know what is.

I haven't truly cared for another person in over eight years. Fucking eight years. It's been so goddamn long since I've felt an inkling of something for another person. And now, on a goddamn island, I have to like someone who lives over three thousand miles away from me.

Good job, Beck. Way to fucking pick them.

Taking a deep breath, I glance in the mirror. The corners of my eyes are weathered, my face almost drained, but there is a spark of hope in my eyes—hope for tonight—despite not being the man Rylee thinks I am.

Fuck, she must think I'm some goddamn knight in shining armor, swooping into her hotel room with the cure for her migraine. I want to be that man. I want to be the man everyone looks at and thinks he's a good human, but that's not how I feel.

I feel like a goddamn fake.

Someone checking the boxes on how to be a good person, hitting all the marks for people to like me, but deep down, I know my soul is tarnished. I'm not the man I'm perceived to be.

I'm ashamed.

I'm an illusion, a torn individual with a charismatic personality.

And yet, I can't stop myself from flirting with Rylee, from taking what I so desperately want—one night with her. One night with those light blue eyes staring up at me, seeing the man I wish I was. *Someone worthy of her.*

Taking a deep breath, I pull my phone from my pocket and dial Cal's phone number.

"Beck, how are you?" his gruff voice answers.

"Good, Cal. How about you?"

"Doing well. The wife and I are about to go to dinner."

"Ah, sorry about interrupting. I wanted to give you a quick call before I head to the wedding."

"Yes, I meant to text you earlier. Sorry about that. How are you feeling?"

I nod even though he can't see me. "I feel confident, in control. I'm going with a girl I met here."

"Is that so? Having a little bit of fun on the island?" His jovial tone is different from his normal straight-to-business attitude, and I like it. He almost seems like a friend right now rather than a guardian angel. And yes, I truly believe Cal is my guardian angel. *Without him in my life . . . No, don't go there.*

Chuckling, I shift on my feet, head tilted down. "Just a little. But I wanted to let you know I'm feeling good and will be drinking water the entire night."

"That's good. Have you had any cravings since you've been down there?"

"No." I shake my head. "None, I truly think I've put drinking behind me."

"You might think that, but the craving will always be there, even if it's buried deep within you right now, it will always be there. Got it?"

"Yes, sir," I answer, hearing the toughness in his voice once again.

"Okay, have fun tonight, and if you need me, you know how to reach me."

We say our goodbyes and I stuff my phone in my back pocket. I adjust my waistline and belt and roll up my sleeves, because keeping them down was a joke. I check the time and see that we have about half an hour before the ceremony, and it will take ten minutes to walk to the venue. It's time to pick up my date.

With a deep breath, I walk out of my room and take the few steps to Rylee's where I knock on the door and stick my hands in my pockets while I wait for her to answer.

From the other side of the door, I hear her moving around the room, and I can also hear the slew of curse words popping out of her mouth after there's a clunk on the floor. My lips turn up in time for Rylee to open the door.

Holy . . .

Shit . . .

She looks . . .

This is going to be one hell of a night.

She's dressed in a teal low-cut dress that drops to her feet with a killer slit kissing her panty line. From beneath the slit, there's a line of lace that matches the dress color, which I can only assume is her underwear. It must be a whole ensemble because it matches perfectly. I'm growing harder by the second.

Her hair is curled in light waves and half up and half down. There is a white flower behind one of her ears, and she lined her eyes with black, making them bluer than I've ever seen.

Fuck me.

She looks like some exotic island princess, and it's making it very hard to remember what the hell we're about to do, because all I want to do is back her up into her hotel room and lick every damn inch of her body.

"Hey, I dropped my clutch. That's why it took me so long to answer. Are you ready to go?" She looks me over and casually licks her lips, not hiding her feelings at all. It's refreshing coming from her. "You look good, Beck."

I don't say anything. Instead, I wrap my arm around her waist and pull her in close. I place a very gentle kiss on her lips, a whisper of a touch. I needed one small taste, something to get me through the night without losing my goddamn mind over this woman.

When I pull away, I rest my forehead on hers. "Fuck, Rylee, you look stunning."

"Really?" Her voice is small. *How the fuck can she not know?* She's . . . there are no words, but fuck. How can she question this?

"Yes, so fucking beautiful, you're making it hard on me here. I want to take you to this wedding, fulfill the wedding crashing promise we have, but damn it, all I want to do is peel this dress off your sexy body and fuck you on every surface of your hotel room."

Her breath catches in her throat, and she takes a deep breath. "I, uh, I got the dress from Macy's."

And once again, she has me laughing from the pit of my stomach. I shake my head and give her one more chaste kiss before pulling away and sliding my hand into hers.

"You really know how to make a man feel good about the compliments he's handing out."

We walk hand in hand down the steps of the hotel and onto the street toward Whitehead Street. "Telling a girl you want to fuck her all over a hotel room is hardly a compliment."

I pull her close and nuzzle into her ear as we walk. "Then clearly you've been hanging around the wrong men. Stick with me, Saucy. I'll show you what it's like to be worshipped."

A gorgeous smile passes over her lips while she continues to move forward. *Maybe, just maybe, she'll be mine all through the night.*

I sure as fuck hope so.

◇

"She's incredibly beautiful," Rylee says, her eyes full of hearts.

Normally I wouldn't be so affected by a wedding, especially since I have a failed marriage under my belt, but the newlyweds were so prolific in their vows and so honest. I don't think I've ever seen a man stand up in front of a large group of people and proclaim his love like that for a woman he so passionately and desperately needs in his life. It was heart-warming, and it made me want to fist bump the fuck out of that guy. He spoke pure poetry to his new bride and even shed a tear.

He's in love. He has the type of love I've never shared with another soul, certainly not Christine.

At first, I thought I had that kind of love with her. We were high school sweethearts, after all. But it didn't take long to work out that's all we really were, and when reality struck, we realized we got married way too early; we went down a treacherous path that carved our tumultuous and rocky future.

But it was refreshing to see love at its finest and truest form. It gave me hope, not for me, but for future generations.

"That was a truly touching ceremony," I say honestly.

"It really was." Rylee pulls her phone from her clutch and starts typing away. Curious, I look over her shoulder and see that she's typing in her notes app.

"Attention, everyone. The bride and the groom would like to invite you to cocktail hour while they take pictures. Drinks and appetizers are being served over by the pool. Please join us."

"Don't mind if I do," Zoey says, dragging Art along with her.

"I smell beef," Chris says, his nose leading the way with Justine trailing behind.

Victoria takes a look at her watch and says, "I'm going to head back to the hotel. You're not going to ditch my friend, are you?"

I shake my head. "I'm stuck to her all night, don't worry."

Victoria gives me a curt nod before taking off, leaving me alone with a typing Rylee. I wait a few minutes before I finally ask, "Are you writing your novel over there on your phone?"

She doesn't answer me.

So this time, I poke her. "Hey, do you want a drink?"

Nothing, just more typing, her fingers moving a mile a minute.

"Yeah, beautiful night. The sky is so clear, I agree."

Nothing.

"Planned on fucking you against the window of my hotel room tonight. I keep picturing your tits pressed against the sliding glass door as I enter you from behind."

Type. Type. Type.

I lean forward now, my scruff tickling her jaw. "I've thought about it ever since I met you. I got off from the image in my mind this afternoon while in the shower."

Type. Type. Type.

Oookay.

Getting closer, I pull her earlobe into my mouth and nibble on it before saying, "If you don't acknowledge me in the next few seconds, I'm bending you over these reception chairs and spanking that sweet ass of yours until you cry out in pleasure."

Her body goes stiff when my hand slides up the slit of her dress.

"What's going on?" She truly sounds clueless.

"Uh, have you not heard anything I've said to you?"

"What? No, sorry." She types a few more things and then sticks her phone in her purse, giving me all her attention. "I had the most brilliant idea and wanted to make sure I got it all down." She links her hand with mine, and I welcome the warm connection. "What were you saying?"

I shake my head and lead her toward the pool where the food and drinks are. "Nothing, you'll just be surprised tonight." We pass a few servers handing out pre-made drinks, but I bypass them and take Rylee straight to the bar. "What would you like?"

She looks over the selection. "Hmm, how about a rum punch?"

Signaling to the bartender, I say, "Can I get a rum punch and a water?"

When I turn back toward Rylee, her brow is pulled together. "Why aren't you getting a drink?"

It's a question I get asked whenever I'm around people who don't know my situation. Adults drink socially, that's what we do, and it looks odd, especially at an event like this, when you're holding a glass of ice water rather than a glass of alcohol. I get it, and honestly, I'm not mad about it. I was the one who dug this grave and have to sleep in it.

"I don't drink." I keep my answer simple, short, and to the point, trying not to open up the floodgates for other questions.

But when you're hanging out with a creative mind, it doesn't seem as easy to move past what I don't want to talk about.

"You don't drink? But, haven't you had a drink since we've hung out?" I shake my head. I would have remembered that drink, because it would have been eight hard years going right down the drain.

"Nope, always water. It's all I drink besides coffee in the

139

morning and an occasional soda, but that's rare. I think this afternoon was the first time in a few months I had a soda."

"Really? Wow. Is it because you're a health nut or something?"

Clearing my throat, I answer, "Something like that," just as our
drinks are put on the bar counter. I toss a tip in the jar in front of
me and hand Rylee her drink.

"You're hiding something from me." She eyes me suspiciously.

"Yeah, I am." I take a sip of my drink. "But it's not something
that's necessary to talk about now, same as the way you've been
hiding something from me."

I'm not stupid. I can read people really well, and there is a
reason Rylee isn't fully enjoying her time in Key West. She's
holding back. I see part of Rylee living life freely, but there are
other times where I see her put restrictions on her fun, on letting
loose, and I can't quite put my finger on it, why she's being so
reserved. But I know it's important. *To her.*

"I'm not—"

"No lying, Rylee. You don't have to tell me what it is. I'm not
here to quiz you about something you don't want to talk about. I'm
telling you I know there is something important in your life you're
not telling me, and that's okay. This is supposed to be fun, right?"

She bites her bottom lip and nods. "Yes, fun."

"Good, then let's have fun. First things first, we need to find a
server who's passing around those beef tenderloin things, because
hell, do they smell good."

"I want a coconut shrimp. I could smell them during the
ceremony."

And just like that, we're back to normal again.

"So that was your stomach making all those noises?"

"Guilty." She tips her drink in my direction and takes a sip,
looking around the place.

The house is beautiful. Small, but gorgeous, with its wrought
iron details, and a definite coastal feel with its bright yellow paint
and shutters. Before we were seated for the ceremony, we took a

quick look around the house. Victoria and Rylee were both over-whelmed with excitement, and I became caught up in their joy.

"Look at this place. It must have cost so much back then."

Not only did he have a beautiful house and grounds, but Hemingway saved six-toed cats and had built a rather impressive pool that, according to the fact plaque, was a bitch to build. "They had to break through coral to build this thing, and before Key West had fresh water piped in, they had to drain the pool then pump salt water in every three days."

"Seriously?" Rylee asks, leaning over to check out the plaque. I take that moment to place my hand on her lower back and pull her in a little closer.

Just in time too, because an older couple steps next to us, a chatty disposition written all over their gleeful faces.

"That beef tenderloin is to die for, have you tried any?" the man asks me.

"Not yet, I'm hoping to flag down a server soon."

"You won't be sorry." He holds his hand out. "I'm Gregory, and this is my wife, Tess."

I grip the man's beefy hand and give it a firm shake only to return it to Rylee's back. "Gregory, nice to meet you. I'm Beck and this is my wife, Rylee. We're newlyweds."

"Oh congratulations. How wonderful. Were Tiffany and Del at your wedding?"

I give him a sorrowful look. "I wish. We had a tiny ceremony out on the rocky cliffs of Maine's harbor. It was quaint and perfect for us. We celebrated with a lobster cake."

"Lobster cake?" Tess looks between us. "I don't think I've ever heard of a lobster cake before, did it taste good?"

"Did it have chunks of lobster in it?" Gregory asks, joining in with his wife.

Well, aren't they cutely obtuse?

I hold back the bold laugh desperate to escape. "Ah no. I guess I was a little deceiving there. I meant the cake was in the shape of a lobster. The flavor was strawberry with fudge, isn't that right, sweetheart?"

"Oh yeah," Rylee finally chimes in. "This guy wanted lemon, but I held strong with my choice of strawberry, and thank God I did, because everyone raved about it."

"And yet they would have raved about the lemon and you didn't give them a chance."

"No one raves about lemon," she deadpans.

"That's not true, I was raving lemon up a storm the other day. Lemon is where it's at, am I right, Gregory?" I give the man a little nudge with my elbow, but he shakes his head.

"I have to disagree with you there. Lemon is not my favorite."

You and me both. In reality, I would easily pass on lemon and dive right into strawberry with fudge. Hell, I hope Tiffany and Del have strawberry with fudge cake.

Tess takes a sip of her drink and asks, "So how do you two know the bride and groom?"

Ehh. With panic in our eyes, Rylee and I glance at each other. It was a topic we never discussed before we came. Rookie mistake.

"Badminton," Rylee blurts out, swallowing hard after, as if she couldn't believe she said that.

"Badminton?" Tess asks as her eyebrows crease together.

Rylee nods, panic still in her eyes. And instead of being the gallant gentleman that's wooed this woman since we met, I leave the explaining to Rylee because frankly, I want to hear all about this. Plus, it's fun to watch Rylee create. Almost beautiful. Right then and there, you can see her mind spinning with all the possibilities of interesting badminton stories.

"Yes, badminton." She laughs, as if she's about to tell the funniest story ever so I gear up, sip my water, and wait for the show. *Ever the storyteller.* "Oh it was so silly. You see, I'm a huge fanatic about badminton. Grew up playing my entire life, almost went to the Olympics for it." Oh Christ, she's really going for it.

"Really?" Gregory asks. "Wow, you must be really good." *Oh, this guy is not a smart man.*

Pretending to do a few swats with her imaginary racket, Rylee says, "See that? Called that the Ry-whack. They still teach it in my hometown. It's a stroke named after me, nothing too special, but when you're least expecting it, boy, can I hammer that cock."

Involuntarily I snort, causing water to shoot up the back of my throat and out my nose. I cover my face as I cough and try to catch my breath. Rylee pats me on the back, a giant smile on her face as she says, "You okay there, big man?" She turns to Gregory and Tess. "This guy, weirdest thing, he has a hard time swallowing without snorting it back up his throat and through his nose. We've been to the doctor a few times. He's going to a specialist when we get back." She pats me some more. "Don't worry, honey, we'll be sure to figure out your snorting water problem. It won't be like this forever."

"Oh, that's sweet." Tess clasps her hands together and stares at us as I wipe my nose.

Gregory continues the story. "So you met while playing badminton?"

"Yes." Rylee perks up again. "It was a wet day, and as you can tell, water doesn't mix well here with Beck. It's like if it rains, he starts to melt, can't handle it. But he was putting on a good show for me, making an absolute fool of himself trying to hit the shuttlecock with the Ry-whack, but talk about uncoordinated. He's better suited sorting and wrapping pennies. It's his hobby actually. Loves packaging pennies."

"What a lovely pastime." Tess smiles at me.

Oh hell.

Packaging pennies? Where is she getting this stuff? And I might not fawn and drool over sports like other men I know, but I sure as hell know how to play them. This girl is getting herself into some major trouble with her storytelling. Just wait until it's my turn.

"Yes, he has a collection of packaged pennies, at least five thousand dollars of pennies stuffed in the garage. I'm like, turn those pennies in, honey, and let's get a freaking jet ski." Rylee lifts her hand for a high five, which Gregory cautiously delivers. Rylee shakes her hand and then makes a fake gun motion at him with a wink. "Nice snap there, Gregory. Impressive."

"Uh, thank you."

"Gregory, Tess, how are you?" A woman wearing a leopard-print dress, bright red lipstick, and her hair up in a cocoon of curls coos from the side, pulling Gregory and Tess's attention away from us. Thank God.

We wave and slowly back away, my grip tight on Rylee's upper arm. When out of earshot, I lean down and whisper in her ear. "What the hell was that?"

She pokes my stomach. "Having a little fun. What, you don't wrap pennies for jollies?"

"More like silver dollars." I bite down on her ear, causing her to gasp, the sound so sweet.

"Oh, I see what you did there, made a reference about your penis."

Halting in my pursuit, I pull away and she gives me a smarmy smile that says, "Game on."

"Is this really happening? Are we really going to spend the night telling lies to these innocent wedding attendees to out-best each other?"

"If you don't think you can handle it—"

"Oh, Saucy, I might not lie, but I have no problem in playing along with your storytelling. I might not be an author, but I can tell a good fucking story."

She eyes me over her cup. "Then game on, Wilder."

"Judy and Dwayne, nice to meet you." I shake the hands of two strangers, putting on a show.

"Nice to meet you too. How do you know the bride and groom?"

"A nursery." I say, taking a sip of my water.

"A nursery? That seems like an odd place to meet since Tiffany and Del don't have kids."

"Ohhh, sorry about that, Dwayne." I pat the old guy on the back. "I meant a plant nursery. We were shopping for a tree to put in our front yard. Such a hard decision, you know. Should we go with the classic maple, or do we want to bring a Colorado feel to our front yard and plant an aspen? Or what about the cherry blossom?"

"Or evergreen," Judy points out.

"Exactly, Judy, exactly. God, what a decision. We spent hours in that nursery, fighting over what tree would look best. Rylee over here, she thought why not plant our fake Christmas tree in the front and call it a day."

"Oh that's a horrid idea," Judy says with disgust. "Why would you ever think that?"

"She's partial to plastic," I say, and then point to her breasts, which garners a giant whack to my stomach.

～

"Yeah, Everest, crazy, right? What a trip that was, huh, honey? Oh." Rylee cringes and covers her mouth. "Sorry, sore subject for this guy. He had such a bad case of altitude sickness after the first thousand feet he had to be airlifted off the mountain by helicopter. They wrapped him up in space blankets like a little sushi roll and took him to the nearest hospital where the nurses had to revert back to bottle-feeding him for a few days. He was delirious. Can't blame him."

"Bottle-feed? Why didn't they use an IV?" Kerry asks, in awe of Rylee's story.

"Oh they did, but he also needed something in his stomach and refused to eat. He truly thought for a couple of days he was a baby." Speaking from behind her hand, she shout whispers, "They had to put him in a grown-man's diaper to keep everything . . . contained."

"Oh dear."

"Quite a mess. Thankfully I was scaling the side of Everest and didn't have to watch my husband lift his butt to have his diaper changed. I think that would have put a dent in our sexual relationship, you know?"

"Oh yes, I don't think I could get that image out of my head," Kerry answers, giving me a once-over.

I grind my teeth together, putting on a good smile as Kerry, in her purple crushed-velvet ensemble, casts judgment.

"Had a hard time sucking from the nipple of the bottle." I decide to join in on the conversation. "They had to bring in the elephant-sized bottles for me."

"What? Why?" Kerry's hand is to her chest.

I thumb toward Rylee. "Was so used to sucking on her thumb-sized nips, I couldn't get used to small ones."

"Oh dear." Kerry stares directly at Rylee's chest, as I happily sip away at my water and pop another beef tenderloin into my mouth while Rylee shoots daggers in my direction.

～

"**W**hat the hell are you two doing?" Zoey asks, murder in her eyes.

Rylee flinches from the tone of Zoey's voice. It's venomous, like she's about to strike any second. "Whatever do you mean?" The innocence is completely transparent. No one believes us at this point. Not that I blame them with the amount of lies we've told in the last hour. How we have so many different stories to tell strangers is frankly impressive. I think we should get an award.

Leaning in close, her left eye twitching, she says, "I just finished talking to my aunt who told me about this couple who sucks on elephant nipples while hiking Everest with their plastic boobs. When I asked my aunt who they were talking about, she pointed to you two."

I can't help it. I fucking laugh and hard, as does Rylee.

146

"Stop it, this isn't funny. Someone truly believes you two met Tiffany and Del at a swingers club that you bought outright with a bunch of wrapped-up pennies. What the hell?"

I'm crying.

I'm crying, laughing so damn hard. Legit tears are forming in my eyes as my stomach cramps.

"Dude, when were you airlifted off fucking Everest?" Chris asks, coming up from behind me.

Justine steps up next to him. "And when in the hell did you find the time to build a one-hundred-acre chicken sanctuary?"

Oh, I forgot about the chicken sanctuary.

Rylee and I hold on to each other, laughing the entire time as our friends surround us, clearly not happy with our shenanigans.

The music fades and the DJ steps up to the microphone. "If the guests could please take their seats, we're are going to welcome the wedding party."

"This isn't over." Zoey points at both of us.

"I want to know more about the chicken sanctuary. Should I invest, man?" Justine is pushing him toward his seat as Chris motions with his fingers to text him.

I wipe under my eyes and glance at Rylee, who's laughing as well. When our eyes meet, we pause for a second and then start laughing all over. That was the most fun I've ever had at a wedding.

CHAPTER THIRTEEN

"Okay, I don't think I can eat another bite." I push my plate away and take a deep breath, grateful my dress is flowy since I'm currently sporting a food baby. "I'm completely stuffed."

"Well, I wouldn't say completely stuffed." Beck wiggles his eyebrows at me as he wipes his face with a napkin.

This man.

Our plan for seating was simple. We were going to check out the seating chart and scan the tables to see if any guests didn't show up, but unfortunately for us, everyone came, most likely because Del and Tiffany are the cutest couple ever.

So when we couldn't find any seating, Beck decided on the next best thing: bar-height tables on the porch of the famous house. This is going to sound super corny, and I know some may roll their eyes at me, but to be standing here, under the stars, in a romantic setting, on the same rock Hemingway once stood on, feels magical, like all the words are floating around me, ready to be grabbed and put on paper.

I'm inspired.

I'm enamored.

I'm spending my last night in Key West throwing caution to the wind and soaking every last moment up.

"How good are you at dancing?" Beck asks as the DJ starts playing a Bruno Mars song.

"Depends. How good are you at dancing?" I eye him up and down. His chest peeks through the undone buttons of his shirt. His pants are tight enough for me to see every deliciously defined part of his lower half. There is no hiding his robust form. When I opened my hotel door to him earlier, I kept trying to pinch myself to see if this was all a dream, but when I didn't wake up, I knew this was reality, a strange yet exciting reality.

Tossing his napkin on his plate, he says, "Back in Malibu, I like to go to an underground salsa club a few times a month." Color me surprised at this little revelation.

"Are you serious?"

"Dead serious. I've got moves, Saucy. The question is, do you?"

Of course he's a good dancer. Why wouldn't he be? He seems to be good at everything he does, even storytelling. "Let me guess, you sing like Harry Styles, cook like Emeril Lagasse, and model professionally on the side like David Beckham as well."

He takes my hand in his and brings me closer to him. "I don't know about the modeling thing, but I'm a damn good cook when I want to be, and if you put me in front of a microphone I'll sing you one hell of a song."

"Figures."

He chuckles and drags me to the dance floor just in time for the start of *Shout*. Classic wedding song, and even though it's over-played most of the time, I still have no problem dancing to it, or singing for that matter. Beck takes no time in moving around me, using me as his own dancing prop, spinning me around, twirling me into his body and then out. When the music picks up, so does his dancing, as well as mine as I try to keep up with him.

Jumping up and down, arms in the air, he's yelling "shout" along with everyone else, and it's as if everything around me slows down and my entire focus is on Beck as he brings the crowd to the dance floor, singing his heart out and directing the wedding party to get low to the ground. *Oh hell. He's too much. Too adorable. Too sexy. Too . . . everything.*

I was right. He's going to be a difficult one to forget.

"A little bit louder now, a little bit louder now." Beck is waving his arms now. "Hey-aye-aye-aye." Mid jump, his eyes connect with mine. His eyes are bright with mischief. His grin widens, his small dimples peek out just for me. His gaze stays on mine, amidst the jumping and the singing, and he holds me captive. Hell if my heart doesn't flip right then and there.

I'm in trouble.

T en songs later, Beck has yet to leave the dance floor, and has now become the life of the party. There have been at least three dance circles I've participated in and held my own with Beck, who has been eye-fucking me ever since I started to really lay the moves on him. The sexual tension between us, the small touches, the heavy breathing is suffocating the dance floor. The way his eyes blaze when he catches a glimpse of the lace panties I have under my dress, or when his eyes focus on the low-cut V of my dress; there is a fire roaring between us ready to explode.

"This is for all my sexy singles and couples out there. Let me see your moves," the DJ says in a low, Barry White voice. The beginning of *Havana* by Camila Cabello starts to play and Beck immediately turns toward me. He's a few feet away, so when we make eye contact, he motions with his finger to come closer, the motion like a tractor beam pulling me in. It's sexy, slow, and seductive, just the song to skyrocket my libido into overdrive. Beck is moving toward me, focused on getting me into his arms.

Determined.

Without a second thought, Beck grabs both my hands and

wraps them around his neck as he starts moving his hips and mine to the beat of the song, our bodies connected, our pelvises rubbing, grinding. Thankfully we're at a wedding where people like to dance, so we're not the only couple on the dance floor, but we're definitely dancing more seductively than others. Just when I start to move in time with Beck, he turns me around, my back to his chest, and splays his hand across my stomach, his head dipping over my shoulder, his lips right next to my ear.

"This dress . . . you're fucking killing me, Rylee." Moving his hand to my side, he slips it under the fabric that's covering my breasts and presses his hot palm against my equally hot skin, his thumb inches below my bare breasts.

"Beck . . . careful," I whisper, unsure if he can hear me or not.

"My heart is in Havana . . ." the music plays. Beck's hips slowly undulate with mine, his pelvis rubbing against my ass, and that's when I feel *him*.

God, he feels good, but what feels even better is the way Beck's thumb barely grazes my bare breast.

"Mmm," I moan, resting my head on his shoulder and reaching behind me to grip his neck. "God, you're good."

He kisses the side of my head, his scruff rough, the way I like it. "Let me show you how good I am, Rylee."

The hand that's not pressing against my stomach travels to the opening of the slit and runs up to my hipbone where he starts to play with that special spot again. I suck in a large gulp of air and flip around so I'm facing him. I grip his cheeks and bring his mouth to mine, lightly pressing a kiss against his lips but pulling away before he can deepen it.

"Fuck, Rylee. What are you doing?"

"What am I doing?" I respond breathlessly. "What are you doing? I can't breathe when I'm near you, let alone concentrate on anything other than the way you're touching me."

"I need you," he mutters, his voice so low, I almost didn't hear him.

"You two need to go back to the hotel before you start

humping on the dance floor," Chris says. "Everyone is fucking staring, even Tiffany and Del."

The interruption shocks me out of the lust-filled haze.

"Shit." Beck takes a deep breath and looks around. From the guilty look in his eyes, I know Chris is telling the truth. I'm mortified. "Time to go, Saucy. The father of the bride is pointing at us."

"Are we about to get kicked out?"

"Looks like it. Let's book it."

Giggling, I let Beck take my hand and guide me out the back, past the pool, through a little garden where a few of the six-toed cats are hanging out, around the house and out the gate. Looking behind us, Beck must spot someone because he says, "Hurry up, Saucy. Seems like they called in the brigade on us."

I run as fast as I can in my heels, hand in hand with Beck, along the streets toward our hotel, past the southernmost point of the United States, and right into our resort. When we slow down, we both struggle to catch our breath. Beck takes a second to scan behind us for any followers.

"Are we clear?"

"Looks like it." Beck lets out a long breath and then chuckles. "Damn, Rylee, you almost got us caught."

"Me?" I point to my chest. "How was that my fault?"

Beck looks me up and down. "I can't be held accountable for what you do with your hands and mouth. You made me forget everything and everybody around us. So basically, it's your fault I didn't get any dessert. That cake looked damn good, too."

"There is no way I'm letting you blame this on me." I walk across the parking lot, toward the ocean where our rooms reside.

"Face it, Rylee. You made the moves, you have to pay the consequences."

I shake my head, humor in my smile. "You're delusional."

As I climb the steps to our second-floor rooms, I feel Beck hot on my tail. It's impossible not to feel him so close to me because his presence is larger than life.

When I reach my room, I turn toward Beck to find his gaze set on mine, his body thrumming with need. "Are you going to bed, Rylee?" His voice washes over me like an exciting chill, and goosebumps prickle over my skin.

"I was thinking about it."

He steps forward and brings his hand to my cheek where he cups my face. "Are you really going to sleep?"

I nod, biting down on my bottom lip. Hating that I can't be bolder, that I let my nerves and brain take over.

"Okay." He presses a light kiss against my head, and although the gesture is simple, very Beck, it touches me deeply. It's a kiss that says *I treasure you* and I want to be treasured. *I want to be treasured by him.* "Have a good night."

And before I can even understand what's happening, Beck's entering his hotel room, leaving me speechless.

What just happened?

Did I misread the entire night?

I mean, the sexual innuendo, the touching, the light kisses here and there . . . were they all for nothing?

More confused than ever, I open my hotel door and set down my clutch. I look in the mirror. Hair's all in place, maybe a little flatter than earlier this evening, but still looking good. I smile, showing off my teeth and make sure there is nothing in them. I test my breath and everything seems on the up and up, so why the hell is Beck in his room and I'm in mine?

Turning toward my bed, I sneer at it. Even though it looks very welcoming, all cushy and pillowy, I have no desire to rest my head on it right now. Instead, I head to the balcony to listen to the ocean. I need something to calm my racing nerves.

I open the sliding glass door and I'm hit by the humidity of the night. I should be used to the weather after dancing for at least an hour in it, but it feels more stifling now than ever, even with the ocean breeze kicking up.

Sighing, I go to sit in my chair when I hear, "I thought you were going to sleep."

Startled, I leap in place and find Beck leaning against his balcony wall, shirtless, pants partially undone. *So, so sexy.*

"God, you scared me."

He pushes off from his spot and walks to the railing that splits our sections where he grips the black metal. "Didn't mean to startle you." He licks his lips and stares at mine. "Couldn't sleep?"

"Didn't even try."

"And why's that?" He's fishing. This is so much harder than I thought, but I try to express myself like I've never had before.

"Because, I thought my night would end differently."

Effortlessly, Beck hops over the railing and leans against it, still keeping his distance. Arms crossed over his chest, his pecs bulging like I've never seen before, he asks, "And how did you see your night ending? I'm assuming not being chased by angry wedding guests."

"Not really." Still in my heels, I toe the ground and say, "Was kind of hoping this guy I can't seem to stay away from would ask to spend a little more time with me before I leave in the morning."

"Hmm." Beck scratches the side of his jaw. "And this guy you speak of, do I know him?"

Why is he making this so goddamn difficult? I swear I can read his thoughts through his intense stare. He's going to force me to say it.

Taking a deep breath, I close the space between us and gently run my fingers up his chest. His chest isn't devoid of hair, but what he does have is trimmed almost all the way down so it has the feeling of stubble. I like it . . . a lot. For some reason it's sexier than a completely bare chest, especially with how strong he is. He's all male, and I love the way he reacts to my touch.

"What would a night in your bed feel like?" I ask him, my legs shaking underneath me.

His eyes sharpen, and the corners of his mouth lift. "A night in my bed?" He pulls me in even closer by my hips and brushes my hair over my shoulder, his hand cupping the back of my neck, his thumb making slow circles along my tendons.

"Demanding, relentless . . . endless. Do you feel this, Rylee, this pull between us, the pull you've been fighting ever since you met me? If you step foot in my room, it's going to combust. I won't be gentle. I won't be able to hold back, at least not the first time."

I take an audible breath when his hand makes contact with the straps of my dress and he starts to loosen them.

"Beck . . ."

"Tell me to stop and I will, but I swear to God, Rylee, if you say yes, I'm going to fuck you until morning."

This night will go down as the best night of my life.

"Fuck me."

A bear-like groan pops out of Beck's mouth as he hops back over the railing and then reaches for me, sweeping me up into his arms.

Oh hello.

When Beck walks us into his room, he shuts the sliding glass door, lowers me to my feet, then spins me and gently pushes me against the door, my hands pressing against the cool barrier.

He undoes the back of my dress, and in one swift movement, the garment falls to the ground, leaving me in nothing but my lace panties and heels.

Beck presses his hand against my lower back and talks to me softly. "Fuck, Rylee. I've been waiting too damn long to see what your tits look like pressed against this window. I've envisioned fucking you against it, hearing you moan my name until you come, then"—he trails his fingers down my ass—"I would take you against the bed, your hands gripping the headboard, your tits bouncing with each and every thrust I steal from you. But all of this can wait because right now, I need to know what you taste like."

Hooking his fingers in my panties, he pulls then pushes them down my legs until they hit the floor as well. I kick them away along with my dress and stand there naked, waiting for Beck.

I feel him retreat for a second before he comes back and gently kicks my feet wider. He crouches behind me, his hands on my ass, when he pops my hips out and squats beneath me.

Oh God, this . . . it's so much . . .

I've never wanted something as much as I want Beck now. *I need him now.*

CHAPTER FOURTEEN

BECK

F uck.
Fucking hell.

I wipe my hand over my face and take in Rylee from behind. From the slope of her back, to the roundness of her perfect ass, to her toned legs propped up in those killer heels . . . She surpasses every fantasy I've had of her.

Crouching down behind her, I spread her legs farther apart to accommodate my broad shoulders, then I slide beneath her. Glancing up, I'm greeted by the press of her breasts against the window, along with her hands, holding her in place.

"Do you like the idea of someone catching us? Of someone seeing the pleasure I bring you, Rylee?"

Her chest rapidly rises and falls, her stomach moving along with each and every breath.

I lightly run my fingers up the inside of her legs, marveling in her silky skin. "Answer me, Rylee. Do you like the idea of being caught?"

"Yes," she answers breathlessly.

"And what if we are? What if someone from below spots us?

What will you do?" My fingers continue to move up her legs until they reach the juncture of her thighs. I rub my thumbs near her sensitive area, lightly teasing her, torturing her.

"I . . . I don't know."

I scoot closer, my mouth inching forward, dry as fuck, desperate for a swipe, one taste of this woman who's thrown me into a lustful tailspin ever since I've arrived in Key West.

"Not the answer I was looking for." I remove my hands and scoot back, which causes her to moan in disappointment. She moves her hips forward but I still her.

"Beck, please."

"Impatient. Does that mean you're wet for me?"

"God . . . yes," she huffs out.

Wanting to see just how wet, I bring my fingers to her slit and ever so lightly press them briefly inside. My fingers slide in with ease. Fuck . . . so goddamn wet.

"Shit, Rylee."

"I told you." Desperation. *Love that.* "Please don't make me wait any longer."

Moving forward again, I bring my hands up her thighs, spreading them even more until I reach her pussy. With my thumbs, I spread her. Glistening and so goddamn pretty. Her breathing picks up even more, a light whimper escaping past her plump lips.

"Tell me, Rylee. Tell me what you would do if someone caught us."

Another whimper, this one almost pained. Call me a dick, but I love how tortured she's feeling right now, because I know within minutes, once she answers the question, she's going to feel so damn good. To encourage her even more, I lightly blow on her clit, causing her hips to buck.

"Fuck, I would scream your name," she answers. "I would let them know how good you make me feel."

If I wasn't so goddamn hard right now, I would have grown at least two more fucking inches from her answer, from the strain in her voice. I'm tempted to keep one hand on my cock, stroking it with each and every lick of my tongue. I want her to grip me, to feel my girth, to tease me like I'm teasing her.

"Beck, please . . . please."

Smiling like a mother fucking fool, I reach out my tongue and very gently flick her clit. The first taste, fuck, it's good—*addicting* —and it blocks out everything else around us. The room turns black, my peripheral vision blurring, my intentions focused on one thing and one thing alone—eating this woman out.

Plunging forward, I lap her up, long languid, flat strokes along her entire slit.

Slow, fast, slow, fast, flick, stroke, kiss . . . suck.

"Oh fuck, Beck, oh God . . . yes." Her knees start to knock against my shoulders, her body shaking under my hands.

I pause, pulling my face away, wanting to see how far she is.

"Wh-what are you do-doing?"

I move my thumb and lightly run it along her slit, loving how fucking wet she is. I don't think I've ever been with a woman who's been this wet, this turned on.

"You're close, aren't you? Are you throbbing?"

"Pounding." She takes a deep breath. "Are you edging me?"

"Maybe." I press down on her clit and her head flies back, her moan so damn loud that I grow so uncomfortably hard. I need some kind of relief, so I grip my cock and squeeze the base, hard. I hiss between my teeth before I press my mouth against her again.

This time, I'm fucking ravenous. Squeezing my cock, I plunge my tongue, lapping her up. A cold sweat breaks out over my skin, my balls ache, and my mouth is on fire from how fast I'm working my tongue along her clit, begging for her to release.

"Fuck . . . fuuuuck." Rylee's hips lightly pound against the glass as they move with my tongue and she screams, the sound echoing through our small room. "God, oh God, yes." She continues to move her hips, burying them over my mouth. My hand still holds my cock, my tongue going along for the ride until she slows her hips down.

I take no time in standing and scooping her up in my arms only to toss her on the bed. Her black hair drapes over her face, but the moment she moves it out of the way, I'm met with the most stated and beautiful eyes I've ever seen.

She takes a deep breath and looks at me, her eyes spending more time on my erection. I swear to God, if eyes could smile, hers just did. And that goddamn tongue of hers, it licks her lips as her legs fall to the side, her heels kicked off in her transfer to the bed.

I nod with my head and say, "Scoot the fuck back and grab the headboard."

"What if I don't want to?"

I start stroking my cock, my body tingling with each and every pass of my hand. "Then I have no problem pleasuring myself in front of you."

"Doesn't that only work when women do that?" She runs her hand down on her wet pussy. My jaw tightens.

Not wanting to break, I continue to stroke and shut my eyes for effect. "You tell me." I groan from the pressure and when I open my eyes up, she scoots back toward the headboard and grips.

So responsive. Love that.

"Beautiful," I say, leaning over her for a brief second to place a chaste kiss on each of her nipples. I retreat to my bag, grab a condom, and toss it on the nightstand. "I'm going to warn you right now. I'm not going to be gentle. I probably won't have much finesse either, but I promise you, after our first round, I'll be better." I run a hand over my head. "You got me so fucking twisted that if I don't get inside you soon, I'll lose my damn mind."

Smiling, she says, "Then what are you waiting for?" She spreads her legs even farther and my mouth waters. I need this woman. I need her so bad.

Picking up the condom, I tear it open and sheath myself, watching how her eyes never stray from my cock.

Hard as stone, I hover over Rylee and press the head of my

cock through her slit, squeezing my eyes shut from how good she feels.

"Rylee, fuck . . ."

I crash my lips to hers and just when I think I might be too rough with my mouth, she matches each and every stroke of my tongue. We mesh, our mouths fusing together, both striving for more, both begging for more. Her hips ride up against mine, her center teasing the fuck out of my dick, warm and soft, enticing.

With my tongue gliding across hers, I grip one of her breasts and squeeze, catching her gasp in my mouth. *Been dreaming about these tits for days.* My fingers find her already puckered nipple. I roll the pink nub between my fingers, loving her involuntary hip movements.

"I want to touch you, Beck."

I start playing with her other nipple. Her breasts aren't huge but they aren't small either. The perfect handful.

"Touch me then."

Moving her hands through my hair, down my neck, to my back, past the slope of my ass, she grips my cheeks and starts to grind them against her pelvis. I accidentally squeeze too hard on her nipple from the feeling of her pussy pressed against my dick. She squeaks but then kisses me lightly.

"Again," she asks, so damn innocently I can't help but listen to her direction. I squeeze her nipple again, this time a little harder. A sharp hiss escapes past her lips as her back arches off the mattress, the look of utter pleasure crossing her features.

Shit, I can't hold back now.

"I need to be inside you." I grip my aching cock and place it in front of her entrance. With one smooth stroke, I squeeze myself in. "Fuck, you're so tight."

She breathes heavily, her eyes wide now. "You're . . . so . . . different."

Chuckling softly, my hips gently moving back and forth, I say, "I hope that's a damn good thing."

"So good." She lifts her hands to the headboard and with a light kiss to my lips, she whispers, "Fuck me, Beck."

Melting into our touch, I brace myself on the bed and start to slowly move my hips in and out of her, glancing down at our connection, loving how deep she can take me, how her legs are spread so far that with each pulse inside her, I bottom out.

So hot.

So tight.

So damn sexy.

Every little moan that passes Rylee's lips is like an electric jolt straight to my cock, spurring me on, driving my hips harder and harder. I grind against her pelvis, swiveling with each thrust, trying to hit all the right spots, and from the look of pure ecstasy on her face, I'm doing just that.

"More," she pants as her hands move to her breasts and pinch her nipples.

There will be none of that. Lowering my head, I nudge her hand out of the way and take one of her pebbled nipples into my mouth where I bite down on the swollen nub. She lifts off the bed, her movement forcefully clenching her around my cock.

Oh fuck.

"Do . . . that again," I grunt out, my eyes feeling like they're about to roll back in my head.

Without pause, she clenches around me, once, twice, three times.

And I'm a goner.

A guttural groan escapes me as my hips still and Rylee pulses around me, milking me so fucking hard that my vision goes black. All I hear are her cries of ecstasy as I bite down on her nipple once more, my orgasm taking over.

My balls ache, my dick throbs, my heart pounds uncontrollably in my chest as I try to catch my breath.

Huffing, sweating, and completely sated, I barely lift up and look at Rylee, eyes closed and a beautiful smile on her face.

Wanting to see those endless pools of blue, I press a light kiss over each eyelid. They flutter open and she meets my gaze.

Fucking gorgeous.

So. Fucking. Gorgeous.

Licking her upper lip, she says, "That was . . . incredible."

Instead of replying, I kiss her, to make sure that this is real, that what we just experienced wasn't a dream, that I truly have this undeniably amazing woman in my arms. *In my bed.*

Her hand curls around my neck, her thumb playing with the short strands of my hair. When I pull away, I kiss her nose and take off to the bathroom where I dispose of the condom. When I come back to the bed, Rylee is sitting up, scanning the room, an unsure look on her face.

Well, not for long.

Tackling her, I bring her down to the mattress and spoon the hell out of her, cupping her body against mine.

"Oh, is this happening?" she asks, sounding light and playful.

"What? Spooning you? Yeah, it's happening. But only until I can gain back some strength, and then, my sexy, Saucy, I'll be taking it nice and slow, making you come over and over."

"Awfully confident, aren't we?"

"Saucy, from the way you react so passionately to my touch, I have no doubt in my mind."

No response, only a nuzzle from her behind, and a contented sigh.

I'm right there with her.

～

There's some rustling next to me, and I barely register the sound in my sex-induced coma. It isn't until a cool breeze hits me that I realize I'm alone. Peering an eye open, I scan the room to find Rylee on the other side of the sliding glass door, quietly shutting it.

Is she leaving?

I lift my head barely to look at the time. Five in the morning. Shit, her early flight. Dragging my body out of bed, feeling satisfying aches from last night, I throw on a pair of shorts that are hanging out of my suitcase and pad across the floor, stubbing my toe on the desk chair.

"Fuck, fuck, fuck." I dance around for a second, swearing until my toe stops throbbing. Limping like an idiot, I make my way out onto my balcony just in time to see Rylee close her door. Before she can lock it, I grab the handle and open it up.

"Ah, what are you doing?" she asks, startled.

"Sorry," I say, my toe still throbbing. "I didn't mean to startle you."

"Uh, that's okay." She's barely wearing the dress she wore to the wedding last night and her shoes are clutched to her chest. "You should be sleeping, Beck."

"Yeah, and you should be next to me." I take a step forward as she sighs.

"I have to get ready for my flight. I have no more than ten minutes before I have to call an Uber. My guess is Victoria is on her way here to make sure I leave *this* room on time."

Sounds just like Victoria.

Awkwardly, I stand there, trying to figure out what to say.

Last night was . . . fuck, I don't know. It was the kind of night you never forget. It was the kind of night that changes your way of thinking.

Going into this trip, I wanted to have a good time, and if I met a girl, hey, bonus. I had no intention of leaving this island with any girl on my mind. But after last night, after these last few days, I know there is no way in hell I can say goodbye to Rylee right now.

I want more of her.

I feel like we're beginning something new, not shutting the door on a brief chapter in our lives.

Looking uncomfortable, Rylee fidgets in place. "Uh, good thing we took a shower early this morning, huh?" She pulls on her hair. "I can roll right into plane clothes and take off."

Ignoring her small talk, I take a step forward and say, "Rylee, we need to talk."

Before she can let me get anything else in, she shakes her head. "No need to talk, Beck. Let's shake hands, thank each other for the amazing night, and go our separate ways."

"What If I'm not ready to go my separate way?"

Sighing heavily, Rylee starts moving around the room, collecting her belongings and shoving them in her bag while she speaks to me. "Beck, don't be ridiculous. From the beginning, we knew this was only a little fling in Key West. Don't be that cliché, wanting more after a promised fling. Come on."

"Cliché? What the hell are you talking about?"

Undoing her dress and letting it fall to the floor, she unabashedly strips in front of me and starts dressing herself in a pair of leggings, sports bra, and long-sleeved T-shirt. I can't help but stare, soak her in one more time before she leaves. "It happens in all the movies. The promise of a vacation fling and then one of the lovers wants more. Can't we call it like it is and be done? Why complicate things?"

Getting a little angry, I say, "Maybe because I want more. Maybe because I want to see where this might go."

She throws her hair in a high bun, her silky black strands binding together. "Don't be ridiculous, Beck. I live in Maine, and you live in Southern California. We couldn't live on two more opposite sides of the spectrum."

"That's just miles."

She packs her small backpack with her phone, laptop, and wallet. "Lots of miles."

"Something we can easily work out."

She shakes her head and zips all her bags up, putting an end to this conversation, especially with what she says next. "And what about all the space between us, not physically, but mentally? There are parts of you that you haven't opened up to me about, like why you don't drink and who this Christine chick is. And there are parts of me you don't know about, dark parts of my life that frankly I'm not willing to share."

She stumps me there. There are parts of me I don't share because I'm too fucking ashamed to share them with anyone new. Yes, I've turned a new leaf in life, but I'm still not comfortable with the man I used to be, nor do I want to share that part of my life, the part I've shut out of the outside world.

Cal's the only one I really talk to about it, but that's only because he won't let me forget, because the minute you forget is the minute you can find yourself back in the same spot. It's what he always tells me.

There is a knock on her door. "You better be up and ready to go. You know I like to get to the airport early," Victoria's voice sounds from the other side of the door.

Shrugging her shoulders, Rylee gives me a sad smile, puts her backpack on, and starts to roll her suitcase to the door.

"So that's it?" I ask, unsure of what else to say.

Knock. Knock. "Rylee, let's go."

"Yeah, Beck, that's it." She opens the door to an impatient Victoria. "Give me one second."

"We don't have . . ." Victoria spots me and her face softens. "I'll, uh, go get an Uber."

Turning away, her wheelie bag rolling behind her, she disappears down the outside hallway, providing me a few extra minutes with Rylee.

Releasing the handle of her bag, Rylee steps up to me and wraps her arms around my waist, pulling me into a hug. And when she looks up at me, those crystal-blue eyes of hers captivating me, a pang of sorrow hits me in the stomach.

Is this really goodbye?

"Thank you for everything, Beck. Thank you for the fun, the memories"—she smiles sheepishly—"the orgasms." Stepping back, she grips my hand and says, "Thank you for showing me how to let go and have fun again. You unlocked a part of me I haven't seen in a while." She squeezes my hand and puts more distance between us, retreating to her bag. "Bye, Beck."

Opening the door again, she gives me one last glance before heading out of the room.

Is this really how this is going to end? With a quick hug and a thank you? After the past few days we've shared together, this is really it?

Fuck, I don't want it to be.

"Wait," I call out, pulling her back by the arm. I clamp my hand around the back of her neck and bring her mouth to mine where I lay sweet kisses across her lips. Her hands wrap around my arms and she matches each movement of my mouth across hers before breaking away.

"I have to go." She presses her fingers to her mouth. With one final glance in my direction, she says, "Bye, Beck," and takes off, out of her room and out of my life.

Forever.

Fuck.

~

"**D**ude, you've barely spoken a word all day," Chris says while peeling back the wrapper to his cheeseburger. "I gave you the first flight because leaving paradise sucks, but now that we're waiting for our second and you didn't want a burger from Five Guys, I'm starting to feel a little concerned."

"Just not hungry," I say, staring at my phone.

"Not buying it," Chris says with his mouth full. "Did you leave something at the hotel? A charger? Dude, we can get you a new one, it's going to be okay, pal." Chris pats me on the shoulder with his greasy hand.

"I didn't leave my charger."

"Oh . . . good then. Want to get some candy bars? I'm feeling NutRageous right now, that and a Take 5. Have you had one of those yet?"

"I'm good, man." I wave him off and scan through my texts, Rylee's name popping up with every scroll of back and forth I do.

"Not even a Milky Way?"

"Leave him alone," Justine says, finally pulling her head out of her iPad. "Can't you see he's upset from having to say goodbye to Rylee?" Leaning toward me, she adds, "By the way, she's a fantastic author."

Don't I fucking know it. I read the book I started the other day on the airplane. It isn't just about sex; it's about the compelling storyline with broken characters. It's beautiful how she can express so much with words.

"Oh, this is a Rylee thing. Dude, I thought you guys were just flinging it."

"We were." I sit back in the uncomfortable airport chair and pass a hand over my face, trying to scrub thoughts of Rylee out of me, but nothing seems to work. She's etched in my brain.

"But . . ." Chris pushes me to say more.

"I don't know, man, what do you want me to say? That I miss her? That I wish there was more to our little fling than a chaste goodbye this morning?"

"Maybe?"

Justine whacks Chris in the arm. "Don't be a dick. Be a friend."

"Ouch." He rubs his arm. "You and I both know I'm not good at this touchy-feely kind of crap. Let me warm up before you start hitting me."

It's fun traveling and hanging out with a married couple, have I mentioned that? Especially a couple who've been together for a little over ten years.

"No need to talk about it." I cut him off before he can try to open me up more than I want to be. "I'm good, just trying to get out of vacation mode."

"See?" Chris motions to me. "He's floating down from vacation mode."

Justine rolls her eyes and pushes Chris out of the way. "You are so obtuse. Do us all a favor and go get your candy bars and some chocolate-covered pretzels for me, yogurt-covered for Beck. He'll want them for the flight." Justine knows me too damn well.

Taking direction well, and most likely wanting to get away from this conversation as fast as possible, he takes off, one of his burger napkins sticking to the back of his jeans.

"God, he's a disaster." Justine chuckles. "I don't know why I keep him around."

"Me neither."

Justine places her hand on my knee and forces me to meet her gaze. "Tell me everything and don't try to get away with saying there is nothing to tell. I wasn't born yesterday, Beck. I know when you're reeling from something, and right now, you're tailspinning. Talk to me."

There is something you need to know about Justine. She's very good at getting what she wants. It's the way she softly speaks to you but with a no-bullshit attitude. The combination is lethal and when you think your mouth is a steel trap, you find yourself divulging your darkest secrets.

I flip my phone in my hands. "I didn't expect to like her as much as I do."

"You guys had an interesting kind of connection. I liked her."

"I agree." I tip my head back and look to the ceiling. "And I can't quite figure out if the connection was from being on vacation and being in the same frame of mind, or if we actually had this cosmic pull to each other."

"Anyone can be in the same frame of mind, especially when it comes to vacation mode, but there was definitely something between you two. What you had wasn't magical vacation mode, it was deeper than that."

"But how was it deeper? We only skimmed the surface when we talked about things. Like she so brutally pointed out when she left, there are things in my life she doesn't know, some dark things, and vice versa. From what it seems, we were both hiding from each other, while enjoying one another at the same time. How is that deep? Seems more shallow to me. Maybe she's right, maybe it truly was just a fling."

Justine shakes her head. "You know connecting on a deeper level isn't just about talking about your pasts and the dark parts of your lives, because that's only a little segment of feeling something deeper with another human. Connecting with another soul is about complementing each other's sense of humor, adventurous side, and of course, sexual chemistry. From observing you two the past few days, you had all three covered."

I can't argue with her. I connected with Rylee more than any other woman, even Noely. And maybe that was scary to her if she felt the same thing.

Sighing, I say, "That's great and all, but it doesn't matter. She really doesn't want anything to do with me past Key West."

"Did she say that?"

I nod. "In a much nicer way, but that was the gist of it. To her, it was a fling, which is fair because that's all it was supposed to be."

"But it was much more to you." *From the very first moment I saw her.*

I nod again. "Hell, I don't want it to be. I'm not ready to expose someone else to my world, especially Rylee, but fuck, there is this pain churning in my gut, telling me that letting her walk away was a huge mistake."

"Eeep." Justine claps her hands together. "Oh, it's so romantic, seeing you all tied up in knots."

I roll my eyes. Not surprised Justine is getting giddy. Ever since I got my life back on track, she's been rooting for me to meet someone. It was one of the main reasons I tried doing the blind dating thing six months ago. After that didn't pan out, she kept nagging me to try again, but I wasn't in the right frame of mind to do so. I'm starting to think I might never be in the right frame of mind.

"I'm not asking for a marriage here," I continue. "I wanted to talk to her some more, you know? Kind of see where this could take us."

"That's fair. What's holding you back?"

I stare at my phone again. "There's over three thousand miles separating us."

"So? You're not committed to living in LA. Who knows, maybe if this turns serious, you can find a cute little art gallery to paint for. Don't let the small, insignificant factors stop you from pursuing something that could be incredible."

I pause to think about her words as Chris comes barreling forward. "I have the goods." He flops down between Justine and me. "Did we figure everything out?"

"Yup, Beck is going to go after the girl."

"Hey, I didn't say that."

"Oh please," Justine scoffs. "It's written all over your face. Stop letting your brain deny it, and let your heart take the lead." She nods at my phone. "Go ahead, text her. You know you want to."

I do, desperately. I've been trying to think of the perfect text to send her that wasn't lame, but that reminded her of the time we had together.

"Oh I'm good at texting. Let me take the lead on this." Chris steals my phone from my hands.

Before Chris can look at the phone, Justine snags it from his grasp. "You are a shit texter. All you do is use GIFs."

"Funny ones."

"You only send storm troopers pelvic-thrusting in the air."

True. If you scrolled through my phone and clicked on my message thread with Chris, the percentage of texts you would see with a storm trooper humping the air is too high to guess.

"That's because a humping storm trooper is pretty much a universal response." He rolls his eyes, as if we're the weird ones. "Believe me, you're going to want me to handle this text message."

While Justine is busy giving her husband a hard time, I steal back my phone, not wanting either of them to participate in texting Rylee.

"Hey, I can help. I'm poetic," Justine complains.

My brows crease together. "I'm not writing her a poem. Christ, that would be weird."

"Why not? I like rhyming. I'm good at it. For instance"—she clears her throat—"pussies are pink, dicks are stiff, spread your legs so I can get one last whiff. See, poetic and enticing."

Chris and I silently stare at Justine, utterly confused as to where the hell that little poem came from. And slightly grossed out . . .

She motions at the two of us. "See? Stunned you both, so imagine Rylee's response. She'll be flying to LA before you know it with one thing on her mind: your tongue."

"For the love of God." Chris looks around. "No more Rylee Ryan books for you. They're turning you into a pervert."

"Please." Justine laughs. "I was a pervert long before I started reading her books; she's only reminded me of the potential I have inside me."

"Lucky me."

Ignoring the bickering married couple, I check my phone again, kind of wishing there was a text from Rylee, waiting for me. Knowing that's probably not going to happen after how we left things, I'm going to have to make the first move.

Lips twisted to the side, I try to think the perfect—

I got it!

I press on the little camera emblem and find the picture of us in front of the helicopter. I add it to our text message thread and type out a comment with it before I send.

Beck: *Can't stop thinking about that smile of yours. The smile I got to see every day for the past few days, the one that brightened my vacation, the one that seems to be fogging up my brain now.*

Happy, I press send and wait.

And wait.

And fucking wait.

Part Three

RED PANDAS AND ASSLESS CHAPS

CHAPTER FIFTEEN

RYLEE

"Rylee, this is absolutely brilliant. I am head over heels swooning over here," my agent, Aimee, says into the phone.

"Yeah? Do you think it's good enough? Are they going to love it?"

"I have no doubt in my mind. You said you have about thirty thousand words left to write?"

"Yes."

Aimee makes a committal noise and says, "I wouldn't go past thirty. Let's keep the manuscript in the eighty thousand range, okay? Gives us room to make adjustments without dragging the story on for too long."

Ever since I returned from Key West, I've been in the writing cave, pounding on my computer, letting the words flow through me and onto the screen. I hate to admit it, but Zoey's plan of crashing a wedding was brilliant. I was inspired. I fell in love with Tiffany and Del's relationship, and the spark of a love story resurrected something inside me.

I've been writing for the past five days, and it's invigorating. I haven't written this fast since my very first book where I was so damn excited to type out all the personalities in my head that I wrote ninety thousand words in a week.

Key West was good to me.

Very good.

Okay . . . I know what you're thinking, there was more to Key West than Tiffany and Del's wedding. That was a small glimpse of your time on the southernmost island.

And listen, I hear ya. I'll give credit where credit's due . . . I had a vacation fling. I traipsed the streets of Key West with a young buck of a man, all muscly and gorgeous and, yeah, you know what . . . he did do me up against a window, and I'm not mad about it.

But I don't want to talk about him.

Not because I'm upset with him, or because he did something wrong, but because the minute I start to even think about my time with him, my gut starts to churn with regret, regret of cutting him out of my life.

And with every text message I receive from him, my heart sputters in my chest to see what he has to say. It's torture.

After the picture he sent of us in front of the helicopter—the one I saved to my phone and look at daily—I had to tune him out. I was feeling too much, yearning too much, and come on, we live three thousand miles apart. What's the point?

And I meant what I said. We both have baggage, and I'm not sure how that plays into a fling. It doesn't really. The only thing that plays into a fling is sex, and hell, the sex was good. I regret not participating in the sex earlier because more than one night with him would have been unbelievable.

"Are you still there?"

"Huh?" I shake my head. "Oh yeah, sorry . . . just thinking about how to finish this book."

"Ooo, want to share?" Aimee's voice brightens.

"Uh . . ." Think of a plot, think of a plot, think of a plot. "I want to keep it a secret for now. Surprise you."

Aimee chuckles. I feel like she knows I was daydreaming. Surely she must be used to daydreaming authors by now. "As long

176

as these characters get their happily ever after that's all I care about."

Happily ever after. That's what my world revolves around and yet, I struggle to find one myself. How freaking ironic.

"Naturally. I'll talk to you later, Aimee."

I hang up the phone, strap on my backpack, and head out my front door and down the street.

I live in the smallest little coastal town in Maine. It's a tourist destination because of the beautiful historic lighthouses, the beloved Lobster Landing gift and fudge shop, and Monahan's Market one of the most tasteful organic groceries you've ever seen. It puts Whole Foods to shame – and I've gotten to know the ice cream selection well over the years. The owner, Oliver Monahan, is one of the main reasons the town has revived so beautifully.

"Good morning, Rylee." Speak of the devil.

"Oliver, how are you?"

Oliver Monahan, my old friend and local grocer extraordinaire is as handsome as ever, and has an absolute heart of gold. He's also a volunteer fireman, and spends his nights and weekends saving local damsels in distress.

"Good. Getting ready for another fast-paced day at the market. We just not a new order of fudge from Lobster Landing and I know it's gonna go quickly"

"Ooo, you have more in stock? I might have to stop by later, if it's already sold out at the Landing. Please tell me you have my favorite." The market is the ONLY place the Landing will sell their fudge because they are on opposite sides of Main Street and because it helps slow down the traffic in the very busy tourist destination.

"S'mores? Of course. Want me to save a chunk for you?" We cross the street, Oliver placing his hand on my shoulder until the road is clear. Seriously, this guy looks out for everyone.

"Would that be asking too much?"

"Nah, nothing is too much for our resident romance author." He winks at me and starts toward the Market as I walk toward the coffee shop. Pointing at me, he adds, "No kicking old ladies out of their chairs today."

"That was one time," I whine, hating how word gets around this small town.

Laughing, he gives me a salute goodbye and continues down the street.

If things were different, I would go for Oliver Monahan. What stops me, you might ask? Well it's hard to date someone you've spent your entire life seeing as a brother, isn't it? Especially when that someone just went through the nastiest divorce in the history of nasty divorces. Plus, if we did start dating, everyone in town would immediately know, and start asking questions . . . very personal questions.

Walking into the Snow Roast, I'm greeted by Ruth behind the counter and the overhead bell.

"Rylee, good morning."

There's something to be said about a small town and everyone knowing you. Yes, having people in your business is a downfall, but when I'm greeted by a genuine smile and an interest in my little world, it brightens my day.

"Good morning, Ruth. How are you this morning?"

"Oh good. I saw a few of the Knightly brothers jogging around town this morning. Made a couple of passes by the coffee house. Quite the sight." She wiggles her eyebrows, causing me to giggle.

Ah yes, the Knightlys. The Knightly family owns the famous Lobster Landing and their fudge is almost as mouth-watering as those four handsome brothers. But handsome as they all are, we grew up together, and like Oliver, I'm cursed to forever see them as brothers.

I slide a ten-dollar bill to her that will cover a few cups, I grin at her, wondering if she has a soft spot for any brother in particular, but not wanting to pry – this time.

"Let me know if you need anything." She nods to my special corner. "Your sex chair is available if you need to write any of those racy scenes of yours."

Holding back the giant eye-roll and exhale that wants to escape me, I smile kindly. "Thanks, Ruth."

Walking to my corner, I set down my cup of coffee, open up my backpack, and pull out my laptop just as my phone vibrates in the front pocket.

Once I set up everything from my earphones to my notebook to my water bottle, I look at my phone and my heart starts to beat rapidly in my chest.

Beck.

Should I? Should I tempt myself to see what he has to say today? Or should I ignore it, avoiding all torture of what he's up to?

Hmm . . .

Who am I kidding? I open that bad boy up like it's about to detonate in ten seconds if I don't read it.

Beck: *Good morning, Rylee. Did you know sometimes I have to wake up at the ass-crack of dawn so I can get into exhibits for touch-ups before park goers arrive? Today I'll be hanging out in the red pandas exhibit. They had babies a few months ago, and we're getting the exhibit ready for their arrival. Kind of like a* welcome to your new home *painting. What are you up to?*

Is it just me, or is it super sexy that this man can not only paint, but is designing a nursery for red panda babies?

I mean, my ovaries are crying right now because he's almost too perfect. Funny, resourceful, kind, can dance—no, he can *dance* —and his tongue . . . his hands . . . his . . . *Stop. Don't go there, Rylee.*

Setting my phone down without an answer, I open my laptop, then take a sip from my coffee. Ooo, still a little hot. That's going to have to sit a few more minutes before I gulp it down.

Reading over the scene I wrote yesterday, I refresh my mind on where the story is going and then glance at my phone.

Focus, Rylee.

Taking a deep breath, I put my earbuds in, turn on my Spotify playlist geared toward the book I'm writing, and place my fingers on the keyboard.

. . .

Okay, here we go, start typing.

. . .

Do all the typing. Type away. Make the words happen.

. . .

Maybe I need a little more coffee.

Picking up my mug, I blow on the steamy liquid and take another sip. Okay, cooling down. That's good stuff right there.

Sighing, I look out the window and watch some of the early morning tourists hit up Patty's Pancake House. They won't regret their decision.

Now watching the people heading to Port Snow's fifties diner, have fun eating food that tastes like the grill in the back. Puke. How that place is still open, I have no idea. All the locals stay as far away as possible besides the older generation who apparently like when their food tastes like they licked an overused kitchen grill.

Did you throw up in your mouth? Yeah, me too.

Okay, focus. I take one more sip. Let's get to work.

One big sniff and a gulp and we're good to go.

Sighing, I place my fingers on the keyboard and stare at my computer.

Red pandas, what do those look like again? Already connected to the Internet, I open up my search engine and type red panda into Google.

Aww.

Look at those little itty-bitty faces. These guys should totally be domestic animals.

Let me see what the babies look like.

I wait for the search results to—

Oh.

My.

GOD!

Stop what you're doing and look at red panda babies. Look at ALL the red panda babies.

They're just so cute and fluffy and those faces . . . I just want to squish them.

Oh, look at that. You can adopt one and get pictures of them every month. Well, how can I NOT do that after seeing these little guys?

I wonder what their exhibits look like? And what goes into an exhibit? Is that paint safe for the animals? What kind of paint-brushes do you need to make that kind of texture? Is that a horse-hair brush? Do they make those still? I wonder what kind of horses have the best hair? Well, black horses are the most stealth in my opinion. But Clydesdales, what majestic animals with their hairy hoof feet and giant asses. God, if I was a horse I would want to be a Clydesdale, hands down. Or would I want to be a mustang? Mustangs are such hot cars, especially the older ones. Doesn't Jay Leno have Mustangs? Or is that someone else? Jay Leno, he likes denim, a lot. Jimmy Fallon doesn't wear a lot of denim, at least in pictures. Hey, wasn't Jennifer Lawrence on *The Tonight Show* last night. . .

One YouTube black hole and an hour later, I have zero words, I've acquired too much information about red pandas, and I know that Jennifer Lawrence and Emma Stone are best friends. Kind of wish they would make their duo into a trio and invite me in with open arms. I think we're best friends and they don't even know it.

My phone buzzes next to me and without thinking about it, I open it up to find a picture of Beck wearing a white T-shirt, a grey sock beanie, leather bracelets, and a paintbrush in hand pointing to the exhibit behind him. He has the same vibe as a younger, more handsome version of Colin Farrell.

God, he's so hot.

Like . . . my nipples are hardening hot.

Beck: *Touching up some leaves. In one of the leaves, I scrolled your name inside. Knowing you, you probably looked up red pandas and are dying over how cute they are. So I made sure you're here with them. I'll take a pic to show you.*

Another text message comes in, and it's of a painted leaf on the wall. You can barely tell, but written along the veins of the leaf is my name, right there, on the wall of the red panda exhibit.

Hell.

Fucking hell.

I press my lips together, leaning my head backward. Did you hear that? That cracking sound? Yeah, that's my icy exterior starting to crumble.

Damn him and his use of red pandas. Damn him and his thoughtfulness. Who does that?

I bite on my bottom lip and pose my fingers at the keys.

Do not write him back, Rylee.

Don't you dare start typing.

Don't you—

My fingers move across the screen of my phone.

Oh you defiant bitch!

My fingers press send, and I immediately hate myself.

That's until I see the little dots appear on the screen, because he's typing back, and damn it, I get so freaking excited that I reposition myself in my chair, getting ready for a long conversation with a boy I shouldn't be talking to when in fact, I should be writing.

But hell if I can hold back any longer.

Seven days.

Twenty-one messages.

Small moments in my days that made me smile, just as he would want.

Small moments that show me I'm not as forgettable as I've always believed myself to be.

Messages that hit their intended mark.

Connection.

With me.

He broke me.

I'm cracked and exposed.

And I think I need Beck to fill me up again.

CHAPTER SIXTEEN

BECK

I wipe my face with the back of my hand. Fuck, it's stifling in here. A little bit of AC wouldn't hurt. I have a mini portable fan with me for instances just like this, but it's doing shit right now to cool me down.

Leaning back, I reposition my pants so they're sitting on my hips again, and look over the mural, making sure I've touched up everything in the small section I'm currently working on. Working in small sections is the easiest way for me to get the job done and done right. Given my background, I want to make sure there is no second-guessing about whether the zoo or museum should have hired me.

That doesn't mean I don't take breaks while working though, especially when they're short little breaks to text Rylee.

That girl is about killing me. I mean, tell me if I'm wrong here, but in my mind, it's polite to text someone back when they've taken time out of their day to correspond with you. But nothing. A week of absolute nothing.

Frustrated, I rake my hand through my hair and then decide to send her another picture, because *why the hell not?* I've already gone past stalker status with my frequent text messages, might as well send her one more.

Turning the camera to face me, I take a picture with my paintbrush and part of the exhibit. Followed up by the little leaf I wrote her name in. Yeah, that was planned to try to get her to talk to me, because what kind of romantic gesture is that? One of a kind. Pulling out the big guns to talk to her.

Standing back, I give the small section I was working on one more look through before I move onto the next section. The good thing about my work ethic is that even though I might take longer in assessing my work, I'm pretty damn fast with the paintbrush, and I have very accurate strokes.

And the funny thing is, I didn't discover painting until—

My phone beeps, and my body stills. I don't text many people other than Chris, and it's rare when we do text. *Because no one really wants to see another storm trooper gif.*

Reaching to my back pocket, I bring my phone forward and squint at the screen. A slow grin spreads across my face.

She cracked.

Thank you, baby red pandas.

I open her text message and smile like an idiot.

Rylee: *Damn you, Beck Wilder. Using cute fluffy animals and sweet gestures is not playing by the rules.*

I bark out a loud laugh and type back a quick response.

Beck: *The minute you refused to reply to my text messages, all rules were thrown out the window. Sorry, Saucy.*

No one around, so I take a seat on one of the exhibit rocks, open my cooler, and pull out a water. As I wait for her response, I relish the cool water rushing down my throat, adjusting my body temperature. If only I could take my shirt off and douse myself with the water. Pretty sure the zookeepers wouldn't enjoy that.

My phone beeps and just like that, another smile pops up on my face.

Rylee: *I feel like you've never played by the rules. You're always pushing the limit.*

She's got me pegged.

Beck: Someone has to push the limit in order to help people break through their comfort zone. Without people like me, the world would be pretty damn boring, don't you think?

Rylee: You're a different kind of person, Beck.

Beck: I hope that's a good thing.

Rylee: It's a dangerous thing.

Beck: You aren't living if you don't have at least a little danger in your life.

The little dots appear, but then they disappear. She's pausing. I feel like I can see her right now, that mind of hers working a mile a minute. That creative mind producing all different ways this little situation between us can work out.

Not wanting her to shut down again, I type her a quick text.

Beck: Are you in the sex chair right now?

An immediate response.

Rylee: It's an INSPIRATION chair.

Beck: Lol. Send me a picture.

Rylee: No.

Beck: Come one, I sent you a picture of my office. It's your turn.

Rylee: I don't think you deserve a picture after your brutal tactics to get me to respond to you.

Beck: Brutal tactics? I don't consider sending you pictures of a red panda exhibit brutal. Dramatic much?

Rylee: Drama is my life . . . so yes.

Beck: Stop deferring and send me a picture.

There is a pause in her text, and I hope she's taking a selfie. Might sound weird, but fuck, I want to see her face again. Desperately I want to see her face again.

A picture comes in, and I nearly fall off the rock I'm sitting on.

What the hell?

I look closer and start chuckling to myself while I shake my head.

She sent me a picture all right. She sent me a picture of her damn feet up on a chair in the coffee shop. Not exactly what I was looking for. Then I read her comment with the photo.

Rylee: *You wanted a picture of my office. So here you go. Enjoy, big guy.*

Foolishly I grin and adjust the beanie on my head.

Beck: *Can't wait to submit this to foot fettish dot com. *rubs hands together* here come the big bucks. Famous author, Rylee Ryan. I can see all the money already.*

Rylee: *DON'T YOU DARE!*

I laugh even harder, the sound echoing in the little exhibit, reminding how long it's been since I've actually felt this light, this carefree.

It's been a long fucking time.

A week to be exact.

"This is beautiful, Beck. It looks so fresh and clean in here. The blues you added to the sky are amazing, and it gives the exhibit so much more dimension."

"Yeah, I thought the plain blue was looking a little dull so I added some things. I'm glad you like it, Aly."

"Absolutely spectacular. Such a wonderful place for these little babies until they can be transferred into the outdoor exhibit. This will be perfect."

"Good, I'm glad." I pull on the back of my neck and ask, "Do you see anything you want me to touch up? I went through twice to make sure everything was okay."

Aly, the zookeeper for the red pandas, takes a look, closely inspecting every inch of the wall. She shakes her head. "No, it looks great." Turning toward me, a gentle look in her eyes, she asks, "Would you like to meet them?"

"Seriously?" My brow shoots up in surprise.

"Yeah, I feel like it would be nice for them to meet the guy who painted them such a beautiful nursery."

Excited because well, baby animals, I say, "Hell yeah, I want to meet them."

Chuckling, she opens the small door to the back of the facility where all the behind-the-scenes work takes place. "Come on, I think it's feeding time. I might be able to get you to hold a bottle."

She doesn't have to twist my fucking arm.

And this isn't the first time I've gotten some one-on-one time with the animals—naturally, under the watchful eyes of the zookeepers. My first encounter was with a boa constrictor, and that was a bit scary. But hell, those snakes are badass. Ever since then, whenever they ask, I always say yes. My least favorite? The monkey who shit on my shoulder, the little fucker. I swear to God, he leaped off me and then laughed, hand over his mouth and everything. Later that day, I painted a middle finger of leaves in his exhibit. You wouldn't be able to tell as a zoo visitor, but I know, and I think that punk of a monkey knows too, because when I walk by him, he eyes me, pretty sure wanting to make my shoulder his toilet again.

I'm led down the hallway into a quiet zone where there is a makeshift sign on the door that reads: Baby Panda Nursery.

Quietly, Aly opens the door and guides me in. There are two zookeepers sitting in chairs each with a fluffy little red panda in one hand and a bottle in the other.

Fuck me.

I'm a pretty strong guy, you know, masculine and all that shit. I work out and do all the male things, but I'm a fucking fool when it comes to animals. Like melt in a puddle, drop to my knees, and worship the damn things if given the chance.

One look and I'm melting inside.

"Would you like to hold her?" one of the ladies asks.

"Fuck yeah," I answer, not caring that I'm swearing in front of the babies . . . or women.

I spend the next half hour holding, feeding, and playing with the little guys while the ladies educate me on red pandas and their risk of becoming extinct. I take pictures with plans for them later and then thank the ladies for one of the best half hours of my life.

Returning to the exhibit, I clean my paintbrushes, making sure to wash out all the paint, put my supplies away, and pack them into the provided locker. Unhooking my motorcycle helmet from inside the locker, I tuck it under my arm, and take my phone from my back pocket. Using every lethal weapon I have, I send Rylee a text.

Beck: *Guess who I got to hang out with today?*

I attach a picture of me feeding Daly, one of the baby pandas.

I don't have to wait very long for a response and the response is fucking amazing.

Rylee: *You bastard! Why would you rub that in my face? OMG, she's so cute.*

Chuckling, I text her back on my way to my bike.

Beck: *Her name is Daly, and she fucking loved snuggling on me. Jealous?*

Rylee: *Clearly, I want to hold a baby red panda.*

Beck: *No, I'm not asking if you're jealous of me holding a baby red panda. I'm asking if you're jealous that Daly is snuggling up on your territory.*

Rylee: *My territory? Pretty sure I didn't lay claim on you.*

Smiling, I straddle my bike and send her one more text before I take off.

Beck: *The minute you came all over my cock, moaning my name, you laid claim. Just waiting for you to reclaim it.*

I put on my helmet and I'm about to put my phone in my pocket when she responds. I laugh in my helmet, fogging up the shield.

Rylee: *You're going to be waiting a long time, Wilder.*

◈

B eck: *What are you wearing?*
  Rylee: *Such a lame way to open a text conversation. You can do better than that.*

Beck: *You think so? I thought that was a good starter, but how would you open a text conversation?*

Rylee: *Maybe something like, how was your day?*

Beck: *That's far too common. I wanted something different, intriguing.*

Rylee: *So you went with what are you wearing?*

Beck: *Well I mean, you're talking to me now, so it seems like it's working.*

Rylee: *...*

Beck: *Does that mean you're naked?*

Rylee: *That means I'm wearing a Snuggie.*

Beck: *... with nothing on underneath?*

Rylee: *You're absurd.*

～

B**eck:** *I had a California burrito today that I'm pretty sure I would have married it if it were legal.*

Rylee: *California burrito? What's that?*

Beck: *Ryyyyleeeeee! Fuck, it's so good, but not better than your taco, so no worries.*

Rylee: *OMG, don't say that.*

Beck: *It's true ...*

Rylee: *Just tell me what's in the burrito, Wilder.*

Beck: *Carne asada, sour cream, cheese, and French fries with a side of guac. So damn good.*

Rylee: *French fries?*

Beck: *Yes.*

Rylee: *I hate you.*

Beck: *Because you want one, don't you?*

Rylee: *Desperately.*

～

Beck: *Had a dream last night that your hunk souvenir was thrusting its box in my face.*
Rylee: *That's concerning. Did you like it?*
Beck: *I mean, I couldn't turn away.*
Rylee: *Very concerning.*
Beck: *The bow was flopping around, all red and glittery.*
Rylee: *Extremely concerned.*
Beck: *Glad to see that you still have feelings for me. Couldn't bear to see me bat for the other team? I see right through you, Saucy.*
Rylee: *That's not what . . . damn you.*
Beck: *Caught red-handed. Want me to send you some shirtless pictures of me to curb your appetite.*
Rylee: *Our correspondence is done for the day.*
Beck: *[Picture sent]*
Beck: *Look at those abs.*
Beck: *[Picture sent]*
Beck: *That smile, come on, tell me you think I'm hot.*
Rylee: *You're . . . God, you're so hot.*
Beck: *Bingo Bango*
Rylee: *Annnd that just ruined it.*
Beck: *Yeah, the minute I sent that text, I knew.*
Rylee: *LOL, at least you can admit to your faults.*
Beck: *Honest always. Especially with you, Saucy.*

"**C**ome on in," Justine says, sounding more formal than our usual casual relationship. "We are so glad you joined us, Beck. Can I take your helmet?"

Eyeing her suspiciously, I hand her my helmet and leather jacket. "What's going on?"

"We're so happy you could make it to dinner."

Looking over her shoulder, I see Chris talking to a nervous-looking woman who's sitting up straight, hands in her lap.

Glancing back at Justine, I hide behind their entryway wall and say, "What the hell are you up to, Justine?"

Glancing over her shoulder, she leans in and whispers, "That's Sierra. She works with me and get this, she's single."

"Shocking," I mock. "And what the hell is Sierra doing here, in your living room, dressed nicely, and looking nervous as hell."

"Ah, you think she's dressed nicely? Why don't you go tell her?" Justine tries to drag me toward the living room by my arm, but I stand firmly in place.

"Why are you trying to set me up with a coworker?"

Giving up on her attempt to move me, she puts her hands on her hips and huffs. "Because, Beck, it's been three weeks since we got back from Key West, and you're all grumpy and whatnot, chasing after Rylee. At first, I was gung-ho about making it work, but you can't keep texting her and get no response. It's time to move on. Sierra is perfect for you. She likes art . . . children's book kind of art, but art nonetheless, and she's ridden a bike before, not a motorcycle, but an actual bicycle, but close enough. And hey, she has boobs, so there's a plus."

I roll my eyes. Boobs are always a plus, but not in this instance; I don't want to hang out with Sierra. She's probably a nice girl, but it wouldn't be fair to her. And maybe I should have told Justine and Chris about how Rylee and I have been texting every day, but I wanted to kind of keep it in the dark . . . for reasons like this. She'd want to butt in, and I don't think I'm ready for the inquisition that comes along with wanting to be a part of my love life.

"Did you hear me, Beck? Boobs, she has boobs."

"Well aware, Justine." I pass my hand over my hair, the short strands tickling my palm. "I'm not into blind dates, okay?" Not anymore. I reach for my helmet, but she swats my hand away.

"You can't leave. She knows you're here. It would be rude to leave, especially after I told her she's here to see you. Do you want her to feel bad about herself?"

Ughhh.

Note to all you married people out there trying to hook your friends up: don't, okay? Just don't. Unless they ask for it. Because then shit like this happens and we, the daters, are put in awkward situations.

"Well, that's not my damn fault. That's yours. You shouldn't have set this up without asking me first," I whisper-yell at her.

"What's your problem? I'm doing you a favor here. You need to move on."

"Why would I want to move on when Rylee is talking to me now?" Yup, the cat's out of the bag, but kind of had to go there. I don't want to end up on any other blind dates thanks to Justine.

Standing tall, a little shocked, she asks, "What? Rylee's texting you back?"

"Yeah, for two weeks now."

"Eeep! Really?" Justine encases my hands and jumps up and down. "That's amazing. Does she love you? Are you going to go see her? Are you dating? Oh my GOD. Have you had phone sex yet? Please tell me you have. I need all the details. When you come on phone sex, do you show her? I've never had phone sex before."

For fuck's sake.

I drag my hand over my face. "It's only talking right now, Justine. No need to shriek." I press on my ear. "How does Chris deal with that?"

She doesn't answer me, instead she says, "So, no phone sex?"

"No, no phone sex. Sorry to disappoint. We're just, you know"—I swallow hard, hating this word—"flirting."

Why do I hate that word, because . . .

Justine squeals and runs in place, head turned down, her hair falling over her face as she shakes it. Can you tell she's a bit of a crazy romantic?

"Oh my God, a love story for the digital era. Have you texted her today?"

"Yeah." I shrug casually, not mentioning how I text Rylee good morning and good night every day. I can keep that to myself.

"Can I see?" She intrusively reaches for my back pocket, but I sidestep her. "Let me see."

"No. That's private, Justine."

She curls her lip to the side. "Then how do I know you're telling me the truth and not just trying to avoid meeting Sierra? Because she's a really nice girl, and I don't want to hurt her feelings because you're being a dick."

Sighing, I reach for my phone and unlock it. "I'm not being a dick." I open up our message chain and hold it far enough away that she can see we've been talking but not close enough that she can read our messages. I honestly don't care too much about privacy at this point in my life, but what I really don't want is for Justine to see how Rylee turns me down on a daily basis. If it was any other guy, I'm pretty sure they would get a complex. But me, I know she's playing incredibly hard to get.

"Can I read them?"

"No." I pocket my phone and then wave my hand at Sierra. "Now what are you going to do about her?"

"What?" Justine shouts. "You're kidding. Ugh," she grunts.

What is happening right now?

"Beck, but you promised," she shouts again. And then says, "Chris! Beck can't stay for dinner. He came by to say he has to work extra hours at the zoo tonight."

"What?" Chris asks, standing from his seat and excusing himself. When he reaches the entryway, he looks me square in the eyes and says, "Run, man. Run the fuck out of here. The girl has been collecting clipped toenails since she was twelve. Get the fuck out of here right now."

Justine gives an embarrassed smile with a shrug. "She has boobs?" she says as more of a question.

"Boobs can't eclipse everything, Justine, especially a clipped toenail collection." I place my helmet over my head and leave, thanking the dating gods I didn't have to follow through with that setup.

CHAPTER SEVENTEEN

RYLEE

Beck: *Do you collect anything weird?*
I pause mid-sentence and read Beck's text.
I'm going to admit something, just between us ladies. I've been spending way too much time texting Beck, to the point that I've slightly fallen behind on my edits for this damn book. But it's like an addiction I can't curb. I see his name on my phone, and I have to answer. I try to tell myself *no, answer later*, but before I know it, my hand goes rogue on me and it's unlocking my phone.

And this morning is no exception.

Rylee: No, never really been someone who likes to collect things. Well besides my hunks. What about you?

Beck: I used to collect bottle caps, but I don't anymore.

Rylee: Bottle caps, like from bottles of soda?

Beck: Yeah, weird, right? But I would stack them up and crash my cars into them. There was a legit reason.

I smile to myself and envision a younger version of Beck stacking up bottle caps and tearing through them with monster trucks, or something like that.

"What's the smile for?" Oliver sits next to me, startling my attention from my phone.

"Oliver, hey. Gosh, I didn't see you there."

"I can see that." He nods at my phone. "Who you talking to? Secret admirer?"

Smirking, I answer, "He wishes."

"Oh damn." Oliver chuckles. "Ruthless, Rylee."

I shrug and put my phone down, giving my attention to Oliver. "How are you doing?"

"Slightly chaotic. On top of the Market, the firefighting alone is a lot of work. But then there's all of the community outreach. Basically going around to the senior houses in town and changing fire alarm batteries and testing them."

"Ah, the joys of a small town." We both laugh, knowing exactly what it feels like to grow up in such close quarters to everyone around you.

"Hey, you guys." Zoey comes strolling up to us, carrying her giant canvas bag full of the materials she needs to write and illustrate her books. And I'm not talking paints and papers and all that. No, she writes and illustrates on her iPad. It's impressive. It's everything else like a candle, a throw blanket, a neck and head massager, her essential oils, her water bottles, one for ice water, one for tepid. It's truly an absurd thing to watch her set up. But once she's done, it's like observing magic in the making. She's so focused, so precise with everything she does. When she's in the zone, she doesn't get distracted, not even by her phone. *Like me.* Art knows if she's at Snow Roast and really needs something, he'll either call me or Ruth to get Zoey's attention.

"Oliver, I haven't seen you in a bit. How are you?" She plops down in the chair across from me. Waving her finger between us, she asks, "What's going on here? Are you two finally dating?"

"What? No," I say, feeling embarrassed.

Can you tell I haven't quite told Zoey, or Victoria for that matter, about my texts with Beck? I don't know why. Maybe because I'm afraid they'll encourage the bad behavior I've been taking part in.

"Say that a little faster next time." Oliver laughs next to me.

"Sorry." I can feel my cheeks redden. "I didn't mean it like that. I mean, I didn't want you to feel weird because you're hot and you have forearms, and it would be like dating a mouse if you were with me, and I should shut up now."

Chuckling, Oliver says, "Dating a mouse?"

I shrug. "I ramble a lot. I can't be held accountable for what comes out of my mouth."

"It's true. She's terrible at speaking a lot of the times." Zoey starts casually pulling out her "must needs" for writing, as if she didn't make Oliver and me incredibly uncomfortable.

"It's bad. Sorry, but no, we're not dating, Zoey."

Looking over at Oliver, she asks, "Still on that dating hiatus?"

Leave it to Zoey to bring up things people don't talk about. Well, that people only talk about behind closed doors.

Pulling on the back of his neck, Oliver taps my knee and says, "I'll catch you later, Rylee." He pats Zoey's shoulder on the way out, leaving without answering Zoey's question.

When he's walking outside, down the sidewalk to his shop, I turn on Zoey. "Was that really necessary?"

"What? It was a simple question."

"It was rude." I hate how she can be so bold sometimes, especially when it's at someone else's expense.

She shrugs and puts her headphones over her ears. Rolling my eyes, I turn back to my phone to feel it vibrate in my hand.

And of course, my heart skips a beat.

Beck.

He's calling.

Why is he calling? We don't call, we text.

Should I answer it? Hell, I want to answer it. I want to hear his voice one more time. Is that desperate?

Maybe a little?

But I don't care at this point. Making sure Zoey is engrossed in her music, which it looks like it from the way she's mouthing lyrics, I swipe to answer and turn to the side, trying to be discreet.

"Hello?"

There's a pause and then, "Hey."

Oh God. One little word. How, with one monosyllabic word can he shoot a serum through my body and make every one of my muscles turn into noodles?

"Hey," I reply, not being clever at all.

"How are you, Saucy?" And there is it, his nickname for me, said in his beautifully delicious voice that rolls through my ear and down my body like it did when we were in Key West.

I swallow hard and take a deep breath, trying to rid the nerves gathering in the pit of my stomach. It's just Beck. There's nothing different here . . . other than images of him hovering over me—pulsing inside me—that keeps fogging my brain.

"I'm doing all right. How about you?"

This is awkward, oh so awkward. I'm tense, I'm on the verge of stuttering, and I'm sweating. I am legit sweating in my elbow pits.

He chuckles, and the low rumble hits me hard in the gut, setting off a wave of butterflies. "Great now that I get to hear your voice." He sighs, and I can envision him scratching his jaw, his scruff scraping across his fingers.

"Is that why you called? To hear my voice?" I briefly close my eyes, trying to calm my racing heart.

I shouldn't be engaging in this conversation. I already told myself this was over, we weren't doing this, but here I am, once again giving in and feeding on Beck like a starved woman. *And that's exactly what it has been like.* I only had him for a few days. They were some of the best days I'd had in such a long time, and I really enjoyed talking with him, laughing, being generally ridiculous with him. The stupid things we came up with at the wedding. Keeping a straight face with each ludicrous answer he came up with. I have friends, but I've missed him. *His* friendship. And since returning from Florida, at times, the daily silence has been . . . noticeable.

"Yeah. Is that okay?"

"It shouldn't be, because we decided to say goodbye in Key West."

"You decided," Beck says. "I had other ideas about how we should correspond after we left."

"Good job following through on that by the way." I chuckle.

He joins me. "Never said I was good at listening. And hell, you should know this about me already, Saucy. I do what I want."

If that isn't the truth . . .

"Yes, you've made that quite clear."

"As long as we're on the same page. So, tell me, are you naked right now?"

"What? No. What is with you?" I laugh. "I'm at the coffee house."

"Ah, hanging out in the sex chair, huh? Getting it on with your keyboard? Diddling those keys to climax?"

I roll my eyes, mirth pulling at my features. "You're ridiculous."

"Nah, not ridiculous, just a damn good time. Now tell me, Rylee, have you spiced up your current work in progress with any real-life experiences, maybe a little fucking against a sliding glass door?"

"Oh, that would make you the happiest mother fucker, wouldn't it?"

"More like the jolliest mother fucker. Tell me . . . did your hero have your heroine naked, breasts pressed firmly against the cold window, while he lapped every last drop from her drenched pussy?"

Well . . .

I take a deep breath and clear my throat. *God, that had been spectacular.*

I eye my computer, twisting my lips to the side, hating myself right now. "Maybe."

A loud laugh pops out of Beck, which only irritates me. Okay, I should have never said anything.

"What's so funny?" Irritation blooms at the pit of my stomach, overtaking the butterflies.

"You."

"Why? What did I do?"

Zoey lifts her head, mid mouthing a lyric and spots me talking on the phone. She gives me a questioning look.

I point at the phone and mouth, "Mom." Giving me the side-eye with a nod, she returns to her work, thankfully.

"You're so goddamn damn proud it's ridiculous. You know you can give in, right? It's okay to feel things about me. It's okay to admit you had a fucking blast in Key West, and it's okay to admit you miss me."

"I don't miss you." *Lie.*

"Fucking liar." There's so much humor in his voice that once again, butterflies.

"I don't. You know, you're very forgettable."

"Bullshit. If I was forgettable then why have you been texting me?"

"Throwing you a bone?" *You and I both know that's not the truth.*

"I don't believe that for a second, but nice try, Rylee."

Sighing, I lean back in my chair, propping my leg on the table in front of me. "Are you going to irritate me, or are you going to say something to make me swoon?"

There's some shifting on his end of the phone before I hear, "You want to be swooned?"

"Doesn't every girl?"

"Not being a girl myself, I'm not quite sure what every girl wants since you all are so damn different, but hell, if you want to be swooned, I can make you swoon. Is that what you really want, Rylee?"

Crap, I don't even know at this point.

I know I don't want to start anything with someone who lives so far away, because that's long distance, and not close to being easy. But then again, this man, he's starting to consume me. To the point that when I hear my phone ding with a text message and it's not Beck, I'm disappointed. *Slightly depressed.*

What I do know is quitting Beck isn't what I want. My heart wants more time, but my brain is wary, for all the right reasons.

Unfortunately, it's my heart that's calling the shots right now. Feeling shy, I say, "Maybe."

Beck clears his throat, his voice turning serious. "You want to be swept off your feet? I can do that, Saucy, I can easily do that."

I'm about to answer when Zoey tosses a mechanical pencil and hits me in the boob. "Are you talking to Beck?"

"What? No." I lie.

"Yes, you are." Zoey motions at my face. "You're all red, and you're rubbing your legs together. You're talking to Beck."

"No, I'm not." Clearly my lie isn't very convincing, because Zoey is pushing all her things to the side and snagging my phone from my grasp before I can stop her.

She holds the phone in front of her and puts it on speaker. "Beck Wilder?"

Chuckling, Beck answers, "Zoey."

"What are you doing calling my friend? I thought she was moving on."

"Looks like your friend has failed to mention she's been talking to me for the past two weeks."

Zoey raises an eyebrow at me. "Is that right?"

"Maybe," I answer, feeling my cheeks warm with embarrassment again.

"Is that why you won't give Oliver a chance?"

"Oliver, who's Oliver?" Beck asks, sounding slightly concerned.

"Just one of the hottest guys in town. Besides the Knightly brothers, of course. Wouldn't you agree, Rylee?"

"Uhh, I don't know." Killing Zoey right about now actually sounds like a really good time.

"Looks like I have some competition then. I wasn't aware I was going to have to bring my A-game, Rylee."

"Ehh, yeah, Oliver is.... errr... attractive." *Don't say that. Even though he is, don't say that.*

"Attractive, huh? Interesting."

Then there's silence and talk about uncomfortable . . . Zoey's specialty. Why am I friends with this woman again?

"Hey listen, I have to go. Zoey, always a pleasure." And then he hangs up.

Shrugging her shoulders, as if nothing happened, Zoey tosses me my phone and gets back into position.

"Uh, are you going to explain what that was?" I'm fuming. I should be relieved she kicked Beck off the phone, but that's not the truth.

She starts drawing on her iPad with one of those magical pens. "Just helping a girl out."

"How was that a helping a girl out?"

"Trust me, I lit a fire under Beck's ass. Give him two days. Guaranteed that guy does something to make you swoon over him. No doubt in my mind."

"How can you possibly know that?"

Zoey barely lifts her head to look in my direction. "Easy, because Beck looked at you the way Art looks at me. He's a fool for you, Rylee." The look.

It's always about the look. Lizzie Bennett taught me that years ago. *It's always about the look.*

∾

T*wo days later . . .*
    I set my glass of wine on the side table, kick my feet up, pick up my remote and press on. Within an instant, the fire in my fire pit roars to life.

Ah, the perfect summer night.

Fire pit, check.

Wine, check.

Hot guy . . .

Well, that's to be debated. Thanks to Zoey's loud mouth, I haven't heard from Beck in two days and yeah, I'm freaking sad about it. I didn't think he could be scared off that easily, but I guess I was wrong.

"Hey, are you back here?" Victoria calls out from the side of my house. I don't have a fence. It's more like I share a huge yard with a bunch of neighbors, even though we have distinct property lines we don't worry about.

"Yeah, by the pit," I call out.

Victoria rounds the corner, holding a very poofy garment bag and a small package in her hand.

Oh hell. This isn't going to be good.

"Hey, look what I have." She waves the garment bag in hand and tosses the small box to me. "That was on your front porch."

I take one look at the address label and once again, my heart stills in my chest.

Beck.

How the hell did he get my address? I can give you one guess. *Zoey.* That master manipulator.

Ignoring Victoria for a second, I tear open the box and pull back some tissue paper to reveal . . .

"Oh my God." A snort pops out of me as I pull out a hunky merman ornament. But taped on his face is a small color picture of Beck, grinning like a fool. There is a letter attached at the bottom, so I quickly read it.

Rylee,

Saw this little gem at a Farmers Market in Malibu. Instantly thought of you but decided to spice him up a bit. Abs are spot on, aren't they? Bulge is a little off in size, needed to stuff him some more, but we'll let that go. Bet you that your boy Oliver didn't get you one of these. Point, Beck.

Call me.

I read the note at least three more times, noting how legible is handwriting is. Very sharp in place, as if he's spent years upon years perfecting it.

"Wait, this has Beck's face on it." Victoria holds up the ornament. "Is this from one of your readers? How do they know who Beck is?"

"It's from Beck, Victoria."

"Uhh . . . am I missing something?" She sits on the chair across from me, garment bag still in hand. She hands me back the ornament, seeming really confused. Looks like Zoey doesn't have the big mouth I thought she did.

I fold the note and put it in the box along with the ornament. "I've been talking to Beck recently."

"Is that so?" Victoria knowingly smiles. "I knew you wouldn't be able to cut off your interaction with him. There was something electric between you two. I'm actually surprised you held off this long."

"Seriously?"

She nods. "Yeah, it wasn't hard to see that you two shared something special. I was actually a little surprised when you decided to quit him cold turkey. I don't think he's the kind of guy you can wave goodbye to." *Spot on, Victoria. He isn't someone you can easily walk away from or say goodbye to.*

Victoria never really talks about feelings, or guys for that matter, because it's not her jam. She would rather talk about the intricacies of a World War I musket than a relationship, so I'm a little shocked she's being so open now.

"Where is this coming from?" I take a sip of my drink and set it on the tabletop of the fire pit.

She shrugs and plays with the zipper of the garment bag. "I don't know. After we talked in Key West, I thought about your situation some more. You deserve happiness. It's been a rough year—"

"Everyone has rough years. I don't want to keep using that as an excuse to go after some guy who lives on the other side of the country."

"I'm not using that as an excuse. I'm making a statement. You had a rough year, Rylee. It's time to take a breath and enjoy the life you have, the one you strived to keep. If anyone knows about life being too short, it's you, so live it to your fullest. I'm glad you're talking to Beck again because it shows me, as your friend, that you're moving on from your past and taking a chance on living. I say go for it."

Taking in deep breaths, I look to the sky and close my eyes, willing the threatening tears to stay put. Victoria doesn't like crying. She hates it, in fact, so keep it together, woman.

Not wanting to talk about Beck or my situation anymore, I say, "What's in the bag?"

Victoria pauses. I can sense her wanting to continue this conversation but instead, she moves on, and the stark sound of a zipper being undone opens my eyes. Oh hell.

The garment bag parts and a turn-of-the-century dress, frills, gigot sleeves, and the ugliest fabric that looks like it's been starched at least five times in a row appears. *Oh my God.*

"Uh, what is that?"

A devilish smile crosses her face. "Do you remember our little deal? If I went to Key West, you'd come to my historical ball with me. This is your dress."

Yup, I knew I wasn't going to like the reason Victoria was here. "You can't be serious?"

"Oh, I was very serious when we made that deal. I don't want to go to the ball by myself."

"Well, it's not like you went to the wedding with me. You didn't even stay through the reception. How is this fair?"

Victoria shakes her head. "It's not my fault you met a guy and happily traipsed around with him every day. I held up my end of the bargain." Holding up the dress, she says, "Now it's your turn."

Knowing she's right, I sigh, hating every ounce of the deal I made that seems to be more in her favor than mine. How was I supposed to know I would end up meeting Beck? "Fine, when is it?"

"In an hour."

"What?" I sit up in my chair, leaning forward. "An hour? Why the hell are you telling me now?"

"Because if I told you any earlier, you would have come up with some excuse why you couldn't attend. With this carefully planned-out sneak attack approach, I know you're not doing anything and can go to this ball with me."

God, she's so fucking smart. That's Victoria though; she thinks of every possible route a situation can go and takes the surest route. Something I probably should have done before I made this plan.

"Fine." I huff and stand, taking the bag from her. I turn off my fire pit and point my finger at her. "I don't care what you say, I'm wearing makeup."

"But—"

"If you want me to go, I'm wearing makeup. That's final. I'll be waiting for you in half an hour."

I walk away as Victoria calls out, "Hair instructions are in the bag; try to stay as close to the design as possible." Shouting now, she adds, "We want to look authentic."

Mumbling to myself, I say, "Oh yeah, I'm going to be authentic. Real fucking authentic."

In my house, I take the gown to my bedroom where I start to get ready. This isn't my first time going to one of these terrible balls where I have to talk like I'm from that era. It's dreadful, and I'm always called out for talking about things I shouldn't. Sorry if I think playing some Bruno Mars instead of the organ would put a little more pep in people's step. Bruno Mars was created for a reason: to make us thrust our hips together on the dance floor.

God, Bruno could sing in my ear all day.

But that's not the case for the people attending the ball. They prefer someone to pound out a concerto on an out-of-tune piano. Painful, so freaking painful.

I pull out the instructions for my hair and immediately turn my nose up at it. Yeah, I'm not doing that. A low bun is all she's getting. Sorry, Victoria. Maybe if I'm not "authentic" enough, I'll get kicked out. One can only hope.

Getting ready is only going to take me a few minutes with my new plan of attack, so I pick up my phone and dial Beck, nerves bouncing around in my belly.

I have yet to initiate our contact. Until today, he's always reached out first, but now that the ball's in my court, I have to make the effort.

I don't know why it makes me so nervous, but it does.

I put the phone on speaker and sit on my bathroom counter, listening to the phone ring, and ring, and ring.

Should I leave a message? I wasn't prepared for a message. Why does leaving a voicemail seem so much harder? Maybe because I ramble and say stupid things and will end up saying something like I dream about your dick and wish—

"Hey, Saucy." Beck sounds out of breath when he answers.

"Uh hey." Did I interrupt him doing something? Like . . . you know, *DOING something?*

No, no way. Beck isn't that kind of guy, so get that thought out of your head.

"Rylee, are you there?"

"Oh . . . yup. I'm here. Sorry. Was thinking about you having sex." See, rambling and saying what's on my mind. That's exactly what I'm talking about.

Chuckling, Beck answers, "Is that so? Was I doing a good job?"

"What? No. I mean yes . . . I mean . . ." Flustered, I hang up the phone and drop it on the bathroom counter, as if it's on fire. I step away and place my hand on my forehead, trying to comprehend my inability to call a man and not act normal.

That was embarrassing.

Like, mortifying and yup, look at that. He's calling back. Of course he is, because he's nice and interested and wants to talk to me.

Damn him for being so perfect.

Sighing, I answer, "Hello?"

"Hey there." There is so much humor in his voice, it releases some of the tension in my shoulders.

"What's up?" Taking the casual approach this go around.

Chuckling some more, Beck asks, "Are you nervous to talk to me on the phone, Rylee?"

I should be used to his blatant directness, but it's still taking some time to comprehend. I've never met anyone like him, so to the point, no messing around.

I want to be the same with him.

"I am. You make me nervous."

"Because I'm so goddamn attractive you can't think about me without fumbling over your words?"

Okay, sarcasm works for me. "Don't be a dick."

He barks out a laugh and then soothingly says, "Don't be nervous, Saucy. It's just me. You know what you're going to get when you talk to me on the phone. General interest in your day, some blatant flirting, and of course the begging for a selfie. How many times can a guy really ask?"

"You have pictures of me, so you'll survive."

"I want more. Come on, I know you got the package, my tracking number told me so. FaceTime with me, let me see that smile of yours."

I bite on my bottom lip, trying to comprehend where this is going.

"FaceTime seems too intimate."

"So, maybe I want to get intimate." His response is instant, no stumbling, no pauses.

"Intimate seems pointless because we live so far away."

"Sometimes you have to take a chance on something that makes you happy, regardless of the unknown."

And just like that, his words resonate with me.

Taking that chance, I press the FaceTime button on my phone and hold my breath.

Within an instant, Beck's face comes on screen. Oh my God, I really forgot how attractive he is. How attracted I am to him. I love his gorgeous smile and how his eyes show sincere happiness, amidst the cocky mischief. *How I wish I could hug him right now.*

"Hey Saucy." His voice is low, smooth, just how I like it.

"Hey," I answer shyly.

I take in his background. He looks like he's in his bedroom, and he's definitely not wearing a shirt because his shoulders are bare. There isn't anything on his walls, but he does have white curtains over his windows, which is a bit surprising. I never would have pegged him to be a man bothered with window decoration.

"There's that beautiful smile I've been dreaming about." He sits on his bed. "Now tell me about the package you received. Is it everything your little heart desired? Is he the most handsome of the mermen you have?"

I chuckle, feeling a little more at ease. "He is definitely the most interesting."

"And handsome."

I laugh some more. "Of course the most handsome. I like that he's holding a paintbrush, very fitting."

"I thought so myself. But can we agree that the bulge needs to be bigger? I'm packing some heat here and that merman is not representing me properly."

"Maybe he rolled it up like a sushi roll and tucked it behind his scales. Shifters and such can do that."

"Shifters?" He makes a confused face.

"Never mind." I brush it off, not wanting to get into that conversation. Too many questions are involved when trying to explain paranormal romance to someone. "I love the ornament though. Thank you; that was really sweet."

"You're welcome, Saucy. I'm glad you like it." He lies down on his pillow and holds the camera above him. I catch a flash of his broad chest and my mouth waters. "What are you up to tonight? Got any big plans with any guys I didn't know about like Oliver?"

I give him a sideways look. "Nothing with Oliver."

"That's what I like to hear."

"But I do have plans," I say quickly.

"Yeah?" The hand that's behind his head lightly brushes through his hair that is longer than I remember. "What kind of plans? Do they involve me and getting naked on FaceTime?"

"No, nice try though." I scoot back on the counter and lean against my mirror. "I have a date."

His brow pinches together and call me a bitch, but I kind of like playing around with him since he's played with me so much. It's only fitting. "A date? Tell me about this date."

I purse my lips together. "Let's see, there will be music and dancing."

"Oh yeah? I love dancing."

I know, and he's sexy as sin when he dances. There is something to be said about a man who effortlessly shows his skills with no qualms and no holding back. That's Beck; live in the moment and express yourself. It's what makes him so addicting, and it's what makes him impossible to cut loose.

It's why I'm talking to him right now, giddy as hell to see him, to hear his voice.

"So much dancing." Choreographed dancing from the 19th Century, but I'm not going to let him know that. Dancing that I sure as hell won't be participating in. "And food, because you know, what's a date without food?"

"Got to have food," he answers. "What else is there going to be?"

Hmm . . . let's see, there will be paper fans waving over massive amounts of ringlets cascading down the up-dos of each and every woman—except me—in the venue. Maybe I'll skip that detail.

"Drinks, yup. I'll be drinking." And that's the freaking truth. The minute I walk through the doors of that ballroom, first stop is the bar and instead of a glass of wine, I'm going to ask them to duct tape two bottles of champagne to my hands. And if anyone asks what I'm doing, I'll introduce myself as Madame Boozehands of Soon to be Drunkville.

"Huh, so dancing, drinking, and food. Sounds like you're going to a wedding without me. You wouldn't do that to me, would you?"

There is a pounding in my hallway that's quickly picking up pace and before I can see what it is, Victoria bursts through my bathroom door, looking frantic and thrusting a piece of paper in my direction.

"Victoria, what the—?"

"Oh thank God. You haven't started your hair yet. I gave you the wrong instructions. I gave you the hairstyle of a servant, not of a middle-class woman. What the hell was I thinking? Here, read the instructions carefully and if you need help let me know right away so I can do it for you. You know what, maybe I *will* do your hair. It has to be right for tonight, and I have my dress in the car so we can get ready together. I don't want to be late to the historical ball. Dance cards fill up quickly, and I want to make sure we don't miss out on any of the dances."

What terrible, terrible timing.

Exhaling a long breath, I turn my phone to Victoria and say, "Say hi to Beck."

Startled, Victoria squats to look into the phone like it's a microscope. "Oh, Beck. Sorry. I didn't know you were talking on the phone with Rylee."

I don't have to look at the phone to know that not only is Beck smiling like a damn fool, but he's already calculating the ribbing he'll unleash on me when he next gets the opportunity.

"Hey Victoria. So you must be the date our friend Rylee is talking about."

"Oh, yup." Victoria pushes her glasses up on her nose. "We're going to a historical ball tonight. Do you want to see her dress? I picked it out myself. It's very authentic."

"There is nothing more I want to do than see her dress right now."

My nostrils flare . . . Ass.

Excited, Victoria unzips the garment bag and pushes it over the shoulders to show off the maroon and tan frilly, poofy dress I'll be wearing.

"Wow." He pauses. "I'm going to need a picture of Rylee in that."

"Don't worry. I'll take one with her phone and send it to you. But we should go, because I have to do her hair, and I really want to make sure it's accurate for the era we're representing."

"Totally get it. Don't let me keep you. It was good seeing you, Victoria."

"You too."

I turn the phone back to me where Beck is gleaming with joy . . . on my behalf. With a wink, he says, "Looking forward to that picture, Saucy. I'll talk to you later." And then the phone goes blank.

That devil of a man. Ugh, I could scream at Victoria, letting the cat out of the bag. I mean, to her defense, she didn't know I was trying to pull a fast one on Beck, but still, gah . . .

Beep.

A text . . . from Beck.

"Okay, sit down on this chair, and I'll get to work." Victoria motions for me to sit, which I do. There is no getting out of this anymore. This is really happening, and there's no doubt in my mind Victoria will make sure Beck gets a picture of me. "Beck is so nice. I'm glad you're talking to him again."

"Yeah." I huff and open my text message.

Beck: *I hope your date goes well tonight and you get lucky with Victoria.*

So fucking cheeky.

Rylee: *Me too, twenty bucks says she's a better lover than you.*

Ha! Take that. I giggle to myself, very pleased with my response.

Beck: *Send me video and I'll let you know my opinion on the matter.*

Of course he has a smart-ass comment to follow up.

Rylee: *Your opinion isn't warranted.*

Beck: *Okay, then call me after. Bet she can't make you come all over her face like you did on mine.*

My body heats up and I'm immediately embarrassed when my mind jumps back to our night together, my naked breasts pushed against the glass, Beck's powerful shoulders spreading my legs, and his entire mouth pressed against my center, making me come so goddamn hard I nearly blacked out.

"Are you hot?" Victoria asks. "Your head is getting all steamy. Want me to turn on a fan?"

"Yes," I practically moan.

"Eh, that sounded a little sexual. Are you okay?"

"Fan, Victoria. Just get the fan from my bedroom."

"You're being weird . . . are you . . ." She leans over my shoulder. "Are you sexting right now? While I'm touching your hair?"

"No!"

"Let me see then." Victoria reaches for my phone, but I pull it close to my chest. "Ew, you're sexting while I touch your hair and getting horny over it. Do you realize how creepy that is?"

"I'm not sexting." My entire body is on fire from humiliation. I don't have to look in the mirror to know how red my cheeks are right now.

"Then let me see."

"No. It's not for your eyes."

Staring me down through the reflection in the mirror, she says, "Are you making fun of me in your texts?"

"What? No!" Ughh, I sigh and say, "I was tricking Beck, telling him I had a hot date, and then you came in and spoiled that. Now he's saying he hopes I get lucky with you tonight since you're my date and I said"—I take a second to catch my breath—"I bet you'll be a better lover than him." I cringe in time for Victoria to smack me on the arm.

"Ew, don't talk about me pleasuring you. What is wrong with you?"

The question for the ages.

Before I can answer, she takes off toward my room for the fan. Oh poor Victoria. How she got caught up in Zoey's and my brand of crazy, I have no idea. Some days, I really think she wishes she could trade us in.

For the next half hour, Victoria works on my hair in silence. I don't text Beck, and instead I plot in my head, going over all the different feelings I want to evoke from my characters. When it's time, I slip into the over-starched dress, let Victoria button me up in the back, and stare in the mirror.

What a vision.

What an absolutely *horrifying* vision.

Tall turtleneck and shoulders for days, this is some hot shit. I will say this, though. Victoria created an accurate portrayal with my hair. A loose bun on the top of my head and curls framing my face.

You know . . . I kind of look like . . .

"Oh dear." Victoria says from the side of me, fully costumed, eyes raking over my entire appearance.

"Are you seeing what I'm seeing?"

She nods and bites on her finger. "It's uncanny, almost spot on with the teal circle broach."

"Yup." I nod. "I'm Cinderella's wicked stepmother."

"Dead on." Patting me on the shoulder, she snags my phone from the counter and says, "Smile for Beck."

The flash goes off and there is no time for me to stop her. She sends that puppy right on over to him without my permission. She's been hanging out with Zoey for far too long.

"Hey, did I look good in the picture?"

"Eh, not really, but we don't have time to make the picture perfect. Let's go." She tosses me my phone and takes off down the hall. "We are not going to be late. Dance cards, remember?"

"How could I possibly forget?" Following behind her, because I'm nervous she will cut me if we're late, I check the picture to see what she sent and stop in place. "Oh my God. Victoria. I have four fucking chins in this picture."

"Four? Huh, I only counted three."

"I seriously hate you right now."

"Hate me on the way to the ball. Come on."

Blowing steam out of my nose and ears, I follow her into her car, irritated now more than ever when my phone beeps with a response.

"No phones allowed. They didn't have such devices in that time period."

"Yeah, and you weren't alive during that time period either, maybe I should get rid of you, huh?" There is a bit of crazy in my eyes, and I know when she sees it, because instead of pressing the matter, she drops it and starts her car as I read my message.

Beck: *I would still fuck you. I would fuck you hard with that dress pushed up and over your hips, my cock buried deep inside of you.*

Oh God. My skin starts to heat up and my four chins are slowly becoming less of an issue.

My phone beeps again.

Beck: *Can you thank Victoria for the spank-bank material?*

I roll my eyes and look out the window, the slightest of smiles turning up my lips. *And that would be a hell, no.*

CHAPTER EIGHTEEN

BECK

"There's my girl," I say once Rylee answers the phone.

Patting her hair down and tucking it behind her ear, she brings her knees to her chest and shyly smiles. "Hey you."

Hey you. Those two words, so familiar, so comforting. She's slowly letting her guard down with every text, every call, every FaceTime date. It hasn't been easy. This is only the third time I've actually gotten to talk to her on FaceTime, but for now, I'm going to take what I can get.

"How's the book?"

She nods and looks to the side. "It's going well. Just tightening up some things, but I'm sure my editor will have some more notes for me to go over though. Happens every time."

"When do I get to read it?" I wiggle my eyebrows. "You know, looking forward to reading that window sex, as I really want to make sure you're accurate and all."

Chuckling, she answers, "You can read it when it comes out."

"What?" I lean back on the couch and prop my hand on the arm. "I don't get an early read of it? What kind of crap is that? Since I was the inspiration and the creator of sex against the window, you should be happy I'm not looking for a cut of the profits."

Shakes her head. "You're so ridiculous."

"Come on, why not read it to me right now? A little story time might be nice before bed."

"Not going to happen."

"Why not? Is it really dirty?"

She bites her bottom lip and nods.

"Fuck?" I blow out a breath. "Like really dirty?"

"Like verbatim of our night."

And I'm hard.

Hands down, that night with Rylee blows any night I've ever shared with a woman completely out of the water. I've never been with someone so responsive, so reactive to my every touch, my every move. It was addicting trying to figure out what other noises I could cause her to make, what touch made her that much wetter, that much more needy. Playing her body, moving over it, tasting it, hell, I think about it every damn day and yearn for more.

For so much more.

"Kind of killing me, Rylee."

She shrugs absently. "You asked. I just told you the truth."

"We need to change the subject or else we're going to have a big situation on our hands, and what I really mean is I'm going to have a big situation in my hand."

She rolls her eyes. "Oh Beck, you can be so corny sometimes."

"Would you rather me say my cock is hard as fuck and I'm going to start jacking off if we don't change the subject?"

She takes pause, her chest moving faster than before. "I mean . . . maybe, wait, no." She shakes her head. "No cock talk."

"How about vagina talk?"

"No genitals."

I cringe. "Genitals is such a fucking awful word. You know how people don't like the word moist? It's genitals for me."

"Genitals? Really? Mine is cream."

"Cream?" I laugh. "So if I say ice cream you cringe?"

The corners of her mouth tilts up. "Let me be more specific. I don't like the word creamed."

"Ah." I nod. "So the term, I just creamed myself is not part of your vernacular?"

She dry heaves and shakes her head. "Ugh, so gross. Why would that be part of anyone's vernacular?"

"You got me, Saucy." Switching gears, I ask, "Did you get any of that clam chowder you were talking about the other day?"

"Ugh, no. They ran out by the time I got there, so I had to settle for chicken fingers, even though it wasn't close to the same."

"Chicken fingers? Not even in the same food group. What happened?"

"The other soups at this place are pure crap and so is the rest of their food. I literally only go there for their clam chowder and biscuits; it's a lethal combination. But I wasn't about to walk out and not get anything because that's rude."

"So you settled for chicken fingers."

"Exactly." She sighs heavily. "That's what happens when you're stuck in a scene and don't beat the early birds to the clam chowder pot. Don't worry, next Wednesday I'll be the first one in line when the dinner menu rolls out."

I can't hold back my smile. Rylee's life is so different compared to mine. Living in a small town compared to living in one of the biggest cities in the United States, it's such a stark contrast, and for some reason, I find Rylee's way of living a hell of a lot more fascinating than mine.

"Do you like living in a small town?"

She twirls a stray lock of her hair. "It has its ups and downs, but I think the ups outweigh the downs. It's where I grew up, so I know almost every person who lives here, and if I've never really talked to them, I've heard about them from someone. We're always talking about each other, always up in each other's business, but we also look out for each other. Since we're a tourist spot, we make sure to keep an eye out for one another."

"That's nice. Built-in camaraderie. I definitely don't get that in

California. But hey, got to love the road rage only Californians can offer. Bet you don't get that in your small town."

Laughing, she shakes her head. God, I love that sound so damn much. "No road rage, but when Mrs. Braverman decides to cross the street, the whole town knows to stop and wait, because it's going to be a five-minute process. If we rush her, she will—no joke —stand there in the road until she's ready to walk again."

"Seriously? Is this the same lady who took your sex chair?"

"Inspiration chair." She absentmindedly licks her lips, and I can't help but focus on how wet and plump they are. What I wouldn't give to taste them again. "But yes, that was her. She's a squatter and everyone knows it, so we do the best we can to not bother her."

"Just bribe her with candles and incense."

"Of course."

Lying on the couch, she holds the phone out so it's almost like I'm lying with her. I imitate the pose.

"What was your favorite part of Key West?" I ask, loving how her pure blue eyes look so peaceful, content. She really is gorgeous.

"Favorite part?" She quirks her lips to the side, putting some serious thought into my question. "Honestly?"

"Yes, honestly."

"You're probably going to hate me, but when we played cornhole. It was fun and sexy with how you stole little touches here and there. That entire game I felt on fire and then we won and . . ." She shakes her head. "It was a fun, out-of-body moment for me."

"Why would I hate you for that?"

"Because, I didn't say something like when you made me come all over your face."

A low rumble pops out of my chest. "Yes, that was a fucking awesome moment, but that wouldn't be mine either."

"No?"

"No." I shake my head.

"Then what was your favorite moment?"

The image has been on replay in my head for the past few

weeks. "My favorite moment, hands down, was when I found you sitting at the bar alone, staring at the bar top, stirring your drink, because in that moment, there was an opportunity in front of me that was about to throw my entire equilibrium upside down. It was a life-changing moment."

She smiles. It's a slow smile, but it's fast becoming one of my favorites. And for once, she doesn't come back with a smart-ass reply. She's silent. But her smiles speaks volumes. *Yeah, life-changing moment.*

~

Steam billows from the sink as my pasta drains. Sauce is ready, garlic bread is in the oven keeping warm, and there's a nice glass of milk waiting for me on my table.

I check my watch for the time and quickly pull out a plate, pile some noodles on it, top it with some sauce and parmesan cheese—well, a lot of parmesan cheese—and pull the bread from the oven where I break off a few pieces for myself.

Rushing over to the table, I set the mood lighting, including a tapered candle I bought from the store today, play some music, and position my phone as it rings.

Rylee.

Fuck, seeing her name across my phone still sends a sense of excitement through me. I answer her FaceTime request and can't contain the smile when she comes on screen. *God, how I want to kiss that beautiful face, those luscious lips.*

"Hey, Saucy."

She looks flustered, her hair a mess, her face flushed, and splashes of red all over her white shirt.

"Ugh, why did you pick such a hard recipe?" She presses her forehead into the palm of her hand, her eyes still focused on mine.

"What do you mean?"

Moving her phone, she shows me a plate of what looks like

half-cooked spaghetti, chunky sauce, and charred garlic bread. Oh hell.

"I've never made homemade sauce before, my noodles weren't cooking for so long because I didn't know the burner wasn't on, and my oven practically scorched my bread. And who makes sauce with real tomatoes?"

I chuckle. I know I shouldn't but can't help it. Rylee is a bad cook and for some reason, I find it endearing, especially since she at least gave it a go. A few days ago, I proposed the idea of eating dinner together. I gave her what I thought was an easy recipe to follow so we could both eat the same thing. Seems like my night of cooking went a little smoother than hers.

"Uh, it said canned tomatoes."

"No, it didn't." She pauses and looks to the sky. "Did it?"

"It did."

She exhales heavily and sits back in her chair. "Ugh, I'm sorry. I was working through this scene today in my book, and I swear it sucked all my mental capacity. When I realized I was supposed to cook dinner tonight, I was rushing. I'm almost positive this is going to taste like a cat ate it and then threw it back up on my plate." *Gross fucking visual.*

"Why are you apologizing?"

She shrugs. "I don't know." She plays with her fork in her spaghetti. "I've never done this before, had a FaceTime dinner date. I wanted to make sure I did a good job, you know, impress you a little. All I accomplished was tie-dying my shirt with the most likely under-seasoned spaghetti sauce." *This girl. Too adorable.*

"You wanted to impress me? That's sexy." I lean back in my chair and cross my arms over my chest.

She motions to her body. "You call this sexy?" *Fuck, yes.*

"Every single time I see you," I answer, not even skipping a beat. *And every time I close my eyes and see you in my mind.* She casts her eyes downward and what I wouldn't do right now to lift her chin, to force her to focus those irises on me. *How can she be so insecure about herself?*

"I'm just unsure of what this is between us, Beck. Whatever it is, I'm not good at it."

"You don't have to be good at it, Saucy, you just have to be present. The good happens along the way."

She visibly sighs, her tense shoulders relaxing, a light smile playing across her lips.

"You're so freaking . . . ugh."

I laugh. "I hope that's a good thing."

"It is." Shaking her head and hands, like she's erasing the moment, she says, "Let's start over."

Playing along, I say, "Okay, do you want me to call back?"

"Yeah, call me back."

She's so goddamn cute. I hang up and give it a few seconds before I set my phone up again and call her. When she answers, she's no longer wearing a spaghetti-stained shirt. Instead—*and fuck, it's even better*—she's *only* wearing a red lace bra. There might be food somewhere too, but fuck. Red. Lace. Bra.

My eyes narrow and my dick grows hard, immediately pressing against the zipper of my jeans. This is the one time where wearing no underwear is an issue—when you have a hot-as-hell woman you can't get enough of FaceTiming you topless. Fuck, it's been too goddamn long since I've been able to touch her.

I clear my throat, and say, "Are you trying to kill me, Rylee?"

She looks at her breasts that are spilling out of her bra and giggles. "Sorry, I guess I didn't think this through. I was going to change my shirt but you called back so quickly, that this is what you got. Want me to go put something on?"

She goes to stand and I say, "No!" I shake my head. "No, I want you to take more off."

She tilts her head to the side and gives me a *get real* look. "I'm not about to sit here naked for you while you eat your delicious spaghetti meal and I choke mine down."

"I wish you were choking down something else right now."

With mirth in her eyes, she gives her head a shake. "You're ridiculous."

"And you're hot, so take your bra off."

"I'll take my bra off if you take your clothes off."

Done. Before she can protest, I pull my shirt over my head, toss it to the ground and reach for the zipper of my jeans, my cock excited for the release.

"No." She laughs. "I was kidding. Keep your clothes on."

I pause, fingers playing with the zipper of my jeans. "It doesn't bode well for me that you want me to immediately dress myself when I strip down. What are you trying to say? Does my body disgust you?"

"Oh my God, don't be a drama queen."

"Me, a drama queen?" I clasp my hand to my chest in mock disgust. "I'm not a drama queen, and you're avoiding my question. Does my body disgust you?"

Looking up through her eyelashes, her voice soft and serious, she says, "You know damn well your body doesn't disgust me."

And that look, that one right there where she very carefully bites on her bottom lip, causes a low groan to come out of me.

Fuck.

Fuck, fuck, fuck. I want to touch her, fuck her, hold her.

"Rylee," I groan, "you can't look at me like that when I can't do anything with it."

Sighing, she leans back in her chair and studies me. "This is stupid, so why *are* we doing this when we can't touch each other?"

I see the doubt in her eyes, the hesitation.

"Because we enjoy each other's company." Wanting to pull her back into the moment, I nod at our food. "Let's dig in, and you can tell me more about your new book."

We spend the next twenty minutes talking plot and laughing hysterically at the cringe-worthy dinner Rylee prepared. I've never done plotting before, but it's damn fun, throwing out suggestions that are either entirely too terrible for her to consider or ideas that actually inspire her. Even though her laugh hooks me every time, it's the way her eyes light up when I prompt a valuable train of thought for her that really turns me on. *Smart and beautiful.*

Leaving my plate at the table, I take the phone to my bedroom where I flop on my bed and place one of my hands behind my head. Instead of her bedroom, Rylee sits in what looks to be her living room.

"What did you work on today?" she asks, speaking of my painting.

"No assignments today actually, so I worked on some individual stuff."

She perks up, and even though I love seeing how interested she is in my profession, it's hard not to be distracted with how her breasts sway with each and every movement. I've had a fucking hard-on from the minute I rang her back, and it's painful.

So fucking painful.

And she probably has no fucking clue.

"You have your own paintings?"

I nod, trying to focus on something other than the alluring girl in front of me. "Yeah, painting isn't just a job for me, it's therapeutic."

"Can I see what you worked on today?"

I cringe. "Yeah, you don't want to see that."

"I do." She nods vigorously. "Please, will you show me?" Side note, ladies. Boobs wiggle when you nod and/or giggle. *Yeah. Don't ever stop.*

How the hell am I supposed to say no to that? When she looks at me like this—impatient desire to see something of mine —I'll pretty much do anything for her. She's guileless, and having such sincere yearning *in* me, in what I do, does so much for my long-lost heart. It will be her lethal weapon when it comes to me.

"Shit, when you ask like that . . ."

I get up as she cheers and claps, excited she's getting her way.

Since I only have a one-bedroom apartment, I paint in the living room, so I take her to my easel and turn the phone around, showing her a half-finished picture of an aging and balding man. I use oils with unconventional coloring. For this skin tones, I chose

223

to paint with purples and greens, combining the colors to show the depth in his skin.

"Oh my God, Beck. That is amazingly beautiful."

"Thanks," I answer softly, feeling slightly self-conscious.

"Do you know that man?"

I nod, but I don't want to get into how. *Yet*. "Because my work requires me to paint landscapes, when it's just for me, I focus on portraits. It's a good balance, I never get sick of it, of painting that is."

"Makes sense." She shakes her head in disbelief. "It's beautiful. You are so talented."

"Thank you." I scrub the back of my neck. "Want to see another?"

"Yes, please." She's excited, which excites me. Picking up one of the canvases leaning against my couch, I prop it up against the living-room window. It's a painting of a woman with bright red lipstick, high cheekbones, and distraught eyes. Her purple hair swirls all over the canvas. It's one of my favorite pieces. "Oh wow. Look at her hair and the streaks of orange you have in it. It gives it so much dimension."

Encouragement of my art, hearing Rylee describe the details of my painting, seeing what I see when I'm painting, it means a lot to me.

"And the green in her eyes. It's as if it's muddied. Did you do that on purpose?"

"I did."

Sophia. She's a survivor, a strong woman with a muddied outlook on the world who is fighting every day to live a normal life, to forget her attacker, and set herself free from the demons clouding her mind.

"She's beautiful." Rylee pauses. "I'm starting to think maybe you know this woman too."

I nod. "I know of her story. I know everyone's story who I paint."

Rylee twists her lips to the side. "Are these stories of pain?"

I nod, tingles of anxiety rise through me. I don't want to dive too deep into this story, in how I know these people. I'm not ready for Rylee to know that side of me.

Because I'd be damned if after I tell her my story, she becomes one of the tortured souls I paint next.

No, I'm not ready for that. Not sure I'll ever be.

~

Beck: *Are you ready?*

    Rylee: Give me five minutes. I need to get this guy off and then I'll be ready.

    Beck: Please tell me you're referring to a character and not . . . Oliver.

    Rylee: LOL. My character! I have to get my character off and then I'll be ready for FaceTime.

    Beck: Good, I like it when you're specific about who you're getting off.

    Rylee: I can understand that. Give me five.

Walking around my bedroom, I put away my laundry, hang a few shirts, and dust the top of my dresser with the shirt I'm wearing. When I notice how much dust is on my shirt, I chuckle and take it off. I should try dusting more often. Possibly with a duster rather than a shirt.

It's been over a month since I've seen Rylee in the flesh, over a month since I've touched her, and fuck if I haven't felt this goddamn horny before.

We talk almost every night whether it's text or FaceTime, and we keep it to simple things like our likes and dislikes, or ribbing each other. We never delve into our pasts, and when one of us is uncomfortable, we shut down and end the conversation. Sooo, super healthy.

I don't really know what one would call what we're doing, but all I know is that if I go a day without talking to her, I feel empty inside, like I missed out on something great for that day. I never want to miss out on something great, especially where she's involved.

My phone rings and I rush over to answer it. When she pops onto the screen, she greets me with a giant smile. Her hair is piled on top of her head in a bun, loose strands delicately framing her face, and she's still wearing her thick-rimmed black glasses. But what I'm really interested in is the tank top she's wearing without a bra. The tank top is so damn tight I can see the outline of her areolas. I'm hard, just like that.

"Hey you," she says into the phone, her smile capturing me.

"Hey, Saucy." I lick my lips. "You look so damn good with those glasses on."

She tips them up and down. "You like these? I wear them when I've been staring at my computer for far too long. They help my eyes relax. It was a long day editing but I'm almost done, which is amazing."

"Congrats, that's awesome. I can't imagine what it's like to write an entire novel and then send it off, edited and ready for publishing."

"The feeling of accomplishment never gets old."

"I bet." Taking a peek at her cleavage, I say, "Nice shirt choice. You're giving me a goddamn erection with how tight it is."

"Well, I thought it was only fair since you show up on these calls shirtless eighty percent of the time. You know it's not easy over here for me either."

I chuckle, loving how honest she is. "Is that right?"

"Yeah."

Settling on my bed, I ask her, "Tell me this, have you masturbated while thinking about me yet? And don't fucking lie to me."

Pinches her mouth to the side, looking away, almost as if she's ashamed. "I might have."

I groan. "Are you serious?" She thinks of me when she masturbates. *Fucking hell.*

She nods. "I did last night."

"How hard did you come?"

Her cheeks splash with red. "Not as hard as I would have liked to, not as hard as I would have if you were actually here."

Pained, I close my eyes willing my body to calm down, to not get too damn excited.

"Do you ever think about me when you touch yourself?" She looks shy as she asks me.

Is that a joke?

"You're kidding, right? Rylee, do you realize how quickly *and* easily I get hard when I think about you? You're on constant replay in my head, and the minute I touch myself, it's embarrassing with how fast I come."

A wicked smile crosses over her face. "Yeah? Are you hard right now?"

"Hard as fuck, especially since I can see how puckered your nipples are, how almost see-through that tank top is. Yeah, I'm fucking hard."

She lets a few seconds pass before she says, "Let me see."

I raise my eyebrows. "You want to see how hard I am?"

She nods. "Yes, show me."

Are we doing this? Are we about to have FaceTime sex? "Please show me." *She's begging to see my cock. What fool would say no to that?*

"Rylee, if I whip my dick out right now, you're going to wind up with two options: you're either going to have to hang up the phone, or watch me stroke myself to climax. I'm not fucking kidding. You make me so goddamn hard it's almost impossible to ignore how painfully bad I need release."

She sighs and lies back on her bed as well, holding the phone up above her. "Beck, I'm going to be honest. I'm so horny right now and maybe a little drunk." She holds up her fingers. "Well, not drunk, tipsy and throwing caution to the wind." She pulls on her tank top, the collar of her shirt dropping dangerously low on her breasts. She wiggles along her sheets. "God, what I wouldn't give for your hands right now, for your mouth, for your cock."

Confused, since our conversations have been pretty vanilla leading up to this point besides some innocent flirting, I ask, "Where's this coming from, Rylee?"

She grunts and moves her hand around her breasts and pulls on her puckered nipple. She bites her bottom lip and says, "I might have been watching some porn while texting you."

"Porn?" I chuckle. She nods. "So when you were saying you had to get your character off, you were lying?"

"No." She laughs and shakes her head. "When I'm not in my inspiration chair—"

"Sex chair."

She rolls her eyes. "When I'm not in my sex chair and I need to make sure the sex scene is hot enough, I'll watch some porn while I'm writing. It's the perfect way to get me in the mood, but God, it makes me incredibly aroused. Like you with no shirt on, it's making me want to stick my hand down my shorts and find some release."

Fucking hell.

"Saucy."

"Yeah?" Her eyelashes flutter up and she makes eye contact with me.

"Take your shirt off. Now."

Her face softens and a seductive smile takes over her gorgeous mouth. Shifting on her bed, she sets the phone against what I assume is a lamp or clock on her nightstand and reaches for the hemline of her tank. In one fluid movement, she lifts it up and over her head, revealing her magnificent breasts and hard nipples.

I grip my chin, rubbing my fingers across my stubble as I take her in. "Beautiful, Rylee."

She doesn't say anything. Instead, she closes her eyes, presses her head back, and brings her hands to her breasts where she plucks at her nipples. Her mouth parts open as a light, subtle moan escapes her lips. That's all it takes. I reach for my pants just as a frantic and incredibly loud knock sounds at my door, followed by Chris telling me to open up.

"Fuck," I mutter, wondering if I can ignore him.

"What's that?" Rylee asks, lifting her head to meet mine and covering her breasts, breaking away from our moment.

"Beck, I know you're in there. I can see your bike. Dude, I need your help, please open up."

"Shit." I rub my hair. "It's Chris; sounds like he needs my help."

"Oh, yeah, go answer him. Uh, this was stupid anyway."

"Like hell it was." I stand from my bed when Chris's pounding becomes incessant. Rylee quickly puts her shirt back on. "Rylee."

She shakes her head. "I don't know what the hell I was thinking. I'm embarrassed."

"Beck, open up, man."

For fuck's sake.

"Don't be embarrassed, Rylee." I make my way toward the front door. "Give me a second, I'll call you right back."

"Yeah, okay."

Feeling like a giant dick, I hang up and fling my front door open. "Dude, what the hell?"

Chris passes by me, looking crazed. "Thank God you're here."

I shut the door and adjust my jeans before turning around. "What's going on? Is everything okay? Justine, the kids, are they good?"

"What?" Chris shakes his head. "Yeah, they're fine." Reaching into his back pocket, he shows me two white tickets. "Dude, I got tickets to Bon Jovi's concert this weekend. I won them on a radio station contest. Can you believe it?"

Blinking my eyes rapidly, I ask, "Are you fucking serious? That's what you came here to tell me? That's what you practically beat my door down over? Bon Jovi tickets?"

"Yeah, why aren't you excited for me? Living on a prayer, man. This concert is going to be sick. I'm taking Justine; think you can watch the kids for us?" He plasters a huge smile across his face.

"Fuck you." I grab his arm and start to pull him toward my door, his feet dragging against my wood floors.

"What the hell are you doing?"

"Chris, I thought something was wrong with you guys. I was on the phone with Rylee. Damn it." I rake my hand through my hair, the tension obvious in my stiff shoulders.

229

"With Rylee——" Understanding washes over him. "Oh shit, were you having phone sex?"

"Who fucking knows what we were doing?" Her goddamn top was off, and she was pinching her nipples for me. I was about to watch her get herself off. "You can go to fucking hell living on your damn prayer." I open the door and shove him out into the hall.

Before I shut the door on him, he holds up his finger and says, "So is that a serious no to watching the kids for us?"

"That's a fuck no." I slam the door on his face and reach for my phone where I see a text message from Rylee.

Rylee: *Taking a shower and heading to bed. I'll talk to you later. Have a good night.*

Sighing, my chin drops to my chest, I squeeze my eyes shut, and walk to my shower. I wanted to see her. I wanted to watch her enjoy her body, touch the places I can't touch. I wanted to hear her moan as she got closer to release. What I don't want is to know she's having a shower, probably getting what she needs without me there, and once again, shying away from us. *Fuck.*

CHAPTER NINETEEN

RYLEE

"Son of a mother effing bitch," I shout as smoke billows from my oven, clogging my kitchen in a grey haze.

The smoke alarm sets off immediately. No surprise there. It's as if the fog chokes everything in the room. In an attempt to clear out the smoke, I open the windows around the first floor of my house and use a baking pan as a fan, waving it around like a maniac.

I cough a few times, wondering what the chicken I was trying to bake looks like at this point. Probably charred to its very core. No salmonella here. At least I have that going for me.

Broken teeth, now that's a different story.

Smoke alarm still blaring, echoing around my neighborhood, I bring a chair below the alarm, stand on it, and wave my baking sheet frantically, my ear drums ready to rupture any second.

"I get it, you think the house is burning down," I shout. "I can assure you, it's not. So shut the ever loving hell up!"

Beep. Beep. Beep.

"You demon machine!"

Dogs rally with the smoke detector, barking out their displeasure, a car alarm is set off, and the noise echoes horrendously in my head, like a pounding ice pick to the brain.

Beep. Beep. Beep.

"You're a loud mother fucker, aren't you?" I grunt, my arms getting tired and just when I think I'm about to pass out from smoke inhalation and brain damage from the beeping, the sound stops, startling me and sending me careening to the ground.

I land flat on my ass with a plop.

Dressed in a cute flower apron that I thought might give me some super-human cooking powers, hair a sweaty hot mess and plastered to my face, and my baking sheet next to me, looking warped, I sit there, staring at the floor.

"Well," I let out a sigh. "Rachel Ray is a freaking liar. Easy thirty-minute meals, my ass."

From the counter, my phone rings, pulling my attention away from my pathetic attempt at cooking another meal. I don't have to look at the caller ID to know who it is. He calls the same time almost every night.

Not standing from my seat on the floor, I fling my arm to the top of my counter, wiggle my fingers around until I find my phone, and accept the FaceTime call. Always FaceTime, never a straight-up phone call anymore. I think it's cute . . . usually. Right now, not so much.

"Hey," I sigh when his face comes on screen.

Sitting in his living room, he's got a shirt on this go around, a button-up shirt with the sleeves rolled up to his elbows and the top few buttons undone. It reminds me of the outfit he wore to the wedding. Over the past several weeks, I've noticed he's let his hair grow out on top, leaving the sides shaved. I like the new look, and I'd like it even more if I was able to run my fingers through it.

"Hey, Saucy." His face crinkles together when he gets a good look at me. "What's wrong?"

Always perceptive.

"Burnt another dinner." This isn't the first time he's found me in this situation. We tried once making a meal together on Face-

Time, guiding me step by step, and in the end, I still charred the hell out of my meal. I blame my oven. It's a temperamental ass.

"Damn, really? What was it this time?"

"Some chicken bake Rachel Ray believes everyone can make. Well guess what, I'll be writing that lady a letter and shipping her my chicken meal just to prove her wrong. That'll teach her."

"Sure will." He laughs. "Sorry about your meal. Are you going for pizza or lobster bisque tonight?" See, this really isn't the first time he's caught me on a bad cooking night.

"Crackers and cheese. I'm too lazy to go grab something." I stand from my floor and prop the phone against the fruit bowl on my counter so I can start cleaning my kitchen while talking.

"When you say crackers and cheese do you mean—?"

"Goldfish and Cheez Whiz." I nod. "Yup, unfortunately it's a staple in my house."

Shaking his head, laughter in his features, he says, "I should have guessed. At least I've seen you eat this delicacy before and know you have the decency to squirt the cheese on the Goldfish."

"I'm not a monster." I chuckle. Then gasp as someone walks through my sliding glass door, scaring the crap out of me. "Oh Christ, you scared me."

"What?" Beck asks, seeming confused.

Before I can answer him, Oliver says, "Sorry about that, Rylee."

I cringe. There is no doubt in my mind Beck can hear that Oliver is here.

"Are you okay?" Oliver waves his hand in the air. "It's really smoky in here."

"Rylee?" Beck asks, sending a wave of nerves up my spine.

"Uh, yeah, just a cooking mishap." I turn to Beck and give him a quick smile. "Everything is good though."

Being the good guy he is, Oliver comes over to the kitchen and gives me a once-over before opening up my oven, sending another wave of smoke into the air. Oh for the love of God, please don't set off the alarm again.

Pulling out the chicken with an oven mitt, he takes in the

charred chick and says, "Damn, Rylee. What were you trying to do? Turn it into dust?"

Oliver is in clear view now to the phone, giving Beck quite the show as he moves around my kitchen, pouring some water on the chicken, and then taking it outside. "Let me handle this for you."

When he steps out of the kitchen, I turn to Beck and say, "Sorry, he must have heard the smoke alarm going off. He doesn't live very far from me." My explanation is cut off when the phone says poor connection, will resume shortly. Damn you, iPhone.

"There, that should do it." Oliver comes in the house with only an oven mitt in hand. "I left the chicken outside to cool off and remove the smell. Keep the windows open for at least an hour to help with the smoke and please, for the sake of the neighborhood, get your oven cleaned before you cook anything else. Something dripped to the bottom, and that's why there was so much smoke, like double the amount."

"Oh." I nod. "That's why she called for a bigger pan in the recipe."

Oliver shakes his head and squeezes my shoulder. "Stick to the writing, Rylee." He smiles his handsome smile, then takes off toward the sliding glass door. "Holler if you need anything."

"Sure, thanks." Feeling awkward, I turn back to my phone where Beck is waiting patiently, hands clasped in front of him, his forearms flexing from his grip.

Not knowing what to really do, I drop the apron on my counter, pick up the phone, and take it to the couch where I prop it up on my tucked-in knees. There's nothing I can do about the smoke but let it air out on its own, so I devote my time to Beck instead.

"Sorry about that." I wince, hoping . . . hell, I don't know what I hope. It's not like Beck and I are dating, but then again, we talk so much that I kind of feel like I owe him an explanation. "He is a volunteer firefighter—"

"I miss you." Beck's voice is gruff. He grips the back of his neck, pulling on it and rubbing it. "Damn it, Rylee, I miss you a whole fucking lot."

Well, that's not what I expected him to say, but I can't deny the little jump in my heart it's giving me.

"Do you miss me, Rylee? Or is this a one-sided feeling? Tell me now, because if you're not experiencing the same kind of feeling, I have to know. I don't want to keep calling you, and thinking about you every goddamn day, if you're not missing the hell out of me too."

As much as I want to deny my growing feelings for Beck, as much as for my heart's sake I should tell him no, there is no way I can tell him I don't miss him. It's a blatant lie. I feel sheer panic from the thought of him not calling me anymore. This is stupid. I spent a few days with him on an island and over a month with him on the phone, and yet, I feel this bond between us, this electric force pulling us together.

Biting on the inside of my cheek, I nod, unable to squeak the words out.

"No, Rylee. I need to hear it. I need you to tell me." There is a different tone to his voice, a . . . desperation about him that I've never heard before and what's really weird, is that I can feel the same desperation inside me.

Making eye contact with him, I say, "I miss you, too, Beck."

Briefly he shuts his eyes and exhales. "Thank fuck."

"Were you really that worried? Isn't it obvious I miss you?"

"Hell, I don't know, Rylee." He grumbles something as he rubs his hand over his face. "Fuck." Looking at me now, leaning forward, his stare cutting through me, he says, "Meet me somewhere."

"What?" My brow pulls together.

"Let's crash another wedding. Meet me somewhere, anywhere, and we can crash another wedding, maybe spend more time together, see where these feelings are taking us."

"Why crash another wedding?"

"Because, that's what we do." He says it so matter-of-factly, it's hard to give it a second thought.

"I don't know anyone getting married."

"That's the point. We could truly crash a wedding this time."

"But . . . how would we know where to go?"

A devilish smile passes over his lips. "That's easy, the wedding capital of the world. Vegas, baby."

"You want to go to Las Vegas to crash a wedding?" I raise my eyebrows in question. This might be the dumbest idea ever, but I'm actually entertaining the possibility.

"Yeah, why the hell not? We meet up, scour the wedding chapels, maybe take a few pictures with the bride and groom, do a little gambling, and then spend the rest of the time in our hotel room. Sounds like a fucking fantastic time to me."

"You're serious?" I don't know why I asked the question, because I can see it in his eyes. He's locked in on this idea.

"Completely serious. This Friday, let's do it."

"But . . ."

He chuckles. "While you wrack your mind for an excuse, I'm booking a flight." He stands from the couch, propping the phone up on something and quickly returns with a computer. His fingers furiously type across the keyboard.

"Beck, are you really booking a flight?"

Without saying a word, he turns the computer around for me to see the airline flight he's on. Oh my God, he's really doing it. "Better hurry up and get your computer, Saucy. Flights from Maine might be booking up." He looks up from his computer and says, "You know you want to see me."

Damn it, I do. Ever since we turned up the heat and I was ready to masturbate while he watched, I feel as though I've been on pins and needles. So horny. So frustrated. So needy . . . for him.

Gnawing on my lip for all but two seconds, I get up from my couch, grab my computer, and start searching through flights, the impulse decision sending a rush of excitement through me.

"That's my girl." There is a huge grin across Beck's face. *That grin.* I've come to love that grin. Am I really doing this? Are we really going to see if there is more between us than just the mini-vacay jaunt? *Yes. We are.* And to be honest, I love that he wants this. That he wants to see where our feelings lead us.

God, this is going to be so worth it.

"**N**ervous about flying?" the guy next to me asks as he sips from the stir straws of his drink.

"What? No." I shake my head.

"Oh, well it looks like it from the way your legs are bouncing up and down, as if they're trying to create turbulence."

I still my legs and release my grip on the armrests. I couldn't care less about flying. I never get nervous about slicing through the skies in a metal tube. No, the bounce of my legs and the death grip on my armrest is a result of "what the hell was I thinking?" syndrome.

You know when you decide to do something and think to yourself, *this is going to be the greatest thing ever!* And when the time comes for the *greatest thing ever* to happen, immediate questioning and regret pop into your head, drowning you in a roller coaster of "what the fuck am I doing?"

Yeah, I'm there. I'm drowning in my thoughts, questioning my sanity.

"Uh, no, not nervous."

The guy nods his head. "Good, good." He leans closer to me and stirs his drink, rum on his breath. "You know, I was upgraded to this seat. Fancy, huh?"

I eye him up and down, wishing I could sit farther away due to his cheap cologne searing my nostrils. "Oh yeah, that's cool."

"Yup, got the old upgrade." He sips loudly on his straw. "You know they give you free alcohol up here. Want me to order you something? It's on me." He winks, like a dweeb.

I hold up my hand. "I'm good, but thank you."

"Yeah, sure, anytime. I know the waitress. We're tight." He holds his crossed fingers up to me.

"Flight attendant. She is a flight attendant, not a waitress." He needs to be corrected, but doesn't seem to be fazed.

"Oh I know, just joshing around with you." He nudges me with his elbow. "You know, this is when you laugh."

I pick up my earbuds and hold them over my ears. "I laugh when a joke is actually funny." I put in my earbuds and turn up the music on my phone, starting a playlist I created after my Key West trip. The first song to play is *Havana*, the song Beck and I danced to at the wedding, the one where I swear the dance floor was ours and ours alone. Flashes of us plastered against each other play through my mind. His hands gliding up my thighs, his breath caressing my neck, his lips a whisper away from my skin.

Goosebumps break out over my arms and the tension starts to ease in my shoulders as I close my eyes and think of the man I'll be seeing shortly. It will be okay; this was a good idea. Maybe I can get one last fill and move on. Maybe that's all this is—one last hurrah. I bet after this weekend, we won't want to see each other anymore. *Won't I?*

Settling into my seat, I let out a pent-up breath and melt into the leather—

"I got you something." My earphone is yanked from my ear and the man next to me points to a drink beside me. Smiling, he repeats, "I got you something. I like to call it The Brad. Try it."

I eye the drink and then look back at this immature man who frankly shouldn't be touching any part of me. He crossed a line, and I'm about to let him know about it.

Taking my earbud back, and not in a kind way, I say, "Are you delusional? In what universe do you think I'm going to take a drink from you? First of all, I didn't want a drink. Second of all, how do I know you didn't tamper with it? And third of all—I lean in close, my eyes slicing him in half—"touch my earbuds again and I will take those straws out of your drink, pierce your balls with them, and serve them to the other first-class passengers as mini

238

shish ka-balls." To make my point clear, I add, "Leave me the fuck alone."

When he quivers backward, I feel a little bad. But then I tell myself he pushed his luck, so he deserves the little tongue-lashing. Turning toward the window now, I block him off and close my eyes, focusing on one thing. Beck.

～

I stare at my text messages as I ride the train through the Las Vegas Airport to baggage claim. When I turned my phone off airplane mode, I had two text messages waiting for me.

Beck: *Can't wait to fucking see you, Saucy.*

Beck: *Here. Waiting for you in baggage claim*

That last one set off a flutter of nerves, the nerves I thought I already kicked. It's real. It's not just talk over the phone or flirtatious texts. This is really happening. And I haven't told anyone.

Probably not a smart decision, but I couldn't make myself tell Zoey and Victoria. I didn't want to hear their ribbing, and I really didn't want to talk through my decision, because in my mind, I could see them trying to talk me out of it. And maybe I should have had them talk me out of it, given the unsteady situation between Beck and I, but I also feel like I need this wild streak to continue; I need to give myself another chance at throwing caution to the wind.

And that's exactly what this is.

The train stops and I follow the passengers through the exit and past a wall of security doors out into an open room where there are rows and rows of baggage claim carousels. I bite my bottom lip as I search the space, looking for Beck, and when my eyes land on him, my breath catches in my chest.

Leaning against a pole, one leg propped up, in all his sexy, six-foot-something glory, he stands, waiting for me. He's wearing tight-fitting black jeans, black boots, a loose white V-neck shirt, and a grey sock hat. When he spots me, he doesn't attempt to make a move. No, his eyes lock with mine, making a magnitude of promises I'm sure he won't fail to deliver on, and his trademark devilish smile takes over his face.

As I approach, he doesn't shift, and he doesn't even waiver. He waits for me, as if he wants me to make the first move.

Three steps.

Two steps

One.

"Hey," I breathe out, unsure of what to do with my hands.

He tilts his head to the side and pushes off the pillar, coming toe to toe with me. He doesn't say anything. The sounds of our beating hearts fill the silence as he reaches forward and pinches my chin with his index finger and thumb, bringing my mouth to his. It's a light but passionate kiss, his lips taking what they want with just enough pressure to make me want to beg for more.

Growling against my lips, he lifts away, revealing lust-filled hazel eyes, the same eyes I can't seem to erase from my dreams.

"Exactly how I remembered." He places one more kiss on my lips and pulls me into a hug. "I've missed you."

My cheek rests against his chest, his arms enveloping me into his warmth, and for the first time since I said goodbye to him all those weeks ago, I feel at ease, like all my worries are washing away, and I can live in this moment. *How does he do that to me?*

Being honest, I respond, "I missed you too."

"That's my girl." He kisses the top of my head and links my hand with his. Bending down, he picks up a small duffle bag that's at his feet and guides me to the carousel. "I'm going to assume you checked a bag, unless you decided to have a naked weekend in the hotel room, then I'm good with that."

I squeeze his hand, loving how this isn't awkward at all, almost as if we haven't skipped a beat since we parted. "I checked a bag. I'm here to crash weddings and nothing else."

Chuckling, that deep rumbly sound causing me to sigh, Beck says, "I would like to say nothing else is going to happen, but you and I both know that's not the truth." He presses his lips against my ear as he speaks low. "Because I'm going to tell you right now, the first chance I get, I'm going to sink my cock into you and fuck you. For hours."

The way he says the word fuck—with such confidence, such sensual, hidden promises—has my legs shaking beneath me.

Unable to speak, especially with Beck rubbing his thumb along my hand, I spot my baggage quickly and we make our way to the taxi line, which thankfully, isn't very long.

"Where to?" the driver asks. I'm about to open my mouth when I pause. I have no clue where we're headed. I didn't make any reservations.

But I don't have to worry for long. "The Bellagio." Leaning into me, he whispers, "My friend hooked us up."

The taxi takes off and Beck scoots as close to me as possible, his arm stretched out behind me.

"Good flight, Rylee?" he asks, so casually. It's impressive he can seem so chill, especially when I'm shaking with excitement and nerves.

"Sort of. Some college guy was trying to hit on me, I think."

"Is that right?" He chuckles. "Did you shut the poor bastard down?"

"Quickly."

"Man, I feel bad for him."

"Why?" I turn slightly to look at Beck. His scruff looks even thicker, and those lips of his, God, I want to feel them all over my body.

"Because, if I was shut down by you, I'm pretty sure I would cry myself to sleep."

I roll my eyes and playfully knock him in the stomach. "Please, you'd move on to the next girl."

"Yeah, you're right. I would have gone after Victoria."

"What?" Now I turn completely in my seat. *He what?* Beck's laughter carries through the cab. "Are you serious? You would have gone after Victoria if I'd turned you down?"

"Nah, but it's damn sexy seeing that fiery spirit in you again."

241

Infuriating man.

We get checked in to our hotel, and I faintly hear the words suite when the clerk at the front desk speaks to Beck. Just how good of a deal did we receive from Beck's friend? In the elevator to our high-rise floor, we exchange glances, Beck's fingers delicately tracing my back, working their way up and down my spine, slipping under my shirt then below my waistline. I suck in a harsh breath when he starts to play with the lace of my thong.

Tug and snap then a gentle rub of his finger. It's on constant repeat, sending my mind into a whirl of sensations. And thanks to the man in front of us, I'm forced to be on my best behavior.

The elevator stops at our floor and we scoot past the unwelcome passenger, down the hall to our room, where Beck pushes the keycard in to open the door for me. I brush past him, catching his masculine cologne as I walk by. For a moment, I temporarily forget about the sensual attack Beck made on me, and I'm caught up in the beauty of the room.

Windows run the expanse of the large wall, giving a picture-perfect view of the city lights. To the right is a giant bed, fluffy and white, and to the left is a small sitting area and bar. The room is decorated in tans and browns, with touches of black. It's clean and crisp and beautiful.

Stepping behind me, Beck puts his hands on my shoulders and starts to lower them down my arms. His lips press against my neck, and my body starts to tingle with awareness.

"I'm going to take a shower and get ready. I have dinner plans for us, and I've scoped out some wedding chapels. Do you need to shower before we leave?" He kisses my neck again and I'm a little stunned. Don't get me wrong, I'm ready for dinner, my stomach could use something in it, but I thought the minute we stepped foot in this hotel room, Beck would strip me down and make me feel so incredibly good.

But when he parts from me and takes his duffle bag to the bathroom, I'm proven wrong.

The shower sounds off through the partially open door. Beck

was serious? We're . . . getting ready to go out? As I hear him move around in the bathroom, getting in the shower, I contemplate if I should simply shower with him. Is that too bold? To invite myself in?

We only spent one night exploring each other's bodies. I haven't seen him in over a month, so would it be super weird? *Does he want me in the shower with him?*

I nibble on my finger, my suitcase handle in hand, trying to figure out what to do. Deciding to take things slow since we've only reunited, I take my suitcase to the luggage stand and open it up to let my clothes air. Carefully I unfold the black, sequined dress I brought for wedding crashing and lay it on the back of a chair to avoid wrinkles. Next, I pull out my cosmetic bags and grip them to my chest as I take a peek into the bathroom. I can't see anything but billowing steam. How hot does he have the water?

Maybe the shower is partitioned off. Contemplating taking my cosmetics into the bathroom, I decide it won't hurt if I slip in quickly, cast my eyes down, and set my bags on the counter.

Yes, that's exactly what I'll do.

Head held high, plan in place, I slip into the bathroom, keeping my eyes turned down . . . just in time for me to hear a light groan come from the shower directly behind me.

Because my eyes are curious—and don't listen to my brain—I glance in the mirror. And what a sight. A dark outline of Beck's incredible body. I cast my eyes down, focusing on the marble countertop of the vanity. I shouldn't be looking. I should leave. It was supposed to be a quick drop and go, but . . .

I peek up again and notice Beck hunched over, one hand propping his body up against the tile, the other at his waist.

My mouth goes dry as I watch him slowly pump himself, his groan echoing through the bathroom, the steam and sounds coming from him heating my entire body. Like a voyeur, feet cemented to the tile beneath me, I stare into the mirror and watch his silhouette pump his length. Up and down, up and down.

A low ache starts to thrum between my legs, the need for him building, my will for leaving slipping.

I hear him grumble something I can't quite make out, but it sounds a lot like my name, which pulls me toward the shower. On shaky legs, I kick off my shoes and socks, my body moving automatically, my hand reaching for the handle of the shower door.

T-shirt and shorts on, I open the shower door, and the cold air must pull Beck's attention in my direction. Pained eyes meet mine, his hand stills on his cock, and his back muscles ripple from the tension building inside him. He's so gloriously naked, sinew wrapped around the sturdy bones of his body, enticing me inside. Water be damned. I step up from behind him and bring my hands to his back where I hook them around his stomach, and his abs flicker beneath my palms with each inch I lower to his hard-on. I'm silent as I kiss his wet body, his back tight against my mouth, his hand parting from his length, giving me the access I want. With both of his hands leaning against the tile in front of him now, he braces himself as I move my hands to his center.

I grab his hard-as-rock cock and grip the base tightly, rotating my hand, making sure to move my thumb up and down his stiff veins. A low hiss escapes him, and when I grab his balls with the other hand, he bucks against me. I hold him tightly, giving him no wiggle room, as I roll his balls back and forth in my palm, his cock cut off at the root, my squeeze like a vise, trying to pool the blood at the tip as I slowly move my hand to the head. I don't pump. I don't rub. I squeeze and at a snail's pace move upward.

"Fucking hell, Rylee. Goddamn it." His fist pounds against the tile of the shower, his muscles in his back tensing even more. I continue to move my hand up, my other hand rapidly rolling his balls.

"Rylee, please, fuck, I can't take this."

I kiss his back and continue to move my hand up, my squeeze growing tighter with each pass. His breathing becomes labored, and his cock twitches in my hand, as he leans his brow against the tile. When I reach the bottom of the head, I twist my hand at the base.

"Fuck!" he shouts and stands tall, removing my hands. When he spins around, his cock looks heavy, ready to burst, and his eyes look murderous.

He doesn't give me a chance to make a move because he's on me before I can reach out for him again. He plasters my arms against the tile of the shower, bits of water bouncing off his back. Leaning forward, he nips at my lips, pulling on them, giving me no other option but to let him take charge. When he pulls away, he says, "Keep your hands here, Rylee."

Reaching for my shorts, he undoes them and drags them down my legs along with my lace thong. He leaves them on the ground and slowly moves his hands up my legs, past my hips, to the hem of my shirt where he peels the wet fabric off my body.

"We were supposed to wait," he grumbles, working my bra off as well, freeing my nipples as he immediately starts to tweak them with his fingers. I breathe out heavily when he pinches both at the same time. "I had plans of fucking you all over this hotel room tonight, but not right now."

"Why not . . . now?" I practically yelp when he squeezes my boob with his entire palm.

"Because, I don't think after tasting you again I'll be able to leave this hotel room."

Yeah, he might be right about that. It's going to be pretty damn hard.

"Well, you're the one who was jacking off without me."

"To get through the fucking night," he mumbles against my skin. "Seeing you again, fuck, Rylee. It's doing something to my body, something dangerous. I had to take care of myself, to relieve some of the tightness inside me in order to make it through the night with you."

"You should have asked me to help." I move my head to the side as his lips work up and down my neck, my core tingling with need.

"The surprise was better." He lowers his hands and presses a finger against my clit. He slides in easily. "Shit, Saucy. You're ready."

"I was ready the minute I saw you in the airport." And that's the truth, because him leaning against the pole is an image I won't forget for a very long time.

Growling, he hoists me around his waist, spins us around, and presses me against the opposite end of the shower. His erection presses against my ass as I squeeze my legs tightly around him, holding me up since he's once again pinned my arms above me.

He moves his hands down my body, his thumbs rubbing against the side of my breasts as he ravages me with his mouth. Parting my lips, he slips his tongue inside and plunges forward, so aggressive, so needy, so male. *So Beck.*

Everything about Beck is male from the way he's taking me against the tile of the shower, to his hardened cock so thick and enticing, to the way his mouth takes control, moving his tongue expertly against mine.

"Are you on the pill?"

"What? Yes," I mutter, my mind unable to truly comprehend what he's asking until he grunts and lifts my hips up, his cock pressed at my center.

"Tell me now if you don't want this."

Is he insane? Looking him in the eyes, I say, "I need this."

Wasting no time, he brings me down on his cock. Our foreheads press together, our breathing both erratic as I adjust around his girth. I don't remember him being this big. Hell, I don't remember it being this intense, like every nerve ending in my body is set on fire and no amount of water will be able to extinguish the blaze inside me.

"So full," I breathe out.

"So tight," he replies, his voice strained. "I won't last long."

He pumps his hips into me. My body rubs along the tile wall, his mouth is on mine, his tongue busy flicking across mine, and his hands? They're all over my body, searing my skin with each touch.

Relentless.

Slow.

Fast.

A rhythmic pattern of his cock hitting me in just the right spot.

Pulse after pulse.

Toes curling, nipples hardening, deep groans.

My body numbs, my stomach bottoms out, my clit pounds, yearning for release.

"Oh God, yes, more."

Pump after pump.

Groaning, biting, scraping.

Fingertips across my skin, pinching my nipples.

"Fuck," he says, his dick is so hard inside me.

One rub.

Two.

Three . . .

"Yes," I scream as I convulse around him, his dick stilling as he releases right along with me, his cock pulsing inside me.

Light like a feather, my body floats down from my orgasm, tremors ratcheting through me, small little pulses shooting around my nerves.

Head on his shoulder, I catch my breath as he lowers me to the ground. My legs shake. He pulls me into a hug and holds me tightly for a few moments before separating us and grabbing a bar of soap.

What the hell was that?

I've never felt that good.

So sated.

Relaxing into his touch, for the first time ever, I let a man soap me up. It's as if I've been waiting. Waiting for the right man, the man I can trust, and the man I can give myself to freely.

Beck.

"Are you almost ready, Saucy? I'm about to demolish my damn shoe if we don't eat soon."

I fluff my hair one more time and check my lipstick to make sure it's all in place. We might have missed our reservation for dinner due to unforeseen sexual activities, but Beck assured me he'd rather spend the time fucking me than eating dinner. After round three, my stomach grumbled and Beck slapped me on the ass, sending me to the bathroom to get ready.

The plan was to get ready, eat and crash weddings, but after the shower, there was no way we were going to be able to move out of this hotel room without making up for lost time. *Again.* And when he was groaning into my ear from behind, his release taking over the both of us, I couldn't agree more. We needed a little fucking before we could move forward.

I pat down my dress and do a little turn in the mirror to check out my backside. I love how low the dress dips, low enough to make any man lustful. It's so Vegas, so scandalous, and the perfect dress to drive Beck crazy. Especially after seeing him in his black button-up shirt and black slacks, looking sexy as sin.

Taking a deep breath, I walk out of the bathroom and find Beck on a chair, his legs wide, and his forearms resting on his knees as he stares at his phone. When he looks up, he does a quick double take and a slow smile spreads over his lips. Standing and pocketing his phone, he walks toward me, a swagger in every step forward.

Gripping my hips, his eyes then rake over me with hot perusal, his pupils darkening with each pass. "You're trying to get me into trouble tonight, aren't you, Saucy?"

"Whatever do you mean?" I play with the open collar of his shirt, marveling at his bronze skin.

"This dress is going to get me in trouble with every man on the strip tonight." Leaning forward and pressing a light kiss across my lips, he says, "I take no responsibility for any fights I get into."

"There will be no fighting." I walk past him when he catches my wrist and his eyes soften.

"You look gorgeous, Rylee."

My heart sputters in my chest as I feel my cheeks blush. Shyly, I reply, "Thank you."

We take a moment, and an unknown electricity bounces between us, an awareness I've never felt with another man before. I like him . . . a lot, and that's scary.

I shouldn't like him, but I can't help it. I'm drawn to him. I'm addicted to making him smile, and now, to feeling him pulse inside me. And I'm addicted to his mind, the way he lives life so freely, like every day is his last. It's refreshing.

"Come on"—he nods toward the door—"before I rip that dress off you and we do nothing tonight but tangle each other up in the sheets."

"Nothing wrong with that." I give him a wink and pick up my small clutch on the way to the door, Beck trailing closely behind.

After some debating in the elevator about where to eat, we end up hitting a lobster joint called Lobster Me inside the shops by Planet Hollywood. Beck says his friend's husband swears by their rolls. Being from Maine, where lobster is plucked from the sea in the morning and served on your plate that night for dinner, I'm skeptical, especially since Nevada is a land-locked state.

"Come on, admit it, Rylee. This shit is good." Beck takes another giant bite of his lobster roll, his jaw working the food around. Call me crazy, but watching him eat is arousing.

"I'm not sure," I answer, taking another bite of the lobster roll, loving how the flavors pop on my tongue.

"You're such a liar."

Okay, I'm a liar. I admit it; the lobster roll is fucking good. It's more than good, because it's one of the best I've had. And what a sin for me to admit such a thing. I was born and raised in Maine, and not just Maine, but on the coast where I've caught lobster myself. I shouldn't like this lobster roll, I should turn my nose up at it. But holy shit, I can't stop eating it.

"Ha!" Beck pokes my lip where it's turned up. "You like it and you know it. You want another one, don't you?"

I'm halfway through my first lobster roll and, yes, it's crossed my mind to grab another, because that's how good these are.

Ugh, I'm a sham of a woman. I shouldn't be able to return to Maine. My parents will disown me if they find out.

"I mean, it's good." I try to play it casual but Beck can see right through me.

"Yeah, okay. I'll go order another one to split."

"Extra grilled bun," I call out as Beck walks toward the register, his laugh shifting his shoulders up and down.

I'm such a shame to my home state. Thank God, I have this delicious lobster roll to comfort me.

"Have you been to Vegas before?" I ask Beck as we walk to the Vegas Wedding Chapel, well known for their Elvis weddings.

"Maybe too many times, especially when I was younger." His jaw turns tight and I can see the change in his features when he mentions his past. "What about you?"

"A few times for author signings. Spent many a night at Chippendales."

"Love that show. Can't get enough of men's dicks in small fabric slings."

"What?" I laugh. "You've been to a Chippendales show?"

He holds the door open to me and nods. "Yeah, I've done it all, Saucy. Maybe a little too much."

"So does that mean you want to catch a Chippendales show with me?"

"Not even a little."

He kisses the side of my head and directs his attention to the woman at the front desk. It's hard to take her seriously given the Dolly Parton hairdo, the blaring, bright pink blazer, and neon-blue eyeshadow. My eyes are almost watering from the bright, *slightly* over-the-top ensemble. *Welcome to Vegas!*

"Hello, are we getting married tonight?"

The question catches me off guard. I never thought of going to a wedding chapel with Beck and being mistaken for an eager bride to marry her man, but here we are.

Squeezing my shoulder, Beck says, "We've been married for five years actually. We came here to watch our friends, Becca and Charles, get married. I'm Frank, and this is Bitsy, we're super excited to be here."

Becca and Charles. Who the hell are they? And Frank and Bitsy? Good God.

"Oh how wonderful, their ceremony is about to start, so go ahead and sneak right in."

"Thank you." Beck takes my hand in his and guides me through the chapel doors.

"Who the hell are Becca and Charles?" I whisper, scooting into a pew next to Beck. When we sit down, he wraps his arm over my shoulder and pulls me in close.

"No idea," he answers on a whisper. "Just saw the names scrolled on the schedule in front of her."

I turn to look him in the eyes. "Are you really that stealth?"

He wiggles his eyebrows at me. "You have no idea who you're hanging out with, Saucy."

And isn't that the scary truth? I feel like I know him, especially after our month of phone conversations, but I know there is a darker side to him I don't know, a side that's been instrumental in shaping who he is today. A side I desperately want to find out about.

Before I can question him, wedding bells chime and Elvis steps up to the altar and starts belting out a song as the bride and groom walk down the aisle together. Beck twiddles his fingers in their direction as they walk by, pulling a confused look from both of them.

Oh hell. Looks like it's going to be one of those nights again.

"Dr. Pelican and Gloria here for the Barclay wedding," Beck says, putting one hand in his pocket, looking rather dignified.

"Yes, they're over in chapel two. Flamingo hats are on the right, so be sure to put one on before you enter the chapel."

"Oh perfect." Beck presses his hand against his chest in relief. "We left our flamingo hats back at the hotel and I was worried."

"We got you covered," the receptionist answers, her eyes making a dangerous perusal of Beck.

"Come on, sugarplum." Beck presses his hand at the opening of my lower back. "Time to get our bird on."

When we walk away, I lean into Beck and say, "She was totally checking you out."

"Really? I didn't notice, as I kind of had my eyes glued to your cleavage." He presses a kiss against my temple and hands me a flamingo hat. He puts his on and flaps fake wings. "Kaw-Kaw!"

I snort laugh and cover my nose. "I don't think flamingos make that noise."

"They sure as hell stand on one leg and flap their wings though." And to demonstrate his flamingo skills, he does just that, making me laugh all too hard.

"Mr. and Mrs. Gentry, you can sit right here." The usher sits us in a pew behind two beautifully perfect drag queens and a Dolly Parton impersonator.

"Thank ya, kind sir," Beck says in a thick southern accent, tipping a felt cowboy hat he bought from a vendor on the street.

"Anytime. Looking forward to your debut album."

"That's awfully kind of ya." He points at the usher. "Keep that autograph. In a few years it will be worth something."

"I will, sir."

The poor usher will be scouring iTunes trying to find Max Gentry. He might be pissed when he comes up short.

"You're absurd," I whisper. Taking in the setup of the wedding around us, and from the hot pink scattered all over the chapel, I actually think this wedding is going to be a good one.

From the side of the chapel, the groom appears in the brightest pink suit I've ever seen and looking so incredibly happy. I'm going to take a wild guess here and say he's one hell of a guy trying to make his girl happy, and that's all around sweet.

The doors behind us open and a woman in white with hot pink flowers appears. She looks beautiful with her hair flowing around her shoulders, flowers pinned in the tendrils. The Wedding March begins, but is quickly cut out when she motions to her neck to stop the music.

Oh boy . . . this is going to be good. The scene from *The Office* pops into my head where all the characters dance down the aisle at Pam and Jim's wedding. A smile crosses my face as I prepare for the entrance of a lifetime.

But when I think Vegas showgirls are about to burst through the doors as well, I'm utterly mistaken. With the bouquet clutched to her chest, the bride slowly—and I mean slowly—walks down the aisle . . . humming Mendelssohn's infamous Wedding March.

Yes, humming.

Humming to her little heart's content, as loud as can be.

And just when I don't think it could get any stranger, the groom joins in, swaying back and forth, hands linked in front of him.

They hum in unison, eyes locked together, their pitch off, making for an interesting rendition.

That is until Beck joins in next to me. Eyes wide, I turn to him in shock when the drag queens in front of us join in as well and before we know it, the entire chapel is humming together.

Well, okay then. This is by far, one of the weirdest weddings I've ever been to.

N ope.
Nope, nope, nope.

I take that back. THIS is by far the weirdest wedding I've ever attended.

The elderly couple dressed in leather and whips walk down the aisle together as their attendees cheer them on. Next to me, Beck claps and then performs a congratulatory whistle, really getting into it.

When the couple reaches Beck, the balding groom grabs Beck by the back of the neck and says, "Thank you for being here, Pastor Rick."

"I wouldn't have missed it for the world," Beck replies before placing a rough kiss on the groom's head. Leaning past his newfound friend, Beck says, "Edith, you give our boy Erwin here a run for his money tonight, you hear me?"

She points her finger at Beck. "You know I will." Waving at me, she says, "Bye, Marni. Good luck with stripper school; we know you'll do great." Yeah, can you guess who came up with my back-story, once again.

"Thank you and congratulations," I add.

Turning away from us, arm and arm, Edith and Erwin walk off into "the sunset" in assless chaps, their wrinkly old butts swaying back and forth to the music.

Jesus Christ.

I rub a hand over my face. I think my wedding crashing days are soon to be over. Pretty sure I've seen it all.

Once Edith and Erwin are gone, Beck takes my hand and says, "Ice cream?" He says it so casually, as if we didn't just experience a mind-blowing, freaky bondage-type wedding with two old coots.

"You want ice cream? After watching Edith and Erwin's wrinkly butts walk away?"

He shrugs. "Nothing wrong with assless chaps at a wedding. Just means they're marrying the right person for them."

And there he goes, being insightful again.

"You are amazing to me, you know that? Always seeing the good in people, no matter what situation you're in."

"Because there's no need to focus on the negative, it only brings you down." He pulls on my hand. "Come on, Saucy, I'm dying for some mint chocolate chip ice cream."

"Can we get waffle cones?" I ask, trailing behind him.

"Do you even need to ask?" He winks at me and ushers me toward the strip, carefree and handsome as ever.

Part Four

THE TRUTH

CHAPTER TWENTY

BECK

R ylee rustles in the bed, her arms stretching to the headboard. Her little whimpering sounds as she stretches are cute.

When I invited Rylee to Vegas, I really threw the whole wedding crasher suggestion in there to give me an excuse to see her, and even though it was tiring to go from chapel to chapel, trying not to get caught, it was worth it. The amount of times I got to hear Rylee's laugh was beyond perfect.

It's weird that seeing her again in person is stirring up all sorts of feelings, feelings I haven't experienced in a really long time. There is something different about Rylee I can't put my finger on, but whatever it is, I want more.

We both leave tomorrow, back to our opposite sides of the country. Thinking about it rips me apart. It feels like I just got her back, and I'm not ready to say goodbye. Part of me worries that when we do, she'll try to cut me off again like she did last time. I'm not sure I can allow that, not with the connection I share with this woman. *I want more.*

I take a sip of my orange juice and look out the window, taking in the daylight that casts a dirty glow over the city. Las Vegas during the day almost looks like someone stuck a city on Mars. It has an orange glow about it, dusty and dingy looking. But at night, when the lights are gleaming, sin befalls you, and it's an entirely different place.

Soft footsteps approach, and I see Rylee wrapped in a white terrycloth bathrobe, the one I left by the bed for her, walking toward me. Without prompting her, she curls up on my lap, tucking her head in the crook of my neck. I hold her tightly against me, loving how she fits perfectly in my arms.

"What time is it?" she mumbles, her cheek resting on my bare chest. I'm wearing my slacks from last night and they're unbuckled.

"Noon."

She props her head up. "Seriously?"

I nod. "Yeah, you slept in pretty late." We didn't get back to the hotel until past midnight and even then we didn't go to bed right away. I might have spent a few hours worshipping Rylee's body until we passed out.

"You wore me out." She nuzzles against me again and I hold on to her tighter.

"If you're looking for an apology, you won't be getting one."

"Ruthless." I love the feel of her smile against my chest.

I kiss the top of her head and say, "I ordered breakfast. It came about twenty minutes ago, but it's probably cold by now."

"It's okay, I'll eat pretty much anything. I want to snuggle a little longer first."

Hell, I'm not going to complain about that. We rest together, my hand leisurely stroking her hair, her fingers playing with the short stubble on my chest, our breaths synching, our hearts beating as one.

It's the most at peace I've ever felt.

"Do you have any regrets in life?"

I still. *That* question is so unexpected and any peace I felt dissipates. In its place is anxiety, which slowly creeps up the back of my neck. I have so many regrets. The question really shouldn't be if I have any. The question should be how many do I have, and how many altered my life?

Not wanting to get into details, I answer, "I know I seem like a guy who would say something like regrets are what help shape us as humans, but that would be lying. I have some big regrets, some moments in my life I wish I could take back. There's no doubt about that." And to deter her away from those regrets, I ask her, "What about you?"

She pauses, regarding my question. "I mean, I had small regrets that seem ridiculous now like not hiring an editor for the first few months of being an author instead of trying to do everything myself, but big regrets that have shaped me? I don't think so."

"You don't seem like the type to harbor regrets."

"And you are?" Back to me. I knew that was too easy.

I lick my lips and try to think of the best way to put this. "There's an air of darkness that looms over me. I might live life to its fullest, but if you look closely, you'll see regret in my everyday movements. It's like a weight I have to carry around day in and day out. But when I look at you, I don't see that same darkness. I see"—I pause and study her for a second—"a beautifully intelligent woman, maybe a woman with a hint of sadness eclipsing her."

Propping herself up, hand to my chest, she looks me in the eyes and says, "You see sadness?"

I place my finger under her chin and nod. "I do. I don't see it all the time, but there are moments where I've seen . . . sorrow. I'm not sure where it stems from, but what I do know is when you let go, when you let yourself have fun, it disappears and your eyes are clear, full of laughter. It's the way I like seeing you the best, such fucking joy exuding from you."

"And your happiness, is it clouded?"

I press my lips together and close my eyes, my cheek leaning against the top of her head, the smell of her hair melting my muscles.

"It's not clouded when you're around," I answer boldly, but honestly.

She stills in my arms, and I worry I've crossed a line, but when she presses her cheek back against my chest, I relax.

~

Rylee enters from the bathroom, freshly showered, hair wet, still wearing that damn robe. I planned on taking a shower with her but when her editor called about her story, I took a quick shower and left the room to give her some privacy.

"Hey, there you are." She walks toward me, scrunching her wet hair, her tanned legs peeking out past the robe. "Where did you go off to?"

I take her in my arms and plant a light kiss on her lips, my hands playing with the tie of her robe. "Just for a little walk. Thought I'd give you some privacy."

"You didn't have to do that."

"Needed the fresh air."

She cups my cheek. "Is everything okay?"

"Yeah, everything is good." I smile and bring her to the couch where I sit her on my lap and play with her wet hair, twisting it over my finger. "Do you know what you want to do tonight? Maybe crash some more weddings?"

She shakes her head. "I think I'm crashed out. Would it be weird to stay in for the night? Order room service?"

"Hell no. Staying in works for me." All I want is to soak in as much Rylee as I can before tomorrow, before I have to say goodbye for a while again.

"Perfect." She presses her cheek against my chest once again, her legs hanging over my lap, her hair dampening my shirt. She sighs, melting into me.

Clearing my throat, I decide to ask her a question that I can't seem to take my mind off. "So, about this Oliver guy. You close with him?"

She chuckles in my arms and presses a kiss against my collarbone. "We grew up together, went to the same school, hung out on occasion, see each other regularly when we pass each other in town, but close? No, not really. More cordial than anything, possibly friends, but more cordial. Why, are you jealous?"

"Yeah," I answer honestly, "I am. I'm jealous this mother fucker gets to see you almost every day and I only get stolen moments." The day I watched him walk into her kitchen as if he belonged there was torture. I haven't been able to ask her about him. I haven't known what she really thinks about me, about us, *if there is really an us*. So, asking her about the guy she's clearly very comfortable around, the guy Zoey thinks might be into her, yeah, fuck that. I want an *us*. I want more, so yeah, I've been jealous. I know what it's like to feel as if I'm not the one. Not enough.

"Beck." She sighs heavily, and I have a feeling I'm not going to like what I hear next. "What are we really doing?" She lifts her head and smooths some stray strands of hair out of her face. "I get that there is this heavy attraction between us, the kind of attraction you don't experience very often, but is that all there is?"

"No." My jaw tenses from irritation. Is that all she feels? Attraction? "There is a hell of a lot more than just attraction on my end. I feel something for you, Rylee. I have a genuine interest in your life, how your day goes. I crave to talk to you every damn day because I care about you. To me, that's more than just attraction. If I was *only* attracted to you, I wouldn't have taken time off to come see you. I wouldn't be jumping at the sound of my phone every time it beeps, hoping it's you." I scrape my hand down my face, my frustration showing. "I didn't come here this weekend to get laid, Rylee. I came here to see *you*. I text you every day to talk to *you*. I FaceTime you every damn day to see *you*. I'm trying to keep myself immersed in your life from three thousand miles away because I want *you*."

She gives her head a shake and pushes against my chest, sitting up to face me. "Don't you think it's lust driving your actions? You can't possibly be interested in the long run." *That's where she's wrong.*

"I'm interested in the long run," I answer her, looking her square in the eyes.

Her mouth parts, her eyes searching mine. "But there is so much we don't know about each other."

"Then ask me," I shout, my frustration pouring over. "Fucking ask me anything you want."

She tries to scoot off my lap but I don't let her. If we're going to talk, then we're going to talk while we're sitting as close as possible.

Still keeping her distance, she twines her hands together in her lap and softly asks, "Who's Christine?"

Without skipping a beat, I answer, "My ex-wife." To convince Rylee to stay with me, to make this work, I'm going to have to be open and honest with her. I hope she doesn't end up being disgusted with me after.

"You were married before?"

I nod. "For two years. We got married right out of high school. Our families weren't supportive, but we were young and at the time, I thought I was in love. We were foolish, naïve, and immature. After the first year, it went downhill."

"What happened?"

I run my palm up her thigh, my heart pounding dreadfully hard in my chest. "We struggled and when you struggle and are immature, you don't quite fight like adults, or solve problems like adults. We were short on cash every month, we weren't supportive, we didn't have goals, we were the perfect combination of what not to do in a marriage."

"You were toxic for each other."

I nod, continuing my gentle touch against Rylee, pulling courage from her. "Exactly. More toxic than you could imagine. It got to the point that I would end up drinking every night when I got home from my piece-of-shit job."

"You weren't painting then?"

I shake my head. "No, I was working some shitty job at a moving company. It was a complete waste of my life, not at all what I wanted to be doing. But lust clouded my vision, and I ended up in a shitty situation I couldn't get out of." I swallow hard and rub the back of my neck, the next confession is a hard one to share, a difficult part of myself to reveal. "I started drinking a lot. We started drinking a lot. The fights we would get into . . ." I shake my head. "They were volatile, ugly, and so shameful. The names we called each other, the things we said about each other." I bite my bottom lip and Rylee presses her hand against my cheek, her thumb rubbing over my skin.

"Take your time," she whispers, understanding that there's more.

"She started cheating on me. She sent picture after picture of the guys she was with, sent me videos of her banging some random man in a bar bathroom. It spurred me on to drink more. I started drinking during the day, while at work, and the smell of alcohol wasn't easy to hide. I was caught and fired."

Her face grows softer with concern. "I never cheated on her, ever. I said vows, and I held them close to my heart. I didn't touch her after she started cheating though, but what's sad is, I didn't know how to get out of the never-ending circle of hell I was living in. I don't know why she didn't leave me. She didn't want me, so why stay? Why cheat? Why? So I drank more and fought. That was my life, drinking and fighting."

"That's no way to live."

"Tell me about it." I press my fingers into her hips, holding her in place, stilling her for the next part of this story. "One night, Christine came home after sending me the usual disgusting photos, and I was so angry. I was drunk off my ass, we got in a huge fight, and I took off." I pause and take a breath. "I still remember climbing in the car, thinking I shouldn't be driving, I should sleep it off, but I was so goddamn mad that I turned the ignition and drove. I can remember it so vividly: the red light I ran; the bright lights heading my way; the sound of the metal crunching; the brutal force of the airbag slamming into my face." My heart is beating a mile a minute. I chance a look at Rylee and instead of judgment, I see is understanding . . . compassion in her eyes. I feel . . . relief.

She urges me to continue, resting her head on my chest, her hand playing with the fabric of my shirt, her fingers dancing over my erratically beating heart.

"I hit a mother on her way to pick up her son from a slumber party. He got scared and asked to be picked up." My throat grows tight as I recollect the night that changed my entire life. I shake my head, squeezing my eyes shut. "She never had the chance to pick him up. She . . . she died on impact." Rylee quietly gasps, her fingers gripping my shirt tightly. "I can remember sitting on a gurney, EMTs trying to tend to me, but I was only able to focus on the lifeless body being pulled from the car." I clear my throat. "I was tried and convicted of vehicular manslaughter and sentenced to six years in prison."

"You went to prison?"

I nod. "Yeah, and it wasn't fucking pretty. Everything they talk about on shows and documentaries is true. The first day I was there, I was jumped. I had to show I could hold my own, which I did . . . for the most part. The first year, I kept to myself, not responding to anyone. I was angry and reeling, craving alcohol. It wasn't until I met Cal, my sponsor, that I started to make a change for the good. He told me I was going to leave prison at some point, and when I did I had a choice between two paths. I could go back to the person I was, never fulfilling life to its fullest, or I could rise above and make a difference."

Quietly, Rylee says, "And you rose above."

"Not right away," I answer honestly. "But after a few more conversations with Cal, I decided to start participating in some of the educational opportunities prison offered. I learned to speak Spanish fluently, I read every inspirational book that crossed my path, and that changed my focus to philanthropic endeavors. I found a great passion for art, the kind of passion I carried on past prison. Cal saw my talent and called one of his friends at the zoo and recommended me for some part-time work. Because of Cal's recommendation, once I left prison, I was hired and my life changed for the better. I've spent every waking moment trying to be a better person, trying to make things better for the little boy who lost his mom. I'm on a waitlist through the court for a request to be put in contact with him, to apologize, but I doubt he will want to talk with me. I wouldn't blame him."

"I don't know what to say," Rylee says quietly. *Tell me you won't leave me. Tell me you still want to be with me now that you know the truth of my past. Tell me you'll stay.* "It's such a heartbreaking story, but one of hope too."

I kiss the top of her head, feeling a sense of relief from how understanding she is, at least how understanding she sounds. "I know I've come a long way, but there isn't a day that goes by that I don't think about the woman I killed or the son she left behind. I strive to be a better person for them."

She shakes her head, her voice sounding sullen when she speaks. "I can't imagine the type of weight you carry on your shoulders, the responsibility of living out your life in the honor of someone else. Just heartbreaking." She takes pause and then asks, "What happened with Christine?"

"Divorced a few months after the accident. Haven't heard from her since."

"Not even once?"

"Nope." I shake my head. "And I prefer it that way. That part of my life is in the past and I refuse to revisit it. Every step I take is forward, never backward."

"That's a beautiful way of seeing life."

In silence, we sit, my past now hanging heavily over us, the tension in the room starting to grow thick with every word that goes unsaid. Even though she seems empathetic, more needs to be said. I need reassurance that everything is going to be okay, that she's not going to run.

Gnawing on my bottom lip, my arm tightening around her, making sure she can't escape, I say, "Tell me what you're thinking." I have to know. I have to fucking know if she thinks differently of me, if I just ruined any chance I had at being with this woman.

"The pictures you paint, who are those people?"

I shut my eyes, mentally counting all the personal pictures I've painted over the last few years ranging from children to adults. "They're victims of alcohol abuse. People I've met over the last few years, people I've had the honor of speaking with. I have all their stories written in a notebook that I read through at least once a month, reminding myself of the grave and long-term effects careless drinking has on individuals. It's one more way I can remind myself of staying on the straight and narrow."

"Do you still crave alcohol?"

"No." I take a second and add, "I've devoted a lot of my free time to educating youth, talking about my experience, what I've done, how I've affected others with my poor decisions. I'm often a guest speaker at AA meetings, telling my story, spreading the word that there is life after alcohol."

She nods and lets out a long breath. My anxiety increases with every long bout of silence. It's not often I talk about my story with someone I know, about the mistakes I've made, so telling Rylee everything has me quaking beneath her.

I want her to tell me it's going to be okay.

I want her to accept my faults.

I need her to not give a damn about the man I once was and instead care about the man I am today.

To be honest, I never thought I'd find someone important enough to open up to, but now that I'm here, laying all my cards on the table, I've never been more terrified.

Standing in front of the judge, listening to my sentencing was nothing compared to the fear I'm feeling right now. I've come to rely on this woman, to depend on her smile to brighten my day. From her witty sense of humor, to her throaty laugh that makes me want to dive into her soul, I need it in my life. I need her.

"Rylee," I say, my voice strained, my throat so damn tight I'm not sure how I'm able to speak. "I need you to say something, babe. I need you to cut the silence."

She shifts on my lap and lifts off my chest, skyrocketing my pulse to an unbearable rate. Is she leaving?

Lifting her head slowly, she reveals streaks of tears falling down her cheek. With the back of her hand, she wipes them away.

"W-why are you crying?" I ask, stumbling over my words.

"I'm sorry." She gives her head a shake, leaning farther back.

Fuck.

Fuck, she's retreating.

"Just listen, Rylee. I know I'm an alcoholic, but I have it under control, I don't crave—"

She presses her fingers against my lips, silencing me, more tears streaming down her cheeks. Cupping my cheeks, she slowly brings her lips to mine where she lightly presses a faint kiss across them. Our noses touch, our foreheads press together, our breaths mix.

"I can't imagine the weight you hold on your shoulders every day, the sheer magnitude of knowing how you've altered someone else's life. And knowing you, knowing your heart, there isn't a day that goes by that you don't live for that woman, for her son."

Fuck. My eyes start to water and I attempt to look away, but Rylee doesn't let me. She holds me in place, forcing me to listen.

"You need to be proud of the man you are today, the man you've become. You are a product of second chances in life, and you're taking that second chance and turning it into something beautiful."

My eyes shut and tears fall quickly. Rylee catches them with kisses across my lips, searing me with her taste, with her compassion.

Slowly, tears still streaming down my face, I take hold of her hips and reposition her so she's straddling me. Her hands still gripping my face, her kisses become more forceful.

Crashing.

Biting.

Sucking.

Her tongue parts my lips, and her strokes dissipate the knot around my heart. With every touch she unravels the tight hold.

Tongues clashing. Unravel.

Fingers wiping my tears. Unravel.

Hips rotating against mine. Unravel.

"You're such a beautiful soul," she whispers when she lightly pulls away, keeping our heads connected.

My eyes search hers, my chest expanding, my soul connecting with hers.

Scooping her up, I take her to the bed and lay her down. Her dark hair fans against the bright white of the bedding, a stark contrast. She might look hard on the outside, but on the inside, she's empathetic, a quality hard to find in some people. A quality I want in a partner.

From behind, I grab my shirt and pull it over my head. I toss it to the ground and then press my hand against the mattress, my body hovering over hers as I undo the tie of her robe, letting the white terrycloth fall to the side, exposing her soft, silky skin. Gently, I drag the pads of my fingers across her collarbone, between her breasts, down her stomach, across her belly button, and just above her pubic bone, watching how with every pass of my fingers, a wave of goosebumps erupts over her skin.

Her eyes become heady, her legs fall open for me, and she licks her lips, an invitation I crave.

Keeping my eyes trained on hers, the moment so incredibly intimate, I undo my pants and drag them to the floor where I step out. Never breaking eye contact, I grip my rock-hard cock in my hand and give it two strokes before I lean forward and place the head at her entrance.

Her chest rises and falls, her rose-colored nipples pucker, and a light sheen of sweat covers her skin when I rest my cock at her core, waiting, soaking in the moment.

She doesn't force me. She doesn't show her impatience.

She waits.

She keeps her eyes on mine, the rapid pace of her breathing the only inclination of the yearning passing through her.

"You make me feel like a better man," I say, my cock inching inside her. "You give me hope, Rylee." *A few more inches, her eyes close for a second, before focusing back on me.* "You have offered me forgiveness when there was no forgiving needed." *A few more inches, our breathing becoming one.* "You make me want to move on but never forget." *I push forward and bottom out, biting on my lip, her tight channel adjusting around me.*

Not saying a word, Rylee pulls on the back of my neck and brings my mouth to hers where we very slowly—rhythmically—kiss each other, our movements deliberate, with purpose as I move my hips, pushing inside her.

There's no hurry.

There is no urgent rush to climax.

And for the first time in my life, I'm experiencing that all-consuming feeling I've heard about, what people strive for. For the first time in my life, I'm making love. And it's because of her. Beautiful Rylee. *Does she know she owns my heart?*

CHAPTER TWENTY-ONE

RYLEE

The early morning sun peeks past the white curtains, casting an orange light over the room. Tucked in close to Beck, I glance at the clock.

Six. I have a few hours left before I need to catch my flight home, the sheer thought of leaving Beck again is breaking my heart.

My hand around his waist, my head pressing against his chest, I hold on to him tightly, trying to figure out how to make this work, how to talk to him about the future, about the possibility of *us*.

There is no question in my mind that he wants there to be an *us*. That was clear during our conversation last night, and from the . . . lovemaking we did all night and into the early hours of this morning.

We haven't talked much since he spoke of his devastating past, since he poured out his entire soul right in front of me. Instead, we've communicated through our bodies: touching, holding, loving, and accepting. *Healing.* It's what he needed. Every caress of his hand across my skin, every kiss to my lips, to my neck, to my breasts, they were intimate, languid, and purposeful. His strokes inside me were matched with a deeper connection in our gazes, his eyes never leaving mine, his love pouring out of him, his love for my understanding.

I cried.

I cried multiple times, seeing the utter heartbreak in his eyes, but also the promise of what's to come. With every thrust inside me, it was like he was trying to wash away the emptiness inside his soul and replace it with hope.

I want to be that hope. I want to be the one who continues to watch this beautiful man grow. I want to be by his side when he struggles with his inner demons, and I want to be the one who gives him the world, who stands by his side when he speaks of his past, who hugs him when he's struggling.

The one he loves.

I want it all.

But there is one thing I need to know first.

I stroke the light stubble on his chest, his taut chest twitching under my touch.

He groans and kisses the top of my head, pulling me closer into his chest. "Morning." His sexy, half-awake morning voice rolls over me, deep and rumbly. *Waking up alone tomorrow morning is going to suck.*

"Morning," I squeak out, moving my body closer. I kiss his chest not in a sexual way, but to show him I'm still here, that despite his past, I definitely think he's the strongest man I know.

He kisses the top of my head, his fingers tangling with the long strands. "How did you sleep?"

"Perfectly." I bite my bottom lip and try to figure out a way to bring up the topic I so desperately need to talk to him about. "At least I slept perfectly with the amount of sleep I got."

He chuckles. "Sorry, I was kind of ravenous last night."

"Kind of?"

His chest rumbles again, rising and falling with such a delicious sound. "All right, not kind of. I was greedy, but I'm not sorry because last night was"—he pauses, considering his words—"it was everything I needed to heal my heart, Rylee."

My eyes involuntarily shut as his words roll over me. He was so honest, so open. He deserves the same.

"Where do you see your future?" I ask, jumping right into it.

Caught off guard from my abrupt question, he takes a second, his hand still playing with my hair, our naked bodies pressed against one another. "My future? Hell, I don't know. I've never really planned out my future. There's one thing I know though, I sure as hell hope you're in it."

I press another kiss on his chest, more to soothe my racing heart than his. "Have you ever pictured what your life could be? Like, do you want to travel? Or do you want the white picket fence? You know, that kind of future."

"Are you asking if I'll ever get married again?"

No. But I go with that. "Yeah, will you?"

"To the right person, yes. I know my first marriage was a sham, a decision I'll always regret obviously, for many reasons. I don't believe I'm a man who gives up on marriage because his first one was a nightmare. I see that marriage as more of a chapter I had to read through in order to get to where I am today. So, yes, I'd marry again." He chuckles and asks, "Why, you looking to fill the position as wife?"

I laugh against his chest as well and playfully pinch his side.

"Hey, watch it, Saucy." He takes my hand in his and laces our fingers together, bringing the connection to his lips.

"What else do you see?"

He exhales. "Hell, I don't know. If I were to really go for it, if I could really fulfill my dreams, I could see myself owning an art studio with my pictures, every story told underneath, the vivid colors and compelling truths educating people. I can see a wife by my side, accompanying me to AA meetings, showing individuals who struggle that there is hope for a future. I can see a house that isn't perfect, but perfect for my wife and me. I can see the cracks and dents that give the house character, just like my life. I can see children, so many fucking children running up to me, holding my finger, calling me Daddy, depending on me to be the father they deserve in their life, a father full of faults but determined to prove to his children they can make something of themselves."

I swallow hard.

"How many children do you want?"

He doesn't even pause before answering. "At least three, four if I'm a lucky bastard."

I nod, my mouth going dry, my heart racing uncontrollably to the point that I can feel my lungs reaching, straining for air. *Please don't keep talking, Beck. Please don't want—*

"With Christine, I never wanted kids. I didn't want to bring innocent lives into that dysfunctional mess. But with a little wisdom under my belt and a whole hell of a lot of promise, I want to give myself the chance to be a father. I want to prove to myself that even though I come from a damaged and torn-up past, I can still raise kind, loving, and selfless children, the type of children who make a difference in this world. The best kind of difference that understand their worth and the worth of others."

Silence falls between us.

My lungs are screaming for air.

My heart is ready to explode.

My eyes brim with tears. If I blink, if I take one breath, I'll lose it. And I don't want to lose it, not in front of him.

To reassure him, I place a kiss on his chest and say, "Bathroom," before sprinting out of bed and running across the room to the bathroom where I close and lock the door. Falling to the floor, I place my head in my hands and let the pain seep through my eyes into my palms. I try to catch my breath, but my chest is heaving, my body is shaking, and so many tears are falling uncontrollably.

I should have known.

From the very beginning, I should have known.

It's obvious in the way he carries himself, in the way he's so compassionate, sympathetic. His heart really is *that* big.

He's supposed to be a father. He's meant to be a father. *He'll be an incredible father. His kids and his wife will be the luckiest people in the world.*

But it won't be me. Can't be me.

Because despite the love and empathy I can give him, the laughs and the passion, there is one thing I know I can't give him.

Children.

The sorrow is building, the ability to hold it in any longer impossible as a sob bubbles out of me followed by more tears. I'm not quiet, I'm not discreet, and there is no hiding it anymore.

And as I expected, the man I've started to fall for, the man who's become a staple in my life pads across the hotel floor and tries to open the door.

Knocking on it, he says, "Rylee, are you okay?"

More tears. More shaking.

Oh God. This hurts. It's too much. It hurts—

"Rylee . . ."

I shake my head even though he can't see me, my head still buried in my hands, the cold tiles of the floor chilling my body.

"Damn it, Rylee, open the door." More pounding.

But I don't move.

I can't move.

I should never have come. I should never have answered his text messages. I should never have given him my body in Key West. I should have run as far away as possible, like I've promised myself I would do.

Run away.

It's why I've struggled with writing. I'm not stupid. I understand a part of telling stories is mental, if you shut off a part of your life, an intricate part of your life, your writing will suffer.

And I shut off love.

At least I thought I did . . . until I met Beck.

Then he changed everything.

It's so simple: meet a man, fall in love, get married, have kids, grow old together. That's the fairy tale, right? At least that's the "predicted fairy tale."

Unfortunately, not everyone is that lucky. Myself included.

I get it, not everyone wants kids; not everyone sees a future that consists of soccer tournaments on the weekend and sticky hands clawing at your pants, begging for attention. But I did. I saw it so vividly, just like Beck.

"Rylee, please . . . open the door."

I can't. Looking around the bathroom, I see a pair of leggings and a sweatshirt from yesterday and quickly put them on. I tiptoe around the bathroom, gathering my cosmetics, tears dripping onto the marble counter. Taking a deep breath, I open the door and breeze past him.

"Rylee, what the hell is going on?"

I choke on a sob. "I . . . I have to go." I reach my suitcase and start stuffing things inside.

"The hell you do." Beck grabs my arm and pulls me away, hairspray dropping to the floor between us and rolling across the carpet. Lifting my chin, Beck searches my eyes. "Rylee, what are you doing? Why are you crying?"

Closing my eyes, more tears fall as my breath hitches in my chest once again. Beck pulls me into his arms, warming me with his strong hold, an embrace I've grown to adore. *An embrace I may never feel again once I walk out the door.*

"Talk to me. What happened from the bed to the bathroom that has you this upset?"

Gathering myself, knowing there is no other choice, I gently push away from him and zip up my bag. "This isn't going to work, Beck."

"You're running again." Beck blows out a frustrated breath and from the corner of my eye, I see him grab the back of his neck. "What the fuck, Rylee? Is this because of what I told you?"

"What?" I wipe a stray tear off my cheek and shake my head. "No, Beck. This isn't because of you. This has nothing to do with what you told me last night." I gather my backpack, phone, and charger and search the room one last time before turning toward Beck, giving the decency of a proper goodbye.

"Then what? Five fucking minutes ago you were snuggled up against me, kissing my goddamn chest. How could you possibly change your mind that quickly? Is it because I want a family?" I wince and he catches it. "That's it, because I want a family. Hell, Rylee, I don't need one right away. I wasn't speaking of starting one tomorrow, but just knowing it's something I'd like in the future. Christ, you asked me. I simply answered you."

My gaze drops to the floor as more tears stream down my cheeks. "I can't have a family."

"You can't, or you don't want one?" he asks, his voice stern and unforgiving.

Choking back a sob, I take a deep breath and say, "I can't."

"Why the fuck not?" He's spitting fire with every ounce of anger building inside him, and I know this is all my fault. If I acted like an adult—a mentally stable adult, who can hold a difficult conversation—he wouldn't be nearly as worked up, but given the up-and-down roller coaster I've put him through, I can understand why he's being so harsh. He's been so open with me, exactly what I craved, and I'm pulling away. *I'm saying no to an* us.

Shaking my head, I swing my backpack over my shoulder, my throat so tight I can't speak. I pull on the handle of my suitcase and head toward the door, Beck following behind me. When I open the door, he grips the wood from behind me, holding it tightly at the top.

Giving him one more glance, I take in his taut chest muscles flexing with every frustrated breath he takes. His eyes are narrowed at me, his brows pointed down, his knuckles turning white from the death grip he has on the door.

"Why the fuck not?" he repeats, holding me in his glare.

Not able to respond, my past a dagger to my already broken heart, I say, "I'm sorry, Beck."

Disappointed, his head bowed, he says, "Not as sorry as I am."

The door shuts, the loud click of the lock sounding off like a deathly silence in the hallway of the Bellagio. It's like the final nail in the coffin of our story. *Our burial.*

I pause for a second, just a breath to see if he opens the door again, but when I hear nothing from the other side of the door, I take off toward the elevators, my heart dragging behind me.

～

Hood pulled over my head, a coffee in hand, knees tucked, I sit in an airport chair waiting for my flight. Passengers travel past me, suitcases rolling behind them, kids skipping along, not holding hands, and an occasional flight crew buzzing about their layover. Life rotates around me as I sit, stagnant, recollecting on all the mistakes I made with Beck.

Mistake number one: letting him say goodbye to my sweatshirt.

Mistake number two: not requesting a room far away from his.

Mistake number three: falling for a man I had no right falling for.

My phone buzzes next to me with a text message.

Zoey.

I sent her and Victoria a crazed text while waiting in line at security. I'm kind of surprised it's taken one of them this long to get back to me.

Zoey: *Hold on a second, what's happening? You're in Vegas with Beck and he wants kids and you walked out on him? When did you decide to go to Vegas and why didn't I know about this?*

I'm about to answer when Victoria pipes in with a text.

Victoria: *Please tell me I'm not reading this correctly. You flew across the country to be with a man and didn't tell us? That's very irresponsible. You could have been hurt and we never would have known.*

Oh Victoria.

Zoey: *From the text message she sent, I'm going to assume she doesn't need a lecture right now, Victoria. We can tell her how IDIOTIC it is to go somewhere without telling anyone later. For now, let's focus on the facts. You left Beck in a hotel room. Why?*

I type out a response.

Rylee: Rain check on the lecture, I know it was stupid. Despite that, Beck and I decided to meet up this weekend and it was . . . everything.

Zoey: Oh sweetie.

Victoria: He's a very honest and sweet man.

Rylee: The best actually.

If I wasn't so dehydrated, I'm pretty sure I could be crying some more as images of sexy and understanding Beck runs through my head.

Victoria: How was the weekend? What exactly went wrong?

Rylee: The weekend was amazing. It felt like everything was right in the world when I was in his arms. We crashed some weddings but then spent most of our time in our hotel room. Could sense things were getting serious but there was a roadblock in our relationship, our clouded pasts, so I asked Beck point-blank what he was hiding.

Zoey: What did he say?

Rylee: A story for another time. It's far too much to type out. But after, we had the most incredibly amazing night. We . . . we made love. We didn't speak much, but it was an unspoken understanding that we weren't fucking, we weren't screwing each other's brains out like before. We were legit making love.

Victoria: I feel sad for where this is going.

Rylee: I fell for him and I fell hard. It was almost impossible to keep my heart out of the equation, especially after the story he told me. So I asked him what he saw for his future and he went on and on about having a family. He wants a wife and kids. I can't give that to him.

Zoey: Oh Rylee, you can still have a family, you're just going to have to go about it a different way, that's all.

Victoria: Zoey is right. Just because you can't have kids of your own doesn't mean you need to give up on a man who clearly can't get enough of you, who wants to be with you. You can find a solution.

Rylee: You guys didn't hear him. He wants four kids. Four! He has dreams and who am I to stop him from making those dreams his reality?

Zoey: Rylee, I know the operation is still fresh in your memory, that the loss is still burning a hole in your heart, but you have to know not being able to carry your own child isn't a hindrance to stop you from ever being happy.

I take a deep breath and close my eyes, my thoughts traveling back to Beck. He was so sure, so set on having a family, on teaching his children his values. He deserves the world. How could I possibly consider taking that away from him?

Rylee: *It's not going to work out. There are just too many factors keeping us apart.*

There is a pause and then Victoria responds.

Victoria: *But what about all the positive factors pulling you together? Love doesn't come along very often, Rylee. When you feel it, there is only one thing you can do: fall head over heels.*

I cover my eyes with my hand, my throat closing in on itself, my nose stinging, signaling another wave of tears. God, how I wish things could be different, how I wish I had the courage to take a step forward toward a future with Beck, but even though there are options, I will always think in the back of my head, *Beck wanted something different.*

And that something different won't ever include me.

CHAPTER TWENTY-TWO

BECK

Zoey: You need to call me now, jackass.

I stare at the text for what seems like the hundredth time. It's Sunday evening, Chris is on his way over with donuts, and for the life of me, I can't stop staring at the text Zoey sent me.

When I first read it, my immediate thought was something happened to Rylee, but the more I read it, the more I realized what she was doing. She's intervening.

There is no way Rylee kept our story from Zoey and Victoria. Their friendship is too strong. And knowing Zoey, I really shouldn't be surprised by her text, because there is no way she would be able to keep from saying her peace about the entire situation.

But I'm too damn raw to talk to her right now.

Knock, knock.

Thank God.

"It's open," I call out, not wanting to move from the slouched position on my couch.

The door to my apartment opens and when I expect to see

burly Chris walk through with a box of donuts, Justine passes through the threshold, a Danish box in her hand.

Sigh.

Can't a guy get a fucking donut when he wants one?

"You look like shit," Justine says, closing my door and going straight to my kitchen where she grabs two forks, two waters from the fridge, and then plops down next to me.

"What happened to Chris and donuts?"

"You know how he is with feelings, so you're getting Justine and Danish instead." She flips open the box and hands me a fork. "It's raspberry and delightful so wipe that sneer off your face and take a bite."

Before I can stop her, she scoops up a big piece with my fork and shoves it in my mouth. I let the Danish sit on my tongue for a few seconds before chewing and . . . mother fucker, it is good.

With her finger wiggling at me, Justine knowingly says, "See, I told you." Taking a bite of her own, she talks while chewing. "Now tell me what the hell is going on. Last thing we knew, you were having the weekend of your life with Rylee. What changed?"

I exhale and tip my head back so it's resting on the couch cushion. "Everything."

And that's the fucking truth. Not only did my relationship with Rylee end in a flash, but my feelings for her morphed into something entirely more serious than I ever could have predicted when I first met her. Seeing her again, in person, solidified everything brewing deep within my bones.

"Why?" Justine takes another bite from her fork, letting the metal amble in her mouth longer than normal.

"I don't know where to begin."

"Skip the horny details. I'm assuming the first half of your trip was splendid. What happened during the second half? Why am I sharing this Danish with you?"

I let out a heavy breath, sorrow clouding my vision, my fork poised in my hand resting on my stomach. "We started talking about our futures and what we want. Hell, I opened up to her about my past, and I mean I told her everything."

Justine stiffens, her eyes narrowing. "Did she fucking leave because of what you told her?"

"No." I pat Justine's leg, appreciating how protective she is. "She was actually super empathetic when I told her about Christine, the accident, and my time in prison. Incredibly empathetic actually. It wasn't until the morning when we started talking about *our* future that she went rigid on me, disappeared into the bathroom. She was sobbing, Justine."

"Sobbing?" Justine's brows rise. "What the hell did you say to make her sob?" She slaps me in the arm, steals my fork, and then points it at me. "Did you break that girl's heart?"

"What? No!" Why am I the one getting yelled at now? "I told her about wanting to have a family and getting married one day. Isn't that what women like to hear?"

Lip curled, eyes gazing toward the ceiling, her fingers tapping her chin, Justine says, "Well, that doesn't seem incriminating. What did she say?"

"She said she can't have a family." I scrub my face and say, "I kind of blew up on her because it was like déjà vu. She was packing her things and leaving me without even giving me a fucking chance to keep her in my life."

"Hold up." Justine raises her hand. "Did she say she doesn't want a family or can't have a family? Big difference."

My brow pinches together. What is she getting at here? "How is there a difference?"

Justine rolls her eyes and sits up straighter. "Don't be so dense, Beck. If she doesn't want a family, that's her choice. But if she *can't* have kids, that may not be something she can control. So are you sure she said can't?"

I still, my pulse starting to pick up as I try to recollect the words we spoke to each other. "Fuck, I think she said can't."

Justine plants another wallop of a slap to my arm and huffs. "You stupid man. Ugh, this makes sense." Justine shoves a huge bite of Danish in her mouth and continues to speak, bits of pastry flying out of her mouth and hitting my face and shirt. Justine is very comfortable around me. "She confesses that she can't have children. She sobs in the bathroom. You blow up on her. Yeah, no wonder you're in California and she's all the way over in Maine right now."

My eyes race back and forth, my mind working a mile a minute. "Do you think she's unable to get pregnant?"

"Duh! God, welcome to the conversation, Beck." Justine shakes her head. "Men really are stupid."

"Shit." My hand goes to my phone and I open up the screen to Zoey's text. "Shit, shit, shit."

"What?"

I show the text to Justine and once again, she whacks me. "My guess is she's calling to tell you you're an insensitive prick who yelled at a girl who didn't deserve to be yelled at."

Yeah, that's my fucking guess too.

Out of nowhere, Justine swipes my phone and starts pressing buttons only to be followed by the sound of a phone ringing on speaker.

"What the fuck—?"

"It's about time you called me, dickhead." Zoey's voice fills the small space of my apartment and I take a deep breath. Fuck, for a second I thought she was calling Rylee. I can handle Zoey. "You have some explaining to do, mother fucker." Or at least I think I can handle her.

I go to answer her when Justine puts up her hand and says, "Zoey, it's Justine."

"Justine? Oh I'm sorry. I thought this was Beck. You're not a dickhead. How are you? Did you try that brownie recipe I emailed you?"

Brownie recipe? They email? *The fuck?*

"I did. Chris ate half the batch and the kids ate the other half. Note to self: make a big batch and hide them."

"I told you they'd be a real winner."

"They were," Justine coos. "But unfortunately, I'm not calling you to talk about brownies. I, uh . . . I have Beck with me."

"Ah, yes, am I on speaker phone?"

"Of course."

"Hey, Zoey," I sigh, hating this right now.

"Oh hello, Beck. Took you long enough to call me. Had to bring in a friend to help?" *I'm sure I heard her mumble, "Dickhead." Just in case I didn't know . . .*

Grumbling, I slouch on the couch and wave at Justine to continue. I don't feel like a verbal bashing from Zoey right now. Hell, calling her wasn't even my idea, so Justine can take the lead.

Clearing her throat, Justine says, "As you know, our friends snuck away this weekend to Las Vegas."

"Yes, they thought they were so clever, getting away for the weekend without consulting us. Honestly, what were they thinking?"

"They obviously weren't," Justine answers, patting me on the leg.

"Can we just get on with it? Fuck." I rub my brow. What I wouldn't give to *not* be in this situation right now. All I want is to have Rylee wrapped in my arms, looking out over the ocean in Key West. That's when I felt the most at ease, the most myself. And then Vegas. Vegas trumped Key West.

"Hey, why are you getting pissy when you're the one being the asshole? Do you know the kind of hell Rylee has been through?" Zoey's voice gets louder and I match it right back.

"No, I don't. So can someone please fucking inform me? Because she sure as hell didn't. She just ran."

"Because she's scared, Beck." Zoey takes a deep breath. "She told me not to talk to you because in her mind this is over; your relationship is completely over."

I shake my head and look to the ceiling, biting on my bottom lip to prevent me from yelling obscenities. Justine gives my knee a reassuring squeeze, letting me know she's here for me, and even though it's nice to have friends who care deeply enough to sit through relationship agony with you, I want nothing more than to be by myself. *How the fuck was I supposed to know what she meant when she said she can't have kids?* If I'd realized . . . if I had any idea how hard it was for her to hear me talk about my dreams of being a dad . . .

Why run?

And even though I haven't craved alcohol in many years, I know Justine and Chris are still keeping an eye on me.

"So why are you bothering to talk to me then? What's the point if she's tossed our relationship to the trash?"

"Because she loves you, Beck." My eyes start to sting as my skin prickles with goosebumps. If only I could hear that from her. "But she's willing to push that aside so you can have the life she thinks you deserve." *What the hell? What does that mean?*

"I only want her."

"And that's the answer I hoped to hear." Zoey pauses for a second and then says, "This past year for her has been hell. Life-changing hell. We forced her to go to Key West to try and bring her back to life. And then there was you. You were supposed to be a fling, but you kept pursuing, and she saw how she could easily fall for you . . . and she did."

"I don't understand, Zoey. What the hell do I—?"

"She was diagnosed with cervical cancer nine months ago, Beck." My breath catches in my throat and the pieces start to form. *Cancer. Oh Rylee.* Zoey continues to talk and it's almost like my life is in slow motion as she fills me in. "It was aggressive, fortunately she caught it at the very beginning . . ." God, I can hear how this is shaking Zoey. *Fuck.* "She spoke with many doctors and the consensus to beat this cancer was to have a complete hysterectomy."

"Meaning she can't have kids," I finish for her.

"Exactly. At the time, it was a decision she made to save her life. She was in it from the beginning, *remove everything* she told them, but afterward . . . afterward she mourned. For about six months she mourned the loss of ever being able to carry her own child. It was a very tough concept for her to accept. It wasn't until recently that she started to get some color back in her face and enjoy life again. When she was with you, it was the first time in almost a year I saw the true essence of my friend again. She was happy, albeit cautious at times, but she was smiling, and that meant everything to Victoria and me."

Fuck. I take a deep breath, my heart beating so damn fast I feel like I can't breathe. I can't even imagine the kind of emotional battle Rylee has had to fight over the past year. Learning you had cancer, so aggressive it could take your life, and then giving up the idea of having children of your own to save your life? It's unfathomable that an individual would have to make such a decision, let alone Rylee . . . *my Rylee*. With each passing breath, I can feel my heart split in two, from the loss Rylee has suffered through, from the grieving her soul has suffered from.

I ache for her.

I long to hold her, to tell her that her dreams of a family are not over. *That we are not over.*

That I love her.

That even though she's grieving from the loss of not being able to have biological children, her dreams of being a mom can still come true. They'll just have to come true in a roundabout way.

"And she thinks because she can't have kids of her own that I won't want her? Is that what you're telling me? She left before I could leave her?" *I would never do that. Why didn't she trust that?*

Zoey makes an agreeable sound. "Nailed it right on the head. Because she loves you, she wants your dreams to become your reality, Beck. She also doesn't want you resenting her later—hating her —because she can't give you the kids you want."

I let out a long pent-up breath. "That's fucking stupid."

Justine twists her lips and frowns. "Don't call Rylee stupid."

"Yeah, don't call her stupid," Zoey chimes in.

"I didn't call her stupid. I called her thought process stupid.

Christ." I look at Justine. She has tears in her eyes, and I know it's because she understands how this is gutting me. Justine was born to be a mom, so I can only imagine what she's feeling here. *She gets Rylee more than I'll ever be able to.* I can't bear that Rylee thought the only option was for her to leave. It's as though she considers herself less somehow. Her insecurities . . . not knowing how beautiful she is . . . is it all related? I rub my thighs with my palms and lean forward, speaking into the phone more directly. "Just because we can't have biological children together doesn't mean I don't want to be with her, Zoey. There are so many kids out there looking to be adopted. Hell, I'd foster kids if she wanted that. I just want to be surrounded by little minds I can shape and mold. It doesn't matter how we collect those tiny souls. And if she'd given me a chance to speak before running, I could have told her that."

"That's Rylee. Super stubborn."

Yeah, tell me about it.

Standing and grabbing the phone from Justine, I start pacing around my apartment, my mind racing a mile a minute, plans formulating.

"Zoey, can you do me a favor?"

"I don't know." She hesitates. "Does it involve you getting our girl back?"

"It does."

Justine perks up, shoving another big bite of Danish into her mouth, her eyes tracking my every move.

"Then how can I help?"

"Can you get me Rylee's parents' details? I need to talk to them."

"Ah, are you proposing? Are you going to ask for her hand in marriage?" Justine's mouth drops open.

"What? No. I love her, but we're definitely not ready for that step. I'm smart enough to realize that. Can you get me their info, please? I have something important to discuss with them."

"Fine, but are you going to let me in on your plan?"

"Yeah." I pause and push my hand through my hair, staring at Justine. "When you pick me up from the airport."

Justine and Zoey both squeal obnoxiously.

I toss my phone at Justine and head to my room. I have some serious thinking to do. *And packing.*

It's time to get my forever.

CHAPTER TWENTY-THREE

RYLEE

"Heading to the coffee house?" Oliver asks, walking next to me down the small path from our street to Main Street.

"Yeah, wanted a change of scenery. I've stuffed myself in my house for the past week. Thought it would be good to get some fresh air and when I say fresh air, I mean some air infused with coffee."

"I like where your head's at. I have to check a new shipment at the Market, so I'm heading in the same direction."

"Oh, I've been meaning to ask. Word on the street is you've started quite the romance with Mrs. Davenport. I heard she's been after you to cook her dinner ever since you offered the last time you replaced the batteries in her smoke detector." I grin, thinking of the kooky, yet lovable old lady.

"Can a man not pursue an old woman in peace?" He rolls his eyes to the Heavens as he holds the door open to Snow Roast for me and we both laugh, the sound slightly foreign to me. I haven't heard that sound in a week, despite my friends trying to cheer me up with their crazy antics.

I'm sad.

There I said it. I'm fucking sad.

The last month has been like nothing I've ever experienced. I've never lived with a boyfriend, so I didn't know how amazing it is to have someone to talk to every night, someone to joke around with, someone to "share" meals with. It's like Beck became a part of me. Our lives simply blended together and it was . . . seamless.

I looked forward to seeing his face, to hearing his voice, to leaning on him even though we were *physically* so far from each other.

He was a rock.

He was a confidant.

He was a friend . . .

My friend.

I'm not sure I'll be able to forget or let that go. Beck is . . . he's the man that sticks with you forever, and somehow, I knew that the minute I met him. When he was fake crying and saying goodbye to my puked-on sweatshirt, when he took me on a heli-copter ride in an attempt to soften his abrupt departure the night before. The moment he told me good night, perceiving I wasn't ready for more. When he asked me to meet him in Vegas because he simply couldn't take another day apart from me. When he tried to take things into his own hands so I knew he wanted me for more than sex. He's the man who sets the bar unbelievably high so no one will ever reach it. He's the man who makes an indelible impression on your heart. An everlasting impact on your life.

And now he's no longer mine.

Stopping contact with him has been heartbreaking.

Debilitating.

I've spent the last week in bed, doing the bare minimum to keep up with readers, my publicist, and my publisher. *That* is not me at all. I'm always very interactive, very involved, but to say I'm depressed is an understatement. I know this dark feeling too well. For months I grieved and mourned last year . . .

It's so bad that the romantic comedy I'm trying to write has turned into everyone being killed off in the first chapter.

There is nothing funny about your heroine dying from food poisoning.

There is simply no more book to write when your main character goes tongue out immediately.

It's one of the reasons I'm at the coffee house, looking for some inspiration from my favorite chair. Maybe something will strike me.

I'm an observer, a certified creep, who watches every person who passes by. I study them from their choice in clothing to the way they speak, to their mannerisms, and as I watch them, my mind starts racing with what their backstory could be, what they could be doing, or who they might be waiting for.

It's a "talent"—if that's what you want to call it—I've had for as long as I can remember. Thankfully, I get to put that talent to use, which is why I'm out in public.

I need help.

I need something to spark my imagination.

I need one little blip in my life to take my mind off Beck for two seconds and give me a reprieve.

"The usual?" Ruth asks when I walk up.

"Yes, please."

Ruth brings a coffee to the counter and hands it to Oliver. "Do you want an extra for Mrs. Davenport?" She giggles.

"Nah, we'll just share this one." Oliver deadpans and then nods at Ruth. "On the tab?"

"You bet."

"Thanks, Ruth. You're the best."

As Oliver makes his exit, I settle into my seat, thankfully no old ladies to be kicked out, and I set up my computer on my small bamboo lap desk. I take my phone out of my purse and set it on the arm of the chair when I see a text message from Zoey.

Zoey: *How are you doing today? Are you finally out and about? Did you shower? Please tell me you at least put fresh underwear on.*

I swear sometimes she thinks I have no idea how to take care of myself. Leave it to the mother in her.

Rylee: Showered, lotioned, fresh underwear, clean clothes, hair is done, and I'm sitting in the Snow Roast right now, drinking some coffee.

Zoey: Eeep! Okay, be there in twenty. I have some sketches I have to get done and Victoria is doing some serious research today, so I'll let her know where we're at. Writing buddies!!!

Rylee: Writing buddies!!! See you soon

Zoey: P.S. I'm glad you're out in the world today, Rylee. It's good for you. One day at a time.

I exhale heavily reading her last text.

Yes, one day at a time. Seems so easy, right? I feel like I have to take one hour, one minute at a time when my heart starts to ache, when I think about anything that reminds me of Beck.

Shaking my thoughts, trying to start this day off on a not-so-gloomy note, I put my phone down, take a deep breath, and open my computer.

New day, new goals.

First thing to do, resurrect my main character from the dead.

I take a sip of my coffee and poise my fingers on my keyboard, opting for the coffee shop music rather than my own playlist. I'm not in the mood to listen to anything that would even remotely remind me of Beck.

Note to self: make new playlists.

The overhead bell rings to the shop and I glance up to see a man dressed in black jeans, black boots, a black V-neck T-shirt, and leather bracelets on his arm.

HA!

I'm losing it.

It's official. My brain is subconsciously playing tricks on me because that man looks a hell of a lot like Beck.

"Can I help you?" Ruth's voice rings out.

"Uh yeah, can I get your blonde roast please? Nothing in it."

And holy shit. *That voice.* He sounds a lot like Beck too.

"Sure thing. Two dollars."

The man reaches in his back pocket, and pulls out a few bills, then sticks one in the tip jar, the sinew in his forearms flexing with each and every movement.

Ruth hands him a paper cup of coffee and says, "Hope to see you again."

He nods and says, "No doubt you will."

Turning toward me, casual as ever, he lifts his cup of coffee in my direction and says, "Morning, Saucy," and then exits through the same door he just came in from.

What in the ever-living hell?

Quickly putting my computer on the table in front of me, I plaster myself to the window and watch as Beck—yes, Beck Wilder, *my Beck*—looks both ways and crosses the street, coffee in hand, heading down Main Street as if he's lived in Port Snow his entire life.

"What the fuck?" I say louder than expected, drawing the attention of Ruth.

"Uh, do you know him?"

Eyes still trained on Beck, his fine ass walking away from me, I say, "Yeah."

"He came in yesterday and ordered the same thing. I thought he was a tourist, but from your reaction, I'm guessing maybe he's not?"

"I don't know what he is." I fumble for my phone, knocking it to the ground. I tear my eyes away from Beck for two seconds to retrieve it and call Zoey, my face plastered right back to the window while the phone rings.

"Dude, I said give me twenty minutes," Zoey answers.

"Beck is here. Beck, Beck Wilder is here in Port Snow. He just walked in the coffee shop and was wearing all black and those hot bracelets only few men can pull off and he got a blonde roast and tipped Ruth and said hi to me and then took off. He's currently walking north on Main Street, waving to a few people and acting like he owns the goddamn street. What the fuck is happening? Am I in some kind of alternate universe I don't know about? Is this a dream? It doesn't feel like a dream? I legit drank coffee and tasted it. I don't think you taste coffee in dreams? Do you? Ruth, do you taste coffee in dreams? Don't answer that. I don't think you do. This isn't a dream. What the hell is happening?" I speak so fast I don't even know what I'm saying.

"Uh," Zoey pauses and at that moment, I know. I know she knows.

I know she knows, and she didn't tell me she knew Beck was here.

What kind of friend is that?

"Zoey Michelle Platt, you tell me right now what you know."

"Uh, you know, this will be better in person."

"You have five minutes to get your ass in this coffee shop, do you hear me?"

"Noted," she squeaks out on the phone and hangs up.

She better have a damn good story to explain why Beck Wilder is strolling around my hometown, looking better than ever before.

∽

"She doesn't get coffee." I stand from my chair and wave my finger at an out-of-breath Zoey. "No coffee shall be served to her until she sits down and looks me square in the eyes and tells me why she's been omitting information to me."

Ruth backs away slowly from the counter, hands up. "Sorry, looks like the coffee warden has spoken."

"You're not supposed to pick sides," Zoey spits and stalks toward me. She flops in the chair across from me and sets her bag on the floor. Her hair is drenched, she's not wearing any makeup, and I'm pretty sure her shirt is inside out. "I'm here. Go ahead, yell at me."

I lean back in my chair, my hands crossed in my lap. "I would yell at you if I knew what I was yelling about, but to my chagrin, I'm clueless. So would you mind telling me why Beck Wilder is in Port Snow right now and acts like it's normal to see me sitting in this coffee shop?"

She plays with the hem of her inside-out shirt, avoiding eye contact with me. "About that."

"Yeah, about that."

"You see, I might have threatened his life the Sunday you got back to call me."

"YOU WHAT?" I shout, realizing I should probably keep my voice down due to the gossiping hens. I scoot forward in my chair and speak firmly under my breath. "Why the hell would you do that?"

"Because"—she straightens up, gaining a little bravado—"you were hurting and you weren't entirely honest with Beck, and I thought he deserved to hear the truth."

"That wasn't your decision to make."

"No, it was." Zoey leans forward as well, her eyes trained on mine now. "As your best friend, who had to hear the pain in every word you spoke to me on the phone during your layover on your way home, I have all the right in the world to try to educate the man you're in love with on your situation."

"Pfft." I lean back and chew on my bottom lip, thinking everything over. "Love . . ."

"Don't even try to deny it with me. And I'm not sorry, okay? Because guess what? He's here, in Port Snow instead of across the country."

Feeling the weight of that statement, of knowing Beck is only a street away instead of many states, it's overwhelming.

"It doesn't change anything," I quietly answer. "He still wants what I can't give him."

Zoey's face softens, her eyes lovingly looking at me as only a best friend truly can. "Rylee, why are YOU the one who has to give him a family? It doesn't all lie on your shoulders. There are other ways to have a family, so why is that so hard for you to understand?"

"Because." My eyes start to sting and my throat tightens. I bite my bottom lip, trying to hold back the sorrow I've been living with for nearly a year. Noticing the tears welling in my eyes, Zoey sits on the arm of my chair and puts her arm around my shoulders.

"Because why?" she asks, softly, soft enough so I'm the only one who can hear her.

Taking a second to gather my breath, I answer, "Because I no longer feel like I'm complete." *This is too hard.* "I'll never be able to do what is uniquely female." *That was taken from me.* "Because . . . I'm still mourning the fact that I'll never carry a child." *Only the scars represent that loss.* "How can I possibly ask Beck to forgo that experience? To never watch his wife pregnant with his baby?" *He'll hate me, my hollow, fruitless body.* "It's too much, Zoey. He's too good. Deserves so much more—"

"Oh sweetie." Zoey squeezes me tight. "I can't imagine the loss you've been feeling, but until you speak with Beck, I don't think you can assume anything on his end."

"I don't want him compromising his vision to fit my . . . to fit me." *I don't want him sacrificing anything for me.*

Zoey tilts my chin up and looks at me with genuine love in her eyes. "But isn't that what a relationship is all about? Compromise?"

T rying to get any words in today has been absolutely pointless. My mind hasn't been in it, resurrecting a character from the dead has been impossible especially since my fingers wouldn't move across the keyboard. They stayed poised, never once moving as my gaze drifted out the window, trying to catch a glimpse of Beck.

What is he doing here? And why isn't he coming to find me? That's weird. Come to my hometown but don't say hi? Well, he said hi, but that was it. A little explanation would be nice.

But nothing.

Not that he owes it to me, given the way I left.

I pack up my computer, put my phone in my pocket, and make my way through the coffee shop.

"See you tomorrow?" Ruth asks from her perch on the counter.

"Hopefully. Have a good night, Ruth."

I exit the shop and turn toward the Market. This day calls for a about gallon of ice cream. Yes, a gallon. And it wouldn't be the first time I've gorged on an array of the artisanal flavors Oliver always keeps in stock. I'm not ashamed to admit, that, it's my go-to *my life is over* treat.

I push through the doors, grab a basket, and head straight to the freezer area. Oliver immediately spots me from where he stands in the checkout area. His brow creases as he walks to my side.

"Uh-oh. What's wrong?"

"It's going to be ugly, Oliver. Are you sure you want to watch this?"

A blast of cold air hits me as I open the freezer containing row after row of homemade creamy goodness. I reach in and start pulling out pints.

"You know, Oliver, what's with you men? Huh? What makes that little brain of yours tick?"

I toss a pint of chocolate chip cookie dough in my basket, and quickly follow it up with a pint of chocolate caramel swirl.

Still scanning the freezer's contents, I continue, "Why are you so annoying?" Oliver scoffs beside me. "Well, not you in particular, but men. I mean if I say it's over, it should be over, right?"

"Uh . . ."

"And if I want to stop communication"—I throw two pints in my basket—"I should have the right to stop. What's with this"— three more pints—"alpha-male pursuit, huh?"

"You're smart." I tap my head and then toss another two pints – strawberry and cookies n' cream – in my basket, before turning to Oliver. "You date women. You're all about the boobs. Women aren't complicated at all. Very straightforward. We are an easy breed to understand."

Oliver's mouth drops open, his eyes cast toward me, a *get real* look passing over his features. "You're kidding, right?"

"Don't test me right now, Oliver Monahan. Just let me drop a hundred bucks on ice cream." Shaking his head, he rearranges his features into a more supportive expression while I load my arms with even more pints. What flavor is this? I scan the label . . . Key Lime? Oh fuck that. I put that sucker right back where it came from. Meanwhile, the shoppers milling around me begin to back away, some shooting pointed glares at the chaos I'm causing, and I couldn't care less.

Stare all you want.

This is what a crazed person looks like.

Soak it all up.

Take pictures.

Hell, come pose with me, post on Instagram with the hashtag: #PortSnowIceCreamDemon.

"Rylee?" I look toward Robbi, my arms overflowing with pints. "Does this have to do with the guy over there who's staring at you intently, like you're the most gorgeous woman he's ever seen?"

"What?" A few pints fall to the floor as I whip around to find Beck leaning against a pole, arms crossed over his drool-worthy chest, and the most handsome smirk ever lifting up the sides of his lips. "Oh my God." I turn back around, my face burning despite the freezer's frigid air, and dump the remaining pints in my basket.

"I'm going to take that as a yes."

I glare at Oliver, an innocent bystander to this whole madness. "What on earth is he doing here?"

Wide-eyed, probably from seeing this very unflattering side of me, Oliver says, "Uh, I'm going to guess doing some shopping?"

Not wanting to turn around and face him, I ask, "What's he doing?" Oliver turns to look at him when I snap, "Don't look at him." Oliver freezes, unsure of what to do. *Poor men. They have no clue.*

"I'm going to need to look at him if you want me to see what he's doing."

"Make it subtle."

I'm still facing the open freezer, back toward Beck, trying to school my face into a neutral expression —

"Hey, Saucy."

My back straightens, my face blanches, my body stills. My eyes move to Oliver, who's cringing beside me.

From the side of his mouth, Oliver says, "Heads-up. He's right behind you."

My nostrils flare, causing Oliver to back away slowly down the aisle. "Thanks . . . pal." Taking a deep breath, I straighten my shirt and spin on my heel. "Beck, what a surprise. Enjoying your time in Port Snow?"

That damn smirk doesn't disappear. It only grows wider. Leaning forward, he pulls the basket from my hands and inspects its contents. Immediately, I feel my face flame even more with embarrassment.

"No mint chip?" He raises his eyebrows instantly. You have to have about twenty-five pints in there, but you somehow missed the best flavor."

Winking, he hands me my basket, hand lingers against mine, before he steps away and heads toward the exit.

What in the EVER-LOVING HELL IS HAPPENING?

Confused, embarrassed, and slightly turned on, I stare at Beck's retreating back, walking away as if he's lived here forever.

"So, shall I put the ice cream on your tab?" Oliver asks from behind me.

"For the love of God, yes, Oliver." I race out of the building, still clutching the basket. I make a right when Beck made a left, and racing to my house to bury my head in my pillow.

CHAPTER TWENTY-FOUR

BECK

I press my hands into my thighs, nervous as hell, trying to keep my palms as dry as possible.

"Beck?"

I stand and offer my hand to Mr. Ryan, Rylee's father. "Mr. Ryan, it's a pleasure to meet you."

"Pleasure is mine. When Zoey told us about you wanting to sell art in our gallery, I was more than interested to have a different style represented." He smiles, his eyes lighting up like Rylee's when she's excited. "You can only have so many lighthouses for sale until you start to lose your mind."

I chuckle. "Hey, I like a good lighthouse picture, but I get it." I grab my portfolio from the ground and sling it over my shoulder. "I really appreciate you giving me the time to show you my portfolio."

"Of course, of course. Come on back. Mrs. Ryan is finishing up a drink-and-paint class and will be with us shortly."

"Drink and paint?"

Mr. Ryan laughs and shakes his head. "It's all the rage. Drink some wine and paint a picture. It's very big with the tourists, but instead of doing all the same picture, we have a collection of pictures with attached instructions customers can follow. So if you come with a family member, you don't have two of the same picture."

"Oh, that's smart. I like it."

"Mrs. Ryan liked it at first, but I believe she's getting a little worn out with the demand, and coming up with new pictures to be painted."

Hmm . . . I know someone who can help out with that. I will put that little tidbit in my back pocket for now.

"Understandable." I lay my portfolio on the table as Mrs. Ryan walks through the door. Holy shit. Rylee may have her dad's eyes, but she looks just like her mom, from her petite frame to her long black hair, to her feminine bone structure. "You must be Mrs. Ryan."

She takes my hand warmly and gives it a light squeeze. "Beck Wilder, nice to meet you. Please take a seat." She releases my hand and sits next to her husband, and that's when I see it. True, time-tested love. They even still hold hands under the table. "Sorry to keep you waiting."

"No apology necessary. How was the class?"

"Charming." She nods and presses her palm to her forehead, pushing her hair away. "Tiring. Those tourists sure can give me a run for my money."

"I bet, but what an awesome idea."

"Thank you. It's brought in a lot of great business." She waves to my portfolio. "Zoey said you were a very talented artist. Please share with us; we're always looking for new talent."

I take a deep breath and nod. "I'd like to tell you a little bit about myself, because I've learned recently that being honest and open about my situation brings trust." Rylee's parents exchange glances. Not the best way to start an "interview" but after talking with Cal about my grand plan, he said with such big life changes, the best thing I can do for myself is be open and honest. So I'm taking that chunk of advice and running with it.

Clearing my throat, I clasp my palms on the table in front of me and speak directly to Rylee's parents. "Eight years ago, I got behind the wheel of my car, drunk, angry, and on a mission to get as far away from my life as possible." I take a deep breath, my throat already tightening on me. *These are Rylee's parents.* "I was a lost man, searching for solace, for any kind of peace. I searched for it at the bottom of a liquor bottle." I shake my head. "That night, I ran a red light, driving my car right into another, killing a woman on the spot." I swallow hard now. "She was . . . she was going to pick up her son from a slumber party he was too scared to stay at. Rightfully so, I spent six years in prison, sobering up, and changing my life. I learned my passion for art while I was there and read every inspirational book I could get my hands on. When I was in prison, I vowed to make a change, to make a difference in this world. A positive one. And that's what I strive to do every day. I'm often a guest speaker at AA meetings, sharing my story. I talk to high school kids about the risks of drinking and driving, and I also run a non-profit organization to assist families in need." My palms sweat, my leg itching to bounce. "I'm telling you this because I want you to know me, my motivation for my art, and where my inspiration stems from."

Mr. Ryan nods. Both are quiet, and my nerves start to paralyze me as I try not to focus on what must be passing through their minds, what they must be thinking about me.

I flip open my portfolio and turn the photographs of my art toward them to study. They both lean forward and take in the vivid colors and stroke lines. "I'm currently a muralist for some of the zoos and museums in Los Angeles. I work on a contract basis, so I'm very familiar with painting landscapes of all different environments, but my true passion is portraits." They flip through my pictures, the back of my neck heating with each pass of their hands over the pages. *Is this what Rylee feels every time she submits work to her editor and publisher? Like she's giving away a part of her soul?* "Every portrait in this book is of a victim of alcohol abuse. Their story accompanies every face on the back of the pictures. Since these are photographs, you can't quite see the brushstrokes all too well, but I do use a heavy hand with my oils to form movement in the features."

The Ryans nod and continue to look through the pictures, one after another. I'm so damn nervous; my stomach is rolling on me. "Uh, my goal is to move to Port Snow, to possibly find some contract work in Augusta, Portland, and Orono. But I would love to sell my work to you exclusively."

They nod their heads and continue to study my pictures until they get to the last page and gently close my portfolio, pushing it back toward me. I hold my breath, trying to read their faces.

Mr. Ryan clears his throat and pulls on his ear before he speaks. "You have a beautiful eye for color, Beck. Even from the photographs you can see the movement you create in your art."

"Very unique aesthetic that you don't see very often with those vivid colors," Mrs. Ryan adds.

Why do I feel a but coming on?

"But . . ." and there it is. I hold my head firm, my eyes locked on them, not showing any signs of disappointment. I don't want them to feel bad for me. I want them to make this decision honestly. "I can't foresee being able to sell portraits here in the gallery."

Mrs. Ryan nods. "I agree, unfortunately."

Lips pressed together, I take a deep breath, and reach my hand out. "Well, thank you so much for your time. I really appreciate you giving me the opportunity to show you my work."

My heart is breaking in half. Hell, I knew this was a long shot, so I should be proud that I tried at least. I'm going to have to come up with another plan, maybe reach out to the museums and zoos in the area. At this point, I would work for a painting company just to be near Rylee.

Ignoring my hand, Mr. Ryan says, "We're not done here."

"Oh." I take my hand back and settle into my seat.

"I see great talent and passion in you, Beck. I see enormous good in you, and I've always believed in second chances. I think you can be an asset to us." Mrs. Ryan beams at her husband. "Give us a second to talk. We'll be right back."

Hope springs in my chest as I nod. *I want what they have. Love. Devotion. Forever. But will they have anything that will keep me here near my girl?*

~

"How did it go?" Zoey asks as she sits across from me at The Lighthouse Restaurant. She sets her purse on the ground and props her hands on the table.

I can't hold back the smile. "Really well."

She slaps the table and then fist-pumps the air. "I knew it would be. Bruce and Carly are the best, aren't they?"

"They're pretty amazing, but I'm not quite doing what I expected."

"What do you mean? Are you not selling your art there?"

I shake my head. "No, they uh, offered me a full-time job to run the gallery, the paint classes, and help with acquiring new artists in the area. They also hooked me up with a friend they have in Augusta who works with the museums, zoos, and aquariums in the state."

"You're kidding me."

I shake my head. "Nope, they went above and beyond. Mr. Ryan said he wants to enjoy his retirement with his wife, he wants her to paint more, and he was waiting to find someone with enough knowledge to take over the day-to-day work."

"Holy shit!" Zoey claps her hands and leans over the table knocking over the pepper to give me a hug. "That's amazing, Beck. Do they know about Rylee?"

I smile. "When I was leaving, I stopped in the doorway, shaking their hands and told them I was in love with their daughter, and that my master plan is to get her to marry me one day . . . you know, further down the road."

"Gah. What did they say?"

"They exchanged glances and said they knew the stranger in black had to have something to do with the mood swings their daughter has been having."

Zoey laughs and grabs my water, taking a sip. "Oh, I love the Ryans."

"They said a few weeks ago, they couldn't believe how happy Rylee was, and they noticed something must have happened since she's been really quiet lately. When they got the call from you, they knew something was up, but they reassured me the job was purely offered based off my portfolio and experience."

"That's so great, Beck."

I scrub my jaw. "It really is. I can't thank you enough for setting me up with everything."

"Anytime." She waves a hand at me. "And has Victoria been a pleasant hostess? She can get cranky very easily."

Isn't that the fucking truth? Victoria is awesome, but the rules she has for her household, I can't keep them straight. I try not to touch anything unless absolutely necessary.

"She's been great. Very hospitable."

Zoey studies me, her eyes never breaking contact. "Do you really want to lie to me, Beck? Is that what you want to do?"

I chuckle and let out a long breath. "Victoria is very particular, but I'm grateful for a free bed while I try to figure things out."

"And she's not putting the moves on you?"

"What?" My eyebrows shoot up. "No, not even a little."

"Good." Zoey crosses her arms over her chest. "I can see she has a little crush on you, just a small one, but I want to make sure she knows you're taken."

Oh Victoria.

"So maybe I shouldn't let her show me the Amelia Earhart documentary every night?"

"Christ, no. Tell her one time is enough." Zoey shakes her head and pulls out her phone. "That girl, I'm going to text her right now."

I reach over and place my hand over Zoey's to stop her. "Please don't. I don't want her to feel bad. I can handle the documentary. It's fine. I don't want to be rude and look ungrateful, because I'm really grateful for you guys right now."

"We know. The fudge you bought us is thank you enough. Two pounds was really . . . a lot."

I rub the back of my neck. "Yeah, I was unsure of what to get so I bought some of every flavors. I didn't know they had that many flavors. Kind of impressive."

"It's one of the reasons people come to Port Snow. That and the lighthouses and small harbor-town feel. But Lobster Landing is the place to be when in Maine."

"I could tell when I was in there."

The waitress brings our food. Zoey ordered through me prior to her arrival so food would be here, ready for her to chow down. That's how she put it.

Picking up her spoon and diving it into her lobster bisque, she asks, "So what's your next plan?"

"Not sure, yet. I want to find my way around the gallery, and I'm waiting on a phone call from Cal, my sponsor."

"What kind of call?"

I pick at my lobster mac and cheese but don't make any real dent. "Well, given my background, I wanted to see if it was possible for me to be a foster parent. I'm not quite sure they let felons foster kids, or adopt kids for that matter."

Yeah, that was a blow to my whole plan. When I spoke with Cal, he reminded me of the restrictions I have placed on my life, and foster care is most likely one of them.

Zoey slowly looks up at me. "I never even thought about that. Oh shit. So . . . what happens if you can't foster or adopt kids?"

I lick my lips and tuck my fork under my bowl, leaning back in my chair. "Save a lot of money and find a surrogate. I'll do anything to make Rylee happy. It can be some other dude's so she doesn't feel like the baby has more of a connection with me, if it helps."

A small smile passes over Zoey's lips. "Rylee will be able to help you save, if that's what you really want."

"I want whatever she wants."

"So you're really serious?"

I level with Zoey. "Do you think I would drop everything in my life, move across country, shack it up with a historian, and practically beg for a job in an art gallery for fun?" I shake my head. "I'm dead fucking serious about being with Rylee."

"But you've only seen each other in person twice, not even in your own environments."

That's the same damn thing Chris said to me while he drove me to the airport, and I'm going to tell Zoey the same thing I told Chris.

"I'm not sure how you and Art met, but I've been with someone who made me feel like a lesser man, someone who brought me down to their level, someone who was so incredibly toxic for me that I broke. It took about six years to piece myself back together, and since then, I've been cautious when meeting women. Very cautious. Rylee is the first woman I've spoken to about my background. She's the first woman to lift me up, to make me want to strive to be more, to be better than I already am. She's a once-in-a-lifetime person, Zoey. Believe me, I've been through the gauntlet. She makes me happy and she gives me hope for a bright future. I want to hold on to that for as long as I live."

"Well . . . damn." Zoey pats at her eyes. "God, you're a fucking catch. Not a dickhead after all." She clears her throat and says, "Okay, so I know she's seen you, but you're going to have to talk to her eventually."

"I know." I take a big bite of my mac and cheese finally. "I want to have all my ducks in a row before I let it be known I've taken over her town."

Zoey laughs. "Pretty sure she's already aware."

I'm coming for you, sweet Rylee. You're mine forever. Mine.

CHAPTER TWENTY-FIVE

BECK

"These are beautiful, Beck. How on earth did you come up with them so quickly?" Mrs. Ryan asks, passing over the three canvases I brought into the gallery this morning for possible drink-and-paint parties.

I grip the back of my neck, staring at the landscapes of Port Snow I painted last night. I stayed up late, painting in Victoria's garage, draped in white drop cloths, until two this morning, caught up in the strokes and colors. I took pictures of some of the infamous landmarks in the town and put my own spin on them. When I was done, I felt proud. It was like I could see Rylee in every picture I took, in every corner I walked around. I was surrounded by her, and I felt my love for her in every stroke of my brush.

"Inspiration hit me hard last night. I tried to keep the strokes simple, the color mixing basic, and the structure of the painting as elementary as possible without compromising the painting."

"You did a wonderful job." Mrs. Ryan holds up the painting of Snow Roast and smiles to herself, noticing the black-haired beauty sitting in the window. Any tourist would think it's a random person, but the nod to my girl doesn't slip past Mrs. Ryan. "This is my favorite."

"Mine too," I answer honestly. "There's something about capturing people in their natural environment that inspires me, makes me want to paint the truth."

She pats my shoulder. "I couldn't agree more." She brings the paintings to the front window and puts them on display without even discussing it with me. "These unique colors should draw some attention. They're very eye-catching." Turning toward me, she clasps her hands together and asks, "So when are you going to tell my daughter what you're doing here?"

I bite my bottom lip. I knew she was going to ask me this question, I could see it in her eyes the minute she spotted Rylee in the painting.

"Just trying to make sure I have all my ducks in a row before I let her in on my little life change."

"She hasn't said anything to me since you've arrived. I actually think she's retreated into her house, not wanting to run into you. Is there something you're not telling me about your relationship, why she's possibly avoiding you?"

Feeling a little awkward standing in the middle of the gallery having this conversation, I motion to one of the seating areas and ask, "Would you like to sit down?"

"Would love it." We both take a seat and I lean forward, arms rested on my knees.

"I love your daughter, Mrs. Ryan. I want to spend my life with her, but she has this notion that being with her will hold me back from my dreams because she can't have children."

A knowing look passes over Mrs. Ryan's eyes.

"There are other ways to have families, but instead of talking it through, she ran. So I'm here to show her I'm not running. I'm willing to change everything in my life to be with her."

"And what about a family?"

"We'll figure it out, and if it doesn't work out, then we will surround ourselves with our friends' children."

"You'll be happy with that?"

"I'll be happy with Rylee." I take a deep breath. "As long as she's happy and healthy, that's all I really care about."

Mrs. Ryan nods and the bell to the front door dings. We both turn to see Rylee walk through, eyes cast toward her phone. "Mom, Dad said you were training someone new today? What's going—?"

She pauses mid-sentence when she looks up to see me sitting directly across from her mom. Lifting her sunglasses, as if she can't possibly believe what she's seeing, she takes a closer look.

"Hi, honey," Mrs. Ryan says, as if nothing strange is happening.

I love watching Rylee's mind work. It registers from shock to "what the hell is going on" to . . . yup, anger. Her eyes narrow on me, and I can see her feisty side emerging. Fuck, have I missed that side of her.

"What the hell is he doing here?"

"Rylee Lynn Ryan, that is no way to talk to people."

Straightening up, with her hand at her side, she tries to secretly call her mom over with her finger, her head nodding in her direction.

Not being as sly as Rylee, Mrs. Ryan asks, "Would you like me to come over to you?"

Rylee dramatically rolls her eyes. "Yes, Mom. Can I have a word, please?"

I stand, wanting to give them some space. "I was going to get some coffee anyway. Can I grab you anything, Mrs. Ryan? Rylee?"

"A hot chocolate on the rocks would be nice with whipped cream," Mrs. Ryan says.

I gesture to Rylee who shakes her head, her eyes still glaring.

"Okay, I'll be back in a bit. Should I grab a scone to go with that hot chocolate on the rocks?"

"Only if it's from Lobster Landing."

I mirthfully shake my head. "Come on, Mrs. Ryan, I'm not a barbarian. Of course it would be from Lobster Landing."

"Then lemon poppy seed would be delightful."

"Not a problem." I give them a parting wink. Rylee is about to blow a gasket behind me as I leave the gallery and head for Lobster Landing first, then I'll hit up the Snow Roast.

As I'm taking the short walk toward the infamous gift shop, my phone rings.

I take a deep breath and answer the phone. "Hey Cal, how's it going?"

"Good, good. How's Maine treating you?"

"I kind of love it. Got a job at the gallery. I'm going to be teaching some art classes, and there is some possible contract work at the museums and zoos I can score on the weekends. Everything is lining up for me."

"Good to hear. And Rylee, where does she stand?"

"Haven't really talked to her that much. I keep running into her because it's a small town, but I don't really want to make my intentions known until I have answers to all my questions. I have my job situated. I have settled on living arrangements for now but hoping those will change if Rylee decides to take a leap of faith with me. Just waiting on your news to see what my options are."

"Fair enough. I'll be honest, I was a little nervous about flipping your world upside down for the possible chance of being with a woman, but you've gone about this intelligently and you sound happy . . . healthy."

"I am. I feel really positive." I lean against a lamppost, not wanting to take this conversation into a small building where everyone can listen in. Rylee was right when she told me about the gossip in this town. When I was at the grocery store the other day, two women were talking about the rebel-ish stranger lurking around town with the exact description as me. When I made myself known and said hi, they clammed up real quick.

"Glad to hear it. Unfortunately, I don't have the best news."

I sigh, my shoulders slouching forward, my posture shrinking. I knew this was possible. I've prepared myself for it.

"I'm ready for it, just lay it on me."

"Since you were charged with vehicular manslaughter, it really limits your options. Foster care is not an option. Adoption is going to be hard, but there is a chance depending on the social worker you work with and the improvements you continue to make in your life that you can in the next few years get home study approved. But I'm going to be honest. It's going to take a lot on your end to make that happen. It's not going to come easily, and there's a high possibility you'll be turned down."

I nod, pressing my fingers into my brow, trying to massage the tension that's causing my sudden migraine.

"I can understand that. The choices you make always have an impact on your future."

"Which means, the choices you make now, the actions you take to better your life, will better your chances at possibly adopting one day. Keep building your foundation, keep making guest-speaking engagements, and educating everyone about the effects of drinking and driving."

"I will never let those fall through the cracks. They are a main priority in my life."

"Which is very admirable and shows great character, something that will serve you well on your application. But if the times comes and you do decide to take that step toward adoption, I have an adoption advisor that will be critical to have on your side during the process."

"Thanks, Cal." I lean my head against the lamppost. Once again, my decision to get behind that wheel is altering my life. It's a consequence I've had to live with every day of my life.

"But I have some good news." I perk up. "I know you really want to shape and mold kids, that's your true passion." Cal under-stands me to my very core. "So I made a few phone calls and becoming a Big Brother is a very viable option for you."

Huh, the thought of becoming a Big Brother never even crossed my mind.

"Really?"

"Yes, you meet the criteria. The only technicality is the note of violence against others. I spoke with someone in the Portland office and explained your situation, and they thought, given your track record and philanthropic focus, you would be a viable candidate for the Big Brother program, under strict supervision."

"Understandable. But that's amazing. That's actually kind of fantastic. I could really get into doing some work for them and even educational fundraisers." My mind starts whirling with the many possibilities.

"I'll email you the contact information. Her name is Nancy Watson. She's tough, but I think you two will get along."

"Thanks, Cal. Seriously. You went above and beyond to help me out here."

"No need to thank me. Just pay it forward like you always do, and when the time comes for you to be a sponsor, I hope you'll strive for the same relationship we have."

"You've led me with such grace and honesty I can't imagine doing it any other way."

And now I'm starting to get fucking emotional. Leave it to Cal.

"Good to hear." His voice sounds gruff and for the first time since I've known the man, I think I'm hearing a little bit of emotion in his tough-as-nails voice. "Now that you have everything in order, it's time to get the girl. You up for the challenge?"

I chuckle into the phone and pull on the short strands of my hair. "I've never been more ready."

CHAPTER TWENTY-SIX

RYLEE

M y eyes stay laser-focused on my mom when the bell to the door rings, signaling Beck's departure from my parents' gallery.

"What the hell was he doing here? And why on earth is he getting you hot chocolate and a scone?"

My mom pats my cheek with a warm smile. "It's good to see you too, honey. Why don't you sit down? Would you like me to get you a warm washcloth to wipe that sneer off your face?"

Can you guess where I got my sassiness from?

"Mom, seriously, how do you know Beck?"

"Hmm, maybe I should be asking you the same thing? How do you know Beck?" My mom sits back on her chair, which only makes me feel awkward, so I take the seat across from her that Beck was just sitting in. And I swear to my right boob that the space around me still smells like Beck, like his intoxicating cologne. It's . . . frustrating.

He's consuming every last piece of my life, and I don't know what to do with it. I'm hiding out in my house to avoid him, and when I'm not in my house, I see him everywhere, even walking into Victoria's house as if he's living there. When I tried to call her —ten times—she refused to answer. And it's not like I'm about to knock on her door, looking for answers. With my luck, Beck will answer the door wearing an apron from cooking dinner for Lord knows who, probably all his new friends.

How can one man make himself at home this quickly? I feel like everyone knows him and everyone is talking about him— hence the reason to stay at home. I was sick of hearing all the wishful gossiping about the sexy new stranger in town.

I can't seem to shake him, and when I thought I was retreating to a safe space, to get some writing done in my parents' empty classroom—they only do classes in the afternoon and evening— there he is, sitting with my mom, gabbing away and offering hot chocolate and scones.

What the WHAT?

"Well . . ." My mom clears her throat, drawing my attention. "Are you going to tell me how you know Beck?"

"I asked you first," I counter.

"Yes, but I have all day to sit around and do nothing. From the crazed look in your eyes, I'm going to guess you're not at the same leisure as I am."

Gah! Where's my dad when I need him?

"Fine, Beck was the guy I met in Key West. We kind of had a thing for each other but you know how it is. Ideas got in the way, and we kind of broke it off."

"Ah, I see. And what ideas got in the way?"

"It's not important." I wave her off, but instead of letting it go, she presses further.

"What kind of ideas? Because from where I'm sitting, a few weeks ago you were the happiest I've ever seen you, which I'm going to assume is because of Beck. Don't lie to me and tell me it isn't."

"Mom," I groan.

"Don't *Mom* me. You're the one who came into my place of work and started mouthing off to a perfectly nice man, so you better start explaining or you know where the door is."

Ever hear of tough love? My mom has perfected it over the years. She doesn't put up with any sass or denial when it comes to me.

I sigh and place my hand over my brow, massaging my tense forehead. "He has different ideas for the future than I do. And what's the point of getting my hopes up about a man I know I won't be able to . . . fully give him what he wants?"

"Kids."

She says it so upfront, so in your face, but that's who she is. She's never really been one to beat around the bush. She's always straight to the point but shows empathy while doing it.

"Yes, kids. He wants four, and you and I both know that ship has sailed."

With a deep breath, my mom takes my hand in hers. The soft, velvet touch of her thumb fans over the back of my knuckles, a common stroke I've grown accustomed to over the years. It's gentle, sweet, reassuring, but also comes with her two cents.

"Rylee, sweetie, the day you came home and told Dad and me about your cancer, and your options, I remember feeling utterly gutted. How could my child go through such a hardship? It's the question that kept rolling around in my head, followed by the realization that you will never be able to carry a child like I carried you. But guess what?" She lifts my chin up. "None of that matters because you're sitting here, with me, breathing in the same air as me. *You're living.* You need to stop dwelling on what you can't have and start living for what you can."

My eyes start to burn, tears welling up at my lids.

"I love you so much, honey, but you're stubborn as all get out. What I see in that man, when he looks at you, is true adoration. Like you're the one who rises and falls with the moon and the sun every day. You're the one bringing in the light, the humor, and the love in his life." Tears begin to drip down my cheeks, and my mom wipes them away with her thumbs.

"And if he's anything like me, which I'm almost positive he is, he's not going to care about a big family, or the tons of kids you can't have. All he's going to care about is the beating heart in your chest and the air you're able to bring into your lungs. You're alive and you make us happy. That's all we ask for, all we want."

She stands and pats my cheek lovingly. "Now, it looks like he's headed into Snow Roast with a bakery box in hand. You have two choices. You can sit here and cry, let your face get all blotchy and red, or you can go home, think about what you really want. What YOU want, and forget about everything else. You've been through enough for a lifetime, so it's your turn to take what's being offered to you." *But that's the problem. I don't know if the offer I want was ever on the table. He didn't tell me he loved me. He didn't tell me he wanted that family with me. They were his dreams.* But if he's here, what does that mean? Do I have any right to dream too?

Biting on my lower lip to keep it from trembling, I take another deep breath and ask, "Do you really think he'll want me? *Just* me, broken parts and all?"

"I think he'll do anything, and I mean anything, to have you in his life." She squeezes my shoulder and says, "Now go on and get out of here. You don't want him seeing you like this. Next time you run into each other, I want to make sure he sees that charming and beautiful smile of yours instead of your sorrowful tears."

Kissing me on the head, she helps me to my feet, gives me a brief hug, and sends me out the door. Could Beck really be happy with me and me alone? *Dare I hope for that?*

～

I don't leave the gallery and go home like my mom told me to, because why not be the girl with a splotchy face, oversized T-shirt, holey pants, and crazed hair who crouches down behind a mail box and watches for the man she loves to walk out of the coffee shop?

Who doesn't want to be that girl?

She's popular.

She's in with the hip crowd.

She is by no means desperate or crazy, or nasty to poor Mrs. Braverman, who asked for privacy when putting her mail in the box.

"It's mail for fuck's sake," I yelled, taking the mail from her and shoving it down the hole in one giant swoop. "It's not like I'm looking over your shoulder in the voting booth. Now scram, I'm spying."

Not my finest moment.

Honestly, I don't think I've had many fine moments lately.

And I blame Beck. He's driven me to the looney bin.

Legit, I am certifiable right now.

I realize that as I grip the mailbox, talking to it about the troubles of Beck living in this town, making friends with all the locals and barely speaking to me.

Want to send someone straight to the insane asylum? Pull a Beck Wilder.

"I mean, what is he really doing here? For so long? And where is he staying? It's tourist season, which means the bed and breakfasts and inns are booked up."

I stroke the mailbox with my thumb, the blue paint rubbing off the metal. "Have you heard anything around the street? You know, since you're in the thick of things?"

I steady my breathing, half expecting the mailbox to respond to me in my state of delirium.

"Nothing? Not even a little gossip? For someone who has access to everyone's mail in this town, I would have—"

I pause as the coffee shop door opens.

I hold my breath.

Just as Mrs. Braverman pops out holding a cup of tea.

"God damn you, Mrs. Braverman. She's always getting in the

way." She looks both ways before crossing the street and heads toward the harbor, most likely to stare at all the tourists and "accidentally" trip them with her cane.

She's not fooling me. I know her game.

I turn my attention back to the coffee shop just in time to see Beck step outside and hold the door open, Victoria following beside him.

What?

Beck wraps his arm around Victoria's shoulder with the arm that's carrying the bakery box. She smiles up at him and laughs at something as they casually walk together down the sidewalk toward the gallery.

"That harlot," I seethe, gripping tightly onto the mailbox, watching their every move.

Why are they so chummy?

My mind mulls this over as they reach the gallery and say their goodbyes. I see Victoria say something like, "See you at home" but that seems . . .

"Gah!" I spring from my crouched position just as Victoria gets to my trusty mailbox. "You're sleeping with him?" I point my finger accusingly, jumping in her face and causing a scene right there on the sidewalk.

"Sweet Christ!" Victoria holds her chest and pants heavily. "What in the hell are you doing hiding behind a mailbox? Have you completely lost it?"

"I don't know, maybe." I fold my arms over my chest. "Maybe I have lost it. Maybe I'm on the verge of a total and complete mental breakdown, because my best friend, my bosom buddy, my very own frolicsome crony is sleeping with my boyfriend. Care to explain the sexual tension you have going on with Beck?"

Adjusting the height of her turtleneck to hide the redness in her skin from embarrassment, Victoria lowers her voice and says, "I don't believe this is a conversation to have out in the open, on the streets."

"Oh, we're having this conversation, right here, right now." I point my finger to the ground, but Victoria doesn't listen, and instead turns the corner between two buildings and whispers for me to follow her.

Rolling my eyes, I duck away with her and lean against the brick while chewing on pretend gum I don't have, I don't know why, probably because I'm a crazy person. With my arms crossed over my chest, I say, "Explain yourself."

Straightening her dress, she puffs her chest and says, "First of all, last I knew, he wasn't your boyfriend."

"I knew it. You're dating him, aren't you?" I didn't know it actually, but I'm just that crazy to conjure up such thoughts. That's what happens when you're a creative being. The simplest answer is never the one that comes to your head.

Victoria wouldn't do that to me.

Oh, there you are, finally. I finally hear from the logical brain instead of the crazed brain. Since when do I have two brains? Is that normal? I thought there was only a left brain and a right—

"No, and I would appreciate it if you wouldn't think so low of me to think I could date the man you're obviously in love with."

I'm going to blow right past the L-word comment and keep moving on. "Then what were you guys talking about? Why are you going to see him at home?"

Without blinking an eyelash, Victoria says, "Because he's been staying with me for the past week, that's why."

"Judas!" I scream and throw my hands in the air.

"Oh for crying out loud." Victoria shakes her head and starts to walk past me. "You know, Rylee, there are a lot of people who love you, who want nothing more than for you to have everything you deserve." Facing me, she steps close, inches only separating us. "It would behoove you to treat the people who love you with a little more respect, especially since they're the ones helping the man who is head over heels in love with you find a way to be the man you want."

And just like that, Victoria metaphorically drops the mic and takes off down the street, making me feel like the biggest asshole in the world.

Hmm . . . maybe it's because I am the biggest asshole in the world.

But who uses the word behoove *anyway?*

323

CHAPTER TWENTY-SEVEN

RYLEE

A week.

Beck has been in my small town one week, making friends with the locals, becoming ever-so popular with the Knightly brothers, and even Oliver, yucking it up with Mrs. Braverman while feeding pigeons in the park, and telling jokes to the elders at the corner store where they gather for their morning meetings.

I've seen him everywhere.

And yet, he hasn't come to talk to me. Is he waiting for me to approach him? Does he want me to approach him?

From everything I've heard from my parents and friends, and maybe from a quick check-in with Mrs. Braverman—the old coot —he seems to be talking about me to everyone. So why isn't he talking to me?

It's . . . devastating. Seeing him here, seeing that handsome smirk of his, those brilliant eyes, his enigmatic presence. It's a reminder of everything I gave up, everything I walked out on. *Everything I will never have.*

I see that now. I'm not that stubborn. I can admit when I'm

wrong. I got scared, and instead of sticking around to work things out, I was that dumb girl who ran. But I'm human. I'm not perfect by any means.

I have my faults.

I have my demons.

And unfortunately, as strong as I try to be, they still affect me. They still drive me to do stupid things. They still cause me to hide.

It's human nature. *It's me.*

I wish I was stronger.

Scanning my emails, I open one from my cover designer and check out the mock-ups for my next release, studying them intently while sipping tea.

His hand looks weird like that, like it's broken.

Whoa, too many pubes. I don't mind a few strays, but the bush police would write up this picture for sure.

Is that . . . a third nipple? Well, don't we have ourselves a beautiful unicorn?

Knock, knock.

I look to my front door that's open, the screen door offering a light breeze to pass through the small holes.

Zoey is standing there holding a bag.

"Why are you knocking? Come in," I call out, pushing my glasses back on my nose and studying the third nipple that's entirely too fascinating to me.

There is another knock. I glance up, and Zoey continues to stand there.

"Oh for fuck's sake." I stand from my table and walk to the entryway, opening the screen door with a slight creek in the hinges. "Zoey, why—?"

She hands me the bag and then walks away.

"What is happening?" She doesn't say anything, just continues to walk toward Main Street.

Looking at the bag, I let the door shut, clanking against the doorjamb. I open the tissue paper and spot a bag of coffee on the bottom.

Okay.

I pick it up and roll it over finding a Post-it Note.

This is my favorite brew at Snow Roast. Not too rich, but very smooth. – Beck

My stomach drops, my pulse picks up, and my hands start to sweat. I look back at the door and notice Art approaching with another bag.

I set the coffee down and go to the front door, and before he can knock, I open it. Without a word, he hands me another bag with a wink.

I go back to my counter and open it up. At the bottom is a plastic container full of soup. I read the note.

You probably already know this but The Lighthouse Restaurant has amazing lobster bisque, like orgasmic level. But did you know if you ask for their secret cheese sauce on top it brings the soup to an entirely different level? It's my favorite. – Beck

Secret cheese sauce? What? How didn't I know about this?

I'm about to rip the top off the soup and heat it up when there's another knock at my door. It's my dad.

"Hi, Dad." I open the screen door only for him to hand me a bag as well. He leans over and kisses me on the cheek and then takes off.

My eyes start to well up when I bring the bag to the counter.

Inside is a rolled-up newspaper. Today's paper . . . with a note.

The Port Snow Observer is my favorite thing to read in the morning. It's not like a normal newspaper giving you the gloom and doom of the week. It speaks of Tommy Hornbuckle's high-scoring game at Pee Wee football. It shares Martha Gillroy's banana bread recipe, and it speaks of the quirky tourists that are spotted every day. It's intimate and perfect, and I love picking it up and talking to the town elders every morning. – Beck

I shake my head. The Port Snow Observer is by far the weirdest newspaper, but he's right, it's intimate, and one of the reasons why I try to read it at least once a week, if not for a laugh.

There is another knock at the door. *Oliver.* I raise my brow and open the door.

Just like everyone else, he hands me a bag and takes off, a huge smile on his face.

This bag feels heavier, and I have a feeling I know what it is. When I see the three carboard pints inside, my suspicions are right.

I've spent a long time in the ice cream aisle at Monahan's Market. I've tested almost every flavor, and I have to say, mint chip is still my favorite. P.S. The abs have taken a hit from the ice cream, but they're still there, don't worry. – Beck.

I snort-laugh, a stray tear falling down my cheek that I quickly wipe away. The original is to die for actually and probably goes unappreciated with all the different flavors offered.

Knock, knock.

My mom? I don't think I've ever seen her so happy. She's standing at the door, holding a canvas and smiling big. Going to the door, I open it and she hands me the canvas, my heart rate really picking up, my breath starting to become slightly labored. My mom presses a kiss on my cheek briefly and whispers, "He's a very good man, Rylee."

Then she leaves.

I take the canvas to my dining room table and set it down carefully. It's wrapped in paper with a note on the top.

I've been all around this town, soaking it in, taking in every passerby, every local, every popular sightseeing spot marked cleverly by the tourism board. And I've come to find one particular spot that grabs my attention, one place in this town that I can stare at all day and be completely and utterly content. This is my favorite spot to sit and watch the view in Port Snow. – Beck.

With shaky hands, I carefully take the brown paper off the front and bring my hand to my chest when I take in the picture in front of me. A gasp on my lips, I press my fingers lightly against Beck's signature strokes and colors.

It's the coffee shop, neon pinks and greens and oranges making up most of the picture. But there in the window is a distinct figure with black hair sitting in front of a computer.

It's me.

I don't even know what to say.

He's already stolen my heart, but this . . . this . . .

Knock, knock.

I whip around to see Victoria standing at my door with a suitcase at her side. Wiping away my tears, I open the door for her only to hand me the handle of the suitcase and take off.

"Victoria, wait." She pauses and turns. "I'm sorry about the other day. I've been a little . . . lost."

Her face softens and she nods. "I love you, Rylee." With a small smile, she walks away but says, "Open the top zipper."

Not bothering to put the suitcase on a surface, I move it to the side of my entryway, and open it up, fumbling with the zipper in the process. On the very top is a note. Picking it up, I snag a black V-neck T-shirt in process and bring it to my nose where I take a small sniff. The smell of Beck's cologne floods my senses, soothing my shaking bones.

I read the note, Beck's shirt pressed against my heart.

Did you know if you forget to rinse one of Victoria's forks after eating eggs, she begins to lose her damn mind? Yeah, she kicked me out, but I'm kind of hoping I'll be able to stay for a while at my favorite house in Port Snow. What do you say? – Beck

I wipe away a tear and look up to my door only to find Beck standing behind the screen, hands in his pockets, smiling. It's like he's been here this entire time, waiting for me. *Waiting for me to see him.*

Leaving his shirt in his suitcase, I rush to the door and open it, disregarding my not-so attractive loungewear. The minute the screen door opens, Beck's eyes meet mine, and I can't do anything but step into his embrace and rest my head on his chest. His arms wrap around me, tight and strong, and his lips find the top of my head, loving and warm.

"Hey Saucy."

"Hey you." I snuggle closer, gripping his grey T-shirt firmly. I never want to let him go.

"Mind if I come in?"

Glancing at him, his light smirk greets me and I melt. How did I ever think I could say goodbye to this man? How did I convince myself being away from him was smart, that is was the best decision for the both of us?

Because right now, I'm one hundred percent sure we are two lost souls searching for each other, and we happened to meet in paradise.

Taking his hand, I lead him into my home for the first time and guide him past all his gifts and straight to the couch where we take a seat facing each other. I continue to hold his hand as he strokes my cheek with his other.

"I've missed you, Rylee."

I swallow hard and lean my hand into his touch, briefly closing my eyes, tears feeling heavy. "I've missed you, Beck. You being here, not talking to me, but seeing you everywhere, it's been torture." I squeeze his hand. "Why didn't you come to me sooner?"

He wipes a stray tear. "I had some things to figure out first. I wanted to make sure that when I came after you, when I came one last time to convince you to be with me, there was no chance you could say no."

"Beck," I breathe sadly. "I'm sorry about Las Vegas. I never should have run out on you like that."

"And I wish I had been more understanding. I wasn't as cool-tempered and sympathetic as I should have been." His jaw twitches, the muscle pulsing in a sexy manner that makes me want to kiss the spot. "I just got so . . . frustrated. I didn't like being shut out like that. I want to know everything about you, Rylee."

"I know that now, and I'm sorry. Can you tell I kind of suck at this whole relationship thing?"

He chuckles and lifts my chin. "We're not perfect, no one is. There had to be a flaw in you somewhere." Winking, he pulls my head forward and places a very soft kiss on my forehead.

Soaking in his scent, in the way he feels next to me again, I scoot closer to him until I'm sitting on his lap. He strokes my hair casually, the cutest smile on his face.

"So, why are you here?" I ask, hoping for the best.

"Well you see, I had to check Port Snow out, wanted to make sure it was not only a place I could work but a place I could live." Hope springs in my chest.

"And?"

"I love it, Rylee. Just like I love you."

A very unattractive laugh pops out of me. *I'm the epitome of elegance and class.* Overcome with joy, I lean forward and press my lips against Beck's, the salt of my tears mixing with our kiss. "I love you too. I love you so much, Beck."

He groans and moves his hands to my hips where he grips them tightly, deepening our kiss for a brief second before he pulls away and presses our foreheads together.

"Fuck, Rylee. You don't know how relieved I am to hear that."

"I'm sorry I made you doubt yourself. I just . . ." I pause and pull away. "What about . . . what about—"

"I have a job at the gallery. Your parents have been amazing, giving me a ton of responsibility since they want to spend more time on the retirement side of things. They also hooked me up with some contract work in Augusta for some murals." He strokes my hips with his thumbs. "I love it here. It's quirky and perfect, a place where I want to start a family with you."

"But—"

"But nothing. I've spoken with Cal about my options given my background. Adoption may still be an option, surrogacy is an option, and so is becoming a Big Brother, which is good enough for me. All I want is you, whatever comes along after that is cherries on top of the sweetest fucking cake ever."

"Beck . . ."

He silences me and looks directly at me, his eyes unwavering. "Listen to me, Rylee. I'm dead serious when I say being a Big Brother would be sufficient for me. If our family consists of four-legged children, then I'm cool with that too. What I want is you and only you. Do you hear me?"

I press my lips together and nod.

The sincerity in his voice, the way he's dominating me with his words, there is no doubt in my mind he's serious, that this is what he wants. And if we don't have any other additions to our little family other than animals, he'll be okay with that.

"So . . . does that mean you're moving in?"

"Hell yeah." He pulls me closer and kisses me on my mouth, his lips more demanding this time. When he separates, he speaks softly as our noses touch. "But I'm going to tell you right now, I get the right side of the bed and there will be lots of fucking. At least for the next forty-eight hours, there will be lots of fucking and fucking all over this house."

I giggle as he presses his lips against mine again, his hand skirting up my shirt, getting to work on my bra already. He wasn't kidding.

"Beck, screen door," I mutter between kisses.

His head tips back to look at the door and says, "It's fine."

"It is if you want to show up in the Port Snow Observer tomorrow."

This gives him pause. "Shit." He sighs and presses his head against my chest, his hand inches from my boob. "This town is so goddamn in your face, and I weirdly love it."

"I love it even more now that you're here with me."

"Wouldn't change it for anything, Saucy."

He leads me to the door, slams it shut and locks it, and then I guide him to my bedroom where he strips me naked and makes love to me. His mouth, his hands, his body owning mine with every pulse, every stroke, every kiss.

Beck Wilder, the man who mysteriously took over my vacation getaway. I'm an utter and complete fool for him.

It's funny. I write happily ever afters for a living, and this is oddly one love story I never would have predicted or been able to write for myself.

Somewhere along the road, I lost sight of my own happy ending. I had become immersed in my fictional world. I wonder if I believed that only my heroines deserved love. *Only* my heroines deserved a future of bliss without heartache.

And then one day in paradise he appeared. *My* hero. A man with a selfless heart beyond compare, with mischief in his eyes, and ridiculousness on his lips. A man who had the ability to push me outside my cozy world of one into loving and welcome arms of two. A man too good to be true, but somehow mine all the same. *This is where I write The End.* Isn't it?

EPILOGUE

BECK

"Where's the green bag? Did we leave the green bag? Oh my God, Beck, the green bag, where is it?"

My wife wanders around our bedroom, frantic, eyes crazed looking for a bag that is held tightly in her hand.

"Saucy, it's in your hand."

Looking down, she notices the bag and clutches her forehead, falling to the floor. "This was a bad idea. What were we thinking? I'm not ready for this. How on earth will we be able to—?"

"Rylee, take a few deep breaths. Take them with me." I join her on the floor and pull her into my lap. I lean against the wall and stroke her hair as I look at the three bassinets lined up by our bed. So much fucking joy right now, I can't contain it. We breathe in and out together until Rylee's body stops shaking. "We've been to all the classes, we have a schedule set up with the helpers, and we have everything you can possibly need for raising a baby."

"Beck, not a baby, three, three babies!"

"I know." I can't contain the smile. "Three babies, Saucy. We're going to be a family of five. How lucky are we?"

She relaxes when I press a kiss against the side of her head.

"Three babies. Three little ones to call our own. Three little lives we get to mold and shape. Three little souls we get to love and devote our lives to. We're lucky. And I'm not going to promise you it won't be hard, but we have so much help. And when we're sixty and looking back at this moment, we're going to wish we could do it all over again because it's going to be so goddamn fulfilling."

Her head rests against my chest. "This is why I love you, why I married you a year ago. You instill a sense of calm inside of me."

"And here I thought it was my cock you liked inside of you."

"Oh my God." She swats my chest and pushes away. "Way to ruin a moment."

I laugh and pull her back to my chest. "You love it just like I love you, and just like I'm going to love Isaac, Taylor, and Zac."

She shakes her head and dislodges herself from my grip. When I see her pointing her finger at me, a stern look on her face, I burst out in laughter.

"We are not naming our children after the Hanson brothers."

"Come on . . . it's funny."

"No."

"Taylor can be the girl, and Zac and Isaac easily can be the boys. It just makes sense."

"You're deranged." She takes a deep breath and says, "Come on, Stacey is probably already at the hospital."

"Because her mom drives like a mad woman." I stand from the ground and pick up the green bag full of snacks and things to keep us busy while we wait for our triplets to be born.

Yup, triplets. All I have to say is, thank you, prom season.

It was no secret in Port Snow that Rylee and I wanted to have a family, but given my background, we've had a bit of a hard time trying to make that happen. That was until Stacey Higgins approached us, a cliché of unprotected sex on prom night. She has aspirations to go to college and become a marine biologist, and there's no room for triplets in those aspirations.

When she first came to us, Rylee laughed and tried to pat the girl on the shoulder and walk away, but I scooped up the opportunity, found a lawyer, and made it happen. The birth father, Shane, signed the papers quickly not wanting to have to father triplets at such a young age, and Stacey followed closely behind.

Of course once Rylee saw it was a real possibility, she started nesting immediately, which meant we moved out of her little cottage, our love cottage, and into a bigger house on the shoreline —with a fence, of course, for any wandering little kids—and we bought a minivan. Don't believe me? It's black—stealth color—has all the bells and whistles, and I look hot as fuck driving it. We have three car seats strapped inside and lullaby music tuned up on the stereo. We're ready.

We're nervous, but we're ready.

We head out to the black rocket—minivan—and Rylee takes my hand, squeezing it tightly. "What if they don't love me?" She bites her bottom lip. It's a concern she's had ever since we went through the adoption classes. Attachment and bonding has been a big concern of hers.

I cup her chin and meet her watery gaze. "It's impossible not to love you. From the first moment they lay eyes on you, they're going to love you, just like I do. The moment I first saw you, covered in puke, frazzled, and cute as fuck, I knew I'd love you. It was inevitable, and it will be the same with our babies."

I place my lips on her forehead and then help her into the passenger side of the van. When I hop in, I take her hand in mine and kiss the back of it. "I couldn't imagine going on this journey with anyone else but you, Saucy. I'm one lucky motherfucker."

And I mean that.

From a broken and torn marriage, to the worst day of my life, to six years in jail . . . I've come a long way to live in a small town with the love of my life, my best friends, Chris and Justine—only a few houses down now—and three small babies we'll call our own on the way . . .

Hell, life doesn't get better than this. All it took was crashing a wedding to begin the best days of my life and the incredible love-filled—and no doubt chaotic—future ahead of me.

Cheers to the bride and groom!

THE END